ALAN BAXTER IS a British-Australian author who writes dark fantasy, horror and sci-fi, rides a motorcycle and loves his dog. He also teaches Kung Fu. He lives among dairy paddocks on the beautiful south coast of NSW, Australia, with his wife, son, dog and cat. He is the author of the dark urban fantasy trilogy, *Bound*, *Obsidian* and *Abduction* (The Alex Caine Series) published by HarperVoyager Australia, and the dark urban fantasy duology, *RealmShift* and *MageSign* (The Balance 1 and 2) from Gryphonwood Press. He's the award-winning author of over seventy short stories and novellas. So far. Read extracts from his novels, a novella and short stories at his website www.warriorscribe.com or find him on Twitter @ AlanBaxter and Facebook, and feel free to tell him what you think. About anything.

CROW SHINE

CROW SHINE

ALAN BAXTER

Ticonderoga publications

For my dad, John Baxter, who told me to never give up

Crow Shine by Alan Baxter

Published by Ticonderoga Publications

Copyright © Alan Baxter 2016

Introduction copyright © Joanne Anderton 2016

Designed and edited by Russell B. Farr
Typeset in Sabon and Minion Pro

A Cataloging-in-Publications entry for this title is available from The National Library of Australia.

ISBN 978–1–925212–39–6 (limited hardcover)
 978–1–925212–40–2 (trade hardcover)
 978–1–925212–41–9 (trade paperback)
 978–1–925212–42–6 (ebook)

Ticonderoga Publications
PO Box 29 Greenwood
Western Australia 6924
Australia

www.ticonderogapublications.com

10 9 8 7 6 5 4 3 2 1

THE AUTHOR WOULD LIKE TO THANK . . .

. . . so many people are involved in the making of a good book, and I truly hope this is a good book. Writers work in solitude, but nothing is created alone. I have many thanks to give, and I hope I don't forget anyone.

Firstly to Russell B. Farr and Liz Grzyb of Ticonderoga Publications, not only for this book, but for all the great work they do, and for their faith in me, here and elsewhere.

To my agent, Alex Adsett, for her tireless support and relentless front line assaults.

To my writerly friends who have beta read these stories, read early copies of this book, or contributed in some way to this collection or its contents, especially Joanne Anderton, Angela Slatter, Kaaron Warren, Laird Barron, Nathan Ballingrud, Paul Haines, Andrew McKiernan, Lisa L. Hannett. To count myself among you feeds my soul. I know the moment this goes to print I'll realise someone important has been missed from this list and I'm so sorry! Mea culpa.

To all my other wonderful writerly friends not mentioned above, but who are no less a part of my journey, my tribe, my passion. You know who you are and you know I love you. Your support, our community, means the world to me.

To all the editors and publishers who have put their trust, expertise and dollars behind these stories. Great editors are a wondrous breed.

To the literary giants who inspired and continue to inspire me, too numerous to mention.

To anyone who affected my life, whether positively or negatively. Parts of you all live in here. Some of you died in here.

And most importantly, to the two people who make my life worth living and remind me daily that while darkness lurks everywhere, so too does light: Halinka and Arlo, I love you guys more than good single malt whisky.

Lastly, to you, dear reader: Thank you.

CONTENTS

INTRODUCTION

JOANNE ANDERTON

THERE ARE SPACES IN BETWEEN realms, places that ride the fine line between the gritty and the magical, where every choice we make is weighed, and there is very little light at the end of the tunnel. These are the places Alan Baxter takes us to.

The stories in *Crow Shine* explore the nature of these boundaries, and the people and places that balance on their edge . . . or cross them completely. There are choices that must be made, and the consequences of these choices to be endured. An ever-present thread of darkness weaves through the collection, sometimes stark and black and given form, sometimes a creeping sense of hopelessness simmering beneath the surface. And at the heart of every single story is a deep understanding of what makes us human—the good, and the bad.

"Crow Shine" is a story original to this collection and the perfect piece to name it after. It is quintessential Alan Baxter story telling. In it, the main character Clyde and his mysterious Grandpa cross lines both magical and personal. They step into a world somewhere between our mundane reality and a place as black as a crow's wing. Dark magic and soulful music combine to create an intoxicating choice—a drink powerful in more ways than one. We bear witness to Clyde's temptation and understand the choices he makes, even the betrayals, all the while fully aware that he and the people he loves will suffer the consequences. Of course, Clyde is aware of it too, and knows the path he has chosen will bring him darkness. Is he powerless to change course, or just too weak? Are any of us really in control of the decisions we make?

The between places in "The Old Magic", also original to this collection, are completely different—but no less powerful. A eulogy to a life lived too long, the story winds between the present and the past, blending memory and magic. Erin is blessed—or is it cursed?—with magical power that allows her to help others but always sets her apart. As she reminisces about her past and the loves she has lost, we comes to realize that she inhabits an in between place of her own. She exists on the edge of society, perpetually isolated between the real world with its inexorable progression of years, and her own space seemingly out of time. The story is poignant, wistful, and the creeping horror of Erin's situation is so understated we don't even feel it at first. A very human horror of loss, with an ending that feels at once heartbreaking and inevitable.

Whereas "The Old Magic" reflects on a lifetime's worth of difficult choices, "Tiny Lives" focuses on just one. The biggest one. What are we willing to give up for the people we love? "Tiny Lives" is a gorgeous and sad little story about love and sacrifice, told through the image of intricate clockwork toys literally given tiny lives. And then in "Old Promise, New Blood" Alan deals with the consequences of a choice already made. What happens to those left behind? The main character must deal with the fallout of the choice his father made—the dark magic he bargained with, and the son he was forced to sacrifice as a result. *Thank you for not making me choose*, his father says at one point, as the main character's twin brother offers himself up. A sacrifice neither the main character, nor his father, has the strength to make.

This archetypal human weakness is at the heart of "The Darkness in Clara", in which the darkness that is present in so many of Alan's stories is given form. Michelle must deal with the fallout of her beloved Clara's choice to take her own life. As she travels to the small country town where Clara grew up, she is forced to deal with small mindedness and bigotry . . . and something much darker. Remote country towns with uneasy residents and long buried secrets have a long tradition in horror and dark fiction. They are boundary places in themselves—the edge of civilization, where a small human presence struggles against the all-surrounding emptiness. "A Strong Urge to Fly", another original story to the collection, makes use of a similar setting. A tiny town, far from home, right on the edge of the sea. A classic horror story, complete with creepy old woman and her eccentric house full of highly unusual cats, the story offers up a common horror trait—choose to break the rules, and suffer the consequences.

These are only a small selection of stories from a collection that will appeal to those of us who enjoy the darkness, and the bittersweet sting of a not quite happy ending. But we do not take the darkness away with us when we read one of Alan Baxter's stories. He might guide us to those spaces between worlds, and cross boundaries that should not be crossed, and force us to bare witness to hard choices and dark consequences—but that's not what stays with us. Instead, it's the fundamental humanity at the core of every single tale.

Because life is like that sometimes. There is darkness and choices and lines we should not cross but do. Alan's stories grip us, and engage us, and sometimes horrify us, because we have all been there too, in one way or the other.

Joanne Anderton
September 2016

CROW SHINE

CROW SHINE

CLYDE DROVE HIS OLD FORD through dense trees, Robert Johnson on the stereo battling the knock and growl of the almost-dead engine. Tires crunched gravel and hard dirt on the narrow road. When the track ended, Clyde pulled up and left the motor running, enjoying the meagre efforts of the air-conditioning for a moment longer.

He reached into his shirt pocket and pulled out a pack of gum, stared at it in disgust. He hated the stuff. If only he had the courage to ask Melanie out, rather than simply buying shit he didn't need from her over the pharmacy counter. She always looked at him so sly, little tip of the head. She knew, for God's sake. Why was he such a coward? He threw the junk into the passenger footwell.

He'd keep learning from Grandpa, absorb that legendary blues prowess. Then maybe Clyde would feel he had something with which to impress Mel, that made him special enough for her attention.

He killed the engine and stepped from the car into the cruel bayou heat, glanced up into the twisted branches of bald cypress trees, hung with veils of Spanish moss like old men's beards. Sweat instantly trickled down his back.

He reverently lifted Grandpa's rosewood guitar off the back seat, fret-stoned and restrung, fresh from the music store—there was no instrument on God's earth more beautiful—and stalked off through the trees.

As he got close, he smelled wood smoke on the air, thought momentarily about Grandpa's tin and copper still, but the aroma was wrong. His breath caught at the sight of blackened, smoking stumps on the water's edge, a skeletal parody of what had once been his grandpa's secret place. He broke into a run.

Everything was silent devastation, twisted metal and blackened remains, burned almost to nothing. Stark, broken bones jutting from the tranquil water. Clyde desperately hoped the old man was somewhere else.

Movement not a yard away caught his eye as hot sun glanced off the satin sheen of dark feathers and a glistening eye tipped left then right. Clyde frowned at the bird, perched on one sooty stub, disturbed by its calm, its indifference to his proximity. He waved a hand and the crow flapped its wings in response, and cawed. Clyde took a heavy step forward and the corvid hopped to a higher piece of burned wall, out of reach but not much farther away.

"Goddamn you, creature."

Insects buzzed and ticked in the humid air, other wild things whistled and hooted. Nothing else for miles around. Even his daddy didn't know about this place. Clyde himself wasn't supposed to, except for the day after his eighth birthday when he'd followed Grandpa, sneaking and scurrying in pursuit as the aging bluesman ambled out through the bayou.

Then Grandpa had spotted him and his creased face had folded up in a scowl. "The hell you doin', Clyde?"

"Sorry, Grandpa, I was just curious."

"Can't a man have any privacy?"

Clyde had hung his head and one perfect drop of contrition had hit the scuffed and dirty toe of his sneaker.

"Don't snivel, you're here now," Grandpa had said. "Come on in. You tell a soul about this place and I'll have your hide, you understand?"

Clyde had kept that secret for fifteen years, and learned guitar at the man's knee. But he had never shared the crystal clear moonshine that made his grandpa famous. He would sit and watch the old man get drunk while playing the most moving blues in the state. Everyone agreed, no one could hold a candle to Moonshine McCreary.

Always sipping from a clay bottle while he picked the songs of melancholy angels from that rosewood guitar, his voice a gravelly resonance from somewhere beyond this world. The man had skills, but Clyde knew the real power was in the 'shine.

"I shouldn't play for you, boy!" Moonshine would bark, as Clyde would gasp at the drag against his soul. But he'd play on, take a bit more from his grandson, before yelling and sending the young man off home.

"This is my shame, boy," Grandpa had drunkenly slurred late one night, gesturing with the bottle as pale smoke wreathed his grey curls. "When I'm gone, you don't ever let it be yours, you hear? My recipe dies with me."

But Clyde had long since figured it out, and secretly pencilled his notes and sketches, spying as the old man brewed.

He stepped carefully onto the porch of the shack, hoping he didn't go through the burned wood into the swamp beneath. His heart stuttered when he snagged sight of a scorched foot sticking out of burned up denim. He moved around and the rest of Moonshine McCreary was slowly revealed. Clyde jumped as the crow squawked its laughter at him, and then he was crying.

"Grandpa!"

Loss was a tornado through his chest. Despite all the old man had taken, there was no one Clyde loved more. He crouched by the corpse and it was not a pleasant sight. What flesh remained was bubbled and blistered, parts of the man, including his lower jaw, were nowhere to be seen.

The crow hopped down and Clyde tried to shoo it away again, but it danced back out of his reach. Clyde surged to his feet and hollered, swung a foot to kick the foul carrion eater. As it leaped skyward he tripped and fell, but managed to hold the guitar high, away from damage, and scuffed his cheek a little on the floorboards.

He sat up, rested the instrument across his lap, saw his sweat-sheened face mirrored in the deep red, polished surface. His mind drifted to his notebook in the glovebox of his crappy car. Lots of Moonshine's songs, lyrics and chord progressions were in there, along with little scraps of his own inspiration he meant to work on further. And on the front page, a list of ingredients, times, temperatures. The thing Grandpa had guarded with a furious passion. There was a sketch of the still, particulars of its haphazard construction. Clyde knew its energy only worked for the old man, but now he was gone . . . Well, now maybe it belonged to Clyde.

He was guilt-ridden, considering his inheritance not two yards from Grandpa's blackened corpse, but at last it was his turn. He pictured Melanie's smooth curves and a smile tugged his lips. He glanced across at the gruesome remains. Honestly, if Moonshine was going to go, this was probably the best way, accidentally blowing himself to pieces with his secret still.

Clyde knew it wouldn't take much to rebuild and take on the making of Moonshine McCreary's signature blend. He had to hope its power would come to him. The dark bird, high on a blackened beam, laughed and ducked, almost as though it approved of his silent resolution.

Clyde headed carefully off the smoking wreck and made his way back to the car to call the police and his father. Pa wouldn't give a shit, he never wanted anything to do with Moonshine, and gave up warning Clyde away years ago, but he had to be told. People needed to know the legend had died. The blues community state-wide would be in mourning.

◆

THE FUNERAL WAS a circus of local media and milling hangers-on. Everyone wanted to say they'd been there the day they put Moonshine McCreary in the ground. Clyde was seething by the time it was over, but the wake was a much quieter affair. Only family and their closest friends were invited, the location kept secret until passed around by word of mouth at the graveside. *Marie's, one hour.*

Clyde sat in the small lounge room, the smell of coffee and bourbon and Alice's cakes redolent through the house. Fans turned lazily, but did little to push away the heat. He lifted Grandpa's rosewood guitar, that he had refused to relinquish since that dark day, and put it across his knees. The room hushed.

"I'm happy to play for y'all," Clyde said. "I'm nothing like the artist he was. No one was, is or ever will be, but I'll do all I can to bring some honor to his memory."

His fingers caressed the strings and he sang three of his Grandpa's favorites before tears stole his voice.

He endured the hugs and assurances of love, grateful for them though all he really wanted was solitude. As soon as it felt reasonable, he excused himself to go and continue the rebuild in the bayou.

◆

EVEN BEFORE THE still was fully reconstructed, Clyde found some courage to talk to Melanie more often. She was so very sympathetic for his loss and, though he lacked the mettle to actually ask her out, he felt they grew closer over time. He continued to be plagued by a mild guilt as the shack was returned to its former glory, and the still reconstructed. Fresh copper pipes and a new stainless steel boiling vessel were held together by bits of tin and garbage, even some of the scorched remains of its original design. And Mel herself asked sidelong about the old man's famous brew, probing with the curiosity everyone shared; how much did Clyde know? And she even seemed to hint that perhaps he should leave it well alone. But Grandpa's legacy was more important to him than anyone's conservatively cautious mindset.

While he worked in the heat, that damn crow—could it really be the same one?—beset him every day, ducking and dancing, shouting for attention. He began to think perhaps Grandpa had tamed the creature and it was used to human company. But he wondered why he'd never seen the bird before.

"You miss him too?" he asked it one hot afternoon, and it cawed a sad and lonely note.

The ingredients of the 'shine were tricky to source, his income from working the rail maintenance yards and a handful of gigs playing to rowdy bar crowds not likely to make him rich any time soon. Especially hard to find were the strange herbs Grandpa only ever whispered about. He finally discovered them in the third town he tried, nearly an hour's drive from home, in a small, gloomy store where the aged proprietor frowned and scowled as he paid.

◆

THE FIRST DAY the 'shine was ready, Clyde was filled with nerves. He knew Grandpa's nectar would have been no rotgut. No throat-searing jet fuel. The man surely made 'shine as fine as his music and Clyde wondered if his own effort would be as far from Grandpa's as his guitar picking was.

He sipped and paused, and then a wide smile split his face. It tasted better than the most expensive booze he'd ever had. It was perfect. Crow sat on one curling copper pipe and bobbed his head in agreement, croaked a song of celebration. Clyde turned his grin up to the bird and said, "He'd sure be proud of us." And he drank again.

Something snaked through him from his legs up into his groin and gut. A creeping, subtle touch like slipping into a warm creek in high summer. The spread of warmth added power to his mind, seemed to caress him, hold him tight like loving arms. It was more than simple alcohol and Clyde leaned back and sighed. Crow chuckled laughter and Clyde realised he was mimicking perfectly his Grandpa's reaction to the day's first sip. He remembered a conversation from years past.

You always look so damned relaxed when you take that first hit, Grandpa.

The old man had looked serious down at him and said, *It's my curse, son. Don't be fooled.*

Clyde suffered a moment's fear, took one shuddering breath, but Crow laughed again and he shrugged, let the puissant heat envelope him.

After a few more sips, he picked up Grandpa's old rosewood guitar. So relaxed, he had never played as well before, never made the instrument sing like he did that night as his fingers danced and swept with ease. He sounded a lot like Moonshine McCreary as he sat playing into the russet smudge of dawn while Crow bobbed and laughed along.

◆

CLYDE BEGAN TO get better gigs in bigger venues. Places with posters of the greats who had played there before him plastered on the walls, instead of hub caps and beer stains. Where people came from far out of town, drawn by the talent on offer. And he finally balled up the courage to ask Melanie to come listen to him play.

"Well, finally!" she said, smiling at him over the counter.

"I just . . . I guess . . . " He kept his eyes on hers, resisting the temptation to stare at her full curves.

"It's fine. You were scared and that makes me feel special. But I'm glad you finally asked me out. Just promise you'll take me for pie or something afterwards."

Clyde felt red surge up his cheeks and she giggled. "Of course!" he assured her.

"I can't wait to hear you play. You must be much improved since the school band."

"I play a lot better since . . . " He wasn't sure what he almost said. Since Grandpa died? Since I drank his 'shine? "Since then," he finished lamely.

"I'll bet you do. Now get, I've customers to serve. Pick me up?"

"I will. At seven thirty." He turned and smiled an apology to the grinning, red-haired woman next in line.

She winked and actually pinched his cheek.

♦

MELANIE BEAMED AND nodded encouragement from the corner of the low-ceilinged bar. The heat was close, and beer and whiskey filled the air with their tantalising aromas. Cigarette smoke curled and lazed around the crowd, catching here and there in the downlights, then lost again in the gloom as Clyde warmed up with a couple of songs of his own composition. But he intended to transcend his former self with this performance.

"My next song is an old favorite," he said, reaching into his satchel at the side of the rickety wooden stage. He pulled out a clay bottle and lifted it in a toast. A ripple of laughter and soft applause travelled the crowded bar. "My Grandpa made this famous." He swigged. "And this song too!" He stared past the bright lights along the stage edge, into the sea of expectant faces. The world only extended as far as the wooden walls, microcosm, nothing beyond. He took another hit, gestured again with the 'shine, and grinned.

Another swell of appreciation swept the room and, as the heady liquor found his gut, Clyde experienced that warming flush once more. His put the bottle at his feet and began picking out the notes of Grandpa's "Black Wings of Loss", and the sensation flooded his fingertips and his guitar, and rolled out across the patrons like a wave.

Faces in the audience tipped back in rapture, silhouetted bodies swayed and rolled in the darkness, and Clyde bathed in their adoration. It was a palpable thing, thicker in the air than booze and smoke, every bit as physical as the 'shine that warmed his throat and stomach. His guitar sang like the Heavenly Host and his voice was low and perfect. That sensation of drag against his spirit he felt whenever Grandpa had played for him flowed back now, multiplied a hundredfold and more. Everything he gave to the people at his feet they fed back to him amplified and purified, and he rode it like the surge of the finest cocaine. Every nerve thrilled and sang to his ministrations, every soul in the room vibrated in time with his, and fed him.

Before he knew it, three hours had passed, his clothes stuck to his skin with sweat, and he was through his repertoire and gently free-styling a last few melancholy licks. He smiled and let the music slip away. The clientele seemed to rise as if from a dream and they threw rapturous applause at him. He thanked them and sipped more 'shine only to find the bottle empty.

A voice from the crowd called out, "You were the ghost of your Grandpa tonight!" and the applause redoubled.

When he stepped from the stage, Melanie looped her arms about his neck and breathed hot against his throat. "I don't want pie," she whispered. "Take me somewhere private."

◆

THE SHACK WAS the only place he knew. He couldn't take her home where his pa would be full of rancour and questions, and his car was too seedy for the space he felt they needed. When they reached the wooden veranda, Melanie jumped and cried out in surprise.

"Don't mind Crow," Clyde said. "He was Grandpa's pet. Guess he's mine now."

Crow dipped his head and his obsidian eyes glittered in the night.

◆

THE MORE CLYDE played, the better he got, always fuelled by Grandpa's secret blend. And the people's love for him grew, but none so much as Melanie's. As his star rose, the 'shine took back so much more than he ever gave out. Over time, the example of Mel right before him made his choices impossible to ignore. He watched her wither as she loved him, lose weight, lose interest in all other things. He didn't send her away in anger as his grandpa had him, though he knew full well he should. Her love was sweetest of all and he simply couldn't stop.

The bars filled up with adoring fans, crowded ever tighter in the hot, aromatic darkness. Every gig had queues of folk disappointed outside, turned away from a venue already breaking safety codes with numbers. People drew comparisons between his skills and Moonshine McCreary ever more regularly, and soon began to accuse him of being even greater than that great man. He moved from bars to theatres and the lights grew ever brighter.

Articles state-wide lauded his virtuoso talent. A national magazine ran a feature article on the boy who played with a skill and maturity unbelievable in someone only twenty-four years of age. He often cited his losses—mother at age five, grandfather so recently—both such great influences on him, as informing his grasp of the soul of the blues. But he knew it was a lie.

And every time he played, every time he basked in that adoration, he ignored how much it was costing them. Whatever the 'shine catalysed in his spirit, that drew such sweet energy from the crowds, it didn't come without a price. Every little bit of succour he received was a sliver of their very souls, made so clear by Melanie's constant waning presence at his side. Yet he gladly played on.

She quit her job, as he was making good money, playing every night. She talked of marriage and how she had to make sure he stayed hers forever, even while her forever became a shorter and shorter span of time. He knew when she finally creased up and gave the last of herself to him, he would simply find another. He could pick and choose from fawning women, currently held at bay only by Melanie's constant, scorching gaze. He knew too he should resist that, but the 'shine was blinding to his morals even as it was nectar to his soul.

He remembered Grandpa's words as he sipped that day's first draft.

It's my curse, son. Don't be fooled.

Grandpa had insisted his family not come to all his shows, not put themselves out, and he had steadfastly refused to play at home except in the most exceptional of circumstances. *When I'm home, just let me be a man, not a bluesman.*

All those times he had played for Clyde and then grown angry, sent him away with shame in his eyes. Why did Clyde not do the same with Mel?

So many past comments from family about how Clyde must have the metabolism of a racehorse, given all he ate yet remained as thin as rope. But now his body began to fill out even as Mel's continued to waste away. What soul remained untarnished in Clyde ached with the knowledge that everything he built was blacker than Crow's glossy wings.

But still he could not stop.

Until Melanie finally died.

She had insisted he play for her some more after a particularly crowded gig. "Something just for me, sweetness?" she cajoled on the porch of his shack.

And he played. Not for her, damn his soul, but because he knew the sweet perfection of her spirit would be drawn into him and make him even higher. And as she slipped away, as his fingers coaxed the music and the last of her swept into him, her finality hit him like a wave. Crystalline, jagged grief momentarily made him pause, sliced through the velvet redolence of his 'shine-induced delirium. As she expired, Clyde tipped back his head and howled. And Crow laughed.

Clyde carried her skin and bones to his car and hurried to the hospital, but she was cold when he got there. The staff wanted to know what she had taken and he assured them nothing had passed her lips but a bit of liquor. They called the police, who took his statement and then sent him away.

"Go and sleep, Clyde," the sergeant said, one warm, reassuring hand on his shoulder. "You need to rest. Big show at the Emporium tomorrow, right?"

◆

WHILE GRIEF STILL fired his soul, Clyde powered through benighted streets and out into the swamps. He grit his teeth and growled against the physical drag that tried to cease his actions. He grabbed one clay bottle and jammed a rag into its neck. Flame surged into the darkness and he launched that bottle into the shack's open door. Fire blossomed and Clyde ran for his car as the stockpiled liquor blew with a soul-shattering blast. All the 'shine he had went up and the reconstructed still went with it.

As he drove for home, a weight lifted from his soul, but a terrible guilt settled in his mind. He had taken too much for too long, and it had cost Melanie her life. But at least it was ended now. If nothing else, her loss had given him the brief clarity of grief and thereby the power to act. He lamented his Grandpa with a bleak stain of disappointment. That man had enjoyed his 'shine and his success for *decades*. Clyde wound down the window and sped along the empty highway, revelling in the bright, fresh sensation of new-found freedom as tears for Melanie streaked his cheeks.

A flurry of black feathers burst into the window and battered his face, sharp beak and claws sought his soft flesh and eyes. Crying out, one arm striking at the bird, he tried frantically to steer with the other. His tires hissed and skidded and began to slide on roadside gravel. He screamed as the car lifted and spun sideways, then everything was whining metal, smashing glass, and fire.

◆

A SHINY CROW hopped around the twisted wreckage at the roadside as it burned. The night-black creature skipped sideways towards the flames and plucked once, twice, three times, at something on the edge of the carnage.

As blue and red lights appeared over the horizon, the crow dragged a scorched and tattered notepad free of the crash and left it in plain sight on the edge of the blacktop. Then it flew up into the cypress branches above to wait.

THE BEAT OF
A PALE WING

CARLY FOLLOWED 'BIG SILVER' SILVIO across the Volcano dance floor, past the bar and through a heavy door marked *Private*. She smirked to herself at the faces they passed, all the associates frowning, suddenly concerned at the presence of the big boss. His slick, black hair, designer suit perfectly hugging his large, athletic frame, and his hard, expressionless face all spoke volumes. The regular club punters had no idea of the power walking among them.

The door led through an office and out back to a large warehouse. Three men stood on cold concrete, expectant. The one in the middle—tall, thin—lifted his sharp chin in greeting. "Big Silver, so good to see you, boss."

"You can make this happen now, Magic?"

Carly rolled her eyes. He never was much for pleasantries.

Magic Bertoli tipped his head to one side, a strange affirmative. His blond ponytail swung free. "Of course. For you, no problem."

Big Silver pulled his phone from a pocket and dialled. "Bring them around," he said after a moment and hung up.

Magic gestured to the two burly men with him. They went to roller doors leading into the warehouse space. One pressed a button to winch it up while the other casually tucked a hand into his jacket. Trustful as ever.

A sleek black car purred along the alley and into the building. As the roller door rattled closed behind it, the car stopped and a hulk of a man, stretching the seams of a black suit, unfolded himself from the driver's seat. He moved around to the trunk of the car and popped it open. "Where do you want them?"

Big Silver looked to Magic who gestured to the ground right by the car. "Just leave them there."

The big man grunted and reached in. He straightened with a limp, ashen corpse in his arms, a bullet hole like a tiny red flower in the centre of the man's forehead. He dumped the body on the floor. It rolled, revealing an ugly exit wound in the back of the skull. The Hulk pulled another corpse from the trunk, similar, though smaller and older, bearing a comparable mark of execution. He dumped that body beside the first.

Big Silver turned to Magic. "All good here? You can live up to your name right now?"

"All good."

Big Silver pointed to the car, addressed the huge man who drove it. "Take that to the yard and have it crushed, then get yourself somewhere safe and burn those clothes."

"Yes, boss."

"No fuck ups!"

"No fuck ups, boss."

Magic's cronies wound up the roller door, let Hulk drive away. Carly frowned, bothered that such a nice car was being junked. Still, it was details like that which kept Big Silver at the top of this particular game. He turned to her, took her chin in one manicured hand and kissed her.

"I have to go and see some men about some business," he said.

Carly's eyes tightened, her annoyance instant. Her long brunette hair sported an expensive new cut. She wore a brand new dress and knew she looked great in it, her tall, gym-fit body a damn fine piece of work. All for nothing, again. "I thought we were going to enjoy the club tonight. You said . . . "

"I know what I said. Things change."

"Okay." She knew that seeing men about business meant seeing whores in a strip club. She also knew it was pointless to argue.

"You stay here and have a nice time." He turned to Magic. "You'll look after my little lady, right?"

Magic grinned broadly. "Of course. Miss Carly doesn't pay for drinks at my club, boss."

Big Silver nodded and left without another word, strolled through the still raised roller door and into a car at the end of the alley.

Magic waited for his men to close the place up and cocked a thumb back over his shoulder. "Take the lady out front, make sure she has anything she needs."

They nodded and led Carly away. As they shut the connecting door behind themselves, leaving Magic alone in the warehouse with the dead, Carly said, "You boys go on, I know my way. I want to use the bathroom."

When one of them cocked an eyebrow, she added, "I hate using the bathroom out there, with all the coked-up bitches gossiping."

The men laughed and went through into the club. Music boomed briefly through the open door, before returning to a muffled thump as it closed. Carly flicked an eye towards the private bathroom, waited a moment to be sure, then picked her way back to the warehouse door. Fuck Silvio if he was going to leave her alone again. She would finally get to see just what Magic's skills really were. A part of her wondered if he was so good at disappearing people because he ate them.

The door to the warehouse was solid wood on the bottom half, four square panes of glass making up the top. The glass had been painted over, obscuring the view, but a small area a couple of inches across had been scratched or chipped away by something. Carly pulled a tissue from her bag and spat on it, polished the grime away from the gap in the paint. She crouched to peek through.

Magic was on hands and knees, meticulously chalking strange designs on the concrete in a triangle around the two stiffs. The designs were quite simple, but he took patient care in their placement. When he was happy with his work he moved several metres away and chalked a circle, smaller, around himself. Carly took her phone out to video the procedure.

Magic stood in the centre of his circle and pulled a heavy, dark figurine on an equally heavy-looking chain from inside his shirt. He held it aloft and began to intone a strange phrase. It was a language Carly couldn't comprehend, yet he repeated it over and over and the words slowly sank into her memory, heavy with relevance she couldn't explain.

As he spoke, tiny white moths appeared from nowhere and began to flit around him in a dancing cloud. More and more until he was surrounded by a seething mass of fluttering paleness. With a two-armed gesture, like an aircraft traffic controller, Magic pointed towards the corpses in the triangle. The moths swarmed away and surrounded the dead men, flittering over their bodies. As they moved, uncanny colours slipped into the air, drifting and stretching like oil on water. More like stains in nothingness than anything tangible, the colours swam and merged, slowly coalesced into a heavy, undulating cloud of tones and shimmers. The moths winked out, one by one, seemingly consumed by the cloud of colour, and the kaleidoscope descended on the bodies. In the writhing mass of tones the dead men's clothes shifted and danced, and the colour rose again, leaving nothing but empty suits and shirts. Even the bloodstains on the white collars had gone. Four shoes sat, hideous in their sudden emptiness.

The colour swirled within the confines of the chalked walls, rising up in a column and pressing down and out, seeking escape. Carly held her breath, hand trembling as she filmed. Magic intoned another chant, over and over. The stilted words seemed to batter the colour. It twitched and flinched, moved up and down, shifted angrily within its confines before slowly breaking apart and dissipating.

Everything was still.

Magic slumped, panting. Within moments he recovered, took the clothes from the floor. An oil drum stood in one corner and he dumped the clothes into it, doused them with petrol from a battered can and flicked a match in. A ball of orange and black blossomed and crackled as the last evidence was consumed. A minute or two with a bucket and mop to erase the carefully chalked shapes and nothing whatsoever remained of the murderous activity so recently apparent.

Carly stopped her recording, trembling. Magic was well named. She hurried into the club, determined to make good use of those free drinks.

◆

CARLY AWOKE FROM a half-drunk stupor as Silvio crashed home. She winced, instantly aware of the level of his inebriation from the staggering and cursing. He stumbled into the bedroom, began undressing. She squeezed her eyes shut, pretended to sleep on.

"You're not sleeping," Silvio slurred. "I know how much you drank and how wasted you were when you left the Volcano. Which is to say, not nearly enough to be passed out."

Carly's heart sped up. "I'm just really tired, baby."

"I know everything that happens. You know that."

"I know."

He fell heavily onto the bed, began pawing at her hip as she lay curled on her side. Deciding it was better to get it over with than resist, she sat up, turned to face him. "You have a good night, baby?" she asked, forcing a smile.

He looked into her eyes for a moment, his own swimming in and out of focus. With surprising speed he backhanded her cheek, knocked her head to one side. Her teeth rattled together and she tasted blood along with the shock and hurt. "Go the fuck to sleep." Almost a whisper as he fell backwards onto his pillows. He began snoring instantly.

Carly pressed one hand to her cheek, curling up tighter than ever with her back to him. She remembered the love she'd had for him, when he was a player, not the boss. She remembered the sweet, strong, take-no-shit man she'd fallen in love with. She cried herself softly to sleep, wondering where that man had gone.

♦

CARLY ROSE EARLY, spent an extra ten minutes with her make-up to cover the flowering blue stain under her mouth, and left for the day. She wanted to be far away from Silvio for as long as possible. She wanted to be far away forever, but knew it simply wasn't that easy. He wouldn't let her go. And a part of her still loved him. The endless money and royal treatment had held her interest for a long time, but it got to a point where nothing was enough compensation any more.

What seemed like a position of power for so long was slowly revealed as anything but. The emperor wore no clothes and Carly was as powerless as a person could be. She was a strong, smart woman who had let herself become irrelevant. The wife of a mob boss might seem to be top of the heap, but she fondly remembered being the girlfriend of a *caporegime* before his rise. They both had freedom then. Now they were trapped by the confines of hierarchy. Silvio sometimes seemed to hate it even more than she did and it pained a part of her, a part that still cared, to consider the pressure he was under. The responsibility. Regardless, he had the freedom of leadership, at least, even if his life was full of expectation and duty. Her life was nothing except obeisance. For all his talk of respecting the wives, Big Silver had no time for her and no inclination to listen to her counsel. Hell, he didn't even listen to her general conversation any more. She couldn't remember the last time they had talked like a real married couple.

She sat in a cafe, coffee and cake tasting like sawdust and cardboard in her mouth, and wished she had some power back.

Her phone buzzed.

Dinner with Franco and Paulie tonight. Leaving at 6.

She stared at the message. No question of where she was, no concern that she wouldn't show up. Not even a tiny 'x' at the end like he always used to. Just an assumption.

◆

"Do I LOOK okay, baby?" she asked.

Silvio didn't look around. "You look a million bucks, Carly, you always do."

She scowled at his back. What the fuck was a million bucks to him? Pocket change in his empire. "Is there a reason for dinner tonight, or are we just being social?"

He laughed, more a bark of derision than anything like humour. "When is anything just social? We have to talk about the threat from the Baccalieris. They're muscling up too much, something's gotta give."

Carly chewed her lip nervously. "Gonna be a lot more work for Magic, then, eh?"

He turned to look at her, his face hard. She wasn't supposed to talk about this stuff. She was sure he'd rather she didn't talk about anything at all. In his ideal world, she only ever opened her mouth to put his cock in it.

"You know what it is he does?" she asked, trembling as she pressed her luck.

"What do you mean?"

"I mean, do you know *how* he does what he does?"

Silvio's eyes narrowed and Carly's lip throbbed. He stared hard at her for several seconds. Eventually he said, "I don't care how he does it. He's fucking superb and that's all that matters."

"So you don't know?" Carly's heart hammered, hardly able to believe how much she was testing his patience. Clearly some limit had been reached, some unspoken line crossed.

"I know it ain't natural," Silvio said with a twisted smile. "And I know I'm glad he works for me."

He eyes told a different story to his lips and Carly ran out of bravery to push any further. He did know, at least partly, what Magic Bertoli did, but was not going to share it with her. She turned away, feeling angry, impotent, and finished dressing.

◆

THE MEN DISCUSSED the threat from the Baccalieris and ignored the women in the other room. The semblance of a dinner party was a ridiculous parody, lip service to cultural proprietary ignored with every other aspect of the business. Carly tried to engage with the mindless prattle about fashion and hair, and who was fucking who in the lower ranks, but she couldn't even pretend well. They kept asking her if she was unwell and she eventually conceded that she was under the weather, to stop them asking. She kept one ear on the conversation Silvio conducted with the other bosses. She could only catch snippets through the open door, frustratingly small details. Their allegiance went back generations, that much she knew, and this Baccalieri threat was serious, it seemed. For a moment she imagined if all the bosses were women, how different the family affairs might be. Then laughed quietly to herself. Who was she kidding, the women would be heartless bitches, too.

Silvio was sullen and angry in the car going home and Carly braced all the way, wondering when the slaps would start, be they verbal or physical. Or both. But he pulled up the long driveway to their mansion without any attacks and sat staring at the steering wheel.

After a moment of uncomfortable silence Carly said, "Come inside, I'll make you a drink."

Silvio shook his head, almost imperceptibly. "You go in. Go to bed. I gotta see to some business."

Carly didn't move, her slow-boil rage rising again. Silvio turned to look at her and his eyes dared her to do anything, say anything, even move anywhere but out of the car. Somewhere beneath that angry, hostile surface was the man she loved, but he was gone, burned away by duty and a complete lack of respect. She ground her teeth and climbed out of the Hummer. Without sparing her a glance, Silvio turned in the huge gravel driveway and drove back to the road and away.

Carly stood still, shivering with the late evening cold, and a colder sense of purpose sank over her. That line was beyond crossed now. Something had snapped. She fumbled in her bag for the remote and opened up one of the double garages beside the house. She tapped a code into a strong box, which popped open, revealing bunches of keys. She took one at random. It said *Maserati* on the tag. Within minutes the sleek red car carried her at nearly double the speed limit towards the Volcano Club.

♦

"IS HE IN?" she asked the goon at the bar.

"Who?"

"Your boss, dummy. Magic Bertoli."

The goon pointed across the strobing, throbbing dance floor to a roped-off VIP area. Magic sat among sycophants and pretty girls, laughing and drinking. Carly strode across and caught Magic's eye as she mounted the steps. A heavy stepped forward to prevent her access and Magic was there, his hand on the heavy's shoulder. "Let her in."

"I need to talk to you," Carly said.

Magic raised one eyebrow. "I haven't had any word from Big Sil—"

"I don't need his fucking permission to talk to you and you don't need it to talk to me."

Magic raised both hands, palms out. "Okay, okay. What's up?"

"Can we go somewhere private?"

"Sure."

They walked back across the club, through to the offices at the back. Carly felt exposed, obvious. Stupid. But she had to know. Inside the office, the pounding club muffled through thick walls, Magic asked, "So what's up here?"

"How loyal are you to Big Silver?"

His eyes went wide, he looked left and right in panic. "What? Completely loyal, why would you ask?"

She sat quietly for a moment, her face impassive. "He doesn't know I'm here,"' she said eventually. "No one does. Be honest with me. Could you be turned?"

Magic laughed. "You got ideas above your station, little lady. Silvio will kill you when I tell him about this conversation."

She had her answer, and a clear course. "But you won't tell him. I'm not asking because I want you to turn. I want to know that you'll stand behind my Silvio no matter what." She was proud of the strength in her voice. She almost believed herself.

Magic tilted his head to one side, his universal gesture. "Oh, you're scared for him?"

She said nothing.

"This Baccalieri threat, is it? Don't worry about it. Big Silver is one connected *capo*. It's a war no-one wanted, but it isn't one he'll lose. Don't worry, I'm behind Silvio all the way. My loyalty cannot be bought. I owe him more than you'll ever know."

Carly nodded, smiling inside. She'd played that really quite well, even if she did say so herself. For the first time in years, she felt a sense of power returning. "Okay," she said with a nod. "Okay, thanks."

"Don't you worry about Big Sil, little lady. We'll all be fine."

She hated it when he called her little lady. His patronising tone turned her stomach. With a smile like she felt fully reassured, she let Magic lead her back into the club and joined him in the VIP area for a few drinks. It was late when she finally excused herself, but she had no intention of going home.

◆

THE ALLEYWAY WAS cold as hell and getting damp. Carly began to question her resolve, not to mention her sanity, and was about to give up when the roller door to Magic's warehouse shivered and began to rattle up. *Please, please, please,* she thought, watching intently. As the door reached the top, a car nosed out and Carly strained to see. She smiled. Magic on his own, no one else visible in the dark space behind. Before he could clear the doorway and lower it again, she ran forward, affecting an expression of panic. She waved her hands at him to stop.

Magic's face registered equal parts surprise and concern. He rolled down the window and said, "What the fuck, little lady?" just as Carly shot him in the face.

Her purse-sized .22 cracked ridiculously loud in the confined alley and she stared in horror at Magic's brains all over the headrest of his brand new Chrysler. She stood frozen for a moment as all the sound in the city seemed to die. With a gasp of determination she ran to the passenger side and pulled the door open, shifted the car into neutral, ran back to the front and heaved against it. Her feet slipped and skidded on the greasy alley bitumen, but with a will born of desperation she got the car moving, rolled it back into the warehouse. She struggled to regain her breath, arms and legs shaking from the effort. Maybe from shock, too. She punched the button to lower the roller door.

Not pausing to think about it, she ran to the office and accessed the closed circuit TV that watched everything. It only took a moment to locate the camera watching the alley. She wound back the digital recording, eyes widening as the brains left the back window of Magic's car, the flash retreated into her revolver and she staggered back into the darkness of the shadows. She kept the recording going backwards until the roller door closed again, Magic alive and well in his car about to leave for home. She stopped rewinding and hit record, then wiped the machine of all her prints. The time stamp might be out, but there would be no evidence here of what had happened. She smirked, proud of herself. She'd learned a thing or two from her old man over the years.

Back in the warehouse, lights on, she stood for a moment, staring at the car. She still shook, stunned by what she had done. Would this ever work? Swallowing hard, she pulled open the driver's door. Magic sat there, his face still wide with surprise, a seemingly innocuous red hole right beside his nose, just under the left eye. The top and back of his head were another story. Grimacing, swallowing bile, Carly dug into his shirt and pulled free the heavy chain and figurine. *Thank fuck he wears it all the time!* It was even heavier than it looked, carrying a burden of ages. Its dark, carved surface bore an intricate design, a hideous, twisted thing, swollen body with wings and tentacled limbs, a face hard to conceive. It nauseated her to look upon it.

There was blood on the chain and on her hands and arms from where she had retrieved it. Wincing against it touching the back of her neck, she dropped the vile statuette over her head.

The phone video was far from perfect, but it was enough. It had to be enough. She found chalk in Magic's office and began to copy out the strange markings. They were simple enough, really, but even then, a job that had taken Magic mere minutes took her nearly an hour before she was satisfied. A dull panic began to set in that she wouldn't be finished before people began arriving again—cleaners, or boys with jobs, whatever. She pushed the worry away, kept working.

Her circle was easier. It still took a long time, but nothing like the first design. She stood in it and watched the video on her phone once more, listening hard. Just to be sure. With a nod, she pulled the icon out and held it up. Before fear could stay her hand, she began to recite the chant.

The words poured out of her, popping free of her mouth like soap bubbles. As each one emerged, a tiny, white-winged moth burst softly into view. Electricity or static crackled through her, a sensation not entirely unpleasant. Her muscles began to vibrate, her mind buzzed, and more pale moths emerged from nothing and swarmed around her, tickling and fluttering. With a sudden gasp of panic she realised the hideous colours were forming too. A prickle of burning crept across one cheek, another across an eyebrow.

"No!" she screamed. "Him! Take him!" She cast her arms forward, mimicking the action she had seen Magic perform, thought only of Magic and the car, her mind focused on the inside of that triangle. With the mental equivalent of canvas tearing, the cloud of moths surged forward across the gap, sucked into the other space. The disconnection as they passed in was a moment of freedom from incredible power. With it came dizziness and nausea. She shared the gluttonous frenzy as the swarm swirled around the car, pulling the harsh entity of impossible colours and shades from wherever it lived. It consumed the moths, dusty and savoury, and sank over the vehicle, squirmed in through the open door and smothered the corpse inside.

Carly whimpered at the metallic tang of blood, the flavour and scent of still warm human flesh and bone as it was devoured, sharing the hideous sensation as the entity fed. She sobbed as bile rose. The thing slid all over the car, sought out every last molecule of anything human. And then it turned, suddenly crashing up against the invisible barrier of the triangle she had drawn. That she had drawn none too well.

The boundary stretched and flexed. Like paper trying to hold back a wave, it would burst at any moment. She recited the second chant, over and over again, getting louder and more desperate with every repetition. Her will crashed up against that of the entity and they fought as her badly drawn barrier cracked and failed. Wanting nothing more than safety, desperate for success, Carly thought only of sending the hideous thing back to wherever it had come from. As it burst free and crashed up against the circle around her, Carly screamed the chant, staring the writhing mass of colour down, refusing to be beaten. With a sensation like air being sucked out of the room, the thing began to fold in on itself. Its rage was palpable, its hunger all-consuming as it was drawn away by the sorcery she clumsily wielded.

Then stillness.

Carly collapsed, crying, sure she would die from the exertion. It took a long time for her breathing to settle. She dragged herself up and checked the car. It was as clean as it would have been brand new. She drove it back into the corner, where Magic always parked. A glint caught her eye, her bullet sitting on the back seat. With a sound of relief, luck saving her from something she hadn't considered, she pocketed the tiny metal lump, gathered Magic's empty clothes, wiped everything she had touched and locked the car. She returned the keys to the office, blanked the internal security recordings, burned the clothes and mopped the chalked designs off the floor.

She had done it.

She let herself out into the grey, cold light of dawn and walked the four blocks to where the *Maserati* was parked.

◆

SILVIO WASN'T HOME when Carly poured herself into bed. She had to be thankful for small mercies, grateful just this once that he had been out all night. He might not be home for days and wouldn't bother to tell her. It had happened before, until she finally called his cell in a panic and he gruffly told her not to be a nagging wife. Well, fuck him. She let sleep take her.

◆

SHE AWOKE TO Silvio yelling, somewhere downstairs. All one-sided, obviously on the phone. The clock beside her bed said 11:43 A.M. and she still felt bone-tired. Dragging on a robe and staggering down, she saw Silvio pacing the dining room, gesticulating as he yelled. He cast her a look of disdain, presumably disgusted at the lateness of the hour. If only he knew.

She made coffee and toast, gathered herself. *Act normal. Nothing is any different to normal.*

The mantra was still cycling in her mind when Silvio stomped into the kitchen and helped himself to the coffee.

"Everything okay, baby?" she asked casually, chewing on toast. It felt like wood chips in her dry mouth.

"Fucking Magic has done a disappearing act."

Her heart thumped. She hadn't expected him to notice this quickly. Still, what difference did it make? "Disappearing act?" she asked.

Silvio grunted, gulping down the coffee and wincing at the heat of it. "I'm going to be busy all day. This fucking Baccalieri thing needs to be fixed." He stopped, looked at her. "Still, I don't suppose you care, sleeping all fucking day."

She shrugged, smiled sweetly. "I was tired."

He nodded. "Took yourself off to the Volcano last night, eh?" At her wide eyes he said, "I know everything, remember?"

She breathed deeply against her hammering pulse. "Yeah, well, I felt like a drink."

He laughed. "Well, good. Glad you don't need me chaperoning you every time you go out." His eyes narrowed. "Did Magic say anything to you about going anywhere?"

"No. We had a few drinks and talked about nothing in particular. To be honest, I spent more time talking to that girl Selma. She's really sweet, you know." It wasn't a lie.

He turned away. "I'm gonna be in the battle room all day, probably back late. This war starts tomorrow and we gotta be ready."

It was unlike Silvio to be this focused. Or this talkative. The Baccalieri thing had him rattled. "Okay. Be careful, baby."

He grunted and left, not sparing her another look or a kiss goodbye. There was a time when he would never have left without a kiss.

♦

IT WAS VERY late when Silvio came home and fell into bed. Carly woke with a start as he bounced down beside her, whisky on his breath.

"Everything okay, baby?" she said, mimicking the slur of sleep even though she was instantly wide awake.

"Nothing to worry about," Silvio muttered. He sighed, sinking quickly towards slumber.

Carly lay still, listening to his breath settle. She waited several minutes after the snoring started before slipping from the bed. She stepped lightly on the rug, padded across the floorboards of the bedroom and into the dark en suite bathroom. She left the lights off, let her night-vision work for her. With the bathroom door wide, she took her place, held the figurine aloft and began to chant.

It was easier this time, the sensations familiar, the designs better drawn, even on wooden floorboards beneath the rug and on tiles in the bathroom. The moths gathered, fluttering about her. For too long she had been like them, battering against the bright light of Silvio's indifference. Time enough. She cast the tiny harbingers at the bed, watched the foul colours emerge and swallow the swirling insects. It felt good this time, even tasted good, that dry, savoury consumption. The colour descended, snaked in under the covers, and tears streamed Carly's cheeks. They were partly tears of fear but mostly of grief, for the man who had long since gone away.

Silvio thrashed, crying out. He was hard to see among the oily colours, in the dark, through flying bedclothes, but his howls of agony were all too clear. He swore and cursed, the bed rocked and bounced with his rage, and his pain screamed over it all. Carly held the terrible icon high, swallowing against the tastes she couldn't ignore, certainly no longer pleasant. Silvio burst up and met her eye as he struggled on all fours, desperate to escape the bed. Their eyes locked for a moment, half his face already eaten away, as foul colour swirled around him. The entity stripped more flesh, chewed through bone like hot water through ice. Silvio's howls of agony gurgled into incoherent noise as his arms were consumed and his ravaged body dropped, a silent, dead weight. That too passed into the colour and the sheet settled softly on the mattress.

The entity slammed into the invisible wall containing it and Carly began the second chant, her voice almost gone from shock and grief. She screamed and screamed the horrible phrase until the awful entity was sucked away, the room still, silent. Empty.

She sank to the bathroom floor, her breath ragged, miserable at all she had lost, at all she had become. But not any more. There was elation beneath it all. She was taking power back.

It didn't take long to mop up the evidence of the dark magic, wipe floorboards and tiles clean. She showered and made herself ready once the bedroom was back in order. With a grim expression, determined to see things through as planned, she waited until eight A.M., picked up the telephone and dialled. Her heart beat in time to the rings as she waited for an answer.

Eventually a gruff voice said, "Yes?"

She smiled. "Hello, Don Baccalieri. My name is Carly. I have a proposition for you."

TINY LIVES

I TWIST THE TINY COG into place, my old-too-soon fingers gnarled, golden brown and cracked, but true. Complete, I turn the miniature dog over in my hands, the brass and copper of its construction shining in the late afternoon sun. I lift it to my lips, breathe softly into its mechanised heart and it stirs, shifts and wags.

The girl reaches out a greedy hand, eyes alight with wonder and I smile, place the wriggling clockwork puppy on her palm. She hugs it to herself, teeth white in a smile of innocence and immediate love.

"It'll never wind down, really?" the mother asks, eyes wide.

"Never," I reply, as the life draws through my chest like a thick needle through stubborn canvas. I wonder how many more I have in me. The breath is mere delivery, convenience. Something far deeper is taken every time.

"Thank you," she says, handing me so many grubby used notes, as weary as my hands and eyes.

"What do you say to the nice man?" the mother demands of the child.

"Thank you, mister!" the child enthuses and bounds away, her new pet dancing across her hands with tinny yips.

"Khob kun kub, little one," I whisper at her back.

The money goes into the leather satchel at my feet. I wonder when I'll have enough. Soon, I'm sure. I sit back in my tattered deck chair, let the sun bathe my wrinkled skin. My eyes roam the unsteady table before me. Boxes of parts glitter, cogs and tiny pistons, nuts, bolts, brackets and bars. But to me they are all limbs and muscles, nerves and hearts.

A man approaches, smiles unsteadily.

"Is it true?" he asks.

"Is what true, sir?"

"The toys you make. They act as if alive and never wind down?"

I smile. They never really believe, even when they see it. "They are alive, sir, and they will live forever. At least, until the parts wear out."

"Some old Chinese sorcery, is it?" he asks with a crooked smile. He has no idea how offensive he is.

"I'm Thai, sir."

"Ha! Well, there you go." He leans to inspect the compartmentalised case of parts, my neat row of tools in their leather wrap, looking anywhere but into my eyes where he would have to acknowledge the hurt of his words. "Can you make a bird?" he asks suddenly.

"Of course."

"And will it fly?"

"Certainly."

He points to the sign on my table, written when my hand was a lot younger, steadier. "Your price is *very* high."

America, where even the capitalism is subject to suspicion. I smile. "What you buy is absolutely unique, sir."

The chill of the Washington autumn lifts my wispy hair, chills across the back of my hands. The man pulls his jacket tighter. I wish I was back among the warm, humid days of my home, but it's foolish to pine for the past. Instead I am lost in the land of opportunity. But it wasn't for me that we came here. Always for the children. At the thought I smell disinfectant and bleach, see harsh fluorescents and white coats and quickly cast the thoughts away.

"Cash only, eh?" the man asks.

I nod, smile again. Where I come from this much smiling shows nerves, but the Americans seem to think it denotes honesty. Only sharks and the guilty smile this much, but I've learned it can save me a lot of conversation.

"All right, let's see it then!"

It takes nearly an hour to build the tiny hummingbird and test its wings. He's impressed, but scepticism still lives in his eyes. I put the tiny, fragile thing to my lips, breathe into its heart and it flutters up from my palm. The man staggers back and several people gathered to watch gasp and mutter. The bird alights on the man's shoulder and he looks ridiculous as he cranes to see.

"Amazing," he says.

I smile as the life drags again through my chest, snagging against my heart and lungs, adding a wrinkle to my eyes and another layer of weariness in my bones.

"Worth every dollar, buddy!" He hands me a folded wad of bills and I tuck them into the satchel.

Sumalee, my eldest daughter, comes to get me, her face pained at my appearance.

"How many today," she asks.

"Four."

"So we're nearly there?"

I hand her the satchel, its weight pulling against my shoulder like an anvil, though it only weighs a few pounds. "Nearly there."

"You must rest, father."

I nod, but the image of my youngest, Mali, in the hospital tears at me. *She needs rest.* That was how they started to tell us, to lead us to the truth that what she really needed was dollars. Tens of thousands of dollars for surgery. *No insurance,* they cried, aghast, and their interest drained.

♦

It's COLDER AGAIN today, winter coming with relentless certainty. I'm surprised to realise I'm sad I won't see it. Sadder still that I'll never see another sunset in Chiang Mai. Never taste another of Chanarong's sticky rice rolls. But Mali will live, if I hold on a little longer.

Word must be getting around, several people stand impatiently near the spot where I've set up every day for the past month. Sumalee helps me as the people mill about.

"Father," she whispers, and I put a hand on hers to silence the question I know she will ask.

"For Mali," I say. "All of these people. It's enough."

"But can you . . . ?"

"I have to."

Another bird, then a kitten. An obnoxious boy demands a rhino of his fur- and jewel-clad mother and that tests my skills. I've never constructed one before. A puppy and another bird and the day grows old, the sun sinking low. With each enlivening breath I wither a little more. A subtle fears thrills through me. Not for myself, but for her. That I may not make it.

"Please, father," Sumalee says in Thai as I make another kitten. "Let me. Show me!"

"The gift is not something I know how to share," I say, though she already knows.

"Why's she crying," the new owner of the kitten asks as I put life into it. Hot rakes drag through my soul.

I hand over the mewling clockwork cat and smile as it curls in her palm, paws playfully at her fingers. The woman looks down at the tiny life in her hand, astonished, her concern for my eldest daughter forgotten. She hands me a thick stack of bills and I check, add it to the satchel beneath the table. One more and we'll have enough. Mali will get the operation she needs.

Blackness tickles in at the edge of my vision and I realise I'm not breathing. My heartbeat is a staccato throb in my head. Sumalee's face swims into view, her eyes wide, tears streak her cheeks. I was so close. I feel myself drifting away, as if carried like a dried-out leaf on a gentle stream.

"Father? Father, please." She speaks in Thai again and I see Mali in her eyes, stricken, pale. It halts my descent, so briefly, but for long enough. I can't fail.

I reach out, pull myself up with Sumalee's help, drag air reluctantly into my tired lungs. "One more," I whisper, my voice weaker than I expected.

"But, father, you can't . . . "

"For Mali. I must. Help me." I look up to the next in line, forcing a smile from my numbing lips. "What would you like?" I ask in English, ignoring the subtle slur in my words.

"A tiger, please," the man says, tousling the hair of the young boy grinning at his side.

My eyes hurt, throbbing with my irregular pulse. Sumalee holds onto her tears and assists me, steadying the fine tools, selecting the tiny pieces. I can't see by the end, my vision like smoke.

"It's ready?" I whisper to Sumalee.

"Yes, father."

I have one breath left. I'm sure I do. I must have. Suma holds the miniature tiger to me, I feel the copper coolness of it on my lips. I let my last breath go and feel the tiger twitch and stretch its tiny limbs as I sit back.

Sumalee hands it over, thanks the man for the money. My chest tightens, desperate for air I can't give it. The autumn cool gently caresses my face and I close my eyes against the swirling clouds of my vision.

Sumalee slips her hand into mine and I squeeze with the last of my strength. My body is a lead weight in the tattered deckchair. I feel as though I'm sinking through thick sand. Sumalee clears her throat, my tools rattle.

"My father needs to sleep," she says in perfect English, almost no accent from her schooling here. "I'm afraid that's all for today."

I can hear the tears in her voice. They will live for me now, my wife and *both* my beautiful girls.

"Tomorrow?" I hear Sumalee say as I fade. "I don't know, sir." But she does, of course.

ROLL THE BONES

I LOOK DOWN THE BARREL of the revolver, held less than a foot from the bridge of my nose. I've never had a gun pointed at me before. Hard to believe it's happening.

"Please, I think there's been a mistake." The tremor in my voice almost masks the words.

The man sneers. "That right?"

I nod, words clogging my throat. "I'm just a messenger."

"And what's the message?"

The washed-out streetlight shimmers off the rain-soaked edges of the alley. Dirty bricks and rusting fire escapes, over-filled bins and broken glass. Seems like it's been raining forever. "I was told to only tell Mr Armitage."

I wince as the snub-nosed gun dances closer to my face. "And Mr Armitage relies on me to filter out the shit," the man says, rain making tiny rivers either side of his beaked nose.

I should have known there's no such thing as an easy fifty bucks, especially for a street bum like me. Maybe I'll turn around and leave. Give the guy in the diner his money back.

"Well?" the small man barks.

"I was given two very clear directions," I say, trying to hold my voice together. My knees are rattling. "Only give the message to Mr Armitage and don't leave without an answer."

"Who sent you?"

"I don't know. Just a guy in a diner. He gave me some money to deliver a message."

The man seems to waver, his confidence and swagger momentarily dented. "What did he look like?"

I wish he'd move the gun away from my face. "He's a big guy," I say, mind grasping for details. "Well over six feet, broad, very blond hair. He's wearing one black leather glove, but the hand in it seems kinda . . . I don't know, wasted or something."

I stop talking at the look in the gunman's eyes. He's gone pale, skin like cigarette ash. "Where is he?"

I gesture over my shoulder. "The diner . . . "

"Which one?" he shouts, almost knocking my front teeth out with the gun barrel.

"Rosie's. Right across the street."

He spins on his heel and disappears through a door at the end of the alley. I stand in the rain, wondering what to do. The door bursts open again and men pour through it like maggots from the split skin of a corpse. They shove me aside and hurtle down the alley, brandishing weapons and shouting.

I walk to the end of the alley and see them disappear into Rosie's and the gunshots start immediately. Bursts of light and noise punctuate the steamed up windows, screams wail through the night air. There's a crystalline shower of sound as bodies fly out through the glass into the street. Some are diners running for their lives, others are the men with guns, landing in pools of blood that wash away with the rain.

My mind is telling me to get moving, run away, but my legs have grown roots and gripped the soaked asphalt. I'm frozen, watching the macabre light and sound show. One man slumps backwards through a broken window, his face gone. Blood streams down to the pavement below.

Everything goes quiet.

Nothing moves, except the rain streaking past the lights, getting heavier again. I blink water from my eyes and wait. There's an occasional ring as a piece of glass drops, the hiss of the downpour. Then movement inside, one person strolling through the carnage. I can't see any detail, but the size is unmistakable.

The blond man with the strange hand emerges and looks towards the alley. Towards me. A smile splits his face and he nods, crosses the street. He extends that gloved hand and I take it. His fingers feel like hinged metal.

"Thank you," he says.

"I didn't deliver your message, I'm afraid."

"You delivered it perfectly." He points to the door at the end of the alley, still standing ajar. "They came from there?"

I nod, unsure what the hell is going on. For a young man who lives in a box under the freeway, this is one strange evening. I expect this would be strange for pretty much anyone.

"You can go."

I swallow, still trembling. "Who are you?" I ask the question before I realise I'm going to speak.

The man is massive, and seems gentle, but I can see past him, to the bodies on the pavement, to the man with no face still bleeding down the wall. "My name is Montecristo," he says. "You?"

"People call me Skinny," I say. "On account of—"

"You being so skinny."

"Yeah."

"Well, I hope you use some of that money to buy a meal."

"Oh yeah, I will. Rosie usually spares me some scraps, which is why I was there earlier . . . " A thought flits across my mind. "Is Rosie . . . ?"

"She's fine," Montecristo says. He steps past me, walks casually through the door at the end of the alley.

Sirens howl in the distance. I really want to check on Rosie, and Dan and the others, they're always so nice to me. But I don't want to be found in there when the cops show up. My mind is yelling at my legs to make like pistons again, but something is holding me. The door is still open. I should run away. I should take my fifty bucks, enough to eat for days, and just run the fuck away, but I can't. This is all too weird and part of me needs to know what's happening.

I sense an opportunity.

It's very dark beyond the door and smells of cigars and booze. My heart hammers in my throat as I step into the dry warmth.

Muffled conversation makes me freeze. Soft light escapes around a closed door ahead and to the right of me. I shuffle forward, straining to hear.

" . . . all of them?"

"They came at me with guns." That's Montecristo.

"You killed all of them?"

"What was I supposed to do? Kill every other one and hope the rest ran away?"

The sirens outside are getting louder, can't be more than a block away. Makes it hard to hear. I shift closer.

"Armitage, just give it to me." Montecristo again.

"No."

"Come on then, let's do this."

Armitage laughs, a deep booming sound.

The sirens outside wail right up behind me, like they're driving into the building. Red and blue light ripples along the hallway through the half-open door. Shouts and radio crackle flicker through the pulses of sound and I can't hear a thing from the room.

I move closer and the door bursts into the hallway in a shower of splinters. Montecristo slams backwards into the opposite wall, his chest a ragged, open wound. I stagger backwards. Montecristo's head tips towards me, his face twisted in pain. His eyes widen when he sees me and he thrusts something out.

"Take it," he rasps. "Quickly!"

I can't see what it is. I take a step forward.

"Quickly!" The urgency in his voice is unbearable.

I snatch the thing from his hand and run down the hallway as Armitage's rumbling laugh pours through the ruined doorway. Before I duck out to the alley I catch a glimpse of him leaning forward over Montecristo. He's just as big, but all I see is silhouette.

"You tried to take mine, but I'll get yours," he says. "Where are they?"

Standing in the cold rain just outside the door, I'm paralysed with indecision. The police are swarming the street outside Rosie's. Armitage is going to come blundering out any minute. The thing I took from Montecristo is a small leather bag. A couple of hard objects are inside, I can feel their corners and edges.

"Where are they?" Armitage roars.

It spurs me into action. I stuff Montecristo's bag into my pocket and take a running leap at a fire escape hanging over the fetid alleyway. The cold iron is slick with rain and I slip, about to crash down onto the hard ground, but one hand closes and I'm up. I swing one leg over the railing, and scurry to the second floor. The door at the end of the alley slams open, bouncing against the dirty bricks. Armitage stands there, glaring into the wet night.

I melt back against the wall and hold my breath. Armitage walks along the alley toward the police. He stands with his back to me, and I creep up to the third floor. With a sound of absolute disgust he wheels and goes back inside. I let out a breath, clamber up and run for blocks across the rooftops.

♦

I SIT IN the shadows of a roof corner. A gargoyle spits into the indifferent street below. I'm hot despite the wet and cold, gasping for breath, dizzy. I need something to eat. A smile flickers across my lips at the thought of Montecristo's fifty in my pocket. But the smile dies at the image of him, chest blown open from throat to navel. Who could survive that? How could he even have the strength to give me this . . . whatever it is.

A shiver passes through me. Why did I follow him? I know why, really. It's the law of the street; never pass up an opportunity. I thought there was something in it for me. Money maybe, or information that might lead to cash. I'll get out of my box one day, I won't be on the streets forever. At least, that's what I've always told myself, though sometimes I wonder.

I'm partly sheltered by the low wall around the rooftop, but the rain still needles across my legs and feet. Scrunching up tighter into the space, I open the drawstrings of the bag and tip out the contents. Two dice rattle free. They look carved from bone, smooth and ancient. The one spot on each is an intricately carved skull. The other spots are different designs; tiger's heads, curled dragons, stars and moons, clover leaves and eyes. Every one beautiful in style, exquisite in execution.

Why was Montecristo so desperate to give them to me? It seems the only thing that mattered to him was making sure Armitage didn't get them.

You tried to take mine, but I'll get yours.

How had Montecristo managed to draw out Armitage's men and deal with them so ruthlessly, yet fall so easily to Armitage himself? And what the hell is my next move? All I want is a chance to make a dollar, get a proper place to live, enough to eat. It's not so much to ask. These dice, antiques, beautiful and ornate, must be worth a fortune.

Instantly a deep longing drags at my chest, a sense of loss so palpable I gasp. The thought of giving these up is heartbreaking. I don't like the feeling.

"I wish I knew what to do," I say aloud to the rain, and roll the dice on the pressed lead roof. They land on a seven, five and two, and a rush streaks through me, like every adrenalized moment of my life compressed into a single second. I shudder violently. The entire universe is mine for the taking, there's nothing I can't do. The dice sit next to the leather bag and there's writing on it I hadn't seen before, gently pressed into the surface, worn shiny and smooth with use and age. It's hard to make out in the dark. I make my way down to street level and stand in the persistent rain under a street lamp. The writing is clearer.

Toymaker. Argyll.

There's an Argyll Street in town, could it be that simple? The other side of the bag has a strange sigil pressed into it, swirling and intersecting designs that confuse the eye and confound the mind. As I try to see it in more detail my eyes slip and slide away. It makes me nauseated.

I tip the dice out again, rolling them on my palm. They feel alive, warm and aware. They scare and enthral me. I hunker down in the entrance alcove of a closed dry cleaners, away from the rain. "Any chance I could know what the hell is going on?" I say aloud, and roll them.

They come up seven once more, four and three, and my head slams back as the rush hits me and images flood my mind. History swirls by in an instant. I see Montecristo and Armitage, fighting through the ages. I see a small woman, shaking her head in disappointment. I see peoples' lives saved and ruined, a thousand thousand lives and more, turning on the tiny pinpoints of luck and chance. I cry out, my mind stretching beyond its ability to cope with the information pouring through it and the images cease. I collapse onto my hands and knees and dry heave, nothing in my stomach to throw up.

◆

THE FLUORESCENT GLARE of the fast food joint burns my eyes, but I'm past caring. The burger and fries taste good, the giant cup of coke is sweet and cold and delicious. There comes a point when nothing is more important than filling your belly. Once I'm full and my brain is working again I can try to figure out what to do.

Sated, my stomach pressed against the tatty belt that holds up my oversized jeans, I sit back with a sigh. The night outside is still dark and wet, the streets empty at this hour. Even the burger joint is populated by more staff than customers.

My eyes widen as I realise what I'm looking at, across the street. A large shop window displays rocking horses and puppets, board games and costumes. Above the glass, in curling script, is *Argyll Toys*. Something stirs deep inside, a knowledge that I'm beyond some veil. Things are moving and I'm being carried by the current.

The shop doorway is set back in shadow. I push against it, not expecting anything to move, and let out a small sound as it swings open and I stumble in. Catching myself against the jamb I look out to the street. This feels like a turning point. The world out there is cold and wet and hard. Inside it's warm and dry. But will it be any less unforgiving?

I let the door swing silently closed behind me and stand still. Details slowly emerge as my pupils dilate. All manner of toys are crammed into the small shop, stacked on shelves and strewn across the floor; kids' bicycles and rocking horses, water pistols and boxed games, every conceivable kind of ball. A bead curtain behind a desk at the back draws my attention. My ears feel like they're standing off my head, I'm listening so hard, but everything is heavy silence.

Through the beads, a flight of stairs leads up into darkness and I'm tentatively climbing before I've really thought it through. The steps open onto a long corridor, doors along each side.

The corridor is far longer than it should be, the scale completely wrong. I take a couple of steps and stop at a clicking, hissing sound. I can't see anything clearly, but something is moving, some small machine firing up. A series of clicks accompanied by random xylophone notes, ringing loud in the stillness. A shape spreads out of the darkness ahead, glinting with dull gold and copper tones.

With a burst of movement it surges forward, clattering along the hallway. On all fours, dog-like and bounding, dozens of pistons, clacking up and down, hundreds of cogs spinning and grinding, the skittering of brass claws on the parquet floor. And over it all the cacophony of disjointed xylophone notes.

I cry out and stagger backwards, frightened of falling down the stairs, though that's preferable to being eviscerated by the slavering machine bearing down on me. Its jaws spread wide, metal teeth shining. It hisses and wheezes and clatters and clonks, twisting and writhing as it rushes at me.

I stumble down the first couple of steps, lifting my arms for protection. Those dice have led me to a violent death. All I ever wanted was one lucky break.

A voice yells out. "Finbar! Down!"

The machine skids to a halt right before my trembling knees, panting, hissing steam from myriad pistons. It wiggles as its several-jointed brass tail wags vigorously. A figure emerges from a doorway, a tiny woman, barely four and half feet tall, thin and old.

"Give him a pat," she says. "He's a bit over-enthusiastic. We don't get many visitors."

I reach out a trembling hand and gently pat the creature's head and it presses up into my palm, eyes clicking shut.

"He's a good dog, really," the woman says.

My pulse and breathing start to settle. "A toy dog?"

"A clockwork dog. Not a toy. A companion. Like any other dog."

"He's so . . . lifelike," I say, still stroking the smooth brass skull of the thing.

"Well, of course," she says. "He may be clockwork, but he's alive. What's your name?"

"Skinny. Well, that's what people call me. My real name—"

"Your real name is what people call you," she says. "Be careful uttering your true name if you don't have to." She taps the side of her head.

I nod, unsure what she's talking about. "Who are you?" I ask.

"I'm the Toymaker. You'd better come in. Finbar, here, boy!"

◆

WE ENTER A huge room. There's a comfortable-looking lounge area taking up one far corner, a log fire crackling, but the rest is a workshop unlike anything I've ever seen. All kinds of benches and tools scattered around. Furnaces and lathes, pulley rigs and anvils, a thousand other things I can't recognise.

The Toymaker watches me, a slight smile tugging at her lips. Finbar nudges under my hand for another pat. Fear washes through me as I see Montecristo and Armitage get up from chairs in the lounge area and wander over.

Armitage is huge and smug, sneering. He flips a coin casually as he walks. Montecristo isn't dead, his chest shows no signs of being recently blown open, but he doesn't look well. He's just as big as ever, but withered, deflated. Pale and drawn, eyes desperate.

They stand on either side of the Toymaker and stare at me. I feel tiny. Insignificant.

Montecristo reaches out a shaking hand. "Can I have them, please?" His voice is weak.

I pull the small bag from my pocket, feeling the warmth of it, the reassuring weight. I don't want to give it back.

"Just a bloody minute!" Armitage booms. He pulls out a crazy mad gun, twenty times bigger than anything that should fit in the pocket it came from, the barrel a foot in diameter. He moves it threateningly between me and Montecristo.

"What *is* that thing?" Montecristo asks.

Armitage grins. "Mischief made it for me. He owed me a favour."

The Toymaker shakes her head and gestures with one hand. An ornate wrench appears in her gnarled fingers and she taps the cartoon gun. It falls to pieces, clattering at Armitage's feet.

Montecristo laughs despite his weakness and Armitage scowls. "Fucking hell!"

"You should know better than to pull a weapon in here," the Toymaker says. "Or raise a hand anywhere near me."

Montecristo absently flexes his mechanical gloved fingers. I wish I'd run away while the gunshots rang through Rosie's Diner.

I turn to the fading man. "Montecristo, please. Tell me what's happening."

The Toymaker raises an eyebrow. "Is that what you're calling yourself now?"

"It's a good, strong name. I like the feel of it." He turns back to me. "Please, just give me my dice."

"Don't you dare," Armitage says in a low voice.

"Ignore their names, and their entreaties," the Toymaker says. "This is Luck." She points to Montecristo. "And this is Chance." Armitage winks, flips his coin.

"Luck and Chance," I whisper. "They're not the same thing?" The two men scowl.

The Toymaker smiles. "Everything is duality, one thing can never exist alone. Luck is the force of good or bad in a person's life, shaping events, opportunities, circumstances. Chance is the absence of any cause of events, the unpredictable, uncontrolled.

They're similar and different. But," she adds with a sigh, "they're forever intertwined."

Armitage, Chance, leans forward. "Give me the dice, Skinny. I'll have 'em and this'll all be over."

How does he know my name?

"No!" Montecristo, Luck, barks. He staggers with the effort, clearly unwell.

I look from one to the next, out of my depth. "What do I do?" I ask the Toymaker and she shrugs. But there's something in her eyes, some testing look. She's waiting for me to ask a different question. The right question.

"What happens if I give the dice to Monte . . . to Luck," I ask.

The Toymaker smiles. "Then it will all be back to normal, Luck and Chance back out in the world, squabbling like children."

Both of them laugh softly, in spite of the tension.

"Getting people killed!" the Toymaker says, clearly displeased.

"Only our own," Chance says. "They know the risks when they sign up."

"And if I give them to Chance?" I ask.

"Then a fundamental balance shifts. Dangerously so, perhaps. Chaos. Who knows, it's never happened before."

"You two are always fighting." I put a finger to my temple. "I saw it. You've been fighting for . . . well, forever."

They both shrug.

"It's our nature," Luck says. "I thought I'd screw with him again today, but he pulled out that stupid Mischief gun." He turns to Chance. "Seriously, dude, what the hell?"

Chance rumbles a deep laugh. "You should have seen your face. And I nearly had them! If Skinny here hadn't followed you inside . . . "

The real question I've been leading up to hovers on my lips. I'm almost too scared to ask it. "And if I keep the dice?" I whisper.

Luck and Chance freeze, watch me with avid eyes.

"That's the real test, isn't it?" the Toymaker says. She gestures at Luck. "He's waning. Before long he'll be gone, nothing without his dice."

"And if he fades away?"

"You'll be the one with the dice."

"I'll be Luck." Somewhere, deep down, I knew all along it was the case, but hearing her say it is intoxicating. I've felt the power

I could have. I try to imagine the possibilities that might open to me.

The Toymaker is watching me again, her eyes dark and deep. Age and wisdom I can't comprehend lives there. It's clear she won't influence my decision, but it's obvious I have the balance of power. I can shift reality for all or some or me or them.

I don't want to give up the dice. They already feel a part of me. I feel bigger, fuller, my jeans less baggy. I'm growing as Luck fades. But I don't want to be like them. I've never craved power, just a fair go.

"What do I get out this?" I ask the Toymaker. "If I choose not to be Luck, what's my benefit?"

"Nothing. Don't look so crestfallen, life has never been fair. Be Luck or don't, simple as that. Hurry or he'll be gone, and the choice with him. You took the dice."

Luck and Chance. All I really want is a better deal from each.

The law of the street; never pass up an opportunity.

"How about a compromise?" I say. They don't answer. "I was stupid and curious, but all I've ever wanted is a chance." Chance grins. "I just want some luck." Luck smiles softly.

I don't want to be like them.

I tip the dice from the bag, roll their heavy warmth around my hand. "One throw," I say. "I'll roll these and take whatever comes out of them and walk away with it. And maybe then my life will get better."

"Not if you roll snake eyes," Chance says.

I look him right in the eye. "I'm prepared to take that chance."

He smiles crookedly and nods. "Brave lad."

I step back, gesture at my ragged clothes, shoes held together with duct tape, filthy coat. "You really can't get much lower than me."

The Toymaker's eyes narrow. "Be careful. There are far worse lives than yours."

I rattle the dice in my hand, crouch down. "You all let these roll to a stop and show the result clearly. Nobody moves until I'm done."

"That's how it'll go," the Toymaker says, and Luck and Chance sigh and step back.

I can see through Luck, a gossamer ghost in the room. His eyes are wild, desperate. I'll roll in his direction, give him the best chance of getting them back. But it'll be out of my hands by then. The dice tumble around in my cupped palm, life and death circling past my fingers. Out of the box, into a life worth living, that's all I've ever wanted. I've thrown two sevens, can I throw a third? Or a double six? "What's the best result?" I ask.

"Depends on the game," Luck says, sounding a thousand miles away.

"The game of life," I say.

He smiles. "Lucky seven, Skinny. It's always lucky seven."

Three in a row. I can do that. If I believe strongly enough. I deserve it. I've struggled my whole life, I've always tried to be a decent person, even on the street where some people will steal the shoes off your feet or stab you for a cigarette.

This is my time.

I take a deep breath and roll the bones.

OLD PROMISE, NEW BLOOD

I STILL THINK OF MYSELF as a twin, though it's been fourteen years since my father killed my brother. We were twelve when he sat us down on the threadbare sofa for a talk. Twelve years old and inseparable, almost one person in two bodies.

He explained why, our father. Talked of blood prices, old promises, stupid mistakes. He cried so hard and we'd never seen him cry before. But all we heard was, "One of you has to go."

He sobbed as he told us how much he wished it were different, but if one didn't go we both would. We told him that was fine by us, but he wouldn't have it. "Someone *has* to survive," he said. "One, at least, has to cleanse the blood. Then it hasn't cost us everything."

And Simon said, "Then it has to be me." He was the elder, by twenty minutes, and that made him the one. He looked at me. "Brothers, always and forever."

I railed against it, but our father simply nodded. He put a shaking hand under Simon's chin and said, "Thank you for not making me choose."

♦

As I WALK this darkened corridor my heart is strangely calm. My mind is still. All the doubt, all the planning, all the second-guessing, seems pointless now. Even if it's not the right thing, it's the only thing. There's no going back. I know he wouldn't approve, my father, but really, fuck him. Like I owe him any kind of allegiance.

I don't hate him. I've lived a life furious with him, but hate is the wrong word to describe how I feel. I get it. He made a mistake. A terrible mistake that nearly cost him everything. And everyone makes mistakes.

The door at the end of the hall is deep red, as I'd been told to expect. I raise my hand to knock and I'm surprised to see it trembling despite my calmness. It shudders like I'm cold, or struck with a palsy. I grip my fingers into a tight fist and the shaking stops. I rap against the crimson wood, one two three. Pause for a three count and rap again, one two three. I wait. Nothing happens and a weight descends on my mind, everything crashing down around me with the realisation that it was all a joke, all pointless and I've been led along on a merry dance by magi with . . .

I jump as the door clicks open. A two inch gap of darkness appears inside the frame as the door drifts in and stops. I give it a gentle shove. It swings soundlessly all the way, a yawning blackness beyond that threatens to suck me in.

A sharp scratch and a flare and I wince as matchlight blossoms into being. Parts of the room resolve, armchairs, bookshelves, desk, small tables, a standard lamp. In the middle of it all a man so old he looks desiccated by age, his face stark yellow in the light of the flame. Deep wrinkles seem to squirm on his cheeks as he lowers the match to an oil lamp. Light flares again and he turns the wick down, the room settles into a soft glow that doesn't quite reach the edges and corners, thick shadow lurking on the periphery. He sinks into a chair and beckons me in with one crooked finger.

♦

SIMON'S BRAVERY THAT day still shames me. I never once offered to take his place. I shouted and screamed at him not to do it. But he understood it had to be done, there wasn't a choice in the matter. One of us had to go to save the other and I never offered my life for his.

I turned on my father. "Why can't it be you?" and my father hung his head, tears spattering the knees of his worn jeans.

"I've offered," he said in a broken voice. "I've begged, but the deal is fixed. It was made when you two were born, before I knew you. I loved you both. From the moment I found out your mum was pregnant, I loved you. When we learned there were two of you, we had twice the love. But I didn't *know* you. And I . . . " he sobbed so hard the words were lost. He sniffed, drew breath, tried again. "Damn my soul, I loved her so much."

"Mum?" Simon asked, as I stared in disbelief.

Our father simply nodded, crying too hard to speak.

♦

I STAND BEFORE the old man, my eyes straining through the gloom for some kind of detail. I feel awkward, hands hanging limply at my sides. They are trembling again.

The man's eyes are rheumy, wet and loose. His lower eyelids hang away from the eyeball, red and sore-looking. He nods almost imperceptibly. "You brought them?" he asks, his voice paper thin with decades.

"Yes." I reach into my pocket and pull out the muslin wrapped parcel, grubby with specks of mud still clinging to it. I hand it over.

The old man shifts back in his chair, shakes his head vigorously. "No, no, I can't touch them." He points to a sturdy walnut table beside him. "There. Unwrap it."

I lay the muslin down, fold back the sides to reveal the dirty, thin bones inside. My father's hand.

"Have any trouble getting them?" the old man asks.

I shake my head. The gesture is a lie, it had taken months to find his grave and weeks to plan the theft. I was nearly caught, digging up the hard ground one frosty night and abandoned the operation, only to return the next. But this old man doesn't need to know all that.

He leans forward, his face lowering over the bones until his nose almost brushes them, and sniffs. Three quick, short inhalations. He nods again and sits back. "And the other?"

I hand him the envelope with the money. More money than I've ever had before. Hard as the bones had been to find and retrieve, the price had been harder.

He opens the envelope and peers inside, runs a thumb over the wad of bills. "Good. Pull up a chair."

♦

"SHE WASN'T KILLED in a car crash, was she?" Simon said as dad cried. It wasn't really a question, the realisation hit us both with sudden surety. As dad's tears soaked his knees, we knew we would soon be separated and that our mum hadn't died in an accident.

Our father shook his head, taking short, shallow breaths.

"That day we were picked up from school by Aunty Sue, when you told us mum had had an accident," I said. "What really happened?"

My father looked up at us for the first time since Simon had offered himself and nodded. We deserved the truth, his nod said, and he wouldn't shy away from it any more. "She couldn't handle it." His voice gained strength with each word. "What I'd done, it pretty much destroyed her. For years we grappled with the decision, she grappled with her hatred of me and her love for you. She endured my presence for your sake, but she never loved me, not after you were born." He paused, hitched a couple of ragged breaths. "We both tried," he went on. "We searched for any possible way to save you both, even if it meant our lives, but there was no option. That day, when you were ten, she finally cracked. She couldn't bear the thought of what would happen. I tried to tell her she needed to get as much of you both as she could, that we owed both of you as much time and love and attention as we could possibly manage, but she . . . her mind . . . she broke inside.

"I got a call at work that day because the postman heard a car running in the garage when he knocked to deliver a parcel. The garage door was locked. He called emergency services, but it was all too late. Your mother had been in the car, a hose through the window from the exhaust, for hours." His sobs took over his voice again and he sank his face into his hands.

Simon and I exchanged a look and we both felt the loss of our mother more strongly than ever. We knew again the pain of losing her, and her pain at not being able to cope with our father's mistake. And we burned inside knowing she hadn't been able to stay with us until the end. We looked into each other's eyes and we missed our mother and, for a moment then, we certainly hated our father. I don't know if Simon died still hating him or if he'd found any kind of forgiveness. He didn't have long.

"I just loved her so much!" our father said suddenly through his tears. "I loved her more than life and she was dying, haemorrhaging as she gave birth, and the doctors started to panic." His rubbed his palms over his face like he was trying to drag it off. "I couldn't bear the thought of losing her and the doctors said I would. They could save you boys, they told me, but not your mother. And I wished, I wished so hard for her to live."

"And?" Simon's voice was hard and cold as ice.

Our father looked up, eyes red and haunted. "And it came to me. As the doctors worked, the room around me darkened and time froze, everything stilled like a photograph. And it stepped from between shadows and said, 'You really want her to live?' I thought I was dreaming. I thought I had gone mad, but I said, 'Yes! I want her to live!'"

Our father stood up, anger pulsing off him in waves as he paced the small room. "I could only feel her loss in my heart. I loved you boys, but I didn't *know* you. 'What price?' he said and I didn't understand. 'She could live,' he said, 'but I need to be paid. Blood for blood.'" I stared at him. I didn't know what to do. He pointed over my shoulder at the frozen tableau of your mother in the fatal pain of childbirth and said, 'One of them, when they come of age.'" Our father collapsed back onto the sofa, gasping breath between sobs of grief and rage. "And I said yes!"

◆

I PULL UP a wobbly dining chair and sit across the table from the old man, my father's fingerbones on the wood between us. My hands tremble in my lap, but my heart and mind are still.

"Your father made a terrible deal," the old man says. "A dangerous game he played."

I nod, unsure what to say.

"And you play an even more dangerous one."

I nod again. I don't plan to lose my nerve now. They're all gone, my grief and pain has eaten me for years. We've been apart longer than we were ever together, Simon and I, and the pain won't go away. The scars won't heal. One person in two parts we were. Now I'm half a person in one part and it hurts.

"If this fails," the old man says, "he gets you all. I will not allow his presence into *my* life. I'll take no chances for you."

I shrug. "So be it." I'm pleased my voice sounds strong.

The old man stares at me for so long I start to shift uncomfortably on my seat. But I won't give in. He doesn't think I've agonised over this? I don't care now, whatever way it goes will be better than how it is. I need closure, even if that's a new hell. My father may not have been able to find a way, but I have. This option was never open to him. Simon's a part of me, after all. We shared blood in the womb, so much better than what little of himself my father gave to us at conception.

Eventually the old man nods once and stands from his chair. He opens a dresser drawer and takes out a piece of chalk. With slow, careful movements he starts marking the wooden floor around both our chairs with intricate sigils of a kind I haven't seen before. And, despite my father's warnings, his desperate plea, I've seen a lot as I searched the shadows of this world for a way.

◆

"How LONG HAVE we got?" I asked my father and his eyes gave me all the answer I needed.

"He's there with you now," Simon said, staring past my father. "The Devil, sitting on your shoulder, waiting for me." He was always the smart one, Simon. Wise beyond his years. When I looked, I saw it too. A dark, cold smudge in the room. Not corporeal, but indisputably, defiantly there. Smiling.

My father dragged a hand over his face again and shook his head. "There are things older and meaner in these worlds than the Devil, son," he said. "Hungrier and stronger. The kind of things that would bully the Devil in his own hell if they actually gave a shit about him. And yes, it's here, now." He vibrated with fear and grief with every word.

We were both so calm, Simon and I. Every time I recall that horrible day I can never understand how tranquil and accepting we were. I think it must have been some magic of our father's. Or maybe something as simple as a drug in our meal before he told us. I'll never know. But it was time and we accepted that. The evidence was coldly present there with us and it chilled me deeper than my bones.

My father stood and led us down to the basement. I begged him not to do it, regardless of my calm acceptance. And Simon cried too, put his hand in mine and we gripped each other like we would never let go.

And I never once offered to go in his place.

In the cold basement my father stood between us and the stairs, his face a mask of misery. "I've done so many things I shouldn't have," he told us. "Messed with forces and magics I should have left well alone, since well before you were conceived. I opened myself to this and it's cost us all so dearly. If there was another way, I promise I would have found it. But if he doesn't take one, he *will* take all. I tried to go in your place, Simon, I begged and pleaded, but nothing can break the deal. The only way for one of you to survive is for one of you to go and I am so very, very sorry. But one of you *must* survive. We can't let him take everything."

He began to cry again. I hated his tears.

And still I didn't offer to go in Simon's place.

♦

THE OLD MAN slumps back into his chair, the protections drawn. He unrolls a leather wrap, smooth and shiny with age, exposing an array of knives in stitched pockets, from a tiny switchblade to a wicked long machete. He hands me a small, ornate dagger, with jewels in the hilt. The lamplight reflects off the silver blade, glinting across our faces as I turn it over in my hands.

"You ready?" he asks.

It took me so long to find him, so long to find the ritual and someone willing and able to do it, that I've never been more ready. I just want this all to be over. One way or another. "Yes," I tell him.

"There's no going back," he says, his red eyes serious. "Once this begins, once we call it in there's nothing to do but let it play out."

I nervously twist the knifepoint between my fingers. "I know."

"If those aren't the right bones or . . . "

"I know," I say, a little more sharply than I mean to. "I'm sorry, sir, but I know. This is what I want."

"I tell you again, if it goes bad, you'll go. I won't chance myself. Yes?"

"Yes."

The old man sighs. "Then cut yourself and every time I raise my hand, let one drop of blood touch those bones. And you'd better hope your blood is strong enough."

With a nod, I draw the blade across the side of my index finger. My hands are criss-crossed with scars already, from previous excursions into things my father expressly forbade I do. And from practicing for this one. I can blood myself like an expert. The old man starts chanting something. I recognise some of the words, some of the phrasing. I feel the old magic, knowledge older than history swelling into the room. This is rare and powerful stuff. The old man raises his hand, two fingers extended like a blessing, and I drip my blood onto my father's bones. The bones of the hand that shook on the deal twenty-six years ago in a delivery room soaked in my mother's blood. An arcane wind stirs between us.

♦

IN THE BASEMENT that terrible day my father suddenly switched. Something took hold of him. I like to think it was his own will, that he was determined then to see the thing through without any more delay. But I think it was more likely the strength of that evil presence taking command. He drew himself up and sucked air into his lungs. Simon took me in an embrace I can still feel to this day, and held me tight. "Brothers," he whispered into my ear. "Always and forever."

"Always and forever," I whispered in return.

Grief already tore at my gut, yet that uncertain calmness persisted. I wanted to scream and rage, push my father out of the way and run with Simon out into the world and never look back. But I knew, deep inside I knew without any doubt, that my father was right. It would cost us both if we ran from this, and that would be the worst price to pay.

As Simon stepped back from our embrace my father put one hand to his shoulder. His other hand held a large bowie knife. "I love you, son," he said. "I love you so much." And he gripped Simon's shoulder tightly and plunged the knife into my brother's chest.

Simon gasped, his eyes wide, and I screamed. I feel the loss every day, Simon tearing away from me. My father hugged my brother tightly against his body and Simon's gaze met mine, his cheek pressed against my father's checked shirt. My scream withered away as I watched the light slip from Simon's eyes. "Always and forever," I whispered again, as my father lay Simon's body gently on the cold concrete floor, and wept again.

I don't know how long we stayed like that, my father crying over Simon's corpse as I sat numb and frozen. All I can remember is an icy laughter that seemed to echo and bounce around us, sweeping up and back, dancing in a satiated glee that chills me every time I recall it. Eventually it drained away from the room and my father stood and turned to me. "It's done," he said. "On your feet."

I struggled to stand, my legs like tissue paper. The grief, the misery, the sorrow in my father's eyes was horrible to behold, yet still the calmness soaked through me. Surely it had been some magic of his to protect me.

"Don't let the temptations of power distract you like they did me," he said, laying one palm across my cheek. "No matter how much you think you can gain, no matter how powerful you think you can be, it's a game we mortals can never win. We're pawns in the frivolity of greater beings, nothing more."

I wasn't really sure what he meant, not then. I know now and of course I didn't heed his advice, but then I simply nodded and said, "So it's over now?"

"You're the new beginning. It ends here and starts again with you. Fresh, untainted blood at last." My father stepped back, pointed at Simon. "Never forget," he said, and drew the blade across his throat so quickly that for a moment I wasn't sure I'd really seen him do it. His eyes were wide, like he couldn't believe it himself, then his throat peeled open like a scarlet mouth, his lifeblood arced across the space between us. I felt it splatter on the backs of my hands, across my face and neck, hot and thick. As I stared he held my gaze with his and slowly crumpled to his knees and tipped facedown to the floor.

It was hours before I staggered from the house into a life of foster homes and rage, abuse and arcane searching.

♦

THE WIND WHIPS widdershins around the room as the old man chants. His fingers raise and I drip blood onto the bones. It's pooling, spreading out like a flower across the golden polished walnut surface of the table. I make a cut across my middle finger and switch, determined to control the bloodletting perfectly. My only active role in this ritual will not be the thing that lets us down.

I feel the presence rise and my father was right. Older and meaner than sin, pure malice strides through the space, drawing the shadows from the corners with it. Evil howls in the world and things start to shift. From somewhere I feel my father again, for the first time since that basement when he left me all alone. He's still crying.

The evil bends and stretches and, for the first time in fourteen years, Simon is with me. I smile and almost miss the old man raising his hand. Things shudder as I swing my hand back over the table and squeeze free a drop of blood.

The evil howls in anger and my brother is confused, uncertain, aching with such deep pain. *It's me!* I scream through the aether. *I've come to get you back!*

My father's presence rips through me, his grief palpable, but overwhelmed by his anger. *I told you not to!* he cries as he slides through.

The old man signals, still muttering, I drip my blood, and my father is whipped away. *Fuck you, I owe you nothing!* I spit after him. He may not really deserve this, but Simon and I are brothers, always and forever. He should pay the price, not us.

The evil loses its grip on my brother as my father slams into his place. It's screaming its anger, fury at a trade it didn't agree to.

"Now!" the old man shouts, and I drag the knife across my palm, clench my fist over my father's remains. Blood floods across the table, washing the bones into a strange pattern, like a sigil of separation. But something isn't working as it should. The connection doesn't sever, the evil still builds. My father is screaming, my brother cries in my mind and cold, furious malice crawls through the blood and enters my hand. The old man's voice goes up a notch in volume and desperation as he chants, his magic pushes against the rising evil, but it suddenly feels weak, insubstantial in the face of ancient malevolence.

You think to stand against me? a voice booms into my head and my bowels turn to water, my mind freezes solid. That anything can be so all-encompassing, so total and insurmountable, is staggering. I've doomed us all.

◆

BACK THEN, AS I grew up and began the quest my father forbade, searching the dark corners of human existence for the magic, the connections, the secrets best left buried, one lesson stuck with me beyond all others. A woman in a bazaar in Morocco, whose face bore burn scarring that was hideous to behold, said to me, "Never try to renegotiate a bargain."

She taught me a lot, that old witch, and helped me along my journey, but perhaps the lesson that always stuck with me, that I chose to ignore, was the most important after all. I'm a fool, like my father.

◆

THE PRESENCE CRAWLS through my blood lasciviously, tauntingly, making the most of my complete inability to do anything about it. Without words it makes sure I know what it will do to me for eternity, and to my father as well. And to Simon, as it has all along. I've done exactly what my father managed to prevent. For all his mistakes, this thing only got Simon. Now it has us all.

Then the malice screams in rage-filled denial and something slams ice through my arm at the elbow. Pain arcs through me, from fingertips to shoulder, white lightning through mind to groin and back again. I rock back in my chair to see the old mage, his face twisted in desperation. In one hand he holds high his blood-soaked machete, in the other is my severed arm.

The evil screams its rage, but it and my father are carried away, swirling into the aether.

The old man's machete is over my head, ready to sweep down and end me. "Is it gone?" he screams at me.

"I felt it go!" I shout back over the dying winds.

His eyes narrow, his intention to let that huge blade drop all too clear. "Truly gone from you?"

I'm weakening as the stump of my upper arm pumps my lifeblood across my lap, the table, the floor. I let my swimming mind search my body and every trace of the damned thing is out. It took its time to toy with me and that was its downfall. All I can feel is myself, and something else, in the back of my mind, lost and confused, but not evil. "It's all gone," I say weakly.

As darkness closes in, the old man's mind sweeps over and through me, searching. In the last dim moments of consciousness I see his blade sink slowly to hang by his side.

◆

As I come to, the first thing I hear is the old man's rasping breath. He tourniquets the pumping stump of my arm, muttering incantations as he works. My severed arm lies on the floor by his chair, withered and blackened from what it briefly contained. Quite a price, I've paid, but worth it. The magi's magic as much as his first aid is keeping me alive. His eyes flick up from his work to meet mine. "Strong, you are," he says, respect evident in his voice.

"Stubborn is what I am," I tell him.

A flicker of a smile ghosts across his face. "It'll never leave you alone, you know. Not after that. It'll hound you forever, try to cajole you into a mistake, to exact its revenge. And you'd better be careful how you eventually die if you don't want it to win in the end. One thing it certainly has is eternal patience. You have a hell of a burden to carry alone now."

I nod, and smile. "But I'm not alone."

The old man shakes his head slightly. "I suppose not. I hope it was worth it." He bandages the raw end of my arm and I realise his magic is dulling the pain for me. "You'll not have me caught up in all this. A man will be along in a moment and he'll drive you to a hospital and leave you there. You'd better come up with a good story to explain this."

"Thank you." I mean it, I'm genuinely grateful to him.

Can you feel me, Simon? I think to myself.

His voice in my mind is lost, scared, still a twelve-year-old boy. *Jacob? Is that really you?*

Brothers, Simon, I tell him, as a burly man appears and lifts me like I weigh nothing, carries me from the magi's dim apartment. *Brothers, always and forever.*

ALL THE WEALTH
IN THE WORLD

THE TIME-MAKER'S EXPRESSION IS SERIOUS. I can't stop looking at her translucent skin. She must be a thousand years old. Her eyes are almost lost in folds, but dark brown irises glisten, bright and sharp, in the tiny gap. "Nothing without a cost," she says again, voice heavily accented. Eastern European, maybe Russian.

"I know," I say.

"Do you really? Not just money."

"Whatever time you give me has to come from somewhere else. I get it."

The old woman sneers and turns away, busily shuffles among the detritus on her desk. Her tiny apartment is packed with the accumulation of countless years of hoarding. Books and magazines, trinkets and souvenirs, all covered in dust.

She turns back holding a strange device of metal and glass. It's beautiful, finely crafted and delicate. Cogs and wheels, tiny gears that interact with crystal spheres like miniature bubbles. I'm mesmerised by the craftsmanship of it and gasp when she moves away and sits, places it on her knees. She adjusts mechanisms, gnarled fingers sure and swift. She casts an appraising glance up at me, makes another adjustment.

"Speak," she says.

"What do you want to me say?"

"Anything."

"Mary had a little lamb, its fleece was white as snow . . . "

"Enough." Her disapproving expression reminds me of my mother. "Have you any idea how many people choose that rhyme?"

"Lots?" I venture.

"Almost all." She shakes her head, returns to work.

I remember reading that when Thomas Edison built the phonograph, the first words ever recorded were "Mary had a little lamb". I wonder if that simple act has resonated through history ever since.

♦

THE WORLD IS empty and quiet out of time. I had no idea how lonely I would become. The magic restricts a person in space, so the Time-Maker warned me. I chose my house, of course, my comfort. But it's so quiet and still. No radio, no television. No news. No phone calls. No people. *Nothing* is happening. I'm outside time, living day after day in a tiny sliver between one moment and the next.

I have music and DVDs, but they feel so artificial. The inert world outside the windows, bathed in a white mist of temporal paralysis where I can't tread, is too disturbing to look at for long. My eye keeps being drawn to one flower in the bed by the pond, leaning in a soft breeze and frozen there, like it's desperately reaching for the water. It reminds me of her.

As time froze, after I'd rung the Time-Maker to tell her I was home and ready, I had a moment of panic. The fear has dulled to a quiet boredom.

It's a small price to pay, the actual monetary cost notwithstanding. The first couple of days were the hardest, and strange. Meeting her disappeared, but the rest of our brief, torrid affair lived on in my mind. I still know what's happening, because I still remember so much of our time together, but I've no idea how it started. It's a strange dislocation, but I try not to think about it too much.

Will I remember this silent, misty time once all memory of her is gone? I can only assume I will. I'll remember what I engineered. I have to make sure I don't try to find out what it was. There's a note on the fridge door, just in case, large bold letters.

Trust yourself, you needed to forget.

◆

"How much time do you need?" the Time-Maker asks.

"A month."

Her eyes widen, bloodshot yellow and white around hazel. "A month?"

"I know it's a lot."

She sits back in her chair, cups her chin, forefinger across lips. "People come to me for a few hours, occasionally a day."

I shrug, embarrassed.

"You must be very wealthy."

"You will be too, if you give me what I need." I can hear the defensiveness in my voice.

"All the riches in the world can't help some things, eh?" She chuckles, somewhere deep in her chest.

"That depends on you." I gesture to the device.

"Giving a person more time is a delicate operation. If you spend an entire month outside the tempo of the world, you could wreak all kinds of havoc."

"You're getting a conscience?" I ask. "After all the time you must have given people?"

"I have a small and discrete clientele," the Time-Maker says. "They call when they need hours to prepare for a business deal, get a jump start on the competition, or maybe they've forgotten an anniversary. They pick a place, call me, ask for a short time. This is powerful magic, designed for very concentrated use."

"I'm sure there could be quite serious consequences with even the smallest amount."

The old woman nods. "True."

"So, enough with the conscience, eh?"

I can see in her eyes that she wants to ask why. She's thinking about turning me down, but she must be considering the fee. So very much money. "You are well referred from a client I trust. I never thought anyone would pay for so much," she says quietly.

I look around the tiny, crowded, dirty apartment, the Time-Maker's threadbare clothes. I don't ask the obvious question, make the crass suggestion. "I have considerable wealth. I need this."

◆

I REMEMBER NOTHING now of the initial good times, those few amazing days, but finally the horrors are starting to go. Today I'll forget the first time she cut me, in a sudden and inexplicable fit of rage. Grabbing the knife from the kitchen bench, swinging it at me with hate and fire in her eyes. Tomorrow I'll forget forgiving her.

In a few days I'll forget the broken glass, the screaming and the restaurant I can never go to again. So much abuse and anger and violence in such a short time. Those few occasions when I had to fight back and the stain that leaves on my soul. The way my perfect life spiralled into madness so quickly. I'll be a better person when the whole thing is wiped away. Money can't buy happiness, they say. But maybe it can buy respite from things so beyond my control.

◆

THE TIME-MAKER NODS, sits forward over the machine. "When would you like your month taken from? First month of life?"

"Is that how people do it?"

"First hours after birth, a day around one month old, things like that. Most people never use up more than one twenty four hour period of their life, even with several visits. Twenty four hours when they were nothing but a gurgling baby, nothing to lose. Time people think they would never miss. There have been mistakes."

"Mistakes?"

"One regular client thought to scatter the time taken throughout her early life, ended up picking the day she took her first steps. Had to learn to walk again." The Time-Maker looks up me, wags one finger. "Consequences!"

◆

THIS IS HARD, painful. I can't remember anything about her, who she was, what happened between us. All I remember is her pale skin, the blood-filled bath like she lay in wine. Her eyes staring glassy at the ceiling, mouth half-open as though she was trying to cry for help.

What drove her to this? Whatever led her here must have been too painful for me to bear. The note on the fridge keeps reminding me to trust myself. If you can't have faith in yourself, who can you believe? And I'll certainly be glad when this image is wiped from my mind.

She's so beautiful yet her death is so ugly. So violent.

As the day wears on I forget where I was before I found her. I forget finding her. Slowly, the memory of the frantic phone calls, the crying, the police, all wink out of my mind. It's a frightening relief.

♦

I DON'T FLINCH from the Time-Maker's hard glare. "I want you to take from March fourth to April fourth, last year."

She gasps. "You don't want *more* time at all! You want to forget."

"I want it to have never happened to me."

"It will still have happened for everyone else. They'll still remember."

I tap the side of my head. "As long as it's gone from here. I plan to move away, start again. Wealth has a way of isolating a person anyway. There'll be no one to remind me if I go away, cut all ties. There's nothing here for me now."

Her face is sad as she shrugs, adjusts the machine. "I hope it works."

"So do I."

She points to a dusty laptop, a note beside it with numbers and the name of a financial institution. "Funds transfer, please."

♦

I'M STANDING IN my kitchen staring at this note and I can't believe it. I needed to forget? All I have left is this one day. This last, tear-filled day and by tonight it too will be gone. I miss her so much. I love her so much, but I barely know her now. I don't even recall what she looked like. I remember nothing of our time except this deep love and terrible sadness. Am I really so weak? Has my wealth become so great that I'll do something like this, just to be rid of a painful memory?

I remember standing at her graveside, crying, my chest aching with the pain in my heart. Why have I chosen to forget everything that led to this? I recollect her friends and family casting me glares and suspicious eyes. Barbed comments like, *You barely knew her* and *What did you do that drove her to this?* Was it my fault? How did she die? Am I really paying so much money to avoid a memory of something heinous? To hide some terrible guilt from myself? Ease a bit of pain in my life? I'm a monster.

What happened to her? To us? What were we together? We must have loved each other deeply for me to feel this pain on her death, but all in so little time. Just one month. Has it really only been a month of forgetting, or am I misremembering that now? How can I be sure of anything? This cool, white nothing surrounding me feels eternal.

I can't remember what it is I've forgotten and it's driving me insane.

By this time tomorrow the magic will be done, of that I'm almost certain. I won't remember the terrible beauty of this last day, her funeral, all the love and sadness around her, despite their disdain for me. Everything will be gone. I'm a fool.

I drag a notepad and pen from the desk drawer and quickly write down everything I remember before it fades forever. It's all I have left now and I need to make sure I don't lose it, so I *can* get back out there, ask everyone what it is I've done. They'll tell me. I don't have to give away the magic, I can quietly drop hints, ask questions askew, reminisce with them and piece together what it was I was too weak to allow myself to recall. I can fix this.

◆

THE MIST HAS lifted and the world moves on again. I have no idea what it was I paid so dearly to forget, but whatever happened left me with nothing but grief. I'm hollow inside with loss.

There's a note on the kitchen table, frantic scrawls talking about a funeral and love and recriminations and things that make no sense at all. But this aching hole in my heart needs to be filled. I have to go out and find my friends, start asking questions.

I remember the Time-Maker, waggling one finger at me. "Consequences!"

She was right.

IN THE NAME OF
THE FATHER

RAIN BATTERED AN ARRHYTHMIC TATTOO against dirty glass and the old priest cursed the winter breeze slicing through every gap. Lamenting that his hands would never be warm again, he continued to rummage, searching, fingerbones clicking through stretched parchment skin. A door scraped open, watery light pouring through the tatty garage.

"That's enough, Barrett."

Barrett stood quickly, drawing breath as he drew courage. "I know what you're doing! No one believes me, but I know. I won't let you!"

The young priest in the doorway smiled, feral, predatory. "Won't let me? Really, Barrett, as if it's up to you." He drew a long, bright blade from inside his jacket.

Barrett's old knees turned to water. Cursing his age, his fragility, along with the unusual cold that prevented his hands working fast enough, he had no choice but to float to the ground in a haze of fear. Everything slowed, treacle paced. He felt warmth spread through his groin and tears spilled at the final indignity of it all. He began muttering frantically, his reedy voice stronger than it had been in years, "Our Father, who art in Heaven, hallowed be thy name . . . "

◆

"OH, GREG, THERE you are. What were you doing out there?"

Greg kept his hands out of sight, turning to the kitchen sink. "Sorry, love, just throwing out some useless old rubbish."

"You hardly need to go through the garage in this weather. It's been there for a year, it can wait till the rain stops, surely?"

Greg smiled, keeping his body between his wife and the pinkish water swirling across the white ceramic. "Of course, love, it can wait. I'm just a little restless, I suppose."

"Well, don't keep busy by catching a cold! Did Geoff Barrett find you? He came round looking for you again. I don't know why he hangs around so much. He should be enjoying his retirement, shouldn't he?"

"I didn't see him. You can't blame him sniffing around a bit, this was his parish for years. He'll come back if it was important."

"I think he has issues with you. I don't think he likes you."

"That doesn't really matter, love."

"You should head into church, service starts soon."

"I should. You going into town?"

"Yes. I'll see you tonight."

◆

SWEAT ROLLED ACROSS Greg's skin despite the cold. He heaved the axe up, let it fall, a rhythm of labour. Eventually he loaded a gruesome cargo into a wheelbarrow, pushed it through the garage door, his dark shirt and bright white dog collar swinging on the hook as he passed. He trudged across soggy grass and red mud, squinting against the rain. When he upended his load the pigs pushed and shoved each other excitedly, fighting for the choicest morsels.

Leaving the barrow out to be rinsed by the insistent rain, Greg went back into the garage and began gathering bits and pieces from various boxes. Wallets, badges, hats, shoes, ephemeral trophies all. He muttered as he worked.

In the shelter of the garage eaves he flicked a match into a rusting oil barrel, packed with wood, paper and all he had gathered. The match met rising fumes, a concussive orange cloud blooming up.

♦

"Mr Gregory Easton?"

Greg laughed. "You know who I am, Bill!"

"Yes, I know, but this is official police business. Best we try to do it right."

"Oh, sounds serious. You'd better come in."

Bill ducked his large frame in through the front door, taking off his blue peaked cap. "I'm sorry to bother you, vicar, but we need to make some enquiries."

Greg gestured to armchairs in the front room. "Of course. Tea?"

"Er, no, thanks. I'd best keep it brief." Bill sat heavily into a creaking chair. "It's old Geoff Barrett. The staff at Green Havens say he hasn't been seen all day. We know he often keeps in touch with you, so thought it best to check if you knew anything."

"No, sorry. Been missing all day, you say?"

"Yes. The Havens staff say these days he's always going on about things that don't make sense, wandering off, stuff like that. The dementia setting in."

Greg nodded, his face sympathetic. "Well, he's an old man, I suppose. That's why I came to take over, after all."

"So, you haven't seen him?"

"Well, I was working out the back this morning and my wife told me that he'd been around asking for me. But I didn't see him. I figured he'd come back if it was anything important."

Bill took out a notepad and biro. "Right. When was that?"

"About eight o'clock this morning apparently."

"Your wife around now?"

"No, she's in town today. Won't be back until about five."

Bill stared at his pad. "So he knocked on your door around eight, asked for you, then wandered off again?"

Greg shrugged. "That's about it, I suppose. I'll ask Jenny to give you a call if there's anything more to it than that, but I don't think there is."

Bill stood. "Fair enough, vicar. Thank you very much. I suspect the silly old bugger's gone walkabout somewhere and got lost. Comes to something when an old bloke can get lost in a tiny place like this after forty years. Hopefully he'll turn up before anything happens to him."

Greg smiled, moving around to open the front door. "Fingers crossed. Poor old fella."

♦

"I WONDERED IF it was worth the effort, to be honest."

Greg smiled, tucking into his dinner. "It's just a wintery snap, Jen. It'll pass."

His wife shook her head. "I wondered if the roads were going to be passable. Then I spent all day in town worried that I wouldn't be able to get back."

"That's why we have the big four by four, love. You'd be hard pressed to get stuck anywhere with that thing."

"I still can't get used to this, you know. An hour each way to town, most of it not even sealed. I know you're happy out here, doing good work and all that, but I do miss the city."

Greg looked up, his eyes soft, cheek distended as he chewed. "But I'm getting so much more out of this community, love. I'm doing things here I could never do in the city."

His wife smiled. "I know. And I support your choices. You're a good man, Greg."

Greg laughed softly. "And you're a good and patient woman, Jen!"

"I'm sorry if I seem a bit melancholy. I spend the day in town and even that seems like a bustling metropolis compared to being all the way out here. I suppose this weather is making it worse."

"You'll feel better when it dries out and warms up a bit."

"Ha! Then I'll be moaning about the heat and the bloody flies and the red dust all over everything!"

Greg looked up again, a boiled potato on his fork. "It's worth it, Jen. Really it is."

"I know. Just tell me it won't be forever. Like you said at first, two or three years and then we'll look at going back to somewhere a bit less . . . rural."

Greg nodded, not looking up. "Sure, love."

♦

EARLY MORNING MIST drifted, knee high, swirling gently in the cold air. A metallic cough from the diesel engine rattled through the stillness, sending chickens scurrying. "Drive carefully."

Greg leaned out the window, kissed his wife. "I will."

"What time do you think you'll be back?"

"Hard to know, love. Should only take me an hour or so each way if the going's good. I'll try to be back after lunch."

Jenny pulled her cardigan tighter against the early chill. "Got your thermos?"

Greg nodded. "It'll warm up soon. The rain's stopped at least. I'll be fine."

"What are you going to read to them today?"

"I don't know. They like any stories really. The Good Samaritan maybe. It's more just to remind them that we're here and that we care."

Jenny laughed, without humour. "They know we're here, love. They wander in pretty regularly to get their booze."

Greg tutted. "Not all of them, Jen. Come on, don't buy into that stuff. There's a lot of people out there who have lost their way, but I like to think I'm helping them get back on track. And the elders always appreciate my help."

"Just be careful and don't be out too long."

"I won't. See if you can't shake off that grumpy mood before I get back."

Greg drove off across damp mud. Jenny stood, watched him go, her eyes hooded. Casting a slow look around the property she sighed heavily before heading back inside.

♦

THE FOUR BY four stood with the doors open, old delta blues blaring from the CD player. Empty beer cans lay in the passenger footwell.

"You supposed to be a good fella!"

Greg laughed, swinging the shovel again. It rang a hollow thud against the young man's head. He slumped against the ropes holding him tight to the stunted gum tree. Greg leaned on the shovel, watching blood and drool run from the man's wide, dark nose. After a moment he splashed water into the battered face from an old fashioned canteen. The head rose groggily, eyes mixed, unfocused. When he saw Greg's smile the young man's mouth opened wide, a tortured wail ringing across the dry river bed, bouncing around the scrubby hills.

Greg laughed. "Yell all you like, mate. Yell louder! No one for miles."

He swung the shovel again.

◆

"BILL COLLINS CAME round this morning."

Greg didn't look up from his sandwich. "Hmm?"

"He was asking after Geoff Barrett."

"Yeah, he came round yesterday arvo. Apparently the old man wandered off. They found him?"

Jenny shook her head, taking a deep breath. "No, he hasn't turned up anywhere. They've organised a search with all the local police."

Greg shook his head. "Poor old bugger."

"What do you think happened?"

"Dunno. Bill reckons he went wandering off and got lost. The retirement home staff say he's been going a bit doolally lately."

"Don't you care?"

Greg looked up. "Of course I care, love. But what am I supposed to do?"

"I don't know. Bill said I was the last one to see him. After he came looking for you."

"Don't let that bother you, Jen. It's not like there's anything you could have done."

Jenny hugged herself, her face tight. "I could have asked him in for a cup of tea or something. Shown him some human kindness. I just told him you were working out the back and closed the door on him."

"Don't beat yourself up, love."

"But he kept coming around. Saying things like he needed to keep an eye on us and he needed to watch you closely."

Greg laughed. "He just had trouble giving up his parish of forty years to a young city bloke like me, that's all. He was an old man going a bit mad. It's very sad, but it happens."

"Was?"

"What?"

"You said he *was* an old man."

Greg looked into his wife's eyes. "Goodness me, so I did. Maybe I don't hold out much hope if he's been wandering about in the bush for twenty four hours. Frail as he is, you know." Greg sniffed, swallowed hard. "Oh dear."

Jenny stood and came around the table, putting an arm around her husband's shoulders. "It's all right, love." She kissed the top of Greg's head. "You just care too much sometimes."

Greg nodded slightly and took another bite of his sandwich.

♦

"It's not good news, I'm afraid."

Greg frowned. "Come in, Bill, come in."

"What is it?" Jenny asked, voice quavering.

"I'm afraid we're listing Geoff Barrett as officially missing. The search has been scaled back. We've covered a bloody big area over three days and turned up nothing."

Jenny made a small sound of despair, covered her mouth. Greg squeezed her shoulders. "So what now?" he asked.

Bill Collins shrugged. "Dunno really. What are we supposed to do? It's hard to believe that a seventy-five year-old man can wander that far. Of course, there are that many places to get lost out here. We could walk within five feet of him and not see a thing. The case will stay open, but it won't be the first unsolved disappearance around here."

Greg nodded solemnly, squeezing his wife again as tears escaped over her ruddy cheeks.

Bill cleared his throat. "We wondered if you might, er . . . "

"What is it, Bill? I'm here for the community."

"Well, we wondered if you might be able to say something in church this Sunday. Something tactful, you know. Old Geoff was well loved, been here a long time. Especially being who you are, a man everyone trusts, and his successor. It'll be better coming from you."

Greg nodded again. "Of course. We'll make this Sunday a service in his honour."

♦

Jenny wandered around her house, smiling for the benefit of several dozen guests. She served sandwiches, party pies, sausage rolls. She kept boiling and reboiling the kettle for tea. She listened to all the townsfolk gossiping about what might have happened, how the old man was going quickly mad. Was it Alzheimer's, was that just a form of dementia, did it even matter? Where could he have gone, just wandering off like that? And didn't the vicar give a lovely service this morning, such a nice young man, inviting everyone back for morning tea as well. If anyone was going to replace dear old Geoff, at least it was a sensitive and caring young man like Gregory Easton.

By midday Jenny's jaw ached from gritting her teeth in a rictus smile. All these people, stuck out here in the middle of nowhere with nothing better to do than gossip. It wasn't their fault, she couldn't blame them. And she couldn't blame old Barrett for wandering off into the wild blue yonder, for that matter. But she could blame Greg. Why did he have to come out to this godforsaken piece of scrub? She admired his desire to do good, to spread the word, to help people. But she wasn't sure how long she could take it. No matter how she tried she just couldn't get used to it. She would have to be honest with Greg and talk about it.

◆

"Do you have to go out there again?"

Greg kissed his wife's forehead. "These people really do benefit from my ministry, love. It's what I'm here to do."

Jenny sighed. "I know, but you should concentrate on the community here, shouldn't you?"

"I can split my time between the indigenous communities and this one, Jen."

His wife rubbed her eyes. "I think I'm still a little bit shaken up by old Geoff Barrett disappearing."

"It is disturbing, love, I know. But we have to try to carry on."

"Do you have to stay out overnight?"

Greg shrugged. "Well, it's a long way out. It'll take me at least three hours to get there and I want to stick around for a while. I don't want to risk driving back in the dark."

"No, of course not. God, Greg, it's such a long way."

"Nothing will happen to me, Jen. I promise. I'll be back around lunchtime tomorrow."

As Greg headed for the door Jen took a deep breath. "When you get back . . . "

"Yes?"

"When you get back I want to talk about our situation here. I don't know if I can take it, Greg. Not for another two years. Maybe not for another two months."

Greg's face clouded, anger swimming across his features. "I can't just up and leave, Jenny. This community has been through enough upheaval as it is. I've only been here a bit over a year."

"*We've* been here over a year, Greg. Both of us! I don't know if I can stay another year."

"I have to go. I'll see you tomorrow lunchtime."

The door slammed. Jenny stood staring at glossy white paint peeling off old wood, tears streaming down both cheeks. The pigs grunted and chickens squawked as the old diesel engine fired up. With a spin of dirt the sound quickly faded away. She stood alone in the kitchen, hands clasped at her breast, and cried.

◆

GREG RUBBED HIS forehead vigorously, his eyes red. "We had a fight, right before I left."

Bill Collins nodded, lips pursed. "Is there anything I can do?"

Greg took a long, deep breath. "Sort of. Word will spread soon enough, you know how it is around here. I wondered if you might tactfully whisper in a few ears and make sure the truth of it gets out? I don't want Jenny to be the subject of too much gossip. She left me a note."

"Of course I can do that, vicar. What did the note say?"

"Just that she couldn't take it out here, the remoteness of the community. Right after I left she called up her friend from town and had her come out and collect her. She said she was going from there back to Sydney. I found the note when I got back yesterday, and all her things gone."

Bill leaned forward, patting Greg's knee. "A lot of people find it too much to stay out here. You should go after her, mate. She's your wife. The people here will understand if you need a few days away."

"My first responsibility is to the community here, Bill. What would I do if I went after her? I don't think I'd be able to convince her to come back. Maybe I should give her a bit of time to think. Hopefully she'll call in a day or two, let me know where she is. We can talk it out some more."

"Well, all right then. Be sure to let me know if there's anything else I can do."

"I will. Thanks, Bill."

◆

GREG PILED EVERYTHING onto wood in a small depression he had dug behind the pig pen. Dresses, shoes, handbag, purse, diary, anything that seemed relevant. Petrol glittered in the sun as he swung a red can back and forth, dowsing everything. He flicked a match and flames leapt up, hot and powerful. Nylon gathered and twisted quickly in the heat, patent leather blackened instantly.

He smiled and turned to watch the pigs, jostling and shouldering each other noisily. "In the name of *my* Father," he whispered. "My Father, who art the Fallen, hallowed be *thy* name." He picked up his dark grey shirt and clean, white dog collar from the fence, turned back towards the house, stretching expansively as he went. He laughed loud and long, though only the pigs and the chickens heard him.

FEAR IS THE SIN

DARRYL PICKED HIS WAY THROUGH the placards and angry faces, eyes down. He tried not to read the signs, but couldn't avoid them all.

SMUT SMUT SMUT

KEEP SATAN OUT of our Theatre

EXODUS 22:18 - Thou shalt not suffer a witch to live

He watched his worn out shoes overtake each other, saw the tattered trouser legs and equally worn shoes of the protesters. Breathed a sigh of relief as he stepped through the stage door into dim light and the smell of dust and face-paint.

"Darryl, darling, you're late!"

He took off his threadbare hat, gripped it nervously against his chest. "Sorry, Cynthia."

"You're here now. Let's get started."

Other players gathered on the stage, a tense air of expectation in the huge, empty room. Cynthia slumped into a front row seat, a wave of silk dress and long, shining black hair. Emerald green eyes pierced the thespian gloom.

"Right, my lovelies. Today we rehearse the forest scene. Remember, we're transporting these people, these poor desolate souls. We're giving them an hour or two away from everything out there." She gestured expansively at the walls. "Everything horrible stops at those doors. In here it's enchantment. Darryl, take your place. You're scared, but enraptured, remember? Let's go."

♦

"YOU OKAY, SWEETHEART?" Cynthia asked after the rehearsal.

Darryl gazed at his toes, heart hammering. "I'm so grateful for this opportunity . . . "

She lifted his chin on a forefinger, stared deep into his eyes. "You're a prodigy, nothing to thank me for. What's the problem?"

"Those people outside."

"The Jesus freaks? They're harmless, darling. They hide behind old-fashioned religion because they're scared to let go. They're uptight, closed."

"But this show, it is fantasy and . . . and . . . "

"And sex? Fantasy and sex aren't witchcraft." Cynthia's eyes sparkled, her smile weakened his knees. "This is 1936, Darryl, not the dark ages. Those people out there living in tent cities in the park, starving in dirty alleyways, no jobs, no prospects, no hope; we're doing this for them. One penny at the door means everyone can have a break from the horror of reality. Those freaks outside think suffering is godliness. They're frightened fools."

Darryl couldn't bear the intensity of her eyes, looked down. Then he couldn't avoid the swell of her chest, slim waist, curve of thigh, all draped in gossamer silk. "It's not wrong?"

"Would you rather play a straight, boring piece to a mostly empty room, or play something exciting to a packed house? We give the people succour for a penny. And you're a working actor, how many can say that right now?"

She ran one finger softly along his jaw and everything felt okay. She was right.

♦

"DRESS REHEARSAL, DARLINGS! Or should I say, undress rehearsal!"

Laughter and murmurs swept across the stage.

"Opening night tomorrow, let's make it count. And Darryl, when we get to the final scene, when Claire walks out centre-stage naked, you're *supposed* to stare." More muffled laughter. "Don't be embarrassed. You shatter the beautiful illusion of your incredible acting. You're enchanted, she's enchanting, lose yourself in her. And take the audience with you!"

The three suits in the otherwise empty auditorium scowled. As the players took their places, Cynthia sashayed past them, trailing fingers and glances. Surely her enthusiasm alone couldn't stop the show from being closed before it opened.

All the lines were perfect, the lights mesmerising. Darryl lost himself in the surreal, strange words and haunting melodies of the songs Cynthia had taught them. Transported to the decadence of the Underworld, seduction by Claire in her beautiful nakedness began to feel natural.

The show was beautiful. But it didn't matter, not now. The censorship officials would shut them down. He looked past the wings. The three suits surrounded Cynthia, their faces serious. But their eyes danced, alive.

"We will be forced close this production if you push the limits," one said, though his lips twitched in a smile.

Cynthia leaned forward, kissed each of them on the cheek. They drifted away, carried on clouds of subtle bliss.

♦

DIRTY FACES AND ragged clothes in the street shattered the womb-like calm of the theatre. Angry people with angry placards besieged him, hounded him, shouted, *"Decadence, evil, corruption, Satan!"*

"Please," he called out. "Don't be so quick to judge. Don't you want some escape from this terrible reality? Just a penny each, see for yourselves!"

He hurried away under a barrage of abuse and outrage.

♦

"NOTHING LIKE A little controversy to fill a house," Cynthia said. She smiled at the cast, gathered, ready. "They've all parted with a penny they can't afford for this, so give them everything."

In the quiet moments of some scenes Darryl heard the protesters outside, chanting in unison. No one cared. When opportunity allowed he squinted past the stage lights to see hundreds of enraptured faces. People swayed gently in time to the music as the girls sang. He felt their presence as he played his part. *Lose yourself. Take the audience with you.*

Quiet "oohs" and "ahhs" escaped the audience, a thousand eyes almost glazed, unblinking, mesmerised.

Cynthia stood at the side of stage, arms wide, facing the rows of people, hidden only by a velvet curtain. She drew great, deep breaths.

◆

THE AFTER-PARTY WAS raucous. The high of performance and the energy from the audience, was intoxicating. The booze Cynthia supplied made the girls giggle and Darryl soporific.

The morning brought reviews, universally positive. Anyone who had seen the show couldn't praise it highly enough and only those making guesses from the outside continued to protest.

And the Jesus freaks, out in the street, kept up their vigil, kept making their signs and their opposition felt.

Every night another performance, every night a packed house. The positive reviews increased, the queues at the door grew ever longer. Cynthia employed a man to walk the line and count heads, sending everyone past five hundred back to their tents or cardboard boxes. After three nights they started counting to six hundred and the Standing Room Only at the back was packed every time, fire regulations be damned. And the people gazed, swayed with the music, and Cynthia stood at the side of stage and basked in the adoration.

◆

BY THE START of the second week Darryl's inhibitions flowed away. He looked forward to the nudity and the enacted lovemaking, let himself be carried by the ethereal song. Every performance became an exercise in tense anticipation, waiting for the finale. When the girls sang, Claire walked out in glorious undress and the audience collectively moaned. A thin silk curtain swept down, the lights behind threw silhouettes, and the cast play-acted love until the lights faded to black. As the audience cried out for more the girls continued to sing, and Cynthia soaked it all up.

With each performance the silhouette play became less acting, more loving. Darryl's hand stopped miming a touch for the shadows and he drew his palms tenderly over Claire's breasts and thighs. They stopped leaning near each other, smiling while the shadows looked like kisses, and embraced, kissed urgently and passionately.

At the end of the second week, as the lights dimmed, Darryl watched Cynthia lean back, mouth half-open, shuddering in pleasure drawn from the audience. He slipped from Claire's gentle embrace in the darkness and crept across the stage, slipped into the stage-side curtain beside Cynthia. She emanated heat.

He reached out, took her hand, and an electric furnace thrashed through him. He gasped as Cynthia turned. She regarded him with eyes of swirling green, vortices of deepest ocean. Her half-open mouth hissed laughter, a split tongue danced behind her teeth. Darryl felt the audience, became awash with the desire of every person in every row. Their lust, their fear, their guilt, flooded into Cynthia. And from Cynthia into him. It engorged him, filled his soul with burning. And it felt good.

◆

DARRYL WALKED OUT into dull rain and jeers from the Jesus freaks. He smiled, head held high, read their placards. Their abuse faltered in the face of his nonchalance. One pretty blonde, in a nearly clean dress, hair plastered to her face by the crying sky, tilted her head as he caught her eye. He placed a palm, ever so gently, against her cheek, gave her a little of what he'd taken from Cynthia. She sank into him, eyes softening.

"You'd be perfect in the show," he whispered.

"I've always wanted to act, but it's a sin." Her voice trembled near his ear, her breath hot.

"Fear is a sin," he told her. "Let it go."

THE CHART OF
THE VAGRANT
MARINER

REEVE SLAMMED A PEWTER MUG across the drunken sailor's face, knocked him senseless to the floor. He grabbed a handful of the man's greasy hair, hauled him up, and opened his throat with a polished dagger.

"Anyone else care to challenge my captaincy of the *Scarlet Wind* or my ability to lead?" he roared. Spittle flew from the depths of his thick black and gray beard. His eyes were shadowed in his dark skin as he scanned the room.

Heavy quiet sank through the *Mermaid's Tail*, the wharfside pub that was so often our home ashore. The only sound was the water lapping gently at the support poles beneath the floor. Everyone either stared at the pool of blood spreading beneath the unfortunate sailor or looked into tankards or laps. None met the captain's steel gaze. Candlelight flickered off timber walls.

"Then I ask again. Who will join me and replenish the ranks thinned by the Royal Navy? Who'll step up for their share of bounty? The British may try to clean up these waters, but we shall show them their will is unwelcome here!"

A few wary fellows stepped forward and, led by their confidence, more joined them. The promise of wealth has often blinded men to their better judgment and will do forever more, I'm sure. Before long the captain was sat at a scored and rickety table signing tickets for a hearty new crew and I knew we would sail again on the morning tide.

"Boy," Reeve said quietly.

I quickly stood from my place at his feet. "Yes, Captain."

"Take these tickets to the first mate and arrange a measure of liquor for each new soul signed up." He raised his voice. "To show my gratitude and good will." This was met with murmurs and nods of satisfaction. These people thought they had made a good decision. There were far worse captains to serve under, though perhaps not many. A man with vengeance burning inside him cares little for others in the end.

When I returned from the *Scarlet Wind* I saw a scrawny man, deep in his cups, had crawled toward the murdered sailor. He reached out a finger and began tracing a strange pattern in the thick, dark blood pooled across the floor. The design, more than the act, made me uneasy in a way I couldn't explain.

The captain noticed my gaze and followed it, saw the madman drawing. "The hell are you doing there?"

At the sound of Reeve's low voice, the filthy wretch leaped up and scurried away, the pub door banging in his wake. Reeve stared at the marks he'd left for a long moment, then said, "Get him." He could stop a charging stallion with his roar, but my captain usually spoke in a tone so low, it demanded respect. It forced others to silence themselves and concentrate to listen.

I hared out the door and onto the rough-hewn docks. My quarry hurried into the warren of streets that led up toward the town and I gave chase. To lose him would incur Reeve's wrath and I had no desire to risk that. The night was hot and sticky, the whirrs and cries of insects and other nocturnal critters disturbed the dense heat. I would be glad to get back out on the ocean, away from the humid stillness of land. There weren't many of us left after our last run-in with His Majesty's best, so the intake of fresh blood was essential. It was possible to sail a three-masted barque like the *Scarlet Wind* with as few as four or five men—assuming the wind didn't change, but of course, it always did. Most of those lost and a good proportion of the replacements were escaped slaves, a few European mongrels thrown in, men and women of many a mixed breed. Reeve didn't care, he has ever seen the value of all people. A former slave himself, so the rumors go, and it's claimed he ate his owner's heart before taking to the seas. I believe I am the son of slaves myself, but I can never know that for sure as it was Esme told me so, and she's no longer here to ask.

I turned a corner past a stinking tannery and nearly barreled into the scrawny man I chased. He stood motionless, staring at a wall, face twisted in confusion. I drew my small dagger, a gift from Reeve and my only possession, and grabbed the vagrant's elbow. It was slick with sweat and grease. "You need to come with me," I said, as kindly as I could.

He looked at me and frowned. It was no effort to drag him unprotesting back to the *Mermaid's Tail*.

Reeve stared over his tankard as I hauled the man inside. My captain drank and drank but appeared as ever unaffected by the booze. I had seen him drink more than any man should be able, but I had never seen him drunk. His constitution was as infamous as his ferocity.

I pushed the bemused man into the chair opposite Reeve. He sank, resignation writ across his features. His gaze fell to a puddle of spilled beer on the tabletop and slowly he reached out, dragged a finger through the liquid. It was the same disquieting sequence of circles and lines the fellow had traced in the blood. It curdled my mind to look upon it and I turned away.

Reeve leaned forward and the man flinched back, but I put a heavy palm on his shoulder to keep him seated. "Hold there, friend," Reeve said. "Here." He offered his battered tankard and the man looked at it as if it might strike him down. "Drink," Reeve said softly.

A thin and shaking hand reached out, took the mug, and the strange artist swallowed. Cautious at first, then with gusto. When the cup was drained, Reeve took it back. "What's your name?"

"Jenks." The voice was cracked and strained.

"And what's that you're drawing, Jenks?"

The skinny, filthy shoulders rose and fell. Jenks looked at what he'd done as if it was entirely foreign to him. The beer shifted and the lines merged and slowly vanished.

Reeve turned and yelled, "Bella!"

The barmaid staggered in, rubbing at eyes as tired as my own but with a smile plastered on for his benefit. Reeve held out his tankard. "Refill this, and bring another for my friend."

Bella frowned. "Your friend is mad and penniless, yet he always loiters here and begs drinks and food from good folk." She raised a small, scarred fist and Jenks winced.

Reeve caught her wrist. "For now, he is my friend and I will have a drink for him. You know my coin is good. And bring me paper and a pencil."

Bella's expression clearly betrayed her displeasure but she did as she was bid. Reeve offered Jenks the fresh tankard and, when the desperate fellow reached to take it, pulled it away. "You draw me that picture again, here on this paper, clear and true. Then you can have this and as many more as you can swallow."

Jenks looked from the paper to the tankard and back several times before reluctantly picking up the pencil. Eyes squeezed almost shut, as though the act pained him, he scrawled away and the arrangement of lines and curves, clearer than any time before, truly made my stomach squirm and my breath catch in my throat. Even Reeve with his hearty constitution grimaced as he gazed at it. When it was done, Jenks grabbed the tankard and swallowed it down with loud, frantic gulps.

Reeve stared a moment more at the parchment, then folded it away inside his jacket. "I think this is the kind of thing that should not be looked upon too long under the mantle of night, eh, Daniel?"

"I would rather not look upon it at all, sir, even under a blazing sun," I said.

Reeve chuckled softly. "Then perhaps that makes you a wiser man than I." He ordered another tankard for Jenks and said, "Tell me the story of this." He patted his coat by way of explanation.

"Of what?" Jenks asked.

"The pattern you just scribed for me."

"What pattern?"

Reeve frowned, pursed his lips in thought, then, "Tell me the story of your last voyage."

Jenks stared into his ale for a while. "Was a long time ago and only I survived," he said eventually, and drained the brew.

"Tell me how." Reeve waved for fresh tankards and Bella brought them.

Jenks' eyes appeared to glaze and he spoke more clearly than I would have thought possible. "We sailed for an island Captain Jake knew tell of and he said great treasure was to be found there. None of us really believed him, for no one knew where or how he had come by this sudden knowledge. But a crew follows its captain, does it not? Through storms and most inclement seas we sailed, and many thought we were simply straying into the wide reaches of the open ocean. I honestly feared we would never see land again. But after weeks of horrendous journey an island came into view. Stood tall above rabid gray waves like a broken tooth, it did, and the captain said to break out the rowboats.

"Three boats set off and two were smashed on invisible rocks beneath those hellish waves, those men taken screaming to the depths. But still Jake insisted we go on. Our boat beached and we scrambled onto a rocky shore, thankful to have survived that far. A great rending cracked across the waters from behind and we spun to see the *Wistful Lady* split from bow to stern. She bucked and rose and men fell wailing into the waves, and damn my soul I swear I saw thick black tendrils writhing through the timbers as she went down. What kind of monster . . . ? We were all that was left and still old Jake insisted we go on.

"We trudged into a maze of high, sharp rocks, with no idea what we might find other than certain death. Jake led us to a cave mouth, like the iris of a damned cat's eye in the wet, black rock. He forced us to enter and we descended deep into blackness, two damp torches offering a smear of spluttering light to guide us. I brought up the rear and that was all that saved me. The passage opened into a yawning cavern and something glowed an evil, eldritch green on the far wall. A series of circles and lines in a design that made my head hurt and my stomach swim. But I could only catch glimpses of it past the other men as they stood there and stared. And before I got a proper look, they turned upon each other like animals.

"They screamed and howled inhuman, ungodly sounds and ripped and clawed and bit at each other until gore sprayed the walls. I had no thought but self-preservation and I turned and ran, stumbling blind through the black caves until I fell into the pouring rain, the roar of the sea in my ears. I dragged that rowboat back to the waves, leaped in and passed out from sheer terror.

"I have no idea how long I drifted, but luck took me past the rocks, out into the ocean. The weather calmed and, half-dead, starved, and dehydrated, I was found by a passing Spanish merchant vessel. They fed me, watered me, and dropped me in harbor. I will never step off solid land again, I tell you true."

We were silent for several moments after Jenks finished his yarn. He drank his beer, eyes haunted and wet.

"And that's what you draw," Reeve said eventually.

"What's that?"

"The thing you only saw in part in that hell cavern, that's the pattern you draw now. The one you drew for me. Yes?"

Jenks frowned, his knuckles whitened on the cup. "What have I drawn for you?" His confusion and madness had superseded his eloquence once more now he was back in the present.

Reeve stroked Jenks' hair as though the man were a faithful hound. "Drink," he said in his soft, commanding voice, and moved to another seat.

I sat on the floor beside his chair and Reeve patted my shoulder as he drank deep. "Believe him?" he asked me.

"I believe he thinks it's true," I said, for the man's tale bore no hint of artifice. Madness it might be, but deliberate lie it was not.

Reeve nodded. "I think so, too. You're astute for a boy barely in his teens, eh? And I think we have gained something very valuable. You will tell no one of this night's tale, or of this"—he patted his jacket again—"understand? No one."

I nodded, his requests would always bind me. "That crazed thing he drew is valuable?" I asked.

Reeve drained his mug and said, "It's not so crazed, Daniel. It's a map."

I looked up at him, confused. "A map?"

But my captain was not paying attention to me any more. He looked over to Jenks, eyes dark beneath his heavy brow. He sniffed and rose, walked to the madman, and spoke softly. They quietly left the room together. I tried not to consider the possibilities and shortly Reeve returned, slipping his shining dagger back into the leather sheath that hung from his belt.

He slumped into his seat, smiled at me, and raised his tankard. "To Esme, eh?" He swigged, handed it to me for a gulp.

"Always," I replied, sadness tugging at my gut.

Though I had never seen him drunk, the liquor always made him melancholy. "Hair that shone like a raven's wing," he said in a whisper.

I handed back his ale. "Aye, Captain. And her eyes were like emeralds, eh?"

"You remember her nearly as fondly as I, don't you, lad?"

"I do."

♦

WE SAILED ON the early tide. A mass of hungover men and women gathered before the poop deck once we had left New Providence harbor for the open ocean. Reeve gave his customary speech.

"We met in the dark and secret dens where the superior British fear to venture," he began, his soft voice carrying on the warm breeze as each crew member leaned forward to better hear. "Some of you are escaped, or slighted folk, some call you criminals. Well, the law of men be damned. We have no love for those who would rule us, place us under the yoke of order." He barked laughter, which the crowd dutifully echoed. "So we go where we please, we take what we want, and at every opportunity we make His Majesty's finest pay!"

His enthusiasm was ever infectious and fists punched the air, voices roared approval.

Reeve dragged Harkness to his side. "This man is your first mate and whatever he says you can believe came directly from my lips. He'll watch you with a hawk's eye and any man or woman not pulling their weight will find themselves swimming home. Look upon this fellow and fear him, for to cross him is to die. But impress him with your effort, please him, and you will please *me*. And we'll all share in the bounty of our endeavors."

Harkness nodded, smiling wolfishly at the sailors who returned his gaze with trepidation. Where Reeve was big and bushy and authoritative, Harkness was smooth and bald, all hard muscle and aggression. Between them they were a formidable team. Hard to believe that only the three of us and four other crew had survived the last encounter with the Royal Navy. Hard also to believe we had nevertheless won that battle. Or perhaps not so hard to believe, for Reeve's vendetta against those responsible for Esme's death raged and burned inside him like a furnace.

When she was alive, she held her place in his heart, beside his love of gold. He told himself he pillaged and plundered to win and keep her, but she knew better. Knew his greed was his own alone, though loved him still, guided him. Reeve was always captain but it was ever Esme who ruled the ship back then. I wonder what kind of man he might have been if she still lived. When she was gone, the guiding hand that kept the wheel steady was lost. His lust for gold became a lust for blood.

But I approved.

She may have been his lover, but she was like a mother to me. Furious and fearsome, beautiful and brave, she instilled in me a passion for learning, for reading. She showed me I could be something more if I wanted. Her loss left a hole in me, a wound that will not heal. Anytime I feel it might begin to close, I pick at it until it's fresh and bleeding once more. I don't want her memory to ever fade from my mind. I remember her blood on my hands as I held her after a fateful skirmish with the Royal Navy that went so wrong. As she breathed her last, she said, "Love him, but never trust him." And then she died.

The bastard who brought her low took a long time to die, his body hung on the main-mast until the flesh rotted and the bones had nothing to hold them together. The skull still sits in Reeve's cabin, grinning from his desk. Many more have fallen since in a campaign of revenge that will probably never end. We have lost more crew than any other of our kind, yet here Reeve was with another signed up already, drawn by the lure of plunder and freedom.

We sailed for two days and little was seen, no quarter to invade. The weather was hot, the skies blazing blue, and the water clear as crystal, and calm. Hackett in the crow's nest reported no land or ships, and so we sailed on awaiting opportunity. I waited on Reeve in his cabin, fetched him food, poured him liquor, reported any word from Harkness, and, in between times, continued to consume the library he and Esme had built together.

But as time passed, as we sailed further and further from known seas, I realized Reeve paid little attention to his books and less to his crew. He studied that strange thing he had called a map. I did my best not to look upon it, for it still made my insides squirm, but Reeve was obsessed. He muttered about things missing, gaps in the directions, if only that mad fool had seen it all. Of course, had he seen it all, he would not have survived to pass it on, if his tale were to be believed. *This is too much*, I thought, *for a mortal mind to conceive. It saves us from itself. Or it should.*

As I straightened Reeve's bed one day, I heard him mutter again. "Need to fill what the madman missed, find the final heading. Riches greater than gold or British blood, aye." He scratched at the paper with a charcoal stick, frowned and cursed, rubbed out his lines and tried again. Time after time, he sought to stumble upon those missing parts. And what would happen if he did? I wondered.

"Captain," I said nervously, "should we not be on deck, watching for the Navy?"

"They will come whether we watch or no."

I frowned. "Are they not the greatest enemy? We are drifting farther from the waters they patrol. Should we not turn about and hunt them? For Esme," I added quickly at his dark look.

He stared at me with eyes colder than he had ever laid on me before.

"Men went mad from that design," I said in a quavering voice.

"Weak men. Be about your work, boy." He returned his attention to the accursed, all-consuming chart.

That night I woke from my sack in the porch of his quarters to see Reeve stalk past me in the silvery moonlight. Hot and clear, moon and stars bright, he stood on deck and stared up to the firmament. In his hand he held the madman's map and he consulted it, looked up, turned, consulted it again. He searched for something among the stars that might fill the gaps which eluded him. I closed my eyes, tried not to think about it, and slept before he went back inside. Every night after he repeated the action, gazing to the heavens, seeking answers in infinity.

◆

FIVE DAYS OUT, to my surprise, Hackett yelled down to us that a frigate flying British colors had crossed the horizon. Reeve burst into action, for the first time roused from his contemplations. He set up his merchant's flags and raised the ragged, torn sails, the decoys. He had the men head the *Scarlet Wind* on a drifting course to intercept. A deception to make us appear becalmed, a scam he had employed a dozen times.

The crew lolled about the deck, feigning dehydration and weakness even as they held concealed weapons and boarding ropes. As the British hoved alongside, some officer in a glittering uniform called out, asking if we needed aid. Reeve hid while a dark-haired Spanish woman staggered to the gunwale, her voice weak with desperation. "Please, help us! We have been stuck out here so long, our captain dead, most of our crew sick or dying."

"Are you diseased?"

"No, sir, simply starved!"

The other vessel moved to pull abreast and as they drew near, Reeve barked the order. The *Scarlet Wind* heeled over and all our disguised starboard ports fell open and cannon thrust forth, each barking twelve pounds of iron destruction in deafening unison, aimed at the frigate's waterline. Before the British could react, holes punched into their vessel. It leaned to and began to take on water. Reeve yelled and our crew leaped up and swung across, swords rending even as the Navy men desperately tried to bring muskets and pistols to bear.

Reeve himself led the charge, a shining blade in each hand, one his own and the other Esme's. He always played both weapons together since her death. "Slay them all and grab everything you can carry before this rat-infested shit-hole of a ship goes down!" he called.

The battle was harsh and fast, bloody and brutal. Several of our men fell, but all the British died. Reeve took his time with their captain as our crew seized everything of value they could find and repaired to the *Scarlet Wind* as the frigate gave its last heave and sigh and tipped stern first to the deep.

The crew caroused and celebrated with gusto as night fell and Reeve had secured himself another loyal band. They drank the plundered rum, shared the shining coin, and fell into a stupor drifting free by dawn.

Except Reeve, who seemed uninterested in the booty, unfulfilled by the slaughter. He took his map and left the festivities before the night was done and once again studied the skies for clues. His passion for the destruction of the British appeared to wane in the face of this new obsession and all his drive went to it. Each time he studied that thing, another part of him darkened, another moment of his patience wore thin.

He greedily swigged rum as he stared, eyes bloodshot, at the stars.

"You don't want to stow the gold, sir?" I asked him as dawn smudged the horizon and I headed for my rest.

"The crew will manage," he slurred.

"But can you trust their count..?" I began.

Reeve tore his gaze from above and waved the madman's chart in my face. "You think it compares to this? You've read the same books as I, you know the stories of riches beyond dreams hidden by the great travelers of old."

Myths and legends, I thought, and was sure he knew that to be the case. But he clearly thought differently since the mad vagrant's tale. I wondered if the lunacy of the chart had begun to infect his wits and I despaired. But he was more abrupt with me than he had ever been and I learned to steer clear of his attention as much as I could.

◆

FOR SEVERAL DAYS more we sailed on, seemingly directionless, certainly away from land and the possibility of further British encounters. Or any other encounter, for that matter. But I knew Reeve followed what he could of the strange guide he had gained. The crew began to grow restless as the days passed and we moved further from the islands.

Eventually Harkness approached him in the quiet of one evening as I polished silverware, unseen, ignored. "The crew are fretting for our course, Captain."

Reeve's dark face was shadowed, his expression unclear, but his voice was bored. "Is that so?"

"They wonder why we move farther from our prey, east into open ocean. The loot and the enemy are to be found among the islands, no?"

"They are, most likely, but I seek other things. Best not to question your captain."

"And I have never questioned you before, though I must admit to sharing their concern. We are heading not only into open water, but into a region known for dangers. A place where ships go and never return."

"Superstition?" Reeve scoffed. "You take the nonsense fears of these uneducated men and women seriously?"

Harkness stiffened, the implication not lost on him. "Was a time you were a superstitious man yourself, Reeve, and rightly so. We should not tempt the gods or fates."

Reeve flapped a hand. "We tempt no one. Trust in me and those dogs will do likewise. Now begone, I have work to do."

Harkness's eyes narrowed, unaccustomed to being spoken to like that by Reeve. They were as much friends as captain and first mate, but Harkness chose to challenge no further. I felt his dismay and shared it. The captain had ever been driven by a powerful vengeance, though now his demeanor was darker. Where he had been fair, he was becoming mean. Where he had been friendly, he became cold.

Harkness left and Reeve, oblivious, returned to the study of his star chart. Before long, he went out into the night to stare up again.

◆

THE MORNING AFTER Reeve had a moment of revelation with his map, the crew tried mutiny. The captain had laughed aloud and filled in a part of his guide after spotting something in the heavens, and he sat and stared at his new instructions for the rest of the night. When he gave a fresh heading to Harkness the next day, the first mate's face clouded and the crew murmured dissention.

Harkness drew himself tall. "I have followed you for many years and always with loyal service, but this course is one I cannot condone. Those waters are ruled by monsters and death."

"Can't condone?" Reeve laughed. "You think to take command?"

Harkness said nothing, simply raised his chin, and his silence spoke volumes. In a move so fast it belied his bulk, Reeve pulled free Esme's sword and cracked its hilt into Harkness's nose. The man howled and fell, blood pouring from his face. Reeve grabbed a rope and wrapped and rolled Harkness in it before the first mate could put up a fight. Reeve hauled him, trussed up tight, to the rail. With swift strikes he opened several wounds on both of Harkness's legs and crimson flooded the deck as the crew stared dumbfounded and Harkness wailed. Reeve tipped his first mate screaming over the side, the captain's face and muscles straining with the effort as he held Harkness up by the rope, just the poor man's lower half trailing in the waves.

The crew stood stunned. The blood drew sharks and Harkness began to thrash and buck in the water as they found him, but Reeve would not let go the rope. "Anyone else care to challenge my orders?" Reeve shouted over the first mate's high-pitched, agonized screams.

I could see some men wanted to rush the deck and take the captain down, but they lacked the courage. Others' will was broken by Harkness's gurgling yowls. I could not believe Reeve had so quickly and casually sacrificed a man who had been for years and years his second-in-command and his friend. My captain had changed beyond recognition.

Reeve let go the rope at last and the sudden silence was far worse than Harkness's blood-curdling shrieks. "Then it would appear a position has opened on this ship. Any volunteers?"

It seemed a handful of the crew were still loyal, maybe even more so after that display of strength and determination. One man stepped up. "I will take that role," he said in a deep baritone voice.

Reeve smiled, and it was terrible. "Atkins. One of my original men, still with me, still true."

"Aye, Captain."

"Then first mate you are. You know what to do and you know our heading. Make it so."

Without waiting to see if the crew would follow Atkins—knowing, for now at least, they would—Reeve returned to his cabin and his study.

◆

THAT NIGHT THE *Scarlet Wind* followed the dread bearing toward a place in the ocean where even small fry like me knew ships should never go. Reeve's obsession appeared to be taking its toll on his mind and body. For all his strength, he looked somehow diminished by nightfall and tumbled into his bunk clutching the map and fell straight into a deep sleep. For the first time in a week, he didn't stand on deck and study the stars.

From my sack I heard some scufflings and whispers and I was scared, but did not move to look. There was nothing I could do, so I listened until there was only the creak of timber, the slap of the waves, and the muffled clap of rigging. I sank back to sleep.

◆

WHEN I ROSE as the sun lanced across me I found Atkins standing there, ashen and trembling. It turned out he was now the first mate of a four-man crew. When the rest sloped off in the night they had knocked those few loyalists senseless and stolen food and water. It speaks volumes of Reeve's reputation as a killer that after Harkness's murder they were too scared to even try en masse to take the ship from him. They instead took most of our supplies and all but one rowboat. Perhaps that was a small mercy, those mutinous dogs leaving that boat in case the last remaining of us should think to abandon Reeve to his mania. But we were the truly loyal, more fool us.

The captain rose and growled his displeasure, but his voice sounded weak and his eyes were dim above bags even darker than his skin, despite the long night's sleep he had taken. "Move on, there's enough of us to continue," he said.

"Should we not strike for land and more hands?" Atkins asked.

The captain spun, grabbed a handful of Atkins's grubby shirt. "And how far is land, eh? And how close are we to our goal? Do as I say."

"I don't rightly know what our goal is, Cap'n."

"It is to sail that way and ask no questions."

"And should the wind change? We don't have the hands—"

"It will not change." Without waiting for further conversation, Reeve returned to his chart.

That night, we crossed an unseen boundary and entered the region of sea where men knew not to venture. Our small crew, stretched thin, pushed on. Their faces were masks of trepidation, but a modicum of greed lived there as well and that should ever be taken as the lesson of this folly. The tiniest speck of avarice will undo the most determined man.

Reeve stood upon the deck as night fell and held his map. He stared upward and began to laugh and laugh. He ran back to his cabin and through the window I saw him scratch more lines and curves on his design. And I watched the last sanity leave his eyes. I ran to cower behind barrels as he strode out on deck, adjusted the wheel, and tied it off to fix our heading. He called his remaining men forth. As they ran to him, he drew his twin blades and danced between them, severing limb and artery with artistic precision.

He took up their bleeding corpses one by one, opened their throats, and drained them into the waves as an unnatural wind picked up. From my place between barrel and rail I could see the men's blood swirling and gathering against the flow of the currents, growing and spreading in the water. It tied itself into a thick, dark thread, almost black in the night, and wormed across the ocean ahead of the *Scarlet Wind*.

Moonlight silvered the waves as the wind whipped them up and clouds began to roil on the horizon. Starlight glittered from above and lit the trail of blood as it seemed to draw our ship along. Reeve stood in the prow, leaning forward, arms wide, and began calling out words I could not understand and did not like. They felt like nails driving into my ears. In one hand, the mad vagrant's chart flapped like an angry wing. The foul pattern that should never have been revealed. No mortal mind should be able to conceive its instruction. And none would have but for a moment of partial clarity held by a running man, combined with the will of a captain of powerful drive finally finding something to fill the void of love most heinously lost. A man driven. Standing at Reeve's side, shimmering gossamer in the night, stood Esme, terrible and beautiful. Her shining hair streamed in the wind. She reached out and laid one ghostly hand upon his shoulder.

The *Scarlet Wind* plowed on, and dread pirate Reeve sang forth. The blood of his most loyal dragged us forward on stranger tides than any I have ever known and in the ocean before the ship, like a gargantuan yawning maw, a desolate portal to a nether Darkness split open.

My bladder opened, too, and I had seen enough. Realizing the last remaining rowboat was but a few paces away, I clambered in and used my small dagger to cut the rope. The only thing I owned became my salvation from the man who had gifted it to me. Who had been lost, really, since the dark and beautiful Esme fell.

The boat dropped to the churning waves with a bone-jarring impact as a storm howled forth from that unholy rent in the ocean. I grabbed the oars and rowed for my life, forced to watch that from which I ran as I worked. Foul, black, winged beasts surged through that maw and into the stormy sky as the *Scarlet Wind* was drawn into the Darkness. The ship that was my life, my home, with the man who was the closest thing to a father I had ever known, tumbled, cracked, and split as it went over that profane edge.

As I rowed away, powerless but to look across the churning waves into that yawning gulf, the great winged creatures flapped determinedly across the night sky, blanking out the stars with their massive presence. The downdraft from their beats pushed against me as they headed west toward the islands and the New World. Terrible, hungry creatures like no bird or flying mammal I had ever seen, indistinct yet hideous in the night sky. And as they passed I had the inexplicable yet certain realization that these were but heralds for some far more vast and ravenous evil yet to be released. And I wondered, should the madness of any men eventually facilitate that escape, as Reeve had done with these, would that terrible leviathan's shadow ever be removed when it fell across our sun?

I rowed on and on, away from the unnatural swirl, until my muscles were as jelly, my eyes hazy, my mind blank. And then a different kind of blackness stole over me and I fell unconscious to the bottom of the small vessel.

For days I drifted, burned by the sun, starved, desperate for water, and I almost did that one forbidden thing and drank the ocean, when finally a Navy ship came by. British. The irony was not lost on me as they hauled me aboard. I was the son of a merchant, I told them, whose ship had gone down in a storm. They asked how many escaped and I honestly told them I did not know, for how many might have survived that mutinous exodus under the cover of darkness? They smiled on me, fed and watered me, and returned me to New Providence.

Now I am the vassal of their leader, a general with buck teeth, white hair, and a most ridiculous uniform. But he is not unkind and I have a shack of my own to live in when I am not required to wait upon him, or clean, or labor.

And in that ramshackle hut I call my own, I huddle in the shadows of night, listening for those terrible leathery wingbeats. When they don't come, I rise with the sun and bask in its glory all day, dreading the next inevitable night, for one day they will surely make their presence known. Perhaps one day they will lead that which they serve to destroy all we know and hold dear. And I can't help wondering if maybe that is not what the human race deserves for its avarice and hostility.

But whatever may happen or not, I will never set foot again on any vessel that would remove me from this solid, dry land.

THE DARKEST
SHADE OF GREY

1

TOWERING BROWNBRICKS SHIELDED DAVID JOHANSSEN
and the old man from the rain. The red and white neon of a
Coca-Cola sign pulsed like a giant life-support machine behind
them, coaxing hapless tourists and broken people into the plastic
promises of an urban pseudo-Eden. "That's where she was killed,
Mr Curtis?" David asked, clicking on his Dictaphone.

Curtis, a waif of an old man in striped cotton pyjamas, nodded.
Pale, diaphanous colours shivered around the old timer, colours
only David could see. The translucency of the shades around Curtis
showed his fragility and age, but the pale blues and greens were all
calm contentment.

"That's the blood, you can still see it." Curtis pointed to the
stained bitumen. "I was up there, see, and I heard this shouting."
He indicated a first floor window that looked out over the road,
multiple lanes of traffic crawling through the downpour, going
nowhere fast.

David looked up. "That's your apartment?"

"Yup. Lived there over thirty years. I heard this shouting and
carry-on and I could see these two boys yelling and shoving. I

couldn't see the lady, but I could hear her, yelling and cursing back. I tell ya, the language of people these days!"

David laughed. "You can't live in King's Cross for thirty years without getting used to foul mouths, surely?"

"But from people so young? And ladies? The world moves on without us, I suppose."

"I suppose. So you couldn't see the girl? You didn't see them cut her?"

"Nah. But I saw the one lad pull a knife out and then there was scuffling and she was screaming and then it cut short into this sort of gurgling sound and the two boys ran off like scalded cats."

"You came downstairs then?"

The old man laughed, flapping a hand. "Fuck no! I don't come out of my flat after eight o'clock at night any more. I called the police. When they pulled up I did come down and there she was, lying up against that wall with her throat wide open and blood all around her. Soaked in it, she was. I can't believe they haven't cleaned it up."

David shrugged. "They have private contractors for that stuff nowadays. Like everything else, it gets outsourced and then it takes twice as long to happen. The company's probably hoping the rain'll do the work for them and they can get paid for fuck all." He studied the blood stain, sensing the terror and pain that floated around it, an echo of violence. "Anything else you want to tell me?"

Curtis's old eyes, yellow and grey around faded irises, were sad and wet. "What else is there to tell?"

"You hear the argument? What were they squabbling about?"

"Something about drugs and she wouldn't get away with not paying back what she owed. She must have fought back because they all started cursing and hollering and the boys were telling her to get off and stop being crazy. Then they killed her."

David clicked off his Dictaphone. "Okay. Thanks."

Curtis nodded and shuffled back around to the front of his building. "You gonna write a story about it?"

"Sure. But it'll only be a paragraph or two on page three or four I expect. This sort of thing isn't really big news."

The old man nodded again and turned inside without another word. The glass panel door clicked against the security lock as Curtis laboured his way up the stairs one at a time, resignation hanging off every step.

David returned to the blood stain, crouched, put a palm flat against the gritty road. Images and emotions flooded his mind, rocked him back on his heels. She was only young, the poor kid, a teenager. He felt her bravado, her *fuck you* attitude and her fear. She'd sobbed for her mother as she'd held her rent throat closed, hot life flooding through her fingers as the two men fled towards the city. She'd wondered why she wasn't crying tears as she sobbed and called for her mother again, but only a muffled bubbling sound emerged, and then blackness.

David staggered to his feet, stumbling off the kerb. A car horn blared with shattering volume. He threw himself forward with a howl of panic as a wing mirror spanked his hip like a piece of two by four.

"Fucken drunken idiot!"

He didn't look around for the voice and the car didn't slow. Gasping quick breaths, hand pressed to his hip, he limped back to the building, leaned on the wall. "Fuck me."

He rubbed a hand over his face. He found himself doing so more and more recently, like he was trying to wipe something off. Eventually he stepped from the shelter of the building's porch back out into the rain. He headed up towards the red and white corporate god of consumption and the numerous bars in its shadows.

A shiver passed over him. In the shelter of the next building sat a homeless man, hair and beard knotted with grime. The hobo muttered frantically and stared at David with an intensity that froze him to the spot. "Can I help you, mate?" David asked after a moment.

The hobo still muttered, drilling holes through David's soul with large, bright hazel eyes. A miasma of shivers in the air encased the man. The shades kept switching and morphing, yellows of fear, twisted purples and reds of anxiety and confusion, painting patterns of madness and a sense of desperation. David shook himself and walked past. Those hazel eyes followed him, dirty lips muttering, until David tore his gaze away, hurrying up the street.

Today was turning into a real son of a bitch and the sooner he got a few stiff drinks into him the better.

♦

HE GOT BACK to the office more than an hour later, nicely warmed inside from four rapid fire bourbons. He knew he was bitter and twisted, but at least now it was bitter and twisted with the edges filed off. As he turned into the front door of the building something made him look back. On the opposite side of the street stood the homeless man from the Cross. David's heart hammered a quick tattoo of panic against his ribs. "What the fuck?"

Had this weirdo followed him? A ten minute cab ride? David yelled across the street. "You following me?"

The homeless man stared and muttered.

David stared back, unsure what to do. What *could* he do? He turned into the building and headed for the lifts.

As he stomped through the office past reception Mandy raised a hand at him, jabbering away into the headset mic of her switchboard. He stopped, waiting while she rambled about some guy and some bar and some stupid friend.

Mandy was nineteen, blonde and hot as hell. David wasn't quite forty yet, but Mandy looked like a child to him. A child who made his cock heavy as he stared at the swell of her breasts through her white blouse. A child he had often pictured in his mind, naked, sweating and loving him as his hand took momentary care of his frustrations in his bedsit late at night. Or early in the morning. A child who represented everything he would never have again now that he was aging, divorced and broken by a bitch wife, saddled with two hateful kids. All of whom despised him for his 'hoodoo shit'. And his drinking. He stared at the smooth, unblemished flesh of Mandy's cleavage wishing she would hurry the fuck up and tell him whatever it was she had stopped him for.

She looked up, smiled apologetically, holding up one hand again. "Look, babe, I really have to go . . . I'm working! All right, bye, babe." She looked up, tapping a button on her switchboard without looking at it. "I'm *so* sorry, that was rude."

David smiled back, half of him imagining her seeing him as a rugged, desirable older man, gritty and sexy. The other half called himself a fucking idiot. "No worries. What's up?"

"I just wanted to let you know that Miriam, from the post room, she's retiring on Friday and we're having a whip-round." Mandy held out a large manila envelope. "Could you afford a donation towards a present for her? We'll pass a card around later."

David forced a smile, cursing her for stopping him just to beg money for some old bat he didn't even know. He pulled out his wallet and was greatly relieved to see a five dollar bill in there.

Dropping the note into the envelope he noticed coins in the bottom. He could probably have got away with dropping two bucks in.

Mandy almost bounced in her chair. "Thanks!"

He walked into the office, glancing back from the door. She was already talking animatedly on the phone again, probably telling some other friend about the creepy reporter who was always ogling her cleavage. Well, if she didn't like it she could button up her fucking blouse.

Waking his computer, he checked his email. He was soon grinding his teeth, hating Stella all over again. As if it wasn't bad enough that she'd taken the kids and the house and even the fucking dog, now she had to email him shit like this.

You earn more than you're letting on, her email said, *and I'll have a court force you to pay more child support if I have to.*

He sighed heavily, rubbing a hand over his face. His life in the toilet. He angrily tapped out a response. *I'm writing bullshit, hardly deserving of the crap wage I do get. If I earned more I'd move further away from you. See you in court.* He stabbed at the mouse to click the send button like he was driving a finger into her brain through her eye.

Her accusation still rang in his ears, two years on: *you ruined this family with your occult hoodoo shit!* He probably should move away. Only the dog had ever shown an affinity for him. He was jealous as hell of that hound's stupidity. He imagined selling up what little stuff he had, kidnapping the dog and hitting the road. He could wander the country like Dr David Banner, except he wouldn't turn green and solve crimes. He'd turn corners and avoid everybody.

"Johanssen, you listening to me?"

David looked up with a start. Terry, his editor, hung off the doorframe like a well fed, balding gorilla. He watched aura colours swim around the big man, various shades and translucency, dark blue as usual. Grumpy, bitter. "Sorry, what?"

"I said stop daydreaming and get that story wrapped up. Ever heard of deadlines?"

"Right."

He picked up the phone and dialled. A rough voice answered. "Yeah?"

"Amir?"

"No. Who's this."

"David Johanssen."

There was silence and some scuffling for a second.

"David Johanssen, fucken!"

David smiled at the strong Lebanese accent. "Hey, Amir."

"What is it now?"

"Young hooker, teenager, killed last night near William Street. You know anything about it?"

"You calling me a murderer, fucken?"

David laughed. "Don't be a tit. You know you're my go-to guy. Any details for my story?"

Amir made a sucking noise over his teeth. "Nah. I heard about it, but no details, brother. Somebody else's business. Small time shit."

"Okay. Thanks mate."

"You come and see us sometime, ya fucken. Not always about business, eh?"

"Sure man. I will. Thanks." He hung up and wrote a story about a teenager who got her throat cut for a pineapple-deal of smack. He wrote how she cried silently, her lips mouthing 'Mother' as her life flooded through her fingers. He could attribute the details to old Curtis if he had to. Who would ever check? It jazzed up the story. Besides, it was true. He emailed the piece to Terry and sat back in his chair, staring at post-it notes and coffee stains. The minutiae of his life.

After a couple of minutes of nothing he got up, went to Terry's office. He knocked on the door and strode in without waiting for an answer. His editor glanced up, annoyed. David revelled in the tiny victory and hated himself for it immediately.

"What's this?" Terry asked, one tiny white speck of spittle flying from a fat, livery lip.

David scowled. "What's what?"

"This article you've just sent me. This the best you can do?"

David raised his hands, palms up. "It's the best I can do given what there is to work with."

They stared at each for a moment. David watched nervous colours float through Terry's aura. He could tell he had the upper hand. "I'm happy to make any changes you recommend." *That is your fucking job, after all.*

Terry shook his head and leaned back in his overworked swivel chair. A part of David wished fervently for a loud crack and Terry's legs to fly backwards over his fat arse, his sweaty bald head to bounce into the plate glass behind him, shattering it, sending him like an air whale to explode on the pavement below in a modern artwork of blood, guts, and bone splinters. He sucked in a quick breath, dragging himself back to reality. "So that all right then?"

"It'll have to be. Nice bit of blood for page three, I suppose."

"Cool. See you tomorrow."

David was heading back to his desk when Mandy's shrill voice pulled him up short. "You can't come in here! Sir! Errr, sir, please, can I help you?"

He took a step back. His heart did the panic two-step again and the thought of running away screaming like a little girl crossed his mind at the sight of those hazel eyes. The hobo stood motionless but for his mumbling lips. Mandy, Madonna mic held in one hand, wrinkled her nose in disgust. She saw David, her eyes pleading. He cursed under his breath.

Steeling himself he said, "Listen, mate, what's the story, eh?"

"You can tell my story."

David stopped dead, surprised at the sudden clear statement from the muttering man. "What?"

"You can tell my story."

"What story?"

The hobo, the stink of piss, shit, vomit, and alcohol rising off him like a cloud, stepped forward. Involuntarily David took a pace backwards. "I'm watching," the hobo said. "And I'm waiting."

David's eyes narrowed. "Right. Is that the story?"

"I don't know the story, but I know there must be one. You can see things and you write stories. You can help me find it."

David turned to Mandy. "This guy is obviously off his rocker. Call security, eh?"

Mandy nodded, her face horrified. She slipped on the headset mic and jabbed at buttons on her switchboard.

"No, no. Don't do that. Please, you can tell the story."

David held up both hands. "Listen, mate, I don't really know what you're trying to say, but you'll have to leave, okay? You can't stay here. I can't help you."

The hobo looked from David to Mandy, then pushed open the fire exit door. David watched him disappear down the stairs.

"Friend of yours?" Terry's voice was mocking.

David shot him a look of disdain. "Yeah. He wanted to tell me all about his date with your wife last night."

Terry laughed and flipped the bird, disappearing back into his office. David grabbed his jacket. Those afternoon bourbons had long since worn off, and he planned to rectify that forthwith.

♦

IT TOOK THREE more bourbons and a beer to level off the weirdness of the afternoon. After another three shots the melancholy set in. David couldn't remove the image of the hooker's pool of blood from his mind. He was supposed to be the rough, tough, take no shit reporter, getting to the bottom of everything. All he ever got to the bottom of lately was a bottle, and then he started right over at the top of the next one. Perhaps, if he was honest, he had never been a tough guy at all. He stared at the amber liquid in his glass. He thought he used to be a lot tougher and a lot less of an arsehole. Before the hoodoo shit. Before that dinner party with Bradley and Aileen.

Bradley and Aileen's fifth wedding anniversary, with the added celebration of a new pregnancy. "We have to go, David. We never go out any more and Aileen's finally pregnant. Let's get a babysitter."

He was fine with it. He loved his wife, he loved his boys, they all still loved him. "Sure," he said. "Bradley can be a funny bastard."

They laughed and joked and talked about all kinds of stuff. They shared opinions and could disagree without rancour. Just like real grown-ups. They all drank wine, except Aileen. "Have to consider the little one now!"

After the meal Stella pulled out a parcel wrapped in silver and white paper. "Congratulations, you two!"

The happy couple oohed and aahed and unwrapped a little towelling jumpsuit with a bear embroidered on the front. "Yellow, so it doesn't matter if it's a boy or a girl," Stella enthused.

"You don't get presents for yourself any more." David raised his wine glass in a toast. "Your lives are now over. It's all about the kids!"

Stella punched his arm, and everybody laughed.

"Hey, check this out." Bradley retrieved a wooden board and a little velvet covered box.

"Oh, Bradley, don't be ridiculous." Aileen's face twisted in mock disapproval.

Bradley laughed. "Come on, let's give it a go."

The board was light wood with darker wood inlaid. The inlays were the alphabet in an arc, numbers underneath, a circle in each bottom corner, one with Yes, the other No.

"A Ouija board?" David asked.

"The boys at the office got it for me. They said I could use it to figure out if it was going to be a boy or a girl. And when they're a teenager, to try to understand what the hell the kid is doing!"

Aileen shook her head. "It's bloody silly really."

"I've never done this before," David said, intrigued. "How does it work?"

Bradley opened the box, took out a carved wooden arrow head. It had a semi-circle dome on top and another underneath. "It's simple. We all sit around the table, put one finger each on here and ask questions."

"Then what?" Stella looked uncertain.

"Then the spirits answer us!"

David laughed. "Excellent! Come on then, let's have a go."

That was the point. That was the very moment his life had turned to shit. He stood on a precipice and Bradley's Ouija board was the edge. He could have turned around and walked away, but he didn't. He threw himself over.

They cleared the table and turned down the lights. Each of them put a finger on the domed arrow. "Will my baby be a boy or a girl?" Bradley asked suddenly.

"Brad!" Aileen's voice was hushed and annoyed. "I don't want to know!"

"I really don't think it can tell us, love."

There was a moment of silence. David looked around the room. The other three were jolly and happy but he suddenly felt heavy, burdened with a weight of some kind, a sense of expectation. Like something had focussed on him. "Is anybody there?" he asked.

The wooden arrow trembled and skidded across the board. All four people gasped in surprise. "Did you do that?" Bradley asked.

David shook his head. "Look." The arrow rested in the YES circle.

Stella took her hand away, her face angry. "David, stop it. What are you doing?"

"Really, I didn't do that. Put your finger back on."

"No."

"Come on, Stella, this is exciting!" Aileen's eyes held a dare. Slowly Stella reached out her hand and put one finger back on the arrow.

"Ask something else," Bradley said quietly.

David took a slow breath. "Who's there?"

The arrow trembled then began sliding back and forth across the board. The four of them stiffened. The arrow moved smoothly, unnaturally. David read aloud. "L-A-M-A-S-H-T-U. Lamashtu?" The lights blinked, everything black for half a second. Both women screamed. In the blackness David saw a darker silhouette, a human shape.

Stella, Aileen, and Bradley all whipped their hands away, looking accusingly at David. "Fuck, mate, how did you do that?"

"It's not me, Bradley, I promise." David still had his finger on the arrow.

Bradley pushed his chair back a fraction. "David, don't."

"What's the worst that can happen?"

"Dude, seriously, do *not* ask a question like that. Have you never seen a horror film?"

David was still looking at the board, the silhouette in his mind. "Where are you?"

The arrow slid quickly around the board again. I-N-T-H-E-S-E-C-O-N-D-C-I-R-C-L-E-A-N-D-I-T-B-U-R-N-S.

Bradley jumped up, grabbing the board out from under David's hand. "Fuck this, what are you doing?" He snatched the arrow away, stuffed it back into its box.

David felt different, enlivened, exhilarated, opened somehow. Something inside him had changed, static coursed through his veins. Everyone else looked terrified. "What are you going to do with it?"

"I'm throwing it away. It's a bloody stupid thing to have around."

"Let me have it then. I'll take it if you don't want it."

"You shouldn't muck about with this stuff," Stella said. "Just let him throw it away."

"I'll keep it in my study, don't worry about it. I'm just fascinated by it, that's all." He was scared, but his curiosity burned.

That was the night his life had turned to shit, sure enough. David stared at his empty shot glass. He should have listened to Stella, to Bradley. He held up his glass. "Give me another."

The barman nodded once. "With a beer?"

"Fuck it, why not?"

◆

DAVID STAGGERED FROM the bar a little after midnight. "Responsible service of alcohol my arse," he grumbled. The summer night was hot and humid after the air conditioned comfort of the pub. He felt like he'd taken a deep breath of wet sponge. He stood, gathering himself, taking a few more breaths until the sponge was just a hot mist in his lungs. At least the rain had stopped.

He walked, thinking about nothing, staring at the pavement sliding under his feet, not caring where he was going. He ended up walking through a park, down sandstone steps, and eventually looked up. The chattering of fruit bats in the fig trees of Hyde Park surrounded him. William Street stretched away in front of him, a scallop of tarmac and traffic lights, rising up to the red and white flashing neon of the Cross at the other end. *Do I really wanna be here again?* He considered a titty bar. He could barely stand up straight, so it was unlikely he'd be let in anywhere.

"You can see, so you can find the story."

David barked a shout of surprise and anger. The stench of the man floated into his nostrils as he focussed on hazel eyes and a grimy beard. "Why won't the world just fuck off!" he yelled.

The hobo's aroma wafted in a rank breeze. "The world goes on regardless." He began muttering again, frantic whispers.

David tried to hold his breath. "You a philosopher all of a sudden?"

"You look differently, you can see. And you tell stories for people. I'm sure I have a story." The muttering resumed, his eyes wet and glittering.

"Mate, I really don't know what you're talking about. Why are following me? How do you keep finding me?"

"I watch. I see you. Where you are, I go." Mutter mutter.

David shook his head. "Listen, buddy, I'm really sorry, okay, but I have problems of my own. It must be shit to live like you do, but I can't help you. Here, you want some money?" He dug in his pocket, pulled out his wallet. "Fuck knows I have precious little myself, but if it'll help I can give you a few bucks."

The man shook his head, pushing David's wallet away. "We're not all the same. Some are like you, only worse, but some are like *me.*"

David's head spun, the booze soaking his brain. His eyes were heavy and he needed to switch it all off. An image of waking up in a shop doorway somewhere swam across his mind and he turned, swaying and stepping randomly. Among the cars sailing along William Street he could see a yellow light, a beacon of safety. He half fell to the edge of the road and waved a hand. He looked back at the homeless man. "I'm sorry, mate. I can't help you."

The taxi pulled up to the kerb. The hobo stepped forward, taking hold of David's shoulder. He was repulsed by the touch and brushed at the filthy hand.

"You have to help. You will. I'm watching." Mutter mutter mutter.

David held his breath, trapped in the cloud of the man's putrid fug. Unable to help himself, he leaned closer, watching those undulating lips. The words were so fast and whispered they were incoherent at first, but after a moment it became clear. " . . . thine is the kingdom the power and the glory forever and ever amen our father which art in heaven hallowed be thy name thy kingdom come thy will be done in earth as it is in heaven . . . "

David pulled away, eyes wide. "Sorry." He turned and pulled open the taxi door, falling onto the back seat.

"You better not puke in here, mate." The taxi driver's tanned face was hard, angry.

"S'alright. I'm drunk, but I'm fine. Get me outta here."

"That guy hitting you up for money, was he? Fucking junkie."

Through the window David met intense hazel eyes. A cold breeze drifted through his guts, down into his balls.

2

DAVID WOKE, FULLY CLOTHED, DEMONS beating out a syncopated funeral march on his frontal lobes. He groaned, his mouth a festering, greasy trap, and took uneven steps to the bathroom. The need to drink and the need to piss battled until the piss threatened to start without him. He stood, flooding the porcelain, smacking foul lips together in an effort to find saliva. When he was finally done he put his head under the tap and gulped for a long time before digging in the cupboard for aspirin. He showered, dressed, and headed for the door of the single room pit he called home. The Ouija board leant against the wall at the end of his bed. He scowled at it. Why couldn't he chuck the fucking thing away? Maybe it was an anti-trophy, testament to his biggest fuck-up ever. His downfall.

He had used it again and again since that fateful night, communicating with Lamashtu. She would hover at the edges of his mind, coaxing him. He was sure she was female. Every time he felt her near him he craved her knowledge, the things she could give him. The things she promised him. He had tried to explain it to Stella, but she was sceptical at first, then jealous, then angry. When he told Stella about the auras he could see around people, one of Lamashtu's gifts to him, she became scared. It was Lamashtu who had convinced him that Stella was holding him back. Lamashtu who drove wedges into the family. Then it was her who had sent him nightmares and visions. She had driven him to drink. Only when he drank was her voice less powerful in his mind. But the damage was done. The nightmares and the drinking turned him into a monster in his family's eyes. In the two years since Stella had left with the boys he had refused to touch the Ouija board, refused to talk to Lamashtu. Although he suspected she wasn't interested in talking to him any more. Under her spell he had been blind. Now he was ruined, her work done and that was that. He had been played. All he had left was a drinking problem and the ability to see things no one else could. Things, more often than not, that he wished he couldn't see.

By the time he got to work, carrying the biggest coffee he could find, he felt mildly less hellish. As he walked into the building his phone rang, singing electronically from his trouser pocket. He pulled it out, his hand brushing over the bruise flowering across his hip, making him wince. It said THE BITCH across the screen. With a sigh he tapped the answer button. "Yeah."

"Hungover again? You sound awful."

"Good morning to you too, Stella, lovely to hear your voice."

She chose to ignore that. "I got your email. David, let's not take this to court. Really, can't you just be honest about your pay and give us what Joshua and Tyler need for a good life?"

David closed his eyes, tipping his head back, counting to five. "I'm being honest, Stella. My income is assessed, I'm not earning any cash on the side or anything like that. I love my boys, I'm giving everything I can. I'm living in a fucking shoe box for their sake."

There was silence for a long moment at the other end. Eventually, "David, your boys really need all the help they can get."

"And I'm giving them all the fucking money I can," he barked, not even thinking to count this time. "They could probably use a father around them too."

"They don't want to see you. It's not just me. They're scared of you."

"Scared? Come on, Stella."

"They put up with a lot after you changed. They learned to avoid you when you were drinking, learned to ignore your shouts and screams at night. But walking into their room, naked and ranting and threatening?"

David ground the heel of one hand into an eye socket. "I was sleep-walking, they know that."

Stella sounded very tired, very sad. "No, they don't. You told them that. Shit, you told me that, but none of us really believe you. You've changed, David, and the boys are scared of you. Frankly, so am I."

There was silence again. David ached for his boys. He ached for Stella too, if he was honest. And he knew he'd lost them all through his own selfishness. And Stella was right, he had changed. Undoubtedly, irredeemably changed. "I really don't have any more money to give," he said at last.

"Try to find some, please. Stop drinking and start working harder. Get a promotion or something. I can't support the boys properly on the child support I get."

Stop drinking and get a promotion. Sure, it was that easy. She always had been able to say the right thing to really make him angry. "Why don't you get a fucking job? Sitting on your arse, taking all the state help you can get and digging fucking holes in me! They're both in school all day, Josh starts fucking high school next year. They're not babies any more, Stella. Get a ten till three job or something and try fucking contributing yourself!"

The phone went dead at the other end. That was about right. As ever, when the subject gets too close to the bone, just walk away. David took the phone away from his ear, stared at the screen. His two boys, grinning at him in their school play costumes from two Christmases ago. It was the most recent picture he had. He wasn't surprised they were scared of him; he believed Stella about that. His eyes prickled with tears and the pounding in his head intensified, his hangover giving him a beating for his crimes against his family. It was no less than he deserved. Sniffing back his rage and sorrow he walked into the building and headed for the lifts.

His day was a drudgery of phone calls and news feeds, checking wires, drinking as much bad machine coffee as he could manage, trying to ignore the slamming in his forebrain and the nausea in his gut. Lunchtime came around and Mandy offered to do a Macca's run. A double cheeseburger, fries and a Coke made him feel a lot better and that in turn made him feel worse when he thought about it. He used to be proud of his body, his fitness, his vitality. He wasn't fat and wasted yet, but it couldn't be far away. By the time he knocked off he had decided that tonight he wasn't going to drink. He would eat something healthy, hang out at home and not drink. Just to prove to himself that he could. By the time he walked out the front doors of his building, hands shaking, he was questioning his resolve.

"Please, you have to find the story."

David cursed. He saw the hobo the same time as the stench hit his nostrils. "Fuck me, why are you hounding me?"

"Please, tell the story." Mutter mutter.

David shook his head. This was weird and disturbing and he really had no idea what he was supposed to do for this man. But the situation obviously wasn't going away. "What's your name, buddy?"

"I don't know."

"You don't know?"

Mutter mutter.

David shrugged. "Well, I have to call you something. Why don't you pick a name."

Mutter mutter.

"Fuck me. All right, how about Boris? You like that?"

"I don't know what it means."

David laughed. "Neither do I, Boris, neither do I. But if you can't come up with anything better, that's what I'm going to call you from now on. Now, Boris, what the fuck do you want? Really?"

"I'm sure I have a story. You can tell it." Mutter mutter.

David narrowed his eyes, trying to understand. "Tell me more. Tell me what you *want.*" A hazy memory stumbled through the fog in his brain. "You said something about some people being like me and some people being like you?"

The hazel eyes popped wide. "Yes! That's right. Some are like you and some are like me."

David stopped looking at Boris, avoiding the incessant lips. For some reason it was even more disturbing now that he knew Boris was just repeating the Lord's Prayer over and over and over. "What does that mean?" he asked. "What's the difference between you and me?"

Boris tilted his head to one side. "Memories," he said, as if it was obvious. "Some people are like you, broken and lost, but they remember. Some are like me."

"You have no memories?"

"Bits and pieces, images and sounds. But nothing really. I don't know anything about me. But you can see and you can find stories."

There was something in what Boris said that tickled the investigative reporter nerves deep inside David. Maybe this poor, mad hobo could lead David to a story that would stamp his name on the world. Perhaps it could even lead to promotions, more money, reconciliation with Stella and his boys. He stopped dead, his eyes widening. What the fuck was he thinking? Why would his life suddenly become a Time Life drama with a happy ending? He must be as mad as Boris.

But it *was* possible that there was a story here. Besides, this nutcase was obviously going to keep harassing him until he found out. And he was reminded of another question that bothered him. "How do you keep finding me?"

"I can see your light. I want to go to you and I do."

David raised his eyebrows. "Really?"

Mutter mutter.

"All right then. You know some other people like you? People without memories? Can you take me to them?"

Boris smiled and his face was beatific, glowing through his grime. "Yes!"

He turned and walked off along the pavement. David let out a tiny laugh and hurried to catch up. Within a few paces Boris vanished. David froze, staring at the space where the homeless man had stood. His odour, sour and rich, still hung in the air. "What the fuck . . . ?"

He looked around. Not many people were travelling this footpath, and no one seemed to have noticed a man disappear. He turned slowly on the spot, looking all around. As he completed his circle his nostrils filled with foulness and he shouted in surprise.

Boris stood there, looking confused. "You want me to show you? Follow me."

"I tried, but you disappeared. How did you do that? What did you do, exactly?"

"I went to a place to show you a man with no memory."

"I can't do that," David said slowly. "Can we walk there?"

Boris narrowed his eyes, muttering frantically. "All right," he said eventually. He turned and walked off again.

David fell into step beside him, watching closely. "Is it far?"

"Not far. Further like this, but not far."

They walked for block after block, and David wondered just what Boris might consider *far* to mean. Eventually they reached Chinatown. On the corner of Sussex and Goulburn Streets, Boris stopped, staring ahead, still muttering. Though the pavements were busy with foot traffic, a buffer zone of half a metre remained around them. David wondered if the stench that hung around this man wasn't a considered defensive tactic. Maybe David should stop bathing. "Why have we stopped?"

Boris pointed up Goulburn Street, towards the corner with George. "He's coming."

David scanned the crowded pathways, looking for someone like the poor wretch who stood beside him. After a moment a small, bearded man with a mop of dreadlocks welded together with greasy dirt appeared around the corner. He walked along the edge of the path, one foot on the kerb, the other in the gutter. He was chattering away, his mouth and beard dancing a frenzied tango. Every few paces he would lift his knee and stamp into the gutter as hard as he could, shouting, before continuing the walking and chattering. People on the path gave him a wide berth too, casting sidelong glances, some disgusted, some compassionate. "What's his name?" David asked.

"I don't know."

David crossed the street, standing on the kerb to intercept the dreadlocked stamper. Only a metre away, Dreads stamped and shouted, his words incoherent. David winced, wondering how much damage the man was doing to his foot, with his shoe a ragged trainer, split and falling apart. Dreads stopped when he realised David was standing there, looked up sharply. His eyes were wild and scared.

"Don't worry, mate. I wanted to talk to you. Is that okay? What's your name?"

Dreads spotted Boris across the street and hissed, his face twisting in rage.

"What's your name, mate?"

He turned back to David, his nose wrinkled like a child pretending to be a tiger. "Ain't got a name." His voice was thirty years of drinking meths and smoking butts.

"You don't have one or you can't remember?"

"Same thing."

"What can you remember? Why are you on the streets?"

Still snarling, the man tipped his head to one side like Boris had earlier. "Why?"

"Do you remember where you grew up?"

"Grew up? What do you mean?"

David paused, unsure. "Do you remember anything about your life before you were living on the streets?"

Dreads put one hand into the middle of David's chest and shoved him out of the way. He stamped in the gutter, striding on before David could say anything else. Every few metres he lifted his knee and stamped again, until he turned into Sussex Street and stamp-walked out of sight.

David drew a long breath. It was generally well known, though rather less well talked about, that the majority of people living on the streets were suffering from one form of mental illness or another. Most people who were able to operate within society did just that, and the misfits and weirdos ended up homeless. But they weren't weirdos so much as sick, with no one to care for them, to get them the help they needed. David grimaced. Sometimes people weren't very advanced as a species at all, a thin veneer of civilisation barely covering a plethora of failures and atrocities. Maybe it was as simple as that, and these people were more broken in their minds than most. But something still niggled at David's journalistic core. And Boris's disappearing act couldn't be ignored.

David knew from bitter experience that there was lot more to life than most people ever considered. The fairy tales and ghost stories, maybe a lot of that stuff was true. He had recently seen and done more than he would ever have considered possible before, and a disappearing man, while mind blowing on one level, was something he was prepared to accept. But it also helped to convince him that these people weren't simply deranged. Something was going on here.

Another homeless man sat on the opposite corner of Goulburn and George, a hand-written cardboard sign in his lap, a ragged cap on the pavement in front of him. His head hung, eyes downcast, a picture of misery. David jogged between beeping traffic and walked up the street. He crouched, dropping a couple of dollars into the man's hat. "What happened to you, mate?"

The man's his eyes hung under the weight of his sadness. "What?"

"How did you end up on the street?"

"Got taken away from my parents, put into care, and didn't like it. I left for the big city and here I am." He pointed at his cardboard sign. *Homeless and jobless, just looking for a start in life. Please help. God Bless.*

There was a struggle behind this guy's eyes. He was an angry, broken person, certainly depressed, probably suffering something more complicated, with no one to help him. He was an example of the detritus of humanity, and he was different from Boris and Dreads. Very different, though David couldn't really put his finger on why. "Well, best of luck, buddy."

He stood and returned to Boris. "I don't really know what this story is that you want me to tell, but I'll try. You have any idea where I might start?"

Boris just looked at him, muttering away.

"You're a bit different," David said. "You know that you can't remember anything. That stamping guy seemed confused that I was even asking."

"I can remember that I can't remember, so something must be happening. I'm watching for it."

David pushed the thought of a drink into the back of his mind. Maybe this is what he had needed all along, something really intriguing to get his teeth into. "How many people are there like you?" he asked Boris.

"Like me?"

"People who don't remember." He indicated the man with the cap and the cardboard sign. "He's like you, but different, right?"

"Yes, he's like you."

David raised an eyebrow. He wasn't sure he liked that comparison. "But that guy stamping in the gutter. He's like you?"

"Yes."

"And how many others do you know like that? Like you."

Boris shrugged. "Some. I'm the only watcher."

"Can you show me another one?"

"There's one at the Mission."

A few minutes later they stood in front of the Mission Australia Centre. A man with long pale hair and even paler skin crouched on the pavement outside, his back against a wall. "He lives inside as often as he can and spends all day here," Boris said.

David crouched in front of the pale man. "Hello."

Nothing.

"What's your name, mate?"

The pale man's eyes focussed on David's face. "No name." His voice was as light as a wisp of cobweb on the air.

David leaned closer. "How did you end up here?"

"How what?"

"On the street. What happened to you?"

The question appeared to make no sense to him. His gaze slid away, staring through David into the depths of nowhere.

David stood. "Can you show me anything?" he asked Boris. "You said you had snippets of images and sounds. Are they like fragments of memories? Is that the difference between you and these others like you?"

Boris nodded, lips gibbering.

"What do you remember? What images?"

"There's a place that feels familiar."

"Take me there."

The close heat of the summer night made walking sweaty. David's shirt stuck to him, stained at the armpits, back and chest. He was tired and irritable, but his intrigue kept him going. The thought of an air-conditioned pub and an ice cold beer kept surfacing. He pushed it down time and again, knowing it would only pop back up as soon as his thoughts wandered. They walked past Central station and up into Surry Hills, turning off Foveaux Street into a network of narrow lanes and alleys. Boris stopped at the end of one. The left side was all brick walls and boarded-up windows. The right side had roller doors with dirty windows above. Rubbish littered the gutters, a dead rat, dried out and paper thin, pressed into the bitumen in front of them.

"This it?"

Boris nodded, his muttering more frantic, almost audible.

"What is it about this place?" David asked.

"It's familiar. Something happened here. Or something will. It's important."

Boris didn't move, repeating his prayer as fast as he could. David walked up the alley warily. "Come on, walk with me. Tell me what you feel."

Boris entered the alley, his steps heavy, hesitant.

"Let's just walk to the other end. Tell me what you think," David said.

The alley sloped gently upwards for a couple of hundred metres, getting steeper for the last thirty metres or so. They walked slowly, Boris praying ever more desperately until the words merged and blurred. As they reached the steepest incline, a man in a dark suit stepped into the alley. Boris stopped dead in his tracks, his mouth still, his voice silent. David walked on a few paces. "Hey there," he called out.

The Suit approached them casually. A sense of dread draped over David. The Suit's colours were too bright to see clearly, all power and confidence, giving nothing else away. Both men were silent, stock still, eyes locked. David felt like he wasn't even there.

"I'm David Johanssen." His voice sounded reedy.

The Suit's eyes met David's. "I know who you are."

"Do you? Doesn't feel very fair given that I don't know who you are."

The man smiled, a predatory baring of teeth. "David Johanssen, second rate reporter, failed marriage, two boys, ten and twelve, both of whom despise you."

David's knees began to tremble and his balls tightened. The need to drink was suddenly ferocious.

"Alcoholic," The Suit continued. "You played around with magic and got burned. Now you've lost everything and you're desperate for some kind of repentant catharsis. This, I'm afraid, isn't it."

"Who the fuck are you?"

"Let's just say that I'm a company man, here to take care of some business."

"Company? What fucking company?"

The man drew out a shining black automatic pistol and shot Boris in the head. The concussion rang off the alley walls, driving iron stakes into David's ears. Boris stood, eyes wide, a dark red hole in the middle of his forehead leaking a single line of blood over the bridge of his nose. The back of his head had blown open like a sharp, bony flower. He folded to the ground.

David threw his hands up. "What the fuck? Dude, what are you doing? You can't . . . "

"Can't I?"

The alley walls pressed in on either side. The illusion of safety glowed just metres behind the man with the gun, a street running by. A car slid mockingly past as David weighed up his chances of bolting, zigging and zagging in the hope that The Suit would miss until he was in the safety of crowded Surry Hills streets.

"I can do whatever I want as far as you're concerned." The Suit slipped the gun back into his jacket.

David's heart raced against ribs. "You just killed him." Stating the obvious was all he could manage.

"Unfortunately, he could see too much. Much like yourself. You, however, have the option to walk away. Go and hide in the bottom of a bottle again, David Johanssen. It's what you're good at. Forget all about this."

David shook his head, his knees knocking. "How can I forget about this? This was murder!"

The Suit smiled a sad smile. "Who will miss him?"

"I will!"

"And you must walk away. We can take care of you too, if we have to. Just as easily."

"There are plenty of people who will miss me. My family, whether they hate me or not, my job."

"Everyone knows about you and the bottle, David. Don't be naive. It would be child's play to be rid of you."

"So why not just shoot me now?" He was amazed that he had laid down the challenge but the reporter in him, the part always desperate to know the story, had to find some answers.

The Suit laughed. "The Lord said unto Cain, "Where is your brother Abel?" and Cain replied, "I know not. Am I my brother's keeper?" and the Lord said, "Your brother's blood cries out to Me from the ground!" Stupid you may be, David Johanssen, but you are largely innocent. It is offensive to spill the blood of the innocent upon the ground."

"You fucking what? You quote the *Bible* at me while he's lying there with his brains across the road?"

"Walk away, Johanssen."

The Suit turned and left, hands clasped behind his back. For several minutes David stood and stared at the end of the alley. Boris lay on the road, his wide, surprised eyes staring up to the sky, a shining pool of blood making a gory halo around his matted hair. With a cry of despair David turned and ran. His shoes slapped the pavement, his lungs burned from the effort, sweat poured from his face. He raced block after block, tears mixing with the sweat until blackness closed in at the edges of his vision. He slowed, gasping, hands on his knees, swallowing the urge to puke. Voices and carousing sounded ahead of him. The doors of a pub, people on a balcony of the second floor over the street, laughing, drinking, unaware of murder. He staggered inside, drawing deeply of the processed, air-conditioned coolness.

Still gasping for breath he slapped his wallet onto the bar. "Double bourbon, straight, and a schooner of New."

◆

IT WAS WELL after midnight when David staggered from the pub, his vision a blur. He was barely able to stand, yet the image of the bullethole in Boris's head refused to go away. Blood and brains were branded on his memory in an ugly puckered scar that would never heal. A bouncer outside the pub grabbed his shoulder as he fell towards the kerb. "Buddy, you'll get yourself killed."

"Fuggen shit if I care . . . fuggen Boris brains . . . blood and *fucking* company man!"

The bouncer held David as he swayed like a fleshy flag. "How's your luck, here's a taxi. You remember where you live?"

David managed to slur his address.

The bouncer helped him into the cab, telling the driver where to take him. He even found David's wallet and handed the driver a twenty dollar bill in advance. David was grateful. Somewhere deep inside he recognised these acts of kindness and it made him want to weep. The burly goon of a security guard acting so out of stereotypical character, the suited, respectable looking "company man" committing a murder, poor, broken Boris getting his brains blown out. Humanity was one fucked up organism and he was sick of it.

Images blurred and tumbled through his mind as the city lights strobed by the taxi windows, then he somehow managed to find his building, his door, his key, his bed.

3

FOR THE SECOND TIME IN two days David woke fully clothed on the bed, his brain slamming against the inside of his skull. His eyes felt like someone was hammering tiny nails into them. His phone was ringing. "Yeah?"

"You know what time it is, you drunken fucking bum? You coming to work today?"

David stared myopically at his watch, moving his arm back and forth in an attempt to find focus. Eventually he read 9.35. "Fuck, Terry, I'm sorry. Listen, I had a really messed up night last night. I was following up on a great story, but it all turned to shit."

"And that affects your ability to come to work how, exactly?"

"Well, listen, I saw a man killed last night."

"What? You fucking serious?"

"Yeah, I'm serious. I couldn't handle it, I drank too much . . . fuck, Terry, I have to go to the police station today. I don't think I can come in."

He could hear Terry's measured breathing at the other end. "Are you bullshitting me?"

David ran his tongue over his teeth. It was like licking a warm, mouldy towel. "No, I'm serious. There may be a story in it yet, but I don't know. I'll call you back later, okay."

"Find me a story!"

"Yeah."

He hung up. Black spots made random patterns across the dirty white paint of his ceiling, messing with his vision. Was he going to go to the police? *Walk away, Johanssen.* He should probably do just that. What would he tell the police anyway? He pressed the heels of his hands into his eyes, cursing his weakness. Drinking was one thing, but getting this drunk two nights running was ridiculous. He'd be six feet under in no time if this carried on. He crawled off his bed and into the shower, shaved, and took himself to a cafe for a greasy breakfast and as much coffee as he could manage. It was the kind of extravagance that he could hardly afford, but he decided he deserved something to help him back from the brink.

Feeling a lot better full of bacon fat and caffeine, he sat and thought. Going to the police was useless, as he had nothing to tell them. He was fairly convinced that Boris's body would have been tidied up by whoever this "company" was, and that any forensics in the alley, should there be any, would prove useless. Boris wouldn't have left many records. But David felt that he owed something to poor Boris, who suddenly seemed incredibly innocent in all of this. There was also the matter of Stella and the possibility that he could make some more money, give something extra to the boys and maybe get a chance at seeing them again. It was all bullshit, but he had to hang onto something, anything, that might make him feel vaguely human. Something to make him matter. He preferred it when life had been a drudgery of irrelevant stories and staring at Mandy's tits.

Walk away, Johanssen. How did they know so much about him? Who the fuck were they? And what was up with Boris and his lack of memory and disappearing tricks? Like it or not, David wasn't going to be able to let this go. He remembered an old joke: Why do men chase women they have no intention of marrying? Same reason dogs chase cars they have no intention of driving. The same thing applied to David and a good story.

Although this did seem like the kind of story that could get him killed. Boris and his brains floated across his mind's eye again, and he whimpered. That was a trauma that would haunt him forever. The casualness of the killing, the complete lack of concern, lack of emotion. He might be killed just as casually.

Then another thought crossed his mind. *So fucking what?* His life was bullshit stories for a bullshit paper and staring at a nineteen year old's tits for thrills. He had a wife and kids who hated him, a bedsit full of mould, and some weird affliction brought on by fucking with forces he didn't understand. He might as well be dead for all he was worth. Maybe, just maybe, he could find the story here. *You can tell my story.* Death or glory.

◆

DAVID STOOD ON a street corner near the Mission Australia building. The pale blond guy was in his usual place, crouched by the wall, staring into the gaps in the world. David tried to see what wasn't there. Lamashtu might have ruined his family, ruined him, but she had revealed some power in him. It was power he would rather not have, but he had learned to make use of it.

He'd found himself getting drunk in a bar in Newtown a year or so back and a wild, New Age chick had started talking to him, obviously tripping out of her mind. She was all flowing cotton and no bra and he had watched her tits sway under her dress as she talked with her hands. The more he drank the more it amused him, and he started talking about stuff he usually kept private. He told her about the patterns he could see around people, and she had told him he was just so lucky because he could see auras. You could tell all kinds of things about a person by their aura.

She was right. He had learned to read what different colours meant, read a person's emotional state. It would have been nice to know more about her thoughts on the subject, but the alcohol had made him bold and even the acid in her brain didn't stop her being grossed out by a man of nearly forty leaning in for a kiss. She was barely out of her teens. She had slapped him and called him a creep before storming off. When he left an hour later she was all over some uni student, grinding on his hand up her skirt. David had never felt older in his life. They looked like children.

He tried to read the pale man's aura now. A heat haze in washed out colours gently shimmered, telling him nothing. He compared it to other people walking past. That girl was all purples and reds, anxious, that guy was showing depression in charcoal black streaked with blue. He looked back to the pale man . . . nothing. No emotion, no sense of self. Boris had carried a strong sense of desperation, but not this guy. It must have been born of Boris's ability to recognise his condition, while this one was simply lost in his.

David approached him. "Hey buddy."

The man's eyes, palest blue like arctic ice, shifted slightly as his focus changed. "You again."

"You remember me?"

"You were here before."

"I was." He had a short term memory at least. "I asked if you remembered your life before this. Do you remember anything?"

The man slowly tilted his head to one side.

"Any really strong memories? Anything that made you happy or sad or scared?"

The ice-blue gaze slid away again, drifting into nothing.

A deep voice boomed. "Battle not with monsters, lest ye become a monster, and if you gaze into the abyss, the abyss gazes also into you!"

A tall, bearded man stood behind them, smiling broadly. He was dishevelled and dirty, a tangy rank odour drifting off him. His hair was greasy and lank about his shoulders, tiny bits and pieces clinging in it. "Sorry, what?" David asked.

The man's smile broadened. "Friedrich Nietzsche."

David stood, turning to face the man. "Is that right? David Johanssen."

The man laughed heartily. "Billy Patterson. Friedrich Nietzsche is the wise one. Good to know ya."

"You know him?" David gestured towards the pale man.

"Yeah, I've seen him here plenty. Tried to have a convo with him, you know, just shoot the shit, but he can't string a sentence together. Seen some bloody awful shit, I reckon, and it's broken him."

"He ever say as much?"

"Nah. He just has the look about him of someone who looked into the abyss. And the abyss looked back."

David nodded, lips pursed. Was that a possibility? Were guys like the pale man and Boris and Dreads people who had seen something so traumatic that it had wiped their minds? Was it possible that they could have all shared the same traumatic experience? Boris had seemed to think they were all alike at some fundamental level.

Maybe Billy's diagnosis was feasible, but it still provided no root cause. He would need to know what the trauma was to get any answers. He studied Billy's aura, watching the purple of anxiety and madness threaded with a dark, heavy red of anger. Forced happiness greens fought to keep afloat. Billy had a nasty temper buried in there, but he wasn't like the pale man. *One like me, not one like Boris.* David pulled a few bucks from his pocket and offered them to Billy. "Thanks mate. Be nice to him, eh?"

Billy took the coins with a nod. "I'm nice to everybody, me. You have a *good* day!"

"I will."

David turned, walked slowly away, seriously doubting that he would have a good day. With a decisive sniff he headed back towards Surry Hills, to the alley where Boris had died. Boris had said it was important, that something happened there. Or that something would happen there. Perhaps Boris had been foreseeing his own murder.

Rather than walk the length of the alley, David went the long way around and stood at the top of the slope, looking down at the site of Boris's slaughter. Sure enough the road was clean. Much cleaner than any other part of the alley, scrubbed back to raw bitumen, evidence of evidence removed. He looked up at the surrounding buildings. Residential flats, small offices of import/export businesses, and wholesalers. It would be like looking for the proverbial needle to check all these little boxes for traces of the company.

When he reached the clean patch of alley, he pressed his palm to the ground. Faint echoes of Boris, his madness and desperation. He felt Boris notice The Suit and go silent, a sense of terror and wonder.

Boris knew The Suit, but he couldn't place why. He loved this man and his mind stilled at the mere sight of him. Boris was trying to remember why he loved him so much when the gun flashed and something punched him sharply in the head. The last thought that flashed through his mind, *Where do I go now?*

David stood, gently flexing his fingers. A brotherly love, as though they had been family. David turned back to the other end of the alley. He put his palm against the road where The Suit had stood, taking a life as casually as brushing dust off his cuff. A shock bounced through his hand, driving into his shoulder, firing a flashgun in his head. He stood involuntarily, stumbling backwards, tripping over his own feet and sat heavily onto the bitumen several metres away. Gasping for breath, heart racing faster and faster, he thought he would suffer a heart attack and die right there, just centimetres from where Boris had fallen.

The rushing in his body eased slowly. He gulped at the hot summer air, the smell of trash in the alley clearer than ever. His heart rate began to steady. He stared at the spot from where The Suit had fired, where he had tried to put his hand. Beyond the mental shock he had received, all he could remember was a sense of incredible power. Not just ordinary strength, but a preternatural, supernatural authority. If David's own unwanted abilities were measured on a scale of one to ten, it wouldn't matter what he scored. The Suit would be in the thousands.

A tremor passed through David. He held up his palm, searching for answers between the life line and heart line. His whole body tingled, tiny sparks coursing through every nerve. He felt invigorated and violated.

The image of The Suit standing at the end of the alley, gun raised, floated against David's retinas. The shock of the connection had branded the image on David's backbrain, overlapping the memory of Boris and his exploded skull.

David coughed a single, selfish sob. He didn't want these things in his head. He didn't want to be able to see people's fucking auras, or feel what they felt when they died. He just wanted a normal life, whatever the hell that was.

He left the alley. Fuck it all, he was going to have a drink, forget about everything and go back to work tomorrow. He missed Mandy's tits. He even missed the mundanity of the crappy stories he had to cover. Bollocks to all of this.

As he walked something dragged at him. He stopped. Something had hold of his soul and was trying to pull it away from him. There was no pain, but a distinct discomfort. He tried to walk away again and the feeling intensified, nauseating him. He turned, let the sensation draw him back, and the feeling eased. The mental image of The Suit clarified in his mind. He walked out the end of the alley, along the street, turned into another, always letting the sensation guide him. All the time he was getting a clearer image of the man in the suit. Boris's murderer. Some connection had been made in the alley with the shock that had almost killed him.

Whether he liked it or not, he was going to see the man who had killed Boris.

◆

DAVID FOLLOWED THE sensation for a long time, sweating in the summer humidity, cursing everything. A building loomed before him, red bricks beneath peeling white paint. Dozens of old fashioned sash windows, split and flaking, the glass smeared and cracked, a large roller door off to one side. Metal steps led up to a door on the other side of the building, six symmetrical glass windows painted in above a cracked wooden panel. His heart raced. He was here. And something told him they knew he was here. There was really nothing else for it. He walked up the metal steps and banged on the door with his fist, three heavy blows.

Nothing happened. He pressed his ear to the door, heard nothing. He pounded again. "Fuck you." He tried the handle. It turned.

Inside was an office, simply an old wooden desk with a black office chair behind it. Nothing else. Another door led out the back. David ground his teeth. "Seriously, fuck you." He strode across the office and pushed open the second door. It opened into a huge warehouse space. Off to his right was the other side of the roller door he had seen from the street. A mezzanine level circled the walls, six or seven metres above the floor, the ceiling the same distance again above that, grimy skylights shining through the square onto the concrete floor below. Scattered around on the floor were sofas and armchairs, beanbags and beds. People lounged on the furniture, some clothed, some naked. In one corner two guys were enjoying a gymnastic threesome with a young girl, thrusting and laughing. Other couples, threesomes, men and women, men and men, draped over chairs and couches. Others sat around reading, some playing video games or watching a giant plasma TV in the far corner. David stood, mouth agape.

"Walk away, Johanssen. Was that so hard to understand?"

David spun around, an involuntary whimper escaping. The Suit looked angry and resigned. "What the fuck, exactly . . . ?" David gestured behind him.

The Suit stood halfway up metal stairs leading to the mezzanine. David saw movement up there too and looked away, unable to take in any more. "Why didn't you just walk away, Johanssen?"

"You killed Boris, you bastard!"

"Boris?"

"That's what I called him, he couldn't even remember his name. What did you people do to him?"

The Suit laughed. "What did we do to him? We looked after him."

"By shooting him in the head?"

"That was unfortunate."

"Unfortunate? That's a bit of a fucking understatement."

"There are some things that are beyond the control of everyone, Johanssen. And some things you should just leave well alone."

David was unsure what to say, what to do. *Let's just say that I'm a company man, here to take care of some business.* What sort of company was this? This whole place was like a teenager's fevered dream. "Who are you people?" he asked.

The Suit made a rueful face. "There are some things you should just leave alone and some things, Johanssen, that you would not be able to understand. Everything here is both of those things."

The sensation that had drawn David here swelled under his ribs, threatening to burst him open like an egg dropped to a hard floor. He gasped, clutching at his chest. The Suit extended his right hand, palm up, towards David. He grabbed at something invisible in the air and pulled his hand away. David felt as though his heart had been torn out through his chest. He cried out, staggering forward, fell onto one knee. He distantly registered laughter from somewhere in the enormous room. His whole body swelled with agony, brightness flashing through his mind for a split second, then everything went still. He fell forward, catching himself on both hands, moaning as he dragged air into his lungs. The sense of imperative had gone. Any connection he'd had to The Suit was severed. He sat back on his heels, staring up into the man's face, his hatred raw. "Who. The Fuck. Are. You people?"

The man laughed again. "You should be dead, you know. You're stronger than you think."

"Is that right? I feel about as strong as a piss-soaked tissue right now."

"That echo I left behind should have fried you if you went back there. Instead it empowered you, led you to me."

"Lucky break for me, eh?"

"No, not really." A moment of genuine sadness wisped across The Suit's face, like a cloud across the moon.

"You said you were on company business when you killed Boris. What does that mean?" More laughter from the room beyond. David knew he was the only person not in on the joke. "Who are you?"

"You can call me Michael."

"That's a start I suppose."

Michael smiled. "But it won't do you any good."

People had stopped to watch their exchange, the TV ignored, the games paused. Even the people fucking had stopped, completely relaxed in their nakedness, invulnerable. "What sort of company is this?" David asked. He sneered at their smiles and chuckles. "Some kind of secret society?"

Michael laughed again. "Something like that, I suppose."

One corner of David's mouth hitched up in disdain. He wasn't going to keep making a fool of himself. He stood, staring the fucker down even though he felt like pissing his pants. Michael was humouring him. He could be swatted like a fly at any moment, but he wasn't. He was past caring and had every intention of pushing his luck until something broke, even if that turned out to be him. "Well?"

Michael sighed. "You like Shakespeare, Johanssen?"

"What?"

"'There are more things in heaven and earth, Horatio, than are dreamt of in your philosophy.' *Hamlet*, act one, scene five."

"That supposed to mean something to me?"

Michael shook his head, suddenly angry. "There are more things in heaven and earth, David Johanssen, that are dreamt of *by* your philosophies. You broken, weeping, frightened children of the void, asking all the questions and expecting there to be answers. Well, fuck you too, little man. You're nothing, but there are rules. Rules binding both of us. So fuck off." He turned and started walking up the stairs.

David started after him. "Wait a fucking minute, you pompous prick. I need answers and I'm not going . . . "

Michael gestured with one hand. Something unseen lifted David off his feet and slammed him into the wall. He yelped, the wind rushing from his lungs, his head cracking sharply against the plastered bricks. Stars and comets burst behind his eyes. Immediately the mood in the room changed from one of amused observation to determined action. Several men stood and moved in on David. Michael resumed his climb up the stairs, disappearing onto the mezzanine. Strong hands grabbed David, hoisted him, thrashing, into the air. They carried him through the small office and launched him over the metal steps out onto the street. He cried out as his shoulder cracked and he rolled over on gravel and broken glass. Without a word the men turned and closed the door behind them. David writhed on the ground, angry tears squeezing from his eyes. The huge white building behind him cast its shadow across the road. With a sob of pain and impotence David staggered to his feet and hobbled out into the heavy sunshine. He probably needed a hospital, but he'd start with a pub.

4

DAVID SAT IN SOME NAMELESS bar, a shot glass cupped between shaking hands. He was battered and bruised but fairly certain nothing was broken. His shoulder hurt like hell, but he could move it. The booze took the edge off, though he was determined not to get blind.

Walk away, Johanssen. He had tried to walk away, in the alley, and that strange sensation had pulled him back. Pulled him back for a beating. Now that compulsion had gone and he should walk away again. Now he *could*, but was damned if he was going to.

Whatever this thing was, it was certainly bigger than him. Who the hell were those people? Some kind of paranormal old boys' club? Government? High society? They obviously didn't care about anyone else, and he was clearly one of the little people in their eyes. And what of the powers he had seen? Michael, if that was his real name, had tossed him aside like a finished apple core.

"It really depends just how badly you want to know."

A tall, lithe woman stood beside him. She wore a figure hugging black dress, barely concealing every line of her. She leaned one elbow on the bar. His eyes travelled from her stunning face, taking in long, shining black hair, deep inviting cleavage, the smooth rise of one hip, firm thigh, pale skin over long calves. When he pulled his eyes back up she was smiling. "You like?"

David sputtered. "Sorry, I . . . sorry. I'm drunk."

"That's okay. I do tend to have this effect on men." She said the word "men" like an alcoholic might say "whiskey".

"Who are you?"

"Lily." She pulled up a stool and slid onto it, leaning forward, pushing her ample cleavage towards him deliberately.

"Given the last couple of days I've had," David said slowly, "this is almost certainly not what it seems."

"Oh, you can fuck me if you like." She waved the barman over.

David watched, his heart pounding, as the barman's eyes roved down and back, helplessly swallowed by her. "Er . . . yes, love?"

She smiled crookedly. "Red wine?"

David could almost see the steam escaping the poor man's ears. "Sure." He tore himself away and fumbled among the glasses.

"You see," Lily said. "I have this effect."

David's eyes narrowed. "You're an expert at playing it, I'll give you that. You are gorgeous, but you could play it down if you wanted to."

She pouted. "Such a pragmatist, really? I didn't say I didn't like it. So you want to fuck me?"

"More than you could imagine. But with all the messed up shit that's been happening to me, I can't see this ending well."

She shrugged, winking at the barman as he handed her a glass. He didn't even think to charge her. "Good, bad, it's all relative," she said.

"You see, that's what I mean. That's trouble talking right there."

"How badly do you want to know about Michael?"

David shook his head. "No, no. This is messed up, too. How do you know anything about me? How do you know I've been mixed up with this Michael fucker? How did you know I was here?"

"I've been watching you for a long time."

"What?"

"You've had a tough time, huh?"

She leaned forward, taking a handful of David's shirt. She pulled him closer and planted a kiss on him, hot, wet, full lips pressing against his. Every part of his body fired, neurons in overdrive, his heart pumped, his cock hardened. He had never experienced anything so passionate. She took one hand as they kissed, pressed it over her breast, down her side, across one firm thigh, up under the skirt of her dress.

David gasped, pulling away. He ached for her, wanted to drag her to the floor right there and then and fuck her brains out. He felt as though his cock was about to explode. But something terrified him too. Something powerfully bad, addictive, intoxicating. She leaned back, smiling at him, eyes smouldering.

Her aura surged with waves of power, the colours so dark. She was sexual desire personified but so much more than that. She was darkness and rage, vindictiveness and revenge. She was terrifying.

He staggered up off his stool, knocking it over in his haste. He had to get away. Run away before this woman sucked him into a deep blackness that no man could escape. She sat demurely, watching, smiling.

"You're bad, lady. You're fucking incredible, but you're bad."

She laughed and it heated his soul. With a cry like a terrified child David ran, pushing between a couple who cursed him as he burst out onto the street. He ran until he saw a taxi, then fell into pine scented safety and told the driver to take him home.

◆

SITTING ON HIS bed, looking around the one-room hole he called home, David trembled. Images of Lily swam across his mind like the afterburn of looking at the sun. Every curve of her, her scent, her taste. He was still hard. With a sound of dismay he dropped his trousers and beat away until he exploded across the floor, hating himself, disgusted. The images were still there, sliding across his brain. He fell back onto the bed, appalled at what he had become. A man of nearly forty lying in a bedsit with his trousers round his ankles. Wet, heaving sobs erupted from him.

Sometime later he kicked off his trousers, pulled off his shirt and socks and went to the shower in the tiny bathroom off the corner of his tinier kitchenette. He stood under cool water, fighting off the summer humidity, staring at his feet, thinking of nothing. When he returned to the bed he glared at the Ouija board propped up against the wall. The thing that had started it all. The thing that had cursed his life. Driven by sudden fury he stood and lifted one knee. With a remorseful cry he drove his foot down against the board, snapping it against the wall, splinters flying. Sharp pain speared the sole of his foot and was matched by splinters through his soul. The board lay broken, ruined, crooked against the wall. He spent ten minutes picking tiny shards of wood from his foot.

Feeling drained, if not really any better, he reached for his phone. After a few rings Stella answered. "I'm sorry I hung up on you."

That was a surprise. "I wanted to call to say sorry for shouting at you."

"Are you okay?"

"No, not really."

"Oh, David."

There were several seconds of silence. Eventually he had to break it. "I *am* sorry I yelled at you. I've been having a harder time than usual. I know it's hard for you too, with the boys."

"The boys *are* both in school. I could do something. But, you know, when you work you stop getting benefit and it's hard to get work that pays better than the benefit. Sometimes getting a job would actually make me worse off."

"I know, I know. It's a fucked up system. But I really am giving as much as I can."

Silence again.

"What did you mean, harder than usual?" Stella actually sounded concerned. He could hear some of the old Stella in her voice, the Stella who cared.

"I don't want to upset you."

She sighed. "More hoodoo shit?"

"Yeah. But you know what, I didn't go looking for it. It kinda found me and I'm trying to shake it off and I can't."

"David, you need to leave all that stuff alone. I wish you could stop drinking, stop fucking with all that stuff. I wish you could be like you used to be."

"So do I, Stell. Believe me, so do I."

Silence hung again, an aural magistrate judging the weight of his fuck-ups. "I'm worth more to you dead, aren't I?"

"David!"

"The life policy, still in the kids' names if not yours."

"David, shut up. I don't want to hear you talk like that. You may be a useless occultist drunk, but I *don't* want your death on my conscience." Just like the old Stella.

He smiled in spite of himself. "Yeah, I'm just sayin'. I'm worth a lot more dead than alive."

"Most people are these days."

"I'm in something deep, Stella. I'm going to try to leave it alone, but I'm scared."

"Listen to yourself. Don't do anything stupid, David. Maybe we should get together and talk."

"Yeah, maybe we should. But I have to finish this first. I can't just walk away."

Stella's voice was suddenly tight, he could hear tears in her throat. "You're scaring me now."

"I'm sorry. Listen, it'll be okay. I have to sort this shit out and then I'll call you. I'll call tomorrow night and we'll sort something out. I really would like to see you, talk properly. I miss my boys, Stell."

"I know you do."

"I'll call you tomorrow."

"Okay. Call me in the morning."

"I'll call as soon as I can."

"Okay."

"Okay. Bye."

He dropped the phone onto his bed and his face into his hands. The sobbing started again. Great, snotty heaves that only subsided as he slipped into a troubled sleep.

◆

LILY STOOD AT the end of his bed, smiling, her head tilted to one side. David was hard. "I'm dreaming, right?" His voice hoarse.

"Dreams, reality." Her voice was low, tempting. "Like good and bad it's all shades of grey."

She slipped her fingertips beneath the hem of her tight black dress and peeled it up over her head, cast it aside. She stood there, unashamedly naked, watching him watch her. His eyes roved all over her, not a blemish, not a single part of her anything less than perfect. He tried to find her face again, distracted by milky, firm curves, dark nipples. Eventually he met her smiling eyes. She leaned forward, crawled over him, moving like a cat. He arched his back, sucking in air as she took hold of his cock and mounted him. Hands on his chest, hips rolling back and forth, she rode him slowly. "This is what you wanted, isn't it, David?"

"You're bad. You're really, really bad." He curled his hands into the sheets, trying to retain some kind of control. Instead he reached for her breasts.

"Really, David, what is bad? What is good? We don't live in a black and white world. Shades of grey, remember?"

David worked with her, moving with the roll of her pelvis. Never in his life had he felt anything like this. He opened his mouth to speak but could only moan.

She smiled again, grinding deeply against him. His hands found her hips, the perfect curve of her arse, and pulled her down harder, staring at the unbelievable beauty of her. "You may not be able to see me as anything but bad, but I'm not as bad as Michael, am I?"

He shook his head. "Don't know . . . what . . . don't . . . "

"We're all shades of grey, David, even you. But Michael, oh, he's as dark as grey can get, isn't he? He killed your friend."

Half coherent thoughts struggled through the mist of lust in David's mind. Since when did Boris become his friend? "I don't know what to think!"

She began to ride harder, faster. "Don't think, David. You know. Michael is a bad man. He killed your friend. He beat you black and blue, threw you around like a doll. You can finish him and you can be done with all of this."

David panted, heart pounding along with his cock. His body thrummed with impending climax. "Done with it?"

She rode harder and faster. "Kill him, David. Kill Michael. You'll be done with it all. At the very least you'll have avenged the death of your friend. That poor, lost man!"

David breathed out incoherent sounds, electric currents flooding every fibre. His back arched, hips lifting off the bed, lightning cracking through his brain as he came more forcefully and completely than he ever had before. It went on and on, pulse after pulse, wave after wave. After an eternity he collapsed back onto the sweat soaked mattress, droplets coursing across his neck and chest, running in tickling rivulets down his sides. She leant forward, kissed his lips, slid off him. "Kill Michael, David. It's the least you can do. You can strike a blow against the company."

Chest heaving, drawing as much air in as he could, cursing the heat of the night, David tried to form a thought. "The company . . . What do you know about the company?" She was gone. Still buzzing he fell back on the bed and slept like the dead.

◆

THE SOUND OF ringing, atonal and electronic, pushed into his brain. Blinking against the light he rolled over, feeling around the bed, eventually finding the phone. TERRY FUHRER. The time read 9.18. "Shit." He pressed the button to answer. "Hey, Terry. I'm really sorry."

"You didn't call me back and you didn't turn up this morning. Your job is hanging by a thread, Johanssen."

"I'm sorry, Terry. I'm onto something here. I was on it all night."

"It better be the story of the fucking century!"

David laughed. "You know what, it could be. I've uncovered this—I don't know, this group of some kind. They're powerful and they're messing with people. I watched them shoot a guy in the head, for fuck's sake."

"This sounds like bullshit to me, you drunken bastard."

"No, really, this could be massive. Trust me, Terry, yeah? Just give me a couple of days on this."

"Did you go to the police?"

David winced. "Yeah. Yeah, I did. Probably nothing they can do, but I gave my statement. But I don't want to let this go."

Terry sighed. "Don't spend the next coupla days pissed. I want you back in here the day after tomorrow and I want a story that blows my fucking socks off."

David leaned his head back, exhaled loudly. "Thanks, Terry. Really, thanks. I'll see you in a couple of days."

"Yeah."

The line went dead. David held the phone to his ear, listening to the silence. Lily. Was that real? It had certainly felt real. More so than anything ever had before.

It was another hot, muggy day. He showered, standing in cold jets of water, trying to think straight. The board was broken. He needed to be done with all this. He needed to leave all this stuff behind, to close this chapter with Michael. Whatever Lily was, she was right. He had been drawn into this thing and couldn't walk away until it was finished. Michael, whatever else he was, was a cold blooded killer. Whatever this company was, it was getting away with murder.

David would strike a blow. He would kill Michael. That was the one thing he could do to finish this. And it might be the last thing he ever did, but so fucking what? He was a useless drunk worth more to his boys dead than alive. If he somehow survived today, he would have that talk with Stella. But it was the least likely resolution, and that was fine by him.

◆

AN HOUR LATER he stood in a back room, surrounded by boxes of chips and peanuts. A suave young man stared at him laconically, flanked by two hulking Samoans.

"You finally visit and it's for something like this, fucken?"

"Come on, Amir," David said, eyeing the Samoans nervously. "You kinda owe me a favour."

Amir smiled. "You were kind to us in not breaking that story. But we were kind to your bank account in return. I don't think anyone owes anyone anything."

David shrugged. "No, fair point. But I *really* need a favour here."

Amir raised one eyebrow, sucking on his teeth. "This is a big favour, fucken."

"I know."

"It'll cost you."

"How much?"

Amir continued sucking his teeth, staring hard at David. "Tell you what. Because I like you I'll give you this thing. No money now, I know you're worth less than my grandmother in Baalbek." The Samoans laughed as Amir smiled. David agreed with a rueful expression. "So I do this for favour." He ran a hand back over his slick hair. "You owe me big favour now, yes?"

"Well, I don't really know what kind of favour I can owe you, but sure. I'll do my best."

Somewhere deep inside, David knew he was making a deal with the Devil. He knew that one day this would come back to bite him in the arse. Then again, he was in serious doubt that there would be any more days after this one, so what the fuck.

Amir nodded. "Okay." He pulled keys from his pocket and unlocked a safe in the corner of the room. When he turned back he held a pistol, malevolent anodised steel shining dully in the wan fluorescents overhead. He popped the clip and showed David the bullet nestling angrily in the top, silver and brass. "Nine millimetre. Seventeen in there." He clicked it back into the butt of the pistol, turned it over. Taking the top of the barrel he pumped the mechanism, racking a round. "Now it's ready." He thumbed a small lever on the left hand side of the grip. "That's the safety off. Don't forget to leave it on, but don't forget to turn it off if you need to use it!" He handed the weapon to David.

It was cold and heavy in his hand. It felt like power. He flicked the safety back on and turned it left and right, trying to get used to the weight of it. It was heavier than he'd expected.

"You need more ammo?" Amir asked.

David shrugged. "I have no idea."

Amir went back to the safe and returned with a second clip. "Here, take this anyway. What the fuck you need for gun? You're a reporter."

"I have something that needs to be settled."

Amir nodded. "Fair enough. If you fire that, even once, I never want to see it again. Nothing will connect me to that weapon, so don't bring it back here if you touch that trigger."

"Sure. Thanks."

◆

DAVID STEADIED HIS nerves, the pistol a hard weight in his waistband. He felt a strange calmness. Lily's description of the situation lingered coolly in his mind, empowering him. She was right, he was right. The cold steel power of the semi-automatic in his belt was right. Michael was wrong. Boris's death was wrong. He was an instrument of vengeance and justice. One thing in his life would be worthwhile. One thing would atone for the fuck-up he had become. One act would set him apart.

Hot breath in his ear sent shivers through his balls. "Well done, David."

He turned his head to look at her and she put one hand behind his head, pressing a hard, passionate kiss on his lips, her body sliding across his. Somewhere inside he laughed at the thought of striding in there for vengeance with a hard on. The kiss disengaged, and he opened his eyes. She was nowhere to be seen. He turned and strode to the steel steps leading up to the peeling door.

He wondered if the door would be locked this time, but it swung open easily. He drew the gun from his belt and held it tightly along one thigh, flipped off the safety. Stepping out into the open warehouse, he raised the gun, eyes scanning for Michael.

The main room was like before, full of people indulging in decadence. As David appeared they all stopped what they were doing. No one looked especially surprised. David swung the pistol left and right, scanning faces. He looked up to the mezzanine level, about to mount the stairs. If anyone moved he had every intention of shooting them. No one did.

Michael materialised in front him, appearing out of nothing. He was sad. "You really can't walk away, can you?"

David roared in anger to cover his knee-buckling fear and squeezed the trigger again and again. The gun bucked and weaved, kicking with more power than he ever expected. Two scarlet explosions burst out of Michael's chest and a bright red streak tore across his cheek. Further bullets cracked into plaster and whined off the metal of the mezzanine. No one moved.

Michael stepped forward and took the pistol by the barrel. He squeezed and twisted, crumpling the steel like paper, and wrenched it from David's fingers. The wide bleeding gap across his cheek smoothed over with unblemished skin. He gestured behind himself and most of the people in the room fell over, unconscious. Four strong, beautiful men, two of them naked, were the only ones unaffected. They came to stand beside Michael.

David dropped to his knees, nursing twisted fingers, sobbing. "Who the fuck are you?" His eyes were heavy and red.

Michael's face was angry. "Who are we? Who the fuck do you think you are, David Johanssen? You're nothing. You come in here with a *gun?*"

One of the naked men leaned forward. "Control your anger, brother. He's touched."

Michael growled low in his throat, leaning down to look at David as if seeing him for the first time. He pressed one hot, smooth palm to David's forehead. With a louder growl of anger he straightened up, yelling into the air. "Lilith!"

A deep, husky laughter filled the room and David pissed his pants. Lily stepped up beside him, ran one hand lazily through his hair. "Come on, Michael, it was fun," she said, smiling a perfect smile. "He came with a gun!"

Four of the five men looked angry, though there was something underlying that seemed almost amused. Only Michael was pure rage. "You can not play games like this, Lilith. People die!"

She barked a laugh, cold and mean. "You think that's some kind of deterrent to me? You fool. You lapdog. I love fucking with you and yours. What do I care if humans get hurt?"

Michael backhanded her across the cheek. Her head whipped to one side, only to return with blood on her lip and fury in her dark eyes. Michael grabbed David's hair, pulling his head up, forcing him to look at her. "You know who this is?"

One of the other's said gently, 'Obviously he doesn't, brother."

Michael sneered. "This, David, is Lilith. The screech owl. The serpent. The downfall of fucking man! Sometimes called Lamashtu."

David sobbed. Not again. Not the same fucking creature still ruining him. "I don't know what's happening any more."

Michael pushed him away, making him fall onto his side on the cool concrete. "You never did, Johanssen."

Lilith laughed again. Her skin darkened and she expanded, swelling in every direction, her beautiful face twisted into something hideous. The five men grew with her, their skin golden as clothes melted away. Huge white wings swung out from their backs and they fell upon Lilith as she snarled. David cowered, foetal on the floor, crying as he watched them tear her apart. Broken and bloody she laughed again, thrashing left and right. "Such fun to play with you all again!' She burst apart in twists of dark smoke and was gone.

The five men, naked, golden, beautiful, stood before David. Their wings overlapped behind them, reminding David absurdly of the sails of the Opera House. Michael stood in the middle, his eyes dark pools of anger. "You stupid little man."

David stayed down, shaking all over. He felt like a tiny leaf being carried through the crashing white water of a raging river. "How can this be happening?"

"How? It's all you lot. You make all of this." Michael gestured angrily with one hand, seeming to encompass the whole world.

David shook his head. "You killed him. He was just a lost homeless guy. Why would you do that?"

Michael sighed. "Your friend Boris? His name was Raphael. We did all we could for him."

"He was an . . . he was . . . like you?"

"It's not only humans that break, Johanssen. You people and your world, you can break anything. Sometimes you break our kind too. Nothing is immune to madness. Those of us who can't take it are placed in safety here, hidden in human bodies. The stamping man? The pale man? They're ours. Looked after by us."

"Can't you take care of them in . . . your own place?"

Michael sneered. "Can you imagine one of our kind, with our power, with a broken mind? The best we can do is give them space here in a mortal form. This is a good city, a nice place. We care for them here."

"They live as stinking, homeless bums. That's cruel!"

"We tried giving them a peaceful place, away from people, but the isolation broke them further. The city gives them distraction."

"They live here like animals."

"Better we just euthanise them?"

"That's what you did anyway!"

"Only because I had to. Sometimes they're strong and they start to remember. Sometimes we can hide them again, sometimes we can't. Raphael was too strong. Our system here failed him."

"So now what's happened to him?"

Michael's eyes hardened, coldness closing over them. "That's a concept you couldn't comprehend."

One of the others leaned forward. "Michael, it's not his fault. With Raphael, Lilith. None of it's his fault."

Michael turned with a snarl. "None of it, Uriel? Really?"

"He's just a human. Just a curious human."

Michael shook his head. "These fucking people, all the trouble they cause. We can't let him go, we can't let him back among them."

David stayed on the floor, his mind spinning, desperately trying to process everything. The only thought that kept repeating in his mind was, *You fucking fool. You fucking fool.* He watched Michael and Uriel stare into each other's eyes for a long time. Eventually Uriel lowered his gaze, defeated. David whimpered.

Michael turned back to him. He seemed sad as well as angry now. "You really should have just walked away, Johanssen."

Images flashed across David's mind. Michael striding out into the alley, raising his gun. *Let's just say that I'm a company man, here to take care of some business.* "You tempted me as much as she did," David cried, his voice weak and tear-soaked. "You're the one who walked around all kingshit. You're the one who should have made a better job of taking care of Boris. Of Raphael."

Michael pursed his lips. "Maybe."

David's phone rang, shrill and sudden in the echoing warehouse. Michael sneered, raising his hand. Uriel reached out, staying Michael's arm. "Answer your phone, David," he said.

"What?"

"Answer your phone."

Michael dropped his arm resignedly. "This is fucking ridiculous."

The phone kept ringing.

"Answer it."

David fumbled the phone from his pocket. THE BITCH. "Answer it," said Uriel as Michael scowled.

He pressed the button. "Stella."

"Oh, David, thank fuck! You said you'd ring. David, you sounded suicidal last night. I thought you'd fucking hung yourself. What would I have told the boys?"

Tears started from his eyes again. "I'm sorry, Stella."

"You have to sort yourself out, David. Please, for all our sakes. The boys don't want your life insurance."

David avoided the eyes above him, feeling like a fool as his ex-wife ranted at him over the line. "Listen, Stella, I'm really sorry, okay." He couldn't bear to talk to her. He didn't want her to know anything about any of this. "I'll be fine. I'll call you back in an hour or two, okay?" He hated the lie, felt it strike at his heart.

"David?"

"I promise." He killed the connection before she heard the sob he couldn't hold down.

He met the eyes over him. Uriel reached down, helped him to stand. His knees could barely support him. "There's still love there," the angel said.

Michael let his breath out explosively.

David looked from Michael back to Uriel. "There is still love there," the angel repeated, "on both sides."

David barked a humourless laugh. "Love? It's a fucking nightmare. My marriage is a sham. I've damaged it beyond repair."

Uriel smiled. "Where there is any vestige of love, there is hope."

Michael turned away. He gestured to the people lying unconscious around the room and they faded away. The beds and couches, TVs and computer games, drifted into nothingness like mist in a gentle breeze. Uriel smiled again, squeezed David's shoulder. "We'll just go somewhere else," he said softly.

The four angels disengaged from the ground as the room grew visible through them. They lifted up and away and dissipated like smoke. Michael turned, he and David now facing each other in an empty warehouse. Michael shook his head. "You fucking humans." He faded away.

David felt broken and euphoric at the same time. He felt empty, astounded, insignificant. He felt spared even as the urine through his trousers cooled, sticking the material to his thigh. The gun lay on the floor at his feet, a barely identifiable ball of crushed metal. He picked it up, hefting it on one trembling hand. This would have to stay with him now, a trophy of sorts. A trophy to remind him of the anti-trophy he had smashed against his wall. And proof that all this had really happened. If he woke up tomorrow and this wasn't anywhere to be found, he'd know he was having messed up alcoholic's dreams. If it was there everything would be more than real. And he would owe Amir a favour, which meant his troubles were far from over.

He turned from the room, stumbling out through the office into the oppressive heat of the day. The alley seemed fresh. He was dishevelled and dirty, stinking of piss. Unshaven. He looked and felt like a homeless man.

Rolling the crumpled ball of steel around on his palm, wondering what the hell he would write for Terry, he tried to decide if he should have a drink or call Stella back first.

A STRONG
URGE TO FLY

JEREMY WATCHED TREES WHIP BY the train window, a grey-green blur, and wondered if they weren't a metaphor for his life. Zooming past too quickly to appreciate. He wanted to feel in charge of his own destiny and this journey marked the beginning of exactly that. His father had been gruff, but grudgingly respectful of his decision. His mother, of course, had been positively distraught, but she was the problem, after all. This time he'd stood up to her. *You shouldn't upset your mother*, his father had said emptily. But Jeremy had done it anyway and he regretted nothing. In the end, his mother had given in, even helped him find a guest house.

The train slowed. *Beston-on-Sea* said the sign, black paint on rust-riddled white. A tiny place, far from home. He only needed to endure it for six months, maybe a year, surviving in a rented flat on his own, then his point would be made, his autonomy demonstrated. He could start to live like an adult at last. He might even like it here and decide to stay. Regardless, he needed to emerge from under his mother's over-protective wing before he was thirty, and he didn't have much time.

He stepped onto the platform to be buffeted by a briny wind. As he pulled up his collar and dragged his suitcase behind him a voice called out, "Hey ho!"

Jeremy turned to see a round man, bald head and baggy grey suit, waddling towards him, gripping a battered briefcase. The man's trouser legs clapped in the breeze as he extended his free hand. "Donald Bosley. Don't get many strangers here in the winter months. Of course, come summer it's nothing but strangers!"

Jeremy shook Bosley's hand. It was clammy and damp. "I'm here for the start of term next week. I'm . . . "

"Ah!" Bosley exclaimed. "Pickering! Jeremy Pickering, replacement primary teacher for our little school. Damn shame about old Carson and his heart attack."

"You know . . . "

"Everyone knows everything about everyone here, Pickering. You'll soon get used to that."

"Right."

"First placement? You don't look old enough to be out of school yourself!"

Jeremy smiled. "I've done two years of casual stuff here and there since uni. This is my first full-time position."

"Got a place to stay sorted out yet?" Bosley asked.

"I've booked a room at Mrs Oates' guest house for a few days while I look for something more permanent to rent."

"Oh ho!" Bosley said with a wink. "Brace yourself for rules."

"Strict is she?"

Bosley's face hardened strangely for a moment, then shifted back to bland pleasantness. "Come on, I'll show you where it is. Not far from here."

They emerged through a gate and the gusty wind was stronger than ever, carrying with it odours of rotten seaweed and something else altogether more fishy and unpleasant. Gulls screeched in the late afternoon gloom, swooping between lamp posts and rooftops. Beston-on-Sea was a small town, end of the train line. Crossing the road, Jeremy saw all the way along the pebbly beach to where sloping green quickly became sandstone cliffs. Nestled at their foot, on the last vestige of shore, was a caravan and camp site, still and dead. A squall of rain pattered in as they moved away from the coast and headed along the high street. The other end of town was visible already, buildings giving way to paddocks and hedgerows and then undulating up to a horizon lost in grey clouds.

"I commute," Bosley said as they trudged along the pavement. "Always happy to get home. And speaking of home, here's yours.

See you in the pub some time, I'm sure." Without waiting for a reply he stomped off and ducked left to disappear between a closed fish and chip shop and a tiny chemist. Almost as if he didn't want to be seen by someone.

Jeremy looked at all the darkened eyes of shops and cafes. Not a soul roamed anywhere.

"Everything closes early Wednesdays."

Startled, he turned to find a woman framed in the doorway beside him. A hand-painted sign above read *Oates' Guesthouse*. He hadn't even heard the door open.

"Pickering, is it?" she asked.

"Er, yes. Call me Jeremy." He tried a grin, which she ignored.

"I'm Mrs Oates. This way, Mr Pickering."

She disappeared into a darkened hallway. She was thin as a broom handle, sharp-featured, skin wrinkled deep, but she moved lightly. Jeremy hurried after, his case bouncing on the thick pile carpet. A couple of metres into the gloom, Oates turned and hopped up a flight of stairs, lithe as a mountain goat. Jeremy hefted his luggage and huffed behind her. As he came to eye level with the landing above a pair of yellow eyes flashed between the balusters. He let out a little "Oh!" of surprise.

"Don't mind Skittles, he greets everyone," Mrs Oates said. She bent almost double to give the jet black cat a pat on the head, then leaned even further over to kiss him. Her flexibility would have been impressive in a teenager. "There's others. You'll get used to them."

"Are there?" Jeremy asked faintly. Cats. Why did there have to be cats? He looked back at Skittles as he followed Mrs Oates along the hallway and frowned. Was the thing gently shaking its head? Not only cats, but the damn things had nervous tics too.

"This is you." Oates pushed open a heavy wooden door, glistening with at least twenty coats of gloss paint making soft curves of all the old carved details.

The room beyond was larger than Jeremy had expected, paisley carpet and heavy green curtains. A double bed with intricately worked header and footer against the far wall. To one side a three panelled bay window looked out over the high street. Leaning in, Jeremy saw back to the station and the ocean beyond.

"Wonderful view, isn't it?"

He smiled. "It certainly is."

Movement caught his eye. Another cat, this one a tortoiseshell with one brown and one blue eye, had been sitting on the autumn-toned bedspread with that stillness he hated. It watched him for a couple of beats, then stretched languidly and hopped down to slink from the room. "That's Boss," Oates informed him proudly. "He might decide to like you, might not."

"Right." Jeremy's mother had three cats and his loathing of felines was thorough. Though he hated himself for it, when he thought himself unobserved he'd often kick them out of his way. Better kick them than his mother, which was often the temptation. And now, all these miles away, a house with fucking cats. Furry reminders of her and her constant complaints of how much more tenderness she got from the bloody animals than she ever got from him. Love and guilt, in equal measure, a maternal smothering blanket. He reminded himself he would only be here a little while. He took shallow breaths, wondering how much fur would be shed in his living space.

"It's an old house," Mrs Oates said, "so you've got a sink there, mugs, kettle and tea bags beside it for your convenience." She pointed to a bookshelf filled with children's books. "Feel free to enjoy those, but don't take them outside the house, please." Jeremy recognised *Treasure Island*, *Kidnapped!*, several *Biggles* and *Boys' Own Adventures*, all of which might well be worth a fortune at the right bookstore. But he wasn't a child any more. He could shift some aside for his textbooks if he needed the space. "Bathroom and toilet next door," Mrs Oates went on. "You've got it to yourself for now, but if the other room on this floor gets taken you'll be sharing. Not likely at this time of year, to be honest. Three more rooms downstairs, also currently vacant. You're welcome to use the lounge for your relaxing and television, but only BBC. I refuse to allow any of that commercial rubbish in this house."

"Okay." He was perplexed at being told what to watch but once again reminded himself it was temporary. All very temporary.

"I'm on the top floor and that's all mine," Oates went on. "You've no need to go up there and I value my privacy."

"Of course."

"Dinner is at six on the dot every day. Let me know in the morning if you won't be in for your evening meal. Breakfast is seven am, on the dot. Lunch is your own affair. Feel free to use the refrigerator in the kitchen downstairs marked Guests. You'll see each shelf has a number. Yours is four."

"All right."

"Any questions?"

"Any more cats?"

"Oh yes. They'll make themselves known when they want to. It's their home, after all. Besides them and myself, you'll probably have the run of the place until at least March, then I start to get busy."

"Oh, I don't think I'll be staying–"

"Good afternoon, then, Mr Pickering. I'll see you at six o'clock sharp."

Jeremy watched her go. Was she a little deaf or just gruff all the time? He heaved his case onto the bed to unpack. Opening the wardrobe, he jumped and stumbled back as yet another cat streaked out, black and white and wide-eyed. It paused in the doorway and turned, seemed to yearn forward like it wanted to attack him, then changed its mind and fled.

"Who are you?" Jeremy muttered, resisting the urge to swing a foot after it. Was three the limit or were there more? Belatedly, he went to close the bedroom door and saw Skittles right outside, staring at him. He sneered in a low voice, "Hey there, Skits."

The cat's mouth opened a fraction and a low hiss escaped. Jeremy's eyebrows rose and he nodded. "Okay then. We have an understanding."

He stared at the creature a moment longer, then purposefully shut the door. The yellow eyes never left his.

◆

MRS OATES SERVED up a plate of pork chop, boiled potatoes, and broccoli so overcooked it was almost entirely bleached of colour. At least the meat was good. "You're not eating?" he asked, uncomfortable as the old woman watched him.

"Already had mine."

"Right."

"You enjoy your food, eh?"

Jeremy grinned around a mouthful. "Oh yes, always been—"

"Don't speak with your mouth full!" Mrs Oates snapped.

Jeremy stopped, stunned. This woman spoke with his mother's voice. He resumed chewing and swallowed and chose not to say more. Once he'd choked down the last of the broccoli, the landlady nodded and placed a steaming bowl of apple and rhubarb crumble with custard. It was heavenly, the most delicious thing he'd had in years.

Mrs Oates smiled beatifically. "You like a good dessert." It wasn't a question.

Jeremy nodded, but refrained from saying that his mum liked to bribe his favour with good puddings too. He recalled yet again that his mother had found this guest house. He'd just taken it for granted when she had, let her do everything as usual. Now he had the discomforting thought of her and Mrs Oates discussing him, his habits, his failings and foibles. *Hates beans, spends far too long in the bathroom, stays up too late watching rubbish on the television.* Was he out of the frying pan and into the fire? He shook off the paranoia and ate until his spoon scraped the blue of the Willow pattern on the bottom of the bowl.

"Good boy," Mrs Oates said, taking it to the sink.

"Is there a Mr Oates?" Jeremy asked. Perhaps she might warm to him if he showed some genuine interest. Showed her he was nothing like his mother's complaints about him.

"No, dear, never has been. I've found men to always be unreliable creatures."

He wasn't sure how to respond, but knew it wasn't a good idea to ask why she called herself *Mrs*. "I'm sorry," he managed.

"What for? Off you go then. No television or noise after ten."

Jeremy nodded. Another rule that wasn't worth a confrontation. Bosley had been right about this place. A few days at most, he reminded himself, and he'd have found a flat all his own, no cats, no mother substitutes, all the bad TV he could bear. A few days, that was all. In the lounge he flicked on the set, but the BBC held no interest. He retreated to his room to look over lesson plans for the term ahead.

At the top of the stairs he paused. He'd closed his door when he'd gone down for dinner. He was certain. But now it was open and the tortoiseshell, Boss, lay on the bed again. He gave the creature a slightly heavier than necessary shove off the covers and the bastard managed to swipe at his hand as it leapt. There was a thin pink line along his index finger where the unholy animal had got him. He checked the wardrobe to make sure the black and white cat hadn't returned. As he closed the bedroom door, there was Skittles sitting in the hallway, staring.

♦

THE NEXT MORNING'S full English fry-up was ruined by a five cat audience. They perched about the kitchen, on the fridge, the counter, the windowsill. Skittles was there, and Boss. The black and white from the wardrobe was apparently named George, and there were two ginger toms called Ollie and Gimlet. They all watched him with a strange intensity. He couldn't help feeling that they wished him gone. He'd be only too happy to oblige.

"So this is all of them?" Jeremy asked, hoping he didn't sound either nervous or hopeful. The wound on his finger was swollen and stung. Did cats have poisoned claws? Was that real or something he was imagining?

"For now," Mrs Oates said. "You know cats. Like men, they come and go."

"Do they?"

She trained a hard eye on him for a moment, then returned her attention to the dishes.

♦

HIS NEW JOB began on Monday. He'd allowed a few days to get the feel of his new home, but realised he could easily explore the entire town and surrounds in just a few hours. At least the streets were a little busier with the shops open. He couldn't believe there were still places that closed up on Wednesday afternoons. It was archaically charming, but also annoying. He spent Thursday wandering around, nodding hello to people, enjoying the fresh sea air despite the persistent cold and drizzle. He did the circuit twice just in case he missed anything.

After a lunch of egg sandwich and a cup of tea in a small seafront café, he strolled up the hill on the eastern side of Beston-on-Sea to the school. The building was small, grey stone and slate roof, quaint and welcoming, though the doors were locked. He smiled. He thought he'd rather enjoy teaching there, making a difference to young lives. His life would have purpose. He had a meeting lined up with the headmaster on Saturday evening. Dinner and drinks at the man's house, *Let's not start off too formal, eh?* Jeremy decided he was looking forward to that. He must remember to let Mrs Oates know. He spotted a chemist and made a beeline for it. The stinging of his finger had deepened to an ache and the scratch had changed from pale pink to angry red. Surely it was nothing, but he'd get some disinfectant just in case.

Around five thirty in the afternoon the thought of a pint of good ale took root in his mind and he headed for the Rock and Thistle. In the dim warmth of the pub he spotted Bosley, his guide from the train station, halfway through a pint of his own.

"Hello again, Pickering! How do you like Beston?"

Jeremy laughed. "It's lovely, but it's very small."

"Used to somewhere bigger?"

"Much. I grew up in Reading. It's a metropolis compared to this place." He gestured to Bosley's nearly empty glass. "Another?"

When both of them had fresh drinks, Jeremy settled into a padded seat close by the fire.

"So, what do you do around here?"

Bosley barked a laugh. "Around here? Nothing. I take the train to town every day and juggle other people's money. Then back to the pub to forget about it."

Jeremy wondered which town, but it hardly seemed relevant. "This is a nice place to live though, isn't it?"

"Pickering, anywhere can seem nice until you're trapped there. Even heaven would be horrible if you couldn't leave, ever thought of that?"

Jeremy immediately pictured the semi-detached he'd grown up in, his mother's tears, his father's grim frown. Bosley certainly had a point. "Your family here?" he asked. There must be something the man enjoyed.

"Wife died six years ago. Breast cancer. Bloody miss her still, like it was yesterday."

"Oh, I'm terribly sorry."

"Got two kids though, and they visit quite often. Not often enough, of course. I'm hoping for grandchildren soon."

Jeremy smiled. "That's something to look forward to."

Bosley checked his watch and his eyes widened. "It's nearly six! You'd better hurry, doesn't Mrs Oates do dinner on the dot?"

Jeremy waved a hand. "No matter. I think I'll try the scampi and chips here. Another?"

"Not wise to upset Mrs Oates. Everyone is Beston knows that."

"I'm a big boy. Come on, have another."

Bosley frowned, then shrugged. "Why not? I suppose you know what you're doing."

◆

WHEN JEREMY LET himself back into the guest house a little after ten, wobbly and sniggering from the ales, he found himself face to face with all five cats, lined up in the hallway like a furry firing squad. For long moments no one moved, even Jeremy's drunken swaying momentarily ceased. Then the five creatures gently moved their heads from side to side in unison. Surely that was inebriated hallucination on Jeremy's part. The animals rose as one and slunk away. He watched them go, then gasped as he spotted Mrs Oates sat in the gloom of the kitchen, like a statue at the table. She glared at him over a plate of cold spaghetti bolognese. Jeremy gaped, his head swam slightly, then sobriety crashed over him. "You gave me a fright!" he said.

"You're to tell me in the morning if you're not going to be in for dinner," Mrs Oates said.

"Well, I didn't know this morning. I only decided to stay out this afternoon." Bloody hell, she made him feel like a child, scolding him like his mother would. The cats sat around her, glaring. Bastards.

"Not good enough," she said. "Look at this. I cannot abide waste."

"Well, I'm sorry, Mrs Oates, really I am. Cover it and I'll have it heated up tomorrow." Conciliation, he told himself. Tomorrow he was meeting with the realtor. Just be patient.

The landlady rose and drew herself up to her full height. She pointed at the chair she'd just vacated. "You will sit down and eat it cold! Right now!"

Jeremy stared, incredulous. The ales and scampi swirled unpleasantly in his gut. "I'll do no such thing! I'm not a child, Mrs Oates, and I'm certainly not your child!"

He strode from the room, stumbling on the stairs as he headed to his room. At his door, which was open yet again, he paused, sensing himself watched. If the old bat had followed him to continue the argument . . . He swung about.

Skittles sat on the landing, just at the top of the staircase, eyes bright and judgmental. The bastard seemed almost amused. Jeremy barely suppressed the urge to kick it back down the steps. He slammed the door behind him and collapsed on the bed, trembling, feeling twelve years old again, with all the rage and hatred that entailed. It took a few moments for him to realise that he could smell, ever so faintly, the whiff of cat pee.

♦

THE NEXT MORNING there was a gentle tapping at the door. He blinked against the early light that pierced through gaps between the curtains, thankful his pounding head wasn't quite as debilitating as he'd expected.

"Yes?" he said tentatively.

Mrs Oates came in carrying a tray, her face split in a grandmotherly smile that might not have looked so grotesque if they'd not had their set-to less than twelve hours ago. "I brought you some breakfast, as you weren't down at seven."

"Oh, right."

"Perhaps I was a little brusque last night, and I don't want you to feel unwelcome. We all make mistakes." She set the tray across his legs as he struggled to sit up. Coffee, fresh orange juice, bacon and eggs and fried bread that smelled like greasy nirvana. Exactly what he needed. And it covered the stink of cat pee, though he doubted Mrs Oates would notice.

"Thank you, that's very kind." He'd been unfair, he knew. She *had* asked him to let her know if he wouldn't be home for dinner and he *had*, he knew, rather deliberately rebelled against that.

He noticed Skittles, Boss, and either Ollie or Gimlet had wandered into the room and sat around the carpet in various stages of ablutions. The other ginger tom and George were in the hallway, peering intently through the door. As he ate his fry-up he became increasingly uncomfortable with the scrutiny of Oates and her minions. As he opened his mouth to say something, Mrs Oates clapped her hands and said, "Right, I'll leave you to it. Any laundry?"

"Laundry?"

"Yes, I'm doing the washing today, happy to throw yours in."

"Oh no, that's fine, thanks." It seemed a step too far to let the old lady see his smalls.

"Righto then." She smiled and left, leaving the door open six inches. The cats remained, watching. He once again had the distinct impression they wanted him gone and couldn't wait to indulge that desire.

◆

HE TOOK THE tray back to the kitchen after he'd showered and dressed. "I'll definitely be home for dinner tonight, Mrs Oates."

"Jolly good," she said, without turning from the sink.

"I'm off to find a flat today," he said, feeling strangely guilty. "I shan't be in your hair much longer. Ha ha." He didn't actually laugh, but spoke the words *ha ha*. It was the best he could manage.

"Don't be silly, dear," Mrs Oates said. "I'm no more expensive than a flat, and your utilities and meals are included. Not counting lunch, of course."

"Sure. But I'd like a place of my own."

The landlady glanced over her shoulder, eyes narrow and hard. "Don't be ridiculous. How would you cope?"

Jeremy bit back two or three replies. Deciding on silence instead, he moved to leave and saw Skittles glowering at him from the top of the refrigerator. Jeremy scowled back, then stalked off down the hallway. Outside it was gloomy and cold. Heavy rain fell, but it was a blessed relief from the confusing hot and cold vibes of the guesthouse. At least he knew where he stood with rain.

◆

SALLY GRACE WAS the only estate agent in Beston-on-Sea, and it turned out she couldn't show him around until the following morning. He was disappointed there weren't more options, but Sally assured him she would have the three available places ready for his inspection the next day. He would be able to move into any of them immediately, she'd said. He had every intention of picking whichever was the best of the three. *Anything* was better than Mrs Oates' House of Cats and Contradictions.

After a dispirited morning of wandering, he headed to the pub for lunch and was only slightly surprised to find Bosley already there. "Half day Fridays," the round man explained. "Benefits of long service. Join me?"

"Why not."

Jeremy enjoyed a ploughman's lunch and the accountant's

company, though Bosley sometimes tended to look on the dark side of things. They agreed to meet on Sunday for a round of golf, a game Jeremy had never played. Bosley insisted that was a lack to be rectified as soon as possible.

"Better get back in good time today," Bosley said. When Jeremy had shared the story of the previous night's confrontation, his companion had looked a little smug, but also pained. "Seriously, don't annoy the old lady. Get your flat and get gone, but meanwhile, do all you can to keep her happy."

"She's just a weird old woman."

Bosley shook his head. "Is she?" Without another word he hurried away.

Jeremy finished his drink and headed out. The rain hadn't let up, and he hunched against sheets of it as he jogged back to the guesthouse. He arrived at five thirty, bedraggled and cold, but happily drunk from several afternoon pints.

Mrs Oates met him in the hallway. "Goodness gracious, Mr Pickering, you'll catch your death! Get into a hot bath before dinner, you've plenty of time."

"Good idea!" he agreed, and hurried upstairs.

In his room, a large white bathrobe lay on the bed. The clothes he'd thrown over a chair the night before were gone. Jeremy frowned. He checked the drawers, then the wardrobe, anger starting a bonfire in his gut as he found them all empty.

He ran to the stairs and yelled down. "Mrs Oates! Where are my clothes?"

"In the wash, dear."

He gaped like a fish once or twice before he managed, "But I told you not to bother. Most of them weren't even worn, they were clean!"

"It's no bother, dear. And you've travelled. Always best to wash and air clothes that have been packed away."

Glued to the landing, Jeremy trembled with impotent rage. He'd taken a three hour train ride, not a camel-train across the Sahara. He clenched and relaxed his fists several times, at a loss, trying to control the rage that alcohol threatened to set loose.

"They'll be in the tumble dryer soon, dear. You can wear your bathrobe for dinner." She appeared in the hall downstairs, smiling up at him. "Just this once, mind! As there are no other guests."

She ducked out of sight before he could yell at her to not treat him like a bloody child, that she wasn't doing him any bloody favours. *Stop fucking interfering!* he wanted to scream. But it all died on his tongue.

He stewed in the hot bathwater, the steam and heat doing nothing to clear his booze-fuddled brain. He'd left home to escape this shit. His mother's constant coddling, swinging from smothering care to tight fury without warning, the shitty cats who could do no wrong, his shitty father hollowed out by his wife until there was nothing left of him but a distant, pointless shell. Jeremy would not let the same happen to him. Not at home and not here. Tomorrow and those flats could not come quick enough.

The sheer hide of that woman to take his clothes! His anger seethed and he ground his teeth, then jumped, splashing water over the side of the bath at the sight of Skittles on the edge of the sink, gazing down at him.

"How the fuck did you get in here?" he said in a growl. The bathroom door was shut. Had the foul creature been there all along? Was there no peace? Fury melted his thoughts, taking common sense and rationality with them. Jeremy surged up, a tide of bathwater washing over the edges of the tub, and grabbed the stunned black cat by its neck. It squawked and thrashed, but Jeremy gave it no chance, endured flying claws that gouged at his forearms and chest, and plunged it into the hot water. Teeth bared, breath in hard pants, Jeremy used both hands to hold the bastard under.

Finally it stopped writhing.

"Everything all right?" Mrs Oates called. Was she still downstairs or right outside the door?

Anger and inebriation pulsed away as shock ran through him. Jeremy stared at the inert creature floating between his pale feet, its fur gently shifting like seaweed in a current. "All fine!" he said, much too loud. "I just slipped. Everything's fine."

"Dinner in ten minutes."

"Right."

Jeremy gripped the bridge of his nose between forefinger and thumb. What the hell had he done? But a subtle elation rilled beneath the shock. Excitement pushed against the shame. He was, he felt certain, a victim no longer. He looked up at the window, a black square holding back the night. Rain still fell, battering the glass. He climbed carefully from the tub and opened the casement, wincing against the blast of cold air.

There was barely a slap as Skittles hit the grass of the back garden some twenty feet from the house.

Jeremy dried off and donned the robe, feeling regal. He'd vanquished one of his enemies, at least. He celebrated with a feast of stew and boiled potatoes followed by an outstanding apple pie and ice cream. The thought of Skittles dead in the rain and Mrs Oates none the wiser as she served his dinner made him happier than he'd been in years. Let her find the hateful animal in the morning and wonder what had happened.

He found it hard to suppress a smile. It was only a stupid cat, but he was finally standing up for himself. And not for the last time. He revelled in the idea that this was the beginning of his new life.

♦

JEREMY FOUND HIS clothes neatly folded at the foot of the stairs when he came down to breakfast. In the kitchen, Mrs Oates was at the stove. Before he could say anything, she said coldly, "Coffee?"

"Yes, thank you."

She set a steaming cup and a plate of toast in front of him. It was a little too brown, but he chose not to say anything. Today he would pick a flat. He might even sleep in it tonight, if he was lucky. He buttered the toast, not bothering to make conversation. Had she found Skittles yet? He burned to look out the window and see if the corpse still lay in the wet grass, but didn't dare.

"Porridge today," Mrs Oates said, and put a bowl in front of him.

"Thanks. Probably just as well, I don't think my heart could cope with one of your lovely fry-ups every day."

"Heart?" She narrowed her eyes. "I'll put your clothes in your room."

She was gone before he could reply.

He realised he was trembling, and was stunned by the swiftness of his change in mood. He shook his head. She couldn't connect him to the fate of Skittles. But what did he even care? He spooned mechanically, counting the minutes until his ten A.M. appointment with the estate agent.

The porridge was good, creamy and sweet. Better than the toast. He blinked, slow and heavy, his head feeling strangely woolly. He rubbed his eyes and, as he took his fingers away, his vision remained quite blurred. He opened his mouth to say something, anything simply for the sake of speaking, but his tongue felt like a dried out sponge. He managed a "Whu . . . ?" before everything began to go dark.

♦

IRON SPIKES POUNDED his brain when he woke, his mouth still dry, tongue still swollen. Light poured in through a window above him, making him wince. He was pressed down against something hard and cold. As his vision cleared a little he realised he was in the bath, empty of water. He tried to shield his eyes but his hand wouldn't move. Both arms, in fact, were stretched up behind his head. He craned his neck to see his wrists bound in blue nylon rope, tied to the taps above the white ceramic.

He began to panic, and would have screamed but his still-swollen tongue only allowed a muffled whine. He kicked his heels, tried to rise, but the rope holding his arms was short and tight, trapping him in the bath. His body felt heavy, cumbersome, and he was naked. He blinked gummy eyes, trying to see more clearly what seemed to stain his legs and stomach, some dark smear.

Along the vanity, either side of the sink, the four remaining cats sat. Boss, George, Ollie and Gimlet, all in a perfect line, staring at him. They seemed to have deliberately left empty the spot Skittles had occupied the night before. As Jeremy noticed that, the four of them looked pointedly at the space, then back at him. Was that *pity* in their eyes? Their expressions were strangely human in the snub-nosed catty faces. Sudden realisation washed over him. All their hatred, their disdain, wasn't vitriol, but warning. They had been trying to save him.

And he'd killed one of them.

The doorbell rang and Jeremy froze. He listened hard and just heard Mrs Oates say, "Why, hello, Miss Grace."

The estate agent! No doubt wondering why he'd missed their appointment. He couldn't make out what she said, then Mrs Oates spoke again. "No, no, the dear boy left last night."

Jeremy's eyes widened, unable to get a sound past his restricted tongue.

"Apparently changed his mind about the job and everything," the landlady said. "Got the last train back up north."

More muffled conversation then, "Oh, no, dear, sorry, he said nothing about a flat. He just decided to go back to his mother."

Jeremy kicked his heels hard against the tub to make a woeful racket.

Oates's voice drifted up the stairs. "Yes, those cats! Noisier creatures than you might think."

Grace's muffled tones once more, then Oates. "Yes, you know how these young men can be. No problem, you're welcome. Take care now."

Jeremy writhed, making noises that sounded more like choking than cries for help. The four cats sat motionless, didn't take their eyes off him. He stilled as he heard Mrs Oates start up the stairs. His eyes widened at the sight of the dark stain spreading further, thickening, across his naked body, black and soft. It was fur. He winced and moaned as his bones began to ache and creak, to shift and reshape. His mind compressed, thoughts becoming muddy as feline preoccupations rose. But the Jeremy mind remained, pushed back and down but not extinguished. The midnight pelt rippled along his limbs, his hands and feet closed down into rounded paws, his finger- and toenails stinging with sharp agony as they stretched into sharpened points. His face began to twist and contort, shrinking, his eyes moved up and out, his ears stretched upwards. His cheeks prickled as whiskers sprang forth. His remade hands slipped free of the now loose coils of rope as he shrank. The other cats hopped down to the edge of the tub, stalked left and right, mewling softly.

"Boys really should learn to appreciate the efforts a mother goes to," Mrs Oates said from the doorway.

REACHING
FOR RUINS

DOCTOR JOHN ROSENBAUM TRIED TO gauge the emotion in his patient's eyes as she stared into the corner of his office. "What are you thinking, Marie?"

"I'm thinking I don't much like your plant."

Rosenbaum turned to look at the climbing vine, rising from a large terracotta pot. It crawled up the wall on hundreds of tiny dark suckers, waxy green leaves like polished jade hanging heavy as teardrops. "You don't?" It was the first thing to ever survive more than a week in his office, but it was perhaps a little imposing.

Marie pulled her gaze away, laid a haunted expression on the psychiatrist. "It feels . . . wrong."

Rosenbaum smiled, his best put-them-at-ease face. "Would you like to sit over here? Put your back to it."

"I'd still know it was there."

Rosenbaum nodded. *Last session for the day*, he told himself, then he could go home. To an empty weatherboard house in the middle of nowhere. After nearly five months he'd hoped he'd be used to it. But that wasn't Marie's problem. "Okay," he said gently. "Well, let's get back on topic. When did you first feel what you describe as your grip slipping?"

◆

THE NEXT MORNING dawned hot after a close night, the temperatures steadily rising as spring rolled into summer. Dry and dusty, not like Sydney's humidity, but still hard to take. Rosenbaum wondered how searing it would get. Regular periods into the mid-forties were not uncommon he'd been told. Maybe it had been a mistake, running this far away.

He parked under the shade of a huge gum tree, flourishing despite the climate, and frowned as his stomach rumbled. He needed breakfast from the canteen, the cupboard at home surprisingly bare. Still not used to the bachelor life after thirty years being kept and looked after by Rebecca. His wife . . . His ex-wife would no doubt smile nastily at his hopelessness now. But she was far away in Sydney's northern beaches, no doubt entertaining who knew what stuck-up guests. Bitterness was a destructive emotion, Rosenbaum reminded himself, and tried to shake it off.

He stepped out of the car into the heat, and waved across the hospital grounds when he spotted the cantankerous old gardener. "Hey, Henry!"

The wiry man lifted his walnut-creased chin, squinting against the early brightness. "Need another corpse removed, do you?"

"No, quite the opposite. The new plant you gave me seems to be thriving."

Henry leaned on his shovel, brow furrowed. "You lot kill plants faster'n I can replace 'em. That Doctor Hancock left a note on my shed door this morning, and a shrivelled up stick in a pot."

Rosenbaum smiled. "That's why I thought I'd let you know this latest one is doing so well."

"Maybe we've found something a bit tougher this time."

"You should offer one to Jasper. Doctor Hancock. Do you have more?"

Henry nodded, shouldering his spade. "Yep. Got plenty."

Rosenbaum felt the conversation had been declared over. With another smile, he headed for the hospital, an old, dignified sandstone building with a random selection of added modern seventies extensions thanks to a brief era of unexpected funding. It stood in several acres of gardens, well-tended by Henry. Now the place needed more money than it would ever see again and its days were probably numbered.

When he reached his office, Rosenbaum paused in the doorway. The plant had grown overnight, noticeably taller, thicker. He wondered about Marie's concern; the thing did seem somehow . . . weighty. But anxiety made enemies of all things and Rosenbaum needed to distance himself from his patients' issues. And his own. Rebecca was a keen and capable gardener.

He slumped into his chair. Talking of issues, Jack Rickard today, a resident patient. What they would have called an "inmate" in the old days, avoiding jail by living in the secure wing. Rosenbaum reread notes from their last session, braced himself for Rickard's intensity.

A movement at the window caught his eye and he jumped. Henry the gardener peered in, cupped hands shading his eyes. He did nothing to acknowledge Rosenbaum, but stared hard at the plant in the corner. With a look of surprise, almost as if he'd been expecting the doctor to have lied, he turned away and trudged across the grass pushing a wheelbarrow.

◆

JACK RICKARD LEANED back in the chair, legs hanging wide at the knee, hands interlocked behind his head. "I like your new plant, doc."

"Do you?" Rosenbaum watched his patient's eyes closely. "Why?"

"Dunno. Looks healthy. Strong."

"Would you like a plant like that?"

Rickard barked a guttural laugh. "I'm not a fucking housewife."

"But you said you liked it."

Rickard's brow furrowed briefly. "Yeah, well, doesn't mean I want one." He looked away from the plant, his usual sneer returning. "I'm not very good at looking after things."

Rosenbaum nodded, lips pursed. "Hmm. Why don't you tell me why you always so quickly resort to violence?"

"This again?" Rickard's eyes slid back to the plant, his derision melting away to slack-jawed contemplation. Rosenbaum said nothing, observing. Silence hung in the room, present like a third person. Rickard's head tilted slowly to one side, his gaze roaming up and down the tall, dark green plant. His lips shivered, almost whispering something.

"Jack?"

Rickard jumped like he'd been stung. "Because bitches never fucking listen!"

◆

JASPER HANCOCK SAT down opposite Rosenbaum in the canteen, his tray loaded with sandwich, apple and juice box. "Hello, John."

Rosenbaum smiled, one cheek distended with his own sandwich. "Hi. How's things?"

Hancock shrugged. "Life in the madhouse, et cetera. You?"

"Session with Rickard this morning."

"Nuff said. Did you suggest to Henry that I might like some hideous jungle vine?"

Rosenbaum laughed. "Yeah. Hideous?"

"It's horrible! All dark leaves and black stems."

"I thought it was quite exotic. More to the point, it seems quite happy in my office, so anything to get Henry off my back. Hospital policy, got to have greenery."

Jasper's eyebrows rose. "Well, maybe you have a point. It's an ugly thing, but not so ugly as Henry."

◆

AS THE WEEK progressed the temperature continued to rise, but Rosenbaum found himself becoming acclimatised. He could grow to like the place after all, he decided, the dry heat easier than the coastal summer, and the isolation was comfortable.

Under the pleasant breeze of the air-conditioner, he waited patiently while Scott Fleming fumed. He knew the man needed space to vent his feelings, release the valve of anger.

"It's just so hard!' Fleming spat at last. "Why bother?" His Scottish accent seemed to add fury to his words.

"Of course it's hard," Rosenbaum said, keeping his voice in a low, soft register. "It's hard for everyone. But why do you think it's so hard for you?"

"Because it always goes wrong."

"What does?"

"Everything! From a new start in Australia years ago, it's consistently gone bad. My marriage failed, my jobs suck. Even moving all the way out here, I managed to lose a job no one else wanted. I've been retrenched seven times. Seven times! How is it not me? How is that normal? I'm cursed." Fleming's eye twitched as he ground his teeth. Sucking a breath in through his nose he tipped his head to rest on the chair back. His brow creased. "That's new, is it not?"

"What?" Rosenbaum followed the Scotsman's gaze to a tendril of plant creeping across the ceiling. Miniature sucking feet marched over the white tiles, tiny green leaves in a military row beneath. In less than a week the plant had grown rapidly, but this morning it had been a foot short of the ceiling. Now it was six inches across it.

"Yes, it's new," Rosenbaum said quietly. "Do you like it?"

"It's a bit . . . dark."

Rosenbaum nodded. If the "greenery in the offices" policy was supposed to help put the patients at ease, he wasn't seeing it. Except for Rickard, and that wasn't encouraging. "Let's get back to you, Scott."

◆

WHEN FLEMING LEFT the office Rosenbaum stood before the plant. The black trunk thrusting up from the terracotta pot was thicker, more gnarled than before. The vine-like branches spread left and right, climbing the wall like a fan, the whole thing pressed up and out into the room. If it kept going the way it was it would be across the ceiling and over the door within another week. Maybe it was too comfortable inside and not such a good idea after all. He went in search of Henry.

◆

THE OLD GARDENER's hand-rolled cigarette smoke hung fragrant in the musty confines of the shed. A part of Rosenbaum envied the simplicity of the man's life. Rebecca would be appalled by him.

"It's *too* healthy?" Henry asked.

"I'm afraid so." Rosenbaum was embarrassed to admit it. "I don't think it's an indoor species. It's growing too fast."

Henry puffed, blue smoke spiralling around his head, catching in the wispy hair of his ears. "So you want me to take it away again?"

"If you wouldn't mind."

"But everything else I give you bloody dies."

"Why don't plants like it in there?" Rosenbaum asked.

Henry settled back on his stool, affected the air of a teacher. "A lot of things can upset a plant. They react to all kinds of influences; light, water, chemicals, music, feelings."

"Feelings?" Rosenbaum interrupted.

"You can stop smirking. You've heard about people talking to their plants, ain't ya? A plant likes nice soothing voices and music. It responds well to happiness and laughter." He gestured with a tilt of the head. "Not much happiness in that place, eh?"

"Except this new plant seems to do really well."

"Yeah, I don't know why. It's obviously suited to something there. Or you forget to water it just right."

Rosenbaum couldn't help smiling. He figured that was probably the closest thing to a joke old Henry would ever make. "Where's it from?"

"Dunno. Probably a native. I should look it up, maybe. It popped up here in the grounds a while back."

"Popped up?"

Henry pointed with his cigarette, out through a smeared window to the edge of the gardens near the struggling river. "Runs all along that side by the water. Doesn't grow very fast down there, the climate's harsh this far inland. Cropped up one year after days of massive storms and a flood. The river burst its banks. First time I've ever seen that in all my life here. There was hail the size of golf balls, all gritty and dirty looking. Smashed a lot of windows, messed up a bunch of cars. The grounds got thoroughly washed out, stripped all the beds and that. Took me weeks to clean up. That's about when this new thing started growing. But that was a few years ago now. I've ignored it until I started running out of things for you lot in your rooms."

"Don't you think that's a bit strange?"

Henry frowned, shrugged. "You care what I think? Most of you lot don't talk to me much."

Rosenbaum felt a tinge of embarrassment. "Well, I think people are just busy."

Henry sniffed, standing up. "Well. Seeing as I like you, I'll get that plant out of your office later on and replace it with something else."

"Thanks, Henry. I promise I'll do my best to keep the next thing alive."

Rosenbaum left the old man there, staring contemplatively at his cigarette, and strolled through the heat towards his car. *Don't forget the supermarket*, he reminded himself as he went, trying to think what he might buy. Deciding on dinners was a new skill he was having trouble developing.

◆

ROSENBAUM OPENED HIS office awkwardly, briefcase in one hand, coffee in the other. As the door swung in, the coffee hit the rough, brown carpet tiles with a splash of liquid and steam, splattering the doctor's shoes and trousers. He stared in disbelief at the plant, covering the corner of the room in luxuriant growth. Tendrils of dark green droplets snaked across the ceiling, reaching almost to the light fitting in the centre. The plant had virtually doubled in size overnight.

Ignoring the mess on the floor he went in, felt the weight of the thing above him as he passed underneath to see the pot. Its trunk was as thick as his upper arm, twisted and powerful. The terracotta had cracked, overwhelmed by roots pressing up through the soil like fingers reaching from the grave.

The lower limbs were curled, writhing out across the walls. A grey smear caught his eye, the paint peeled off the wall where one branch had been levered away, the tiny suckers ripping out a chunk of the plasterboard. Marks scored the trunk, gashes that had healed and grown over, puckered like old scars. He didn't remember seeing them before. A few threads of cotton hung among the branches and a small, curved handsaw lay on the floor.

Rosenbaum had a strangely compelling urge to lean forward and embrace the thing. With a gasp, he hurried from the room, heading for the gardens.

◆

HENRY'S SHED STOOD empty. No aromatic scent of tobacco, no worksheets from the office on the desk. Rosenbaum stepped back outside, saw Jasper Hancock strolling across the grass towards him.

"He there?"

"No."

Hancock stopped. "If you see him will you ask him to take that plant away from my office? Bloody thing is growing like a weed, I don't like it."

Rosenbaum nodded, mouth too dry to actually respond. Hancock raised an eyebrow, then smiled and walked back inside.

Rosenbaum scanned the gardens. Henry always arrived long before anyone else, up with the dawn, still in his shed after dark. Rosenbaum remembered the first conversation they'd had, standing under that big gum tree in the car park. The doctor had made small talk, trying to be friendly. *Heading home, Henry? Your wife got a hot meal for you?*

Nah. Breast cancer took her a few months ago, but I'm surviving.

Rosenbaum had felt like a fool, such a stupid social faux pas. And he knew his comment stemmed from his own bitterness.

He headed for the administration building.

"Is Henry in today?" he asked the middle-aged woman at the desk. Edith or Edna or something. He could never remember.

She looked up, slid her glasses onto her neatly coiffed hair. "No idea, Doctor. He comes and goes like clockwork, so I imagine he's here."

"He doesn't check in or out?"

"No-one keeps an eye on him. Very reliable, he is. If he's not in his shed he'll be somewhere in the gardens, I expect."

"He drives that battered red Toyota to work, right?"

"Yes. Lives in town and he's driven that thing every day I've known him, and I've been here nearly twenty years."

"He's been here longer?"

"Oh, my word, yes. Much longer. And his car's nearly as old as he is, I'd wager." She smiled, clearly holding the gardener in some affection.

Rosenbaum thanked her and twenty minutes later he'd confirmed the aged Toyota was parked not far from his own car, but Henry was nowhere to be found on the hospital grounds.

♦

THE RIVER TWISTED along one side of the gardens, a glittering snake in the morning sun at the bottom of a deep, dry channel. It would take a phenomenal storm for that to rise high enough to break its banks, Rosenbaum thought. Trees and shrubs lined the near side, edging Henry's manicured lawns. Across the divide, the unforgiving landscape was all orange earth, low scrub and straggling bush in every direction, the town a twenty minute drive to the west. If you could call the small place a town, just a crossroads, two pubs, a few shops. Rosenbaum's new home was another ten minutes past the locality, tiny under the massive vault of sky. But his appreciation of the isolation was growing steadily. It's what he had sought after the divorce, after all. And he was doing good work out here, he reminded himself.

A twenty metre or more section of nearby bank was obscured by the dark green, twisting vine that had claimed Rosenbaum's office. He stared, awe and trepidation swirling in his chest. Further along the river bank more clumps gathered, locked in a frozen dance of growth. They weren't especially tall, but were dense and healthy-looking, their leaves a solid, glossy green, reflecting the hot day. And they stood out, because they all leaned the wrong way.

Other trees and bushes along the riverbank grew upwards, spread softly where Henry hadn't pruned them back. Rosenbaum scanned the sky, traced the line of the sun. His eyes fell back to the vines, all leaning away from the nourishing light. Towards the hospital building, stretching forward like leashed dogs craning their necks to suck in a powerful scent.

◆

JASPER HANCOCK WAVED him over from the entrance to the wards. Clinical white rooms with harsh blue-white lights, echoing somehow with the depression, schizophrenia, psychosis of the patients too damaged to care for themselves, too hurt to be trusted with others. The remote far west of the state was infamous for breaking people.

Rosenbaum waved back as he approached. "What's up?"

Hancock was pale. "You seen the day room?"

"Not recently. Why?"

"Come and look." Hancock turned and led the way along a linoleum corridor awash with antiseptic odours.

People in white gowns wandered the day room, or sat at plastic tables playing board games, doing jigsaw puzzles, scratching at their skin. In the corner a huge vine burst forth from a terracotta pot, the sides of the vessel cracked, leaking soil. The plant fanned across the walls, ten feet to either side, flooded up over the ceiling in a wave. Drops of jade green shimmered over the room. Some of the patients shied away, trying to be as far from the plant as possible.

Others stood beneath it, looking up like a prisoner finally released from solitary, feeling the sun on their face for the first time in years.

Rosenbaum gaped. "How long has that been there?"

"You never come in here?" Hancock asked.

"I do my rounds of the rooms but I never have cause to come in. I don't do groups these days."

Hancock nodded, still staring at the plant. "I do. I had a group in here four days ago. That wasn't there."

Rosenbaum stared, lost for words. It seemed to coax him forward, some strange allure.

"How is that possible, John?" Hancock's voice was strained. "What grows like that? And the one in my office is twice the size it was *yesterday*, stuck to the walls like it's glued there. And have you seen the message from admin?"

"No," Rosenbaum said. "What message?"

"Two patients are missing. Your pal Rickard and old Testa. Unaccounted for, presumed escaped."

"Rickard may have escaped," Rosenbaum mused quietly. "But Testa couldn't walk a hundred metres without needing a long rest!"

"I know. So they're missing, but maybe *not* escaped."

"Missing like Henry," Rosenbaum muttered.

"And two orderlies haven't reported for work this morning, apparently." As Hancock swallowed, his throat made an audible click.

"Really?"

"Is it . . . Is it the plants?" Hancock asked weakly.

"We have to get rid of these things," Rosenbaum said. The vine had a presence, like a predator in the undergrowth, poised, waiting to pounce. "They're not right, they have to be removed." The words tugged against his pragmatic professionalism, but were dense with an innate truth.

"I was going to throw mine out," Hancock said. "But I can't move it. When I tried to pull it away from the wall I felt like it . . . "

Rosenbaum looked away from the plant for the first time as Hancock's voice petered out, saw the man's pinched expression. "Like it what?"

"Like it pulled back."

♦

ROSENBAUM AND HANCOCK stood in the inky shadow of the old gum, hidden in the night.

"Are we sure about this?" Hancock asked.

"I don't see any other option. We're trained to recognise delusion and paranoia, aren't we?" Rosenbaum's eyes were wide in the dark, the whites bright. "We'd recognise it in each other if not in ourselves, yes?"

"There's no other way?"

"There's no time! Think about the rate of growth. And Rickard, Testa, Henry." He had told Hancock more about the gardener, the cotton shreds and the saw. They both agreed on his fate, though their conclusion was unspoken as it threatened their rational minds.

"Is this madness?" Hancock asked quietly.

Rosenbaum shook his head. "I think it's survival."

Hancock was silent for several moments. Eventually he nodded once. "Okay. But we have to time it right, like we agreed. Get everyone out."

"Yes. My office, your office, Sally's office, the day room, the front reception and the courtyard? That's all the places they are?"

"Yep. You take the three offices, I'll do the others, then hit the alarm. Once everyone's out, we finish the job before anyone can stop us. We'll have to try to explain later."

"Good god." Rosenbaum stared into the darkness, towards the river. "Okay. We can help everyone out, and between us we'll send people in the right direction."

"Right." Hancock's voice suddenly held conviction. A decision made, a corner turned. He strode off into the dark, a large jerry can bouncing against his thigh.

Rosenbaum drew a deep breath, headed for the offices, trying not to think of anything but the plan. It was the only way. No one would believe them, not in the little time they had before those things took over.

He walked through dim, empty corridors, the weight of the can in his hand like a tonne of conscience. He pushed open his own office first, gritted his teeth as he tried to ignore the thin curtain of green leaves overhanging the door, covering the ceiling entirely. He strode in, pushed open the window and doused the plant and pot with petrol.

A wave of desolation swept over him, so total, so complete, he whimpered as if in pain. He just wanted to lay down. He wanted to crawl up against the base of the plant and let it wrap him up in its blackened arms and take him away. With a cry he staggered from the room, gasping for air like a man near drowning.

He braced himself, kicked open Sally Kendall's door and walked straight to the window. Her plant was less than half the size of his but its presence no less powerful. He doused the thing, repeating over and over in his head, *My mind is my own. My mind is my own.*

In a cold sweat, trembling with the sour adrenaline of fear, he took long strides to Jasper Hancock's room and repeated the actions. He cried out aloud, "My mind is my own!"

The urge to lay among the twisting black tendrils with their shining dark gems was almost overwhelming. He remembered his patients, Marie's disturbed horror, Rickard's lascivious joy. He was right. They were right. They were doing the right thing.

He ran from the offices, sucking in the night air like a beached fish. He fumbled his cell phone from his pocket and stabbed the button for Jasper. The phone rang and rang and went to voice mail.

Rosenbaum shook his head, muttering, "No, no, no." He waited, listening for the fire alarm, but it didn't come. He dialled again. Nothing.

It took only moments to get to the front office. He ducked behind bushes as a paired security patrol strolled past, chatting quietly amid the twisting smoke of their cigarettes. When they'd passed he hurried to the open window and saw the plant in there, still quite small by comparison to the others. It was dripping, already doused. Hancock had been there.

A jog took him around to the courtyard, a high fence with spikes leaning in at the top like shark's teeth, where patients could get some fresh air and sun without much risk of escape. The vine there was bigger, twisting around the trunk of a small maple beside it. It too ran wet with purpled, glittering droplets. Just the day room left.

Rosenbaum snuck past the security office, sweat soaking his clothes. He ducked below ward windows, used his pass to slip in through a side door, and hurried to the day room. His knees buckled, vomit rising in his throat, at the sight of Hancock suspended in the vines, halfway up the wall, shifting like a flag in a soft breeze. The man was thinned, reduced, the skin on his hands and neck pulled taut and sunken, like he was being emptied, sucked away. He moaned gently, in pain or ecstasy it was impossible to tell.

Rosenbaum's mind swam, the urge to climb up and wrap himself in with Hancock drew him forward a couple of steps. A thought drifted like mist across his consciousness. *Join him? Not save him?* He knew the truth already. Hancock was past saving.

Rosenbaum uncapped his petrol can and threw it at the base of the plant, fuel glittering in the half-light as it turned over and hit the floor, scattering its contents before sliding to a stop. Petrol pulsed out to make a pool before everything was still again. The plant shivered and flexed. The vines creaked as they pushed forward, tiny green leaves reaching. Reaching for him. And he wanted so much to go to it, to accept its embrace.

He cried out and drew a match from his pocket, struck it with shaking hands and threw it into the room. Heat in a concussive blast pushed him backwards. His eyebrows singed, the smell of burning hair stung his nostrils. He had to do it all now, the timing ruined. But the alarms were going, triggered by the sudden fire, claxons shattering the night. Screams and shouts erupted all around.

He retraced his steps and threw matches into the courtyard and the front office, yelling at the top of his voice, "Out! Everybody out!"

Running to the consultation rooms, he heard yelling behind him, security guards hollering at him to stop, panicked cries from inside, all overlaid with the insistent clangour of the alarms. He ran past each window in turn, his own, Sally's, Jasper's. Poor Jasper! Fire burst in a cloud from each office as he flicked matches in and the entire hospital was soaked in noise and smoke and flames.

♦

ROSENBAUM SAT IN the back seat of a police cruiser and watched the fire department douse the blackened ruins of the hospital. Parts of the old sandstone building still stood, though most of the roofs had caved in. Doctors and police tried to control the milling crowd of patients, some enthralled, some shocked. Others were no problem, curled on the grass or rocking beneath trees, stark silhouettes in the floodlights of the fire-fighters.

Horror, confusion, despair swamped the grounds. Not everybody had made it out, headcounts were proving difficult.

Not a chance.

Those had been the fire chief's words when asked about the possibility of survival of anyone still inside. The last conversation Rosenbaum had heard before the car door was closed on him, muffling the chaos he'd caused.

The chief administrator, hair tousled from sleep, approached the car with a police officer, opened the door. His face was white as the moon and just as distant. "Why, John?" he asked, in a voice thin with incomprehension.

Rosenbaum hung his head, tears running down his cheeks, spotting his smoke-stained trousers.

The officer took the administrator's arm and turned him away. The man was muttering something about an acrimonious divorce to the policeman as the car door closed, cutting the conversation off. The sounds of crying and howling were muted once more.

Along the riverbank, massed clumps of twisting black vines stretched forward in the night, reaching for the smoking ruins.

SHADOWS OF
THE LONELY
DEAD

HIS EYES ARE TIGHT WITH pain as he turns away from me, buries his frustration in the pillow.

"Something I said?" I ask nervously. "Or did?"

He shakes his head, rustling against the duvet pulled up tight under his chin. "I'm sorry. It's not you . . . I can't . . . This has happened before, I . . . I don't know why."

"It's okay. We don't have to. No pressure, you know."

He sniffs, turns it into a humourless laugh. "Sorry. I'm damaged goods."

I put a hand on his shoulder, remove it quickly as he stiffens. "Oh, Jake, don't say that, it's okay. It happens to loads of guys, but no one ever admits it. Stay here, just sleep, you know."

He nods. "Maybe in the morning?"

"Sure."

◆

I DON'T PUSH for anything in the morning. Something difficult is happening and I like him too much to scare him off. I make coffee and bring it to the bedroom. He's beautiful, a wave of dark hair half obscuring his face, cheeks dusted with two day's growth. He smiles softly as I creep up to the bed.

"I'm awake."

"Hi there."

We stare at each other for a moment, still getting used to how the other looks, everything so new.

"Sorry about last night," he says. "First time I stay and I can't . . . "

I hold up one hand, pass the coffee with the other. "Doesn't matter. We've got plenty of time, right?"

His smile comes back. There's an edge of melancholy that seems to live behind his eyes, but that smile pushes it away like a breeze behind clouds. "I guess so. Thanks."

"Take your time getting up, have a shower and stuff if you want. I need to get ready for work. I start at ten."

◆

THE HOSPICE IS quiet as I enter. Mary offers me a subtle nod from the reception desk and I push through double doors into the smell of carpets, disinfectant and death. Claire Moyer catches my attention, coming the other way.

"Mr Peters last night," she says. "About three."

I nod. "Thought so. His family there?"

"No. No one."

I shrug and walk on, drop my coat and bag in the nurse's station. Poor old Mr Peters, his daughters stopped visiting about two weeks ago, when he started to spend more time asleep than awake. It doesn't really matter. We all die alone.

Even people surrounded by loved ones are utterly alone as they slip away, the sea of grief around them unnoticed. Death is the only truly personal thing there is. No one can ever understand it, even someone like me. I've seen death take people hundreds of times, held their skeletal hands as the darkness closes in and their breaths stretch further and further apart until they don't breathe again. But I have no idea what it's like.

I check the roster, see who needs medication, bathing, feeding, simple company. I knew Peters was leaving last night. I hope he didn't realise his daughters had stopped coming, but it's surprising what gets through the haze of terminal illness. Even as their minds go and they forget the faces of people they've known their whole lives, moments of clarity spike through the deterioration like lighthouses sweeping the night and they ask, "Where's my wife?" "Where's my son?" And they know they're alone whether those people are there or not and the last of their resolve crumbles as they slide into that stygian unknown.

Edie Sutton is on my list. She needs a wash, and a feed if she's up for it. Doubtful she'll eat, she hasn't managed more than a couple of teaspoons of jelly a day for almost a week now.

I'm surprised to see her awake as I enter, eyes wet and frightened in the glare of spring through thin cotton drapes. I take a sponge lollipop, dip it in the glass of water beside her bed and gently press moisture to her cracked lips. Her chin quivers as the liquid rolls over her desiccated tongue. "That taste good?" I ask quietly.

Her eyebrows rise, the almost translucent skin stretched tight across her skull wrinkling like tissue paper. "Tired." Her voice is barely audible, but you get used to listening for their words, every syllable a struggle.

"Had enough, huh?"

Tears breach her red, sagging eyelids and she nods ever so slightly.

"You can go whenever you like, love," I whisper.

A moment of softening around her eyes. "Can I?"

"Of course you can. You've seen everyone you were waiting to see."

"My Damon?"

"He'll be here at lunchtime." Her son. Visits regularly as he works nearby, sits with her every evening for hours. "Another couple of hours."

She closes her eyes and her exhalation is slow and weak, like heat escaping a long summer day. She'll be gone soon, I'll have to keep a close check. I lift her hand, a collection of brittle sticks loosely attached to an arm like old bamboo wrapped in papyrus, check her radial pulse. Barely there and so slow. I let my mind pass through my touch, search out the decay and failing organs, take the shadows of her dying softly into myself. I can't cure her, but I can collect the scourge, its malice.

A dark stain spreads into me and I store it away.

◆

THE DAY GOES slowly and quietly. It's usually quiet here, except those moments when someone cries out, sudden terror giving voice to weakened lungs as they momentarily face their mortality without the softening armour of fatigue or drugs. Or the howls of grief, sometimes from friends and family, sometimes from the sick themselves. Sometimes both.

I clean up Kathy Parsons, who's been uncontrollably shitting viscous blood onto plastic sheets for more than a week now, check her meds. She exudes the sickly sweet, cloying odour of death. She's terrified. Only forty eight years old, eyes always wide in child-like fear, but she's got a little while to go yet. A little while to reach some kind of acceptance, though not all of them do. Some are gasping in disbelieving horror, even with their last breath. Almost everyone dies scared, especially the young ones. Some people are calm and accepting, content as they drift away, but they're rare, usually very old. Everyone has time to think as they lie here, suspended in the last darkening hours of their life. It's good that some find peace in that mortal dusk.

I reassure Kathy as much as possible, sit with her as a sedative soaks through her struggling veins.

Edie's pulse is almost gone when I check her again an hour later, breaths so far apart every one seems certain to be her last. I call her son to tell him he needs to get here, but his phone goes to voicemail. I leave a message imploring him to hurry if he can.

I pull the chair up beside her bed and take her fingers in my palms, rest my forehead against the back of her hand. Her frailty wafts into me and I soak it up, gather that insipid, creeping death into my cells. It can't hurt me. I don't know why, but it can't. So I collect it. I don't know why I do that either. Because I can. It doesn't heal them or ease their suffering, but at some level I like to think they know I share their pain and that offers some subconscious solace.

Edie's pulse weakens until I can't feel it any more. Her breaths are tiny, sharp intakes, almost imperceptible, more than ten seconds apart. Her exhalations are silent, air leaking from lungs little more than deflated sacks of inert offal.

Fifteen seconds apart. She's going.

Her life leaks into the air and the shadow of her sickness, her fear and loneliness, washes through me and she's gone. I shudder with the gift she's given me. My hands tremble as I stand and move away to mark her chart, dimness swimming behind my eyes.

Her son is hurrying along the hallway to her room as I emerge and his face falls when he sees me.

"I missed her?"

"I'm sorry. Only just. She passed moments ago. But she didn't wake again since this morning."

He barks an uncontrollable sob and tears tumble over his cheeks. We're all five years old when our mothers die. "I can see her?"

"Of course."

I'll send the counsellor down with the relevant pamphlets after he's had some time alone with her.

◆

NOT MUCH ELSE happens through the day, which pleases me. It's terrible when more than one patient dies in a day, as the first one feels somehow cheated of their time in my mind.

Jake is parked outside when I get home, an embarrassed smile twitching his lips. "Hi."

I'm so pleased he's there. "Hi." I had wondered if I might not see him again. Our few faltering dates that led to our first night together had been cautious but full of hope. When something got in his way last night, I worried it would frighten him off.

"Try again?" he says, holding up a bottle of red.

"I'd really like that. I have some steaks in the fridge and wait til you try my potato rosti."

◆

WE GENTLY FUMBLE at each other's clothes, clumsy with nerves and the dull edge of the wine. Edie's death still floats around me, within me, but that helps. I embrace it. Nothing makes me hornier than death. Something about mortality reminds us at a level beyond thought of the importance of contact, of touch, of the life within lovemaking.

I'm not too proud to admit I usually masturbate a lot in the privacy of my home after we lose someone. It's unavoidable, the desperation to feel alive—to feel *life*—especially when I've absorbed the death into my marrow like I do. I hope Jake can see it through this time.

I'm as gentle as I can be, as caring as I know how. He shivers and stiffens with nerves as I run my hands across his shoulders. He looks into my eyes, a nervous smile. "It's okay, I'm sorry. I want to." He reaches back and unclips my bra, lets it drop beside the bed.

"You are so lovely," he whispers.

There's tension, fear, but he keeps assuring me I should continue and so I do and he eventually performs. It's soft and urgent, but electric. Afterwards he grabs hold of me and hugs me against his chest so hard I have to gently force a breath into my constricted lungs.

"That was wonderful," he whispers, his hot breath tickling my ear.

"It was," I say. "I'm glad."

He holds me tight and his breathing changes. He turns his face away. I push away to look at him and tears stand in his eyes.

"I'm sorry," he whispers.

"Are you okay?"

"Yes, really. It's hard to . . . this is difficult for me. But please, don't feel bad. I just can't help it."

"Anything I can do?"

He smiles, leans down to kiss me. "Just keep being so nice to me."

"That's easy."

I settle beside him and turn to let him spoon me, push myself back into the curve of his body. He's so warm and strong and vibrant—the opposite of poor Edie's hard, cool, frailty, all jutting bones and oxygen tubes.

"Was someone less than nice to you?" I ask, biting my lip the moment it's out. Probably not the thing to say.

"Something like that."

I stroke his hand, not game to risk saying anything else, ask for any more of his secrets.

"I'll tell you one day," he says, voice thin with pain.

He holds me tight until we fall asleep. It's good to have someone so alive to hold on to, a beacon against the shadow of all the death in me.

◆

THE DAYS AT work pass slowly and my hours rotate to nights. I prefer the solitude and peace of the night shift, and most deaths happen then. It's strange how people who have been unconscious for days or weeks almost always seem to slip away in the depths of the night, like they know somehow that leaving while the sun shines is unusual. I remember Edie dying in the middle of the morning; her shadow still drifts through me, the echo of her disease. It's all that's left behind, her life and body far away now.

We haven't lost anyone for nearly a week. The orderlies are taking bets on how much longer it'll be. Sam's aiming high, reckoning another few days. Marek is less confident, thinking Mr Patel will die tomorrow. They're both wrong. Jack Oswald will die tonight, maybe in the next two hours, three at the most. I can *feel* it. I've always been drawn to death, always offended by the hopeless indignity of it. And I've always sought to care for the dying, take into myself something of their pain, a memory of their suffering. I was destined for this career.

I pad into Oswald's room, put a hand against his cheek. It's very cool, his eyes flickering gently behind thin, pale lids. I was wrong, it's happening already. No one to ring for old Jack, he has no one to come. "Last of a line and good riddance," he said to me when he arrived three weeks ago.

"You can't be all bad," I'd said, and he laughed.

"Not bad, really. Just not much good either. Never had kids, wife died twelve year ago. Worked fifty years for fuck all and here I am being tucked away in a corner to die alone."

"We all die alone, Jack," I said, an attempt to soften his hurt.

"Yeah, but there's alone and alone, ent there."

Darkness swells up in him. He hasn't woken in five days. He had a drip in his arm feeding him a bare minimum of hydration, anti-nausea medication and painkillers—a poor simulation of normal life while he dies—but we took that out a few days ago. He's a skeleton under linen stamped with the name of the hospice.

He'd asked me the week before to speed it up for him. "Can't you jab me wiv somefing, make it happen? What's the fucking point in hanging on?"

I'd told him I wished I could, and I meant it.

We wouldn't let our dogs and cats suffer like this but we'll happily put our own parents away to wither and waste into ignominy and despair. They deteriorate to frightened babes again as everything they've ever been deserts them, and we think it's the humane, moral thing to do, to let that happen. To watch it happen while we tell them everything will be okay. Which is the worst line of bullshit we ever try to sell in a world powered by lies and deception.

Jack's eyes pop open, a flood of panic blanching his already ivory face. After a moment he focuses on me and nods, a tiny movement of understanding and he's gone. His darkness swells into me, the entropy of his illness drawn up through my hands where I hold his. It adds itself to the blackness I carry inside, that I've carried for so long. Will I fill up one day, no room for any more, and then what?

With trembling fingers I close Jack's eyes and fill out the paperwork. Marek will win the bet. His guess was closer even though they were both wrong.

♦

"I WANT TO tell you why sex is so difficult for me." Jake's face is creased with what looks to me like grief.

"You don't have to."

"I know, but I want to. We've been together a couple of months now and it feels serious. It is, isn't it?"

I nod vigorously. "Oh, I hope so." I really do hope so.

Jake draws a deep breath that shudders on the way down. "I never knew my real dad. He left when I was too little to remember."

I open my mouth to say something, I'm not really sure what, and Jake holds up a hand.

"Let me get this out in one, or I may not make it."

I nod and he smiles, squeezes my hand across the table.

"I don't mind not knowing him. My mum was young and irresponsible. She's always been fucking useless, so I can hardly blame my dad for leaving. It's what I did, first chance I got. She should have protected me, but she couldn't even protect herself." He draws another breath, sips wine. "My mum shacked up with Vic when I was about six years old. She'd knocked around with guys before then but never for long. She did her best by me, even though her best was bloody rubbish. But when Vic came along, everything changed.

"He drank heaps, was always on the edge of violence. Mum told me how much she loved him, but it was clear she was terrified of him too. She said how we needed him to pay the bills and he wasn't such a bad guy. Even with two black eyes and a split lip she'd tell me how he wasn't such a bad guy."

Rage flares in me and Jake can see it in my face.

"Let me finish." He reaches out, strokes my cheek. "You're such a good and decent person, the way you care for the dying, you're so good to me. You couldn't be less like Vic *fucking* Creswell." He drinks more wine, his hand shaking. "Anyway, it wasn't long before Vic started . . . touching me."

I let out a soft sound, part growl, part moan of dismay.

A tear breaches Jake's lashes. "I'm sorry, I need you to know this."

My knuckles creak as my fists clench in my lap. "I want to hear. You shouldn't carry this alone."

Jake nods, sips. "Anyway, he went from fondling and making me do things to him to raping me in very little time."

"You were six?"

"I was probably eight by the time he started that."

He says it like that makes it somehow better than if he were six. "What a fucking . . . "

"He ruled my mum and me, did what he liked to us. My mum should have protected me, but she was trapped too. He would beat her if she tried to intervene. Beat me if I threatened to tell. We lived in terror. When I was fourteen I told mum we had to go, we had to run away. She said we had no money, where would we go?"

"There are shelters," I start to say and Jake nods again.

"Of course, but that wasn't the point. You know what she said to me, after years of beatings and sexual assaults?"

I sigh and shake my head. "She told you she loved him."

"Yep. So I ran away. I have no idea what they're doing now. He could have killed her for all I know. I haven't spoken a word to her since I left. I was on the street at first, then in shelters and care. A foster home took me in when I was sixteen and I was a bastard, doing all the things my mum did and worse, acting like her boyfriends, thinking I was different."

"You're nothing like that," I say. "You're amazing."

He smiles, but it's not enough to chase away the melancholy this time. "My foster mother is a lady called Glenda Armstrong and she fixed me up. Wouldn't take my shit, made me finish school. I was lucky. She gave me direction, I got a job, turned myself around. Twenty five now, finally feeling like I've got it somewhere near together. And then I met you. For the first time I feel something real, instead of just angry fucking because I thought that's all I deserved." His tears have stopped and there's anger in his eyes.

"You should be so proud of where you've come, given where you started," I tell him.

"But I'm scared and you mean a lot to me and that's why it's so hard for me to be intimate, emotional. It's always been an act before, an act of defiance more than anything else, a show of power. But with you, I have no guard and it's terrifying."

I stand, move around to hug him and kiss his hair. "I'm honoured," I whisper. "I'll never hurt you."

"I know."

The shadows of all the people who have died with me mask my vision, make Jake a distant blur. "So many wonderful people die every day, struck down by disease or age," I say. "And yet fuckers like that Vic get to live."

Jake nods against my chest. "There's no justice in the world. We have to hang on to our luck when we find it, because that's all there is."

◆

AFTER NEARLY A week of no deaths we get two in a day. The darkness wells inside me, that delicious blackness I can't help but gather. Sometimes I think it's going to overwhelm me, but there's always room for more. The journey home is muffled by the circling presence of their passing.

Jake comes around not long after I get home, bag of shopping in hand. "I'm going to make us a great dinner tonight. Special recipe! Something Glenda taught me."

"Great! I'm glad we're having a good dinner. I have to go away for a couple of days."

"That's sudden." His brow is creased in concern and it breaks my heart a little.

"There's a two-day course Claire Moyer was supposed to go on, but she's come down with something. Someone needs to go, it's about a new drug administration practice, and they asked if I'd step in. I head off early in the morning to Newcastle. I'll be away overnight, back by dinnertime the next day. Sorry."

He smiles. "Don't apologise. Work is work. Let's enjoy tonight then, eh? Maybe you can lend me your key when you leave and I can get my own cut? Then I can have something ready for when you get back on Thursday?"

I raise my eyebrows, give him a crooked smile. "Your own key?"

"If you think . . . "

I sweep him into a hug. "Of course I think. I'd love that."

◆

IT TOOK A lot of searching to find this place, but hours of free time in a palliative care hospice can be put to good use with a search engine and access to hospital records. Hints from Jake about where he grew up and a keen eye. Plus friends in social services to join the dots. The idea, the realisation, hit me like lightning when Jake told me his story.

There's a broken down car on the front lawn, leaking oil across the dirt like black blood. The house is peeling, the paint reminds me of the skin of a dying woman's lips. I knock on the door, heart hammering against my ribs.

A large figure shimmers through the frosted glass panel and the door swings open. A man stands there in shorts and a stained shirt. He's a tall bastard, muscular, but a beer gut mars anything close to a good physique. He has muddled tattoos on his arms and legs, grey and black stubble across his face like a TV tuned to static. His eyes are dark and mean. "Well, hello, darlin'."

"Victor Cresswell?" I ask.

His eyes narrow. "What?" He glances to my hands, probably checking for a summons.

"*Vic* Cresswell," I ask.

"Yeah."

I hold out my hand. "It's nice to meet you."

His lip curls in a sneer and he takes my hand, squeezing too hard to assert his dominance as he puffs his chest out. "Nice to meet you too, sweetheart. What the fuck is this?"

And I let my darkness out. It rushes through my palm, desperate to escape, and races into him. I feel it gust up his arm, into his chest to nestle in his lungs. It wraps shadowy arms around his liver and coats his gallbladder in an inky embrace. It snakes through his intestines, finds his prostate and slips down into his balls.

A shudder ripples through him as I break our grip and smile, turn away.

"What the fuck was that all about?" he yells as I make my way back to the waiting taxi, a tremor in his voice.

As I tell the taxi to head back to the station he stands in the doorway, one hand rubbing absently at his throat. There's a patina of fear across his face. How much does he suspect? I give him a month at most before the decay begins to set in. Before the tumours start to blossom through his organs. Black, flowering death.

I'm empty inside, somehow hollow but with whiteness swelling into the places where I've collected all that dark over the years. Perhaps I shouldn't have let it all go, should make it last. It's disconcerting, I'm a little lost without the shadows of the lonely dead inside me. I'll have to start collecting again. No matter, at least three at work have less than a week left.

I knew I gathered it for a reason. A shame it took me this long to realise what my purpose is. I have a mission now, giving this unfair blackness to bastards truly deserving of it.

I'm going to be busy.

♦

JAKE IS WATCHING television and looks up in surprise as I enter the house. I'm glad he decided to stay at my place, not his. When the moment's right I'm going to ask him to move in.

"I thought you weren't back until tomorrow," he says, smiling. It's genuine happiness on his face and that warms me.

"We got through the training in one day and finished up in time for me to get the last train back. So here I am." I had taken into account that Vic might be harder to find, maybe not home. It had all been much easier than I anticipated.

"Well, that's a lovely surprise," Jake says, gathering me into a hug.

I breathe deeply of the clean smell of his skin. "Yeah," I say. "Maybe there is some justice in this world, after all."

PUNISHMENT
OF THE SUN

ANNIE SAT AT HER WINDOW, staring across the darkness. No moon and high, thin clouds made the world beyond stygian and dead. Like her life.

She knew the tack shed sat not far away. Beyond that stretched dry, dusty paddocks with dry, dusty horses, ribs like xylophone keys through thin, scabby hides. The orange desolation dragged on as far as hope would last in every direction. Too young to leave this desiccated hole, she grudgingly endured.

A strike of light in the distance and Annie's heart skipped a beat. Her slumped pose in the window became rigid attention as she stared through the dark. Impossible to tell how far away it had been, she grew desperate to see it again.

Then another. Annie gasped, throat thickening with fear. A man, hands cupped around a lighter, his face briefly lit in orange glow and contrasting shadow. She could see two pinpricks of ruddy brightness, glowing and fading, well beyond the yard.

She forced her sight to penetrate the dark. Every time a man drew a lungful of smoke, the cigarette acted like a weak torch, easing back the night. She saw other movement, more than two of them. They carried something, wrapped and heavy, moving easily, unencumbered by the darkness or weight. Across the distance she heard a metallic rattle. They were at the feed shed across the south paddock. She couldn't see it, but every inch of this station lay burned across her mind like a scar. They were putting something in the feed shed.

◆

ANNIE ROSE SOON after the sun. As hot, early light crept across her bed she dragged on shorts and t-shirt and trotted through the house.

Her parents sat at the kitchen table, poring over paperwork. They drank acrid coffee while toast burned under the grill and her father moaned about taxes and levies. Annie headed for the door.

"Where are you going?" her father asked.

"Going to see Pebble!"

"Get back here!"

Annie stopped, set her jaw. She turned back, huffing a deep sigh. She stood in the doorway, framed by sunlight.

"Well?" her father said.

"What?"

"You know very well what! No play till your chores are done."

"I'll do them later."

Her father scowled. "You'll do as you're told!"

Annie gritted her teeth, desperate to investigate the shed. "What difference does it make?"

Her father scraped his chair back, half rising. "The difference is I told you to do them now!"

Annie looked to her mother, eyes pleading. Her mother just shook her head. "Neither of you care about me!" Annie yelled. "You only had children to do all your work for you! I hate you!"

Her father growled, stepping around the table. Annie bolted before he could say or do more, heading into the utility room and the tools for her chores.

◆

AN HOUR LATER she finally got time to herself. Everything seemed to be about cleaning and fixing and tidying. A few more years and she'd be gone.

She skirted the tack shed and climbed the gate of the south paddock. Sunbaked red earth puffed fine ochre dust with every slapping footstep as she ran. She approached the feed shed and slowed. Her heart danced in her throat and a chill leaked down her back. So fascinated by what she'd seen, her only thought had been to find out what those men were up to. Now came a second wave of thought, heavily tainted with trepidation.

She glanced back towards the house, squat and peeling in the already ferocious sun. Perhaps she should tell her dad what she'd seen. But what did he care? Always telling her what to do.

Swallowing her nerves, taking a steeling breath, she opened the shed door. Sunlight flooded into the musty darkness within, dust swirling in the shaft of day. She walked carefully into the gloom, looking all around the huge space. Plastic buckets and battered shovels lined the walls, bales and giant plastic feed bags made haphazard mountains all around. Everything sat as dull as her life. Except for a heavy looking canvas, dumped into a corner.

Annie reached one hand towards it, taking a corner, lifted it back. It lay empty, deflated against the shed wall. She saw a piece of thick, yellowing paper on the floor. It bore a note, hand written in dark red ink.

You slew an elder and your punishment is sun.
Survive this trial and your punishment is served.
Fail to survive and your punishment is served.

That didn't make sense. What kind of punishment was sun? Who was the note for? She sighed, looking around the musty shed. Her eyes narrowed. Did she hear a scrape then, a sound of movement? Sharp lines of incandescence marked gaps in the planks of the walls, painting bright stripes across the floor. She walked among them, looking into the shadows between the feed bags and hay bales. It would take hours to search every nook and cranny.

The distant sound of her dad cursing drifted through the air. She sighed again, and headed back to the house

◆

ANNIE'S DAD WAS furious. Her mum stood in the doorway, hands clasped. "What do you mean, all of them?" she asked.

"I mean all of them! Every fucking car, bike, quad. Even the tractor and the back-hoe. Some fucker's been in and ripped up the engine in every vehicle we own."

"Why?"

Her father spun on his heel, leaning across the yard in his anger. "How do I know why?"

Her brothers stumbled from the house, rubbing sleep from their eyes. Useless, dopey teenagers the pair of them. "Wha's goin' on?" Trent asked.

"Some of your friends having a lark?" Annie's dad yelled. "Someone's been in during the night and ruined every vehicle we've got."

"Why would it be our friends?" Josh, the eldest, seemed genuinely offended. "Maybe it's yours, pissed off that you never cough up for a round on the rare occasion you go to the pub!"

Their dad pulled back one hand, striding across the dusty yard. "Why you little . . . "

"Enough!" Annie's mum's voice cracked across the hot day, freezing everyone in their tracks, always the ultimate authority. "What's wrong with you? Josh, you need to learn some respect. Bill, calm down and call Jerry at the police station. See what he has to say."

Bill pushed past his sons. "As if he'll be any bloody help."

♦

ANNIE SAT AT the kitchen table while her father fumed and her mother cried. Her brothers, quietened, looked on. The ruined remains of two satellite phones sat between them.

"Do any of you know why someone might have done this to us?" her father said. They all shook their heads. "Every vehicle ruined, the phone lines cut and the radio antenna is gone." He pointed at the smashed sat-phones. "To do this they came *in* the house."

Annie thought of the distant cigarette glows in the dark. She'd seen the men there, but hadn't heard anything else. Would they have done this? She fingered the strange note in her pocket, wondering if she should tell her father. But if she could figure this out on her own perhaps they'd all stop treating her like a kid. She bit her lower lip nervously.

"Is this some kind of warning, Bill?" her mother asked.

Her husband gave her a sharp look, said nothing.

"Can't we fix the phone line?" Trent asked.

"No. They've smashed the connection on the roof." Annie's father drew a deep breath, standing. "We need to act. I'll take a horse over to Bradley's place, use his phone to call Jerry and get the police here. They can bring stuff to repair our vehicles and phone. I'll use Bradley's ute to get back. Josh, that puts you in charge."

Josh nodded, looking young and terrified.

Annie's mum looked stricken. "Bill, it'll take you ten hours to ride to Bradley's!"

"What else am I going to do? I can do it in eight."

Josh grunted. "You'll kill the horse. Our nags aren't built or trained for that."

"So be it."

Without another word he headed out, Josh running to catch up.

"It's all right, mum," Trent said, setting his jaw. "We'll look after you."

"You're a good boy, Trent. Help your father."

◆

ANNIE'S RESTLESSNESS BECAME unbearable. "I'm going to feed the ponies."

Her mother looked up, nodded. "Don't go any further than that."

"Okay."

In the yard her brothers were arguing, trying to jury-rig an antenna. Only a year apart in age, everything became more about competition than cooperation. Annie's stomach felt like heavy water. Anger had driven her to hold her tongue. It felt like a terrible mistake. She had to solve this.

She reached the shed and heard scuffling as she pushed the door open. She froze on the spot. Holding her breath, straining her ears, she stood still for close to a minute. Nothing.

She pushed the door wide, walked cautiously in. Everything seemed as it had before. What had she heard moving? It had sounded too big for rats. She stalked through the bales and bags, looking into corners and gaps. As she got deeper into the shed, away from the flood of sunlight through the open door, the shadows grew denser. Gaps in the shed walls here and there still cast bright slashes across the floor and feed, everything in between a soft, dusty twilight. Enough to see by, too dim for detail. Maybe she should open the doors at the other end, let more light in.

She pushed between two stacks of bales and something whipped past with a hiss. The sound like someone in sudden pain, sucking air in through their teeth. A smell of burning hair drifted through the gloom. Annie's heart hammered. She turned in a circle, trembling. Low panic gripped her as she retraced her steps, trying to look everywhere at once.

Outside, the hot day seemed as refreshing as a mountain stream.

◆

HER BROTHERS LOOKED at her disdainfully. "Something in the feed shed?" Josh asked.

Annie nodded.

"What?"

"I don't know. It rushed past me."

The brothers exchanged looks of derision. "Did you get scared by a big, old rat?" Trent asked.

Annie ground her teeth. "What's wrong with you two? Don't you care about all our stuff being ruined? Something's going on!"

Josh barked a humourless laugh. "Yeah, of course. Dad's pissed someone off again and they're fucking with us. He probably owes someone money and all that stuff last night was "a message"."

Annie frowned. "What are you talking about?"

Trent sighed. "Dad's in big debt. This whole station is in trouble. We reckon he's got caught up with a loan shark and they're scaring him into paying up."

Annie looked back over her shoulder. "But what about the thing in the shed?"

"What thing? You're just spooked."

"No! I saw men last night, in the dark. They were smoking cigarettes and doing something over there!"

Josh and Trent's eyes widened in shock. "What?" Josh sounded incredulous. "Why didn't say anything before?"

"Because dad pissed me off and I wanted to figure it out myself to prove I'm not a kid!" Annie looked at the red, dusty ground.

Josh threw his shifter down. "Fuck me, Annie. You *are* a little kid. You should have told dad! When he gets back, you tell him."

She nodded. "What about that?" She pointed at the feed shed. "Someone's in there!"

"Why would someone hide in there, Annie? You're spooked. Go inside."

◆

HER BROTHERS FOUGHT and argued over the radio and eventually gave up. Her mother coped as she always did, making too much food, baking, roasting, boiling things down to jam. Annie worried. Her dad would be furious when he got back.

Her mother ran out of things to cook as the sun began to set. She sat at the kitchen table, hands tormenting a tea towel, staring out across the yard. Annie put an arm across her mother's shoulders. "Dad'll be back soon. It'll be all right."

Her mother smiled, though it did nothing but move her lips. "Sure, honey."

The sun dipped below the horizon, dusky twilight turning everything to deep brown shadows. "It's not really dark yet," Annie said.

Her mother shrugged. "Twilight or dark, same thing."

"Dad'll be back any minute."

"Where are your brothers?"

Annie looked out. "Trying to fix up Josh's bike last time I saw them."

"Call them in for me?"

Annie headed around the house towards the big garage where the ute, bikes and quads were kept. Something whooshed past her in the gloom. With a gasp and a swell of nerves she stopped dead. She saw Trent walking towards her. "Was that you?" she called out.

"What?"

"Something just brushed past me really fast."

Trent shook his head. "Stupid kid."

"Mum wants you two inside."

"Whatever."

A crash and yelp of pain sounded from the garage. Another crash, then a cry cut short. "What the fuck . . . ?" Trent turned. "What are you doing in there, Josh, ya dickhead?"

Annie felt a wave of foreboding spread up her body. "Trent, don't . . . "

He frowned at her. "Don't what?"

She felt fixed to the spot. Trent pushed open the side door of the garage. With a yell like he had been burned he staggered backwards. Annie started to cry.

Trent turned and ran for the house. "Annie! Get inside now!"

"What's happening?"

Trent ran, pumping his arms, face white. "Run inside, Annie!"

A dark blur shot from the shadows beside the garage. Trent arched forward as the shadow hit him in the back, legs still running as he lifted into the air. He screamed, high-pitched like a girl. Annie cried out. Trent hit the ground and a tall, pale man knelt beside him, one hand pressed into Trent's chest, holding him down. The man had blood over his face, dripping from his chin.

Annie screamed again as her mother came running around the house. Her mother's scream mingled with Annie's as the man fell upon Trent, shaking him by the throat like a dog with a rabbit.

Annie's mother skidded in the dust, raising something dark and shiny into the night. "Get off him, you bastard!" Thunder and fire burst out.

Annie winced, closing her eyes against the sound. She opened them as her mother fired the second barrel, but the man was nowhere to be seen. Trent lay still, his throat a shiny black mess in the gloom, his eyes staring wide into the darkening night.

Annie screamed. "He was in the shed!"

Her mother dropped her gaze to stare at Annie. "What? Do you know . . . ?" She whipped away from Annie's side like a sheet of paper caught in a sudden gust.

Tears flooded Annie's vision. Through the haze she saw her mother land near the chicken pens, legs twisted beneath her, mouth crooked in a snarl of pain, unseeing eyes staring at the ochre sand. The shotgun was nowhere to be seen.

Annie fell to her knees, sobbing and gasping. A sucking, slurping began to her left, where Trent lay in the dirt, but she refused to look. Her mind trembled. She wanted to curl up and sleep, never to wake again.

Another sound came distantly to her ears. A chattering rumble drifting on the hot night air. She jumped to her feet, running as fast as she could, waving her arms. "Daddy! Daddy, turn back!"

She saw her father's face behind the wheel, leaning forward, eyes narrow in concern. The ute skidded to a halt and he almost fell from the door, dragging a .303 with him. "Annie, what's happened?"

Annie sobbed, trying to speak. "Men last night . . . someone in the shed . . . Trent and mummy . . . he's coming . . . "

Her father grabbed her, looking hard into her eyes. "Where is everyone?"

Annie cried so hard she couldn't speak. Her entire body shook, her knees threatened to fold up. She felt vomit rising.

Her father picked her up, put her into the passenger seat. "Stay here. Lock the doors and don't open them for anyone."

He ran off into the darkness. Annie shook her head, whispering, "No, no, no."

A howl of soul-tearing anguish echoed back to her. She heard shouts, then gun shots. As her crying hitched to a quiet trembling, everything around the station fell to silence. Complete darkness settled over the ute, impenetrable. She could only see her reflection, gossamer faint in the windows.

Movement outside made her hold her breath. A shuffling, a slight cough. She dropped into the foot well as the passenger's door jiggled, locked shut. The scuffling retreated around the ute. She looked up, eyes widening as she saw the driver's door closed, but not locked.

The door opened and the pale man slipped in, smiling at her. Two teeth extended long over his bottom lip, sharp and shiny white. His face was clean but his shirt front and collar stained a darker blue than the rest. "Hi Annie."

She stayed down, curled as tightly as possible, shaking so much her teeth chattered. He leaned across and unlocked the passenger door, pushed it open.

"I've been watching you, trying to figure it out." He laughed. "I'm too full for more. Even a little one. But I'll see you again . . . one day."

Annie stared, frozen.

"Get out."

She uncurled her legs, sliding off the footplate and dropped to her knees in the dirt. The ute shuddered into life, big engine roaring. With a spin of tyres it drove into the night, leaving Annie kneeling in a cloud of dust. Within moments the darkness and silence had settled over her again.

THE FATHOMED
WRECK TO SEE

IF DYLAN THOUGHT ABOUT IT, he could still feel the sting of the slap across his palm. As if it happened only moments ago. He could see the shock on Catelyn's face, before her eyes creased up in pain. Tears, screaming, accusations. He'd deserved a lot of it. But his rights were out the window after he'd struck her. He couldn't believe he had done it. Like someone else's hand drawing back, slicing through the kitchen's angry air, pinning a red palm print to her cheek.

Next, silence as she packed and refused to meet his eye. Wouldn't say a word. Walked out, slammed the door and made a full stop in his life. An absolute point, unchangeable. And it was his fault. The rock in his chest threatened to choke him again and he knew it wasn't just emotion. He gasped for breath.

He stared at a half-inch of scotch, swirled it around the bottom of the glass, swallowed it. As he rose to get a refill the gentle swell of the ocean under the boat made him stagger. Or perhaps it was the whisky. Either way, he ignored it and drank more. Same as every night for two weeks since she had left. Drinking away his shame. His remorse. His fear.

You love that fucking boat more than you love me! Freedom Spray, *my arse!*

He slumped back at the small, plastic-coated table, glass held in both hands, and stared into the tumbler as though answers swam in the amber liquid.

You'd rather fish than work on this. On us.

It was easier to let her think that. How could he tell her the truth? After her father died so young, lungs blackened and ruined by cancer, and all her haranguing of Dylan to quit. And he had, now. Too late.

Why won't you fight for us? For me? What happened to the man you used to be?

And the scared, broken, angry part of him reacted, slapping at the truth she unknowingly spoke. That he wasn't the man he had been. He was no longer strong nor vibrant. He wasn't her oak any more, always there for her. He trembled, struggling for breath, his lungs thickened and half their size. She would never know the real reason he had become so distant.

With his muscular frame wasting by the day, he couldn't help thinking it was for the best. Better she think him a dick and get on with her life, than continue to love him and watch him die.

Soft music drifted in through the open windows of the cabin, perfect tones lifted in song. Dylan blinked, swallowed the dregs of the whisky. He strained to hear over the sound of water lapping at the hull. The most beautiful melancholy he'd ever heard, floating on the night air. He listened for a while, paralysed. It took him long moments to realise that he wept.

He staggered out onto the foredeck of his fishing boat, scanned the black water. A half-moon dappled the wavelets in shimmering silver. Specks of light on shore dotted the horizon behind him. Dizzy, he held the railing, knelt to steady himself. The voice was clearer, almost crystal, but he saw nothing. A subtle splash and he spun on one knee. Still nothing.

He couldn't understand the words; a fluid language, melodic and gentle, but the sadness was unmistakeable. Longing clawed at him.

"I hear you!" he cried out, his voice ragged, slurred.

Then silence.

"Please, where are you?"

For more than an hour Dylan knelt and wept, but neither song nor singer returned.

◆

THE DOCTORS HAD said maybe one year. The internet said anything from a few months to twenty years, with stories of miraculous recoveries peppering the sobering truths. Believe in Jesus and you'll be saved, said some. Allah, said others. Meditate, eat raw food, sleep ten hours a night. A swamp of conflicting information.

He rubbed his eyes hard and drank coffee, frowning against the harsh light of day. Perhaps he could drink himself to death first and avoid the indignity of wasting away in someone else's care. He imagined Catelyn nursing him, making him comfortable as he died, all the while hating him for putting her through it all again. Sometimes he resented her for the damage she bore already, which stole the opportunity of care from him. Then he imagined her smile. Her softness. He saw the warmth in her eyes when she looked at him, and wondered if he did her a disservice. He remembered that warmth banished by a slap.

He should have told her, trusted in her strength, even as his waned.

He packed up and set the boat towards shore to buy supplies, check in with the real estate agent. Once the house was settled and all the goods and chattels divided up, he planned to bank whatever he had left and live on *Freedom Spray*. Catelyn had always hated that name, sneered at the implication. He understood why, but he'd had the boat before they met. She never seemed to get that. Regardless, a mooring was far cheaper than a mortgage, and he didn't have twenty five years.

As he secured ropes at the wharf, something caught his attention, a sensation like a fishing hook lodging in his soul. For a moment he shuddered, once more assailed by thoughts of rotted lungs and dying coughs. But it wasn't just his fear. He looked up and saw a woman leaning against a scored wooden post, hand shading her eyes as she looked out to sea. Her long hair reflected gold in the sunlight. Like Catelyn's. He took in the curves, breasts, hips, thighs, but images of Catelyn overlaid what was in front of him, surpassing her in every detail. The blonde smiled, stopped him in his tracks. Curious at first, her expression softened, head tilting to one side. One eyebrow rose. "You okay?" she called.

Dylan shook his head, looked away. "No, not really." He closed and locked the boat, grabbed his bag and strode off to buy more food and alcohol, feet slapping the white painted wood of the wharf. Every footstep sounded like his palm across Catelyn's cheek.

◆

DYLAN TOOK THE boat out again that night. Would he do this once it was his only home? In truth, he had never really needed anything more. Offers were coming in on the house already, so he'd find out soon enough. It would be so easy to leave the shore and never return.

He sat in the vast black expanse of ocean, the lights of land far behind, and ate cold beans. And drank. "What's the fucking point?" he yelled, as indifferent stars wheeled overhead.

His leave from work would run out soon and he had no idea what to do then. When he finally gave in and started treatment, he would need more time off. His six foot form would stoop and weaken with the chemo, his hair would fall out. How could a person work through that? His chest tightened, his hands shook, but whether from the sickness, the fear or the drink, he didn't know or care.

The song rose once more, achingly beautiful.

Dylan jumped up, ran to the prow. "Where are you?" His voice struck away the calm stillness. The melody moved through the dark, sank into his heart. "Please," he called, throat constricted. Did this song cause his tears? The booze? Was he just pathetic? "Where are you?" He was so tired of crying.

The music floated nearby and stopped and he turned, glimpsed a beautiful, slim face, long blonde hair spread across the ocean like a fan, then a splash and nothing.

Dylan stared at the empty space. He hadn't drunk that much, not yet. Though he had every intention of drinking a lot more. Had he really seen that? No sight or sound disturbed the night again and he went back below to hide in twelve year old malt.

◆

DYLAN WASN'T SURPRISED to see the blonde on the dock the next morning. For a moment he almost convinced himself it was Catelyn. Could she forgive him? He could be honest with her. But it wasn't his wife. Her position by the post, the direction of her gaze, even her clothing, unchanged. As he tied off she sauntered over, a half smile tugging her lips. "Hi."

Dylan swallowed then nodded, not trusting his voice.

"Do you fish at night?" she asked.

Dylan licked his lips. "No," he said eventually. "I just like it out on the water."

"Is that safe?"

"I don't really care."

She smiled, knowingly. She said nothing more, simply stood and almost gloated. As the moments passed Dylan became uncomfortable. "I need to . . . " He gestured vaguely at the boat.

She nodded and returned to her post, turning to face the horizon once more.

Dylan gathered his things, locked up. Unable to help himself he called out, "What are you looking for?"

"Something lost," she said, without looking at him.

A chill trembled along Dylan's spine and he hurried to his doctor's appointment.

◆

FOR THE FIRST time in his life, Dylan was too scared to take the boat out. He couldn't explain why, but he didn't want to be near the ocean. He wandered around town and ate junk food before walking two blocks to a painfully familiar bar. So many evenings here with Catelyn after a movie, or with Catelyn and friends before a show. He took a few paces inside and changed his mind, turned back, determined to find somewhere else to drown his sorrows.

She smiled as she walked in. She winked and breezed past him. He stood marooned in a sea of people as she pulled out a bar stool and slid onto it, perfect curves stirring him. She drew him towards her without turning around. Her back, veiled by a waist-long fall of hair, beckoned as surely as a crooked finger.

He put one heavy foot in front of the other, desire and danger warring in his mind. She hooked out the stool next to her without looking. He sat down.

"Glenfiddich," she told the barman, tipping her head towards Dylan. "Make it a double."

"How do you know that?" he asked.

"Not taking your boat out tonight?" Her eyes were deep green.

"No," he said distantly. "Thought I might . . . you know . . . land."

She laughed, a light sound like an icy waterfall over rocks. "Land, huh?"

He nodded.

She swallowed the last of her drink and beckoned the barman to refill them both. "Land is overrated," she said, lifting her glass in a toast.

◆

DYLAN WOKE IN his bed. In his bedroom, in his house. He blinked at the ceiling. He didn't remember getting home, or even leaving the bar. The bed felt too big and solid and still. He had grown used to his bunk on the boat. The house echoed with space and emptiness. It rang with absence.

He struggled from the covers and rocked, bile rising in his throat. Deep breaths quelled the feeling, but something wasn't right. There was nausea but no headache, no blindness to the sunlight streaming through the open curtains. He wondered if some magic had cured him, a drinking session heavy enough that it stole his memory but left no hangover. But a deep breath wheezed through his throat into desperate lungs and he shook with the daily realisation that he was wasting away.

Eventually the sickness passed.

Thoughts tripped over each other, seeking some purchase in the vacuum of his recollection. He didn't black out when he drank; he was cursed with remembering every vivid detail and paying for it the next day. Flashes of a kiss, cold skin, a briny aftertaste. Her voice in his ear, soft as a caress.

"Come to the water. Be *found*."

◆

THE DOCK GLEAMED hot and white in the sun, boats bobbing, rigging clapping against masts. She was nowhere to be seen. When he thought of her his blood ran cooler, his brain misted with deep greens and greys, as if the sea had taken up residence there. He tasted salt water on his tongue.

He stood at the post where he had first seen her and gazed out. Past the mouth of the harbour the ocean stretched endless and inviting, as dangerous and mysterious as she was. He wanted to dive in and sink down until the depths swallowed him. And he wanted to turn and run away, pace after pace inland until the sea was as far away as it could be. What had she done to him?

♦

DYLAN MOTORED OUT over calm waters, the summer sun glinting in his wake. In an hour or so it would set, plunging the world into night. He needed to hear her song again. Needed to know what was dream, what was real.

He ignored the compass and heading, ignored distance and time. He kept going away from land until it was dark and no lights could be seen. The sky was still clear; the moon rode high, illuminating the night. One hand gripped the wheel, the other absently pressed and gripped at his chest.

Eventually he decided he was far enough out and dropped anchor. On the curved deck of the prow he sat, whisky bottle in hand. He swigged, forgoing the civility of a glass. A length of rope, secured to the starboard gunwale, lay coiled beside him. He picked it up and tied it tightly about his right wrist. What lay in the depths with her? Salvation? Did it even matter? Perhaps the stains on his lungs were creeping into his brain, infecting his wits, the only things he had left to rely on.

The moon was half set and the bottle half empty when the music slid over him. He gripped the rope until his knuckles whitened. The aria chilled him, quickened his heart and mind, beckoned him. He wanted to leap from the boat, cut into the deep green and never re-emerge. But he clenched his jaw, held the rope, and drank.

She drifted some twenty feet away, bobbing gently. Her hair was slicked back, rippling behind her. She smiled. "You made me come a long way to find you tonight."

Dylan gasped, a beached fish. The rope pressed into his palm, its roughness reassuring, solid, certain. Normal.

"Come," she said. "Join me."

She wriggled, rose up above the surface. Water cascaded over her breasts and moonlight flickered across pearlescence at her waist before she slipped back out of sight. Dylan ground his teeth and drank again. His vision blurred, his tongue swollen with the booze. He waited.

She resurfaced, eyes catching the moonlight and flashing angrily. "Come in," she said, and blinked, her fury melting into a smile so open, so inviting, that he sat up straighter. The rope pulled taut.

She moved closer, stretching to see the deck where he sat. He couldn't take his eyes from her chest, the smooth line of her stomach. She hissed as her gaze fell on the rope. Deep lines darkened her face with harsh shadows. Her teeth sharpened, her hair twisted into dark, greasy seaweed. Dylan cried out, scrambled back in shock.

She swayed, beautiful and calm. Her face smooth, smile straight and bright white in the moonlight, hair drifting on the surface. "Come in. You know you want to."

"Not all palaces under the sea and love among the fishes, is it?" Dylan said.

She swam back and forth, cajoling. "It's whatever you want it to be."

"Is it, though?" He knew she lied, but still longed for her, ached for her. At the mere thought of her he felt the cold embrace of ocean almost manifest on his skin. He sidled forward, his right arm caught behind by the rope. She came to the prow and he leaned forward to see down to her.

"Let go of the rope," she said, her voice sing-song, lulling him. "Let everything go. Come willingly. I'll help you forget."

He leaned further, shoulder protesting. Her body was a wave of motion, dark green scales from the waist down. She grabbed his left wrist, his hand still gripping the whisky bottle. As she yanked he cried out, strained between the securing rope and her incredible strength. She hissed again, fingers extending into claws.

Dylan drove his heels into the deck and pushed back, tried to pull away from her. He gripped the neck of the bottle, refusing to let go, twisted it to break her grasp. The rope bit into his other wrist. A high wail burst from her and she released him, dropped back beneath the surface.

Dylan upended the whisky bottle, gulping until it ran dry.

◆

IT WAS LATE afternoon by the time he reached mooring. His head pounded, his mouth thick with fur, dry. He was scorched by the sun, the skin raw where the rope had bitten into his wrist. He needed a proper feed and a decent sleep. What he needed most was for Catelyn to hold him and tell him everything would be all right. But it wasn't and she never would.

The siren leaned against her post and scowled as he fumbled the mooring ropes. He refused to meet her eye, terrified and intoxicated. She strolled towards him and he watched her long, shapely legs.

"Rather literal, aren't you?" she asked.

"What?"

"For a man who can't quite let go, you're rather literal. Actually tying yourself to your boat."

He saw the rage in her, and the desire. She ached for him, he realised with sudden clarity, as much as he did for her. But his yearning was driven by enchantment. Her own was primal, animal hunger. "I don't know . . . " he started. "I can't trust . . . "

Her face softened, all understanding and sultry invitation. "What's to trust? We could be perfect, you and I. You're lost and alone, and that's exactly what I seek."

She looked up and down the wharf. No one was nearby, no one witnessed the exchange. Dylan gasped as she slipped out of her clothes and sat, her feet in the water. He couldn't focus as her skin shifted gently, green shimmers running up her calves. She dropped into the water and her mouth opened in song.

Dylan clenched his fists at his sides, tried to push thoughts past the pounding in his head.

"Join me," she said, though her singing didn't cease. "You want me," she said with the melody. "You have nothing else."

"Dylan!"

He turned and couldn't believe what he saw.

"Dylan, what are doing?"

He blinked. "Catelyn?"

Behind him, a hiss, feral and furious. He stepped away from the edge of the wharf as sharp, ice-cold talons raked his ankle.

"Is it true?" Catelyn asked. "I talked to your doctor. He rang my mobile because you haven't been answering yours or the home phone."

"True?" Dylan said dumbly.

"He told me you're dying. Dylan, is it true? When he realised you hadn't told me anything he wouldn't say any more."

Dylan nodded. "I didn't know how to tell you. I felt so stupid, so . . . "

"You thought you were protecting me?" Her face showed more anger than concern.

"The way you lost your dad, and kept on at me about quitting . . . "

"You really thought I wouldn't find out?" Catelyn said. "Even if I left?"

"I didn't want you to go. I didn't want to hurt you."

"So you hit me?"

Dylan stared. His chest felt as though it were collapsing in on itself. "I'm supposed to be the strong one," he managed at last. "I'm supposed to look after you."

Catelyn's eyes widened as she looked past him towards the water. "Who's that?"

Dylan turned.

The blonde floated, arms gently paddling out to her sides. "Dylan and I have this thing," she said, with a crooked smile.

Catelyn's eyes narrowed, her face hardened.

"It's not true!' Dylan cried. "She's been . . . stalking me." Though true, it still sounded pathetic.

The blonde began to sing. Dylan's mind softened at the sound; mesmerised, entranced. Catelyn clapped her hands over her ears, blood draining from her face. Her mouth moved without words.

"Stop!" Dylan yelled, looking from the woman in the water to his wife. "Stop it!" And the song dropped into silence.

Catelyn let her hands fall, eyes wide. "What the fuck was that?"

"That hurts you?" Dylan asked. When she nodded, he said, "It's the most beautiful thing I've ever heard."

"Who *is* she? What does she want?"

"She wants to take me away. From this." He gestured at the harbour, his boat, the whole world. "From everything."

"Fuck that, Dylan. You're *my* husband."

He looked into his wife's eyes. And saw the truth there. "Really? She seems to think I'm lost."

Catelyn laughed, a hard sound. "That may be true, but you're *my* lost thing."

"But after everything . . . "

"We're a partnership, Dylan. Can't you understand that? We're supposed to look after each other."

"After what I did . . . "

Catelyn slid her gaze sideways at the blonde in the water. "Why didn't you tell me?"

"I should have trusted you," he said as she wrapped her arms around him. Her smell pushed every fear and doubt from his mind. "I'm so sorry."

She held him tight. "You don't have to do this alone, Dylan."

"I'm so sorry I hit you. I should never . . . "

"You idiot. If you ever do that again . . . " She leaned back, looked into his eyes. "How long?" she asked quietly.

He shrugged. "Months, maybe a year. It's a crapshoot."

Catelyn held him hard. "We'll do this together."

Dylan nodded, revelling in the sensation of her hair against his face. "It's so good to hear that." He pulled away from her, grimacing at the loss dragging on his heart as he moved. And then the lightness of revelation sparked through him and he smiled.

Catelyn's brow creased. "What?"

"I'm a wreck, my love. But I can finally do something right by you. I won't have you watch me decay and die. Remember who I was, before all of this." He turned to the water.

Catelyn cried out as the blonde smiled. Triumphant notes like silver blades spilled out of her and Catelyn staggered, covering her ears. Dylan lifted his arms above his head. At last, he could take control of his future. Still smiling, he dove into an icy embrace.

NOT THE WORST
OF SINS

STARING UP AT THE STARS, I hear the footsteps with plenty time to spare. Two sets, trying to sneak around behind, in the dark beyond the glow of my dying fire. Graham Masters shimmers into view and opens his mouth to warn me, but I just nod and slip my pistol from its holster. So many times, desperate people will try their luck on a hapless traveller. It ain't the first time for me. Won't be the last.

As the steps crunch softly closer, behind the scrubby chalky-pale Chaparral brush, I turn up onto one knee and fire a shot. There's a howl and the pounding of one set of feet. Cowardly bastard ran away and left his friend to his fate. Not so much a friend any more. I aimed low; he should only be wounded. Unless he was crouching, I suppose.

His ragged breath and sobbing mark him out easy. I wander over, pistol resting ready along my thigh. Jesus, he's barely a teenager, not a hint of whiskers on his chin.

"What the fuck you doing?" I ask. Masters stands beside me, shaking his head, unseen by the boy.

The kid's holding hands to his gut. Must have been crouching after all. "You killed me, mister!"

"What you doing creeping up on honest folk in the dead of night?"

"Just lookin' for some justice in the world!"

"Is that right?" I turn around and walk away.

"Poor dumb child," Graham Masters says and I nod.

"You done killed me!" the kid cries out again, but we ignore him and lay down by the fire. I ignore the discomfort deep in my gut too. He gasps and sobs for a good hour before his breath hitches and he bleeds out.

◆

I WAKE IN the darkness with a scream and think I've been dreaming, until I see Masters fighting with the spectral figures. He's shouting and cursing, and I can't make things out too clearly, what with the sleep in my eyes and mind. Masters is grabbing at the ghosts as they claw and scratch, trying to get past him to me. Waves of coldness waft off them. I can smell frosty ground, but it ain't that late in the year yet. My heart hammers and I start to get up.

Masters snarls over his shoulder. "Sleep, boy! Don't give them the power of your attention!"

They've got by him before, and when they claw at me they're so cold it burns. It's hard to ignore the fight. Cursing the whimper in my breath, I turn my face to the earth and squeeze my eyes tight shut. Every night now it's the same, every time getting worse. Pressing my hands over my ears to mask the shouts, I don't know how long before it's over, but eventually sleep takes me.

◆

DAWN SMUDGES THE horizon pale pink and blue as I kick up the embers and set the pot to boiling for some coffee.

"Again last night," I say to the flickering form beside me.

"Ain't nothing for you to worry about."

"They seemed angry . . . "

Masters turns a hard face to me. "Ain't they always, boy? Ain't I always kept them off you?"

Not always, no. But I let it drop. Masters being mad at me all day can be worse than ghosts trying to take me away at night.

◆

THE BUILDINGS STAND like sentinels in the early sunlight. The town is little more than a crossroads, too small to even have a name, by the look of it. I can relate to that. Two streets mark out the cardinal directions, lined with stores and homes made of roughly cut wood, and more properties spread out behind them. People in dusty clothes walk in the shade of awnings, occasionally casting me suspicious glances. They quickly look away if I catch their eye.

I'll ask around and see if any of our leads are good ones. My daddy's had eighteen years of getting lost, having fucked off right before I was born, but a cur like him don't stay hidden for long. He ain't dumb, uses a bunch of aliases, but he did business with Graham Masters not so long ago, so we know all of Pa's fake names. At least the ones he was using before he turned on his own partner. Masters has never told me what their business was, but it can't have been friendly if it caused my sonofabitch father to leave Graham Masters a ghost. I guess Dad thinks moving from state to state will mean he never crosses paths with his past. We aim to prove him wrong in that assumption and put things to rights. Graham Masters for his own reasons, and me for Momma and myself.

The main street is swirling in dust from wagonwheels and horse's hooves as I tie up Old Jack by the saloon. He buries his nose in the water trough, sucking and sucking like he's never had a drink in his life. He's a damn good horse, honest and gentle, and he means the world to me, even if his chestnut brown hide is scraggy and his ribs show through. My gun and my saddle are pretty much all I have besides Jack. And Graham Masters, I suppose, but he ain't an actual thing, regardless of how helpful he's been.

It only takes about a half a minute in the saloon to know the barkeep there ain't going to be any use. He's never heard the names I give him. As I step back outside, a man walks towards me, jaw working as he chews tobacco, and I see the sun glinting off his badge, attitude drifting out from under the brim of his dirty grey hat.

"New in town, eh?" he says, voice like gravel. He seems nervous.

I nod, choosing not to answer such a dumb question with words. Masters beside me says, "Fuck him."

There's an uncomfortable silence that I get the impression I ought to fill. "I ain't planning on starting any trouble here, Sheriff."

He looks me up and down, tips his hat back a little. "You after something specific?"

"Just passin' through."

"That right?"

I smile at him, try to ease his tension some. "I'm on the trail of a man, as it happens, so maybe you could help me out."

"Is that so? Who you looking for?"

"The man uses different names. Danny Calhoun, sometimes. Or Seth Cooper. Maybe Frank Gates?"

The Sheriff's chewing stops dead. He sniffs and spits. "Pretty damn bold, I gotta say. Pretty goddamn bold." He slips his gun from his hip and gestures with it. "This way, kid."

"What the hell? I ain't done nothing."

The Sheriff barks a laugh. "That right?"

"There's some kinda mistake here. I ain't done nothing wrong."

"Why don't you come along quietly and we'll sort all this out."

I cast a desperate glance at Masters, and his face is pure fury. "Do as he says," he hisses. "He'll shoot you down in an instant out here. Go with him and we'll find a way free."

I follow the Sheriff towards the jailhouse, my gut churning as I wonder just what the hell Masters can do to get me out.

♦

THE TINY CELL smells of mildew and something less pleasant. It's dim inside, with sacking over the one small barred window high in the wall, blocking out the fresh air and sunlight. The shackles hang heavy against my wrists, a length of chain swinging between them. I keep hearing talk of a gallows and how they finally got someone they'd been after, and I can't believe they think that's me.

Masters keeps assuring me he'll sort it out, and I have to trust him. I never had anyone to trust before, and I don't think I'll ever get used to it. But I'm doubting him more by the second. The cell door is heavy and new-looking.

A priest comes walking along beside the Sheriff, grinning like a fox. His hair is lank and streaked grey, hanging in rat tails over his ears and brow.

"I suggest you have a chat with this man," the Sheriff says to me. He pulls out a bunch of keys and opens my cell door. The priest steps in, still grinning, his cheeks sallow flaps over a sagging mouth of broken yellow teeth. What the hell is he so damn happy about?

"I don't need no priest!" I say.

The Sheriff ignores me. "You gonna be okay with him, Father?"

"Oh, yes, don't worry about me."

"I'd much rather keep the cell locked and you outside it."

The preacher shakes his head, still smiling. "We'll be fine."

The Sheriff nods. "I won't lock you in with him, but that door there will stay bolted." He points down the hall to the heavy wooden door between the cells and the front office. The only way out. "You knock on that door when you need to come out." He hands the holy man a six-shooter. "If he tries to follow you, even puts one toe outta that cell, don't say anything. Just shoot him dead."

The priest looks like he's going to protest, but the expression on the Sheriff's face brooks no argument. "He's vicious, Father, left two innocent corpses in his wake. And he ain't as clever as he thinks he is, leaving a trail of questions and murder. It was always going to catch up with him eventually."

Two corpses in my wake? I look across at Graham Masters, but he won't meet my eye. His face is a mix of embarrassment and rage. There's more than two corpses in my past, but I think I know the ones this Sheriff is talking about. Masters knows 'em too.

With a shrug, the priest takes the gun and tucks it into the belt holding his black robes closed. "He's just a boy," the holy man says. "But I'm sure this gun will keep him calm while we talk."

"This is your last chance for any kind of redemption," the Sheriff says to me. "Don't fuck it up now."

He walks away before I can protest, and I'm left in an unlocked cell with an armed preacher. The wooden door to the office closes with a heavy *thunk* and I hear the bolt turn.

Masters moves close to me, whispers, "This is your chance. I'll make a distraction, you get past this maggot."

Before I can answer or ask any questions, he's gone.

"What would you like to talk about?" the priest says.

Unsure what else to do, I start by asking him the names.

"No one I can remember," he says, kinda high-pitched.

"You sure?" I say, deliberately loud, like my voice can push away the creep this guy gives me.

"Maybe I can check my donations book. I keep a note of all the generous souls who help the church. But really, you shouldn't be worrying about any of that stuff now." The preacher's eyes linger on me, slide up and down, and he smiles kinda crooked. "Would you like to give something to the church, young man? Before you move on to the next life? It might go down well with . . . you know." He nods upwards.

"I ain't got two pennies to rub together."

"Maybe you could give something else, fine-looking young boy like you?" He steps up, too close, his breath sweet-smelling, like rotten fruit. "A horse or a pig is all well and good, but it's not the same. Oh no, not the same at all." His eyes become suddenly hard, cold. "Besides, you're already damned."

I hear a commotion out front and the Sheriff yelling. There's a gunshot somewhere and the sound of pounding feet. My fists drive the preacher's head back and he staggers away, scrabbling for the gun at his waist.

I hit him again, two-handed, using the metal around my wrists instead of my knuckles.

The preacher doesn't make a sound as blood floods his mouth and chin, rushing from his crushed nostrils. Then he laughs, the unbelievable son of a bitch. "Is that what you like?" he says, high-pitched and breathless.

He draws the gun from his belt, but I'm ready and slap it aside with the chain of the cuffs. The report is loud, and the bullet bites splinters from the side of the cot. Now he looks concerned.

I hit him again and he goes down, tumbling over in a mess of blood and black robes. He comes up onto hands and knees; the gun wavers out in front of him. I grab it and twist it from his grip, hear his fingers snap.

My ragged boot fetches him up under the chin, and his rotten teeth crack and spin across the floor. I drop down on him and keep punching until my knuckles bleed, and his twitching stops.

Masters is right there. "Come on, boy!"

The door at the end of the corridor is unlocked, and I don't have time to ask how. People are screaming in the street and the Sheriff is firing shots into the air, yelling for calm. Whatever Masters did out here has the townsfolk well and truly spooked. Running outside I see Old Jack down the street, the only horse standing calm. I jump on, drag his reins off the rail, and pound out of town before the Sheriff can realise I'm gone.

◆

THERE'S A WHOLE lot of nothing except wide open space and tumbleweeds between that last town and the next. I figured I'd do well to move along quickly, but I meant to buy food and fill my water back there. Now I'm pretty much out of both.. The nights are getting colder and a low fire does little to keep me warm, hungry as I am. My shirt is thick but my denims are ragged. Masters has always worn his fancy suit and shiny shoes, but I guess a ghost has no concerns for weather and seasons. I'm going to need to find a coat and a lot more to eat.

"Quit yer whinin'," Masters says, even though I haven't complained. "You can always eat your horse and walk."

"I ain't eating Jack. He's about the only friend I ever had."

Masters' anger is instant. "That right? And what the fuck am I, boy?" His hand whips out in a slap across my cheek. It's icy cold and stings something fierce, even as it passes right through. Only when he's really angry, he told me before, can he affect physical things. I guess he was mad as hell in that Sheriff's office. "No wonder your daddy walked away from you," he says. "He could see your weakness even before you were born."

"Fuck you, Graham Masters! I ain't weak."

He sneers at me. "Didn't I find you in the depths of your despair, boy? Cradling your crazy Momma while she gibbered in her madness, holding a gun and sobbing your heart up? About to end it all?"

"Fuck you," I say again. I can't meet his eye, so I stare at the shackles hanging off my skinny wrists instead. "I was only sixteen. I was lost. My Momma was . . . "

"You're eighteen now, boy," Masters shouts. "And you got me to thank for that!"

I don't know what to say, so I say nothing, thinking about Momma wasting away like a dead horse by the side of the road, eaten from the inside out by maggots. Except Momma is being eaten up by memories. My good for nothing daddy left her pregnant, no money or family nearby. Dragged her out to the middle of nowhere to start a new life that fell apart before it began. When I swelled her belly, and my daddy's dumbass dream had turned to shit, he just walked away, and she had to beg for everything. I was born in the dirt of the street, and my Momma was reviled by everyone around her. She was too fragile to exist like that, and it slowly drove her mad.

By the time I was five, I'd already had to grow up enough to look after her instead of the other way around, and that was all my daddy's fault. By the time I was sixteen my Momma had pretty much no mind left, and I was sick of it all. Masters is right that he found me in the depths of my despair. And he convinced me to put Momma with the nuns and help him track down my daddy, seeing as we both had a score to settle.

My daddy had killed Graham Masters over a business deal gone bad, so Masters told me, whatever their business might have been. He'd as good as killed my Momma, and he'd ruined my life since before I even entered this unforgiving world. I took the chances Masters offered me, so I oughtta be grateful. It's true he's teaching me to be strong, and I wonder if this is maybe what it's like to have a father.

I'm trembling, but I tell myself it's the cold and the hunger, not fear or hatred.

"I was drawn to you, boy, because we share a common enemy. Your daddy ruined everything for me, fucking *killed* me, and I'm burning with a vengeance. And didn't I light that fire in you?"

I nod, not looking at him. I can feel that furnace churning in my belly every second of every day. It only gets hotter when I think of poor Momma. I look out across the low fire, towards the distant mesas standing like guardians of this desolate land. I'm one tiny person in a harsh and barren world. What chance do I really have of ever finding my hateful father?

"Now shoot the chain between those cuffs, boy," Masters says. "There's room to angle your pistol in there, and I'm about mad enough that I can probably help. Just be careful you don't blow your stupid hand off."

◆

I WAKE IN the pitch dark, and something moves over me. A light of a sort; a glow. The fire has burned away to nothing but a gentle smear of orange in the night, and the cold is in my bones. As I blink awake, rubbing sleep from my eyes, the glow resolves into a face. Then two. They lean over me, eyes wide and terrifying, mouths stretched in silent screams.

My heart races, my stomach turns to water. Fingers rake like icicles across my face and throat, clutching at me, grasping. They drag a tiny sliver of my soul away with each touch. I see it like silvery smoke stretching out of me in ribbons; feel myself lessen every time. A distant wheezing howl escapes their wide mouths, like cries of pain but somehow triumphant.

With a screech, Masters swoops in. He grabs the things and hauls them off, and the fighting starts. Biting down on my fear I scramble away and load more wood to the fire, blowing through numb lips to bring the flames up again. I squint away as Masters brawls with the things that tried to take me while I slept.

A distant howl drags my attention, and I look into the screaming face of one ghost, not distant at all. Masters is grappling with the other, throwing panicked looks at me over his shoulder.

"Don't you let it in, boy!" he screams. "Don't you give it form!"

The ghost reaches for me, its frosty hands dragging the very essence out of me. My mind slides, my vision blurs. I hear the far-off cries of Masters as he's dragged away, fading as he goes.

Swatting at the ghost, my hands slapping through frozen air, I get dizzy. "Graham Masters!" I cry, but there's no answer.

I turn and stagger away, running and stumbling, no idea where I'm heading, just away, away into the morning. Surely it's only minutes now before they've finally got me. Masters is gone, I'm alone in the night.

Don't you let it in, boy!

"You can't have me!" I scream as I run. Icy claws rake my soul through my back; my spine arches like it's going to pop in a dozen places. "You cannot have me!" I howl again and keep running and running until my vision blurs and I fall, blackness sweeping in before I hit the ground.

♦

I WAKE SHIVERING as the soft glow of dawn begins to brighten the horizon. Grey, lifeless scrub stretches away from me in every direction, as empty as my soul. As lifeless as my existence. I might be alive, but I ain't living, not really.

I see movement in the velvet sky above me and squint on the circling black shape of a vulture, looping around like an angel of death. It spirals slowly downwards, joined by another. They land not twenty feet from me and hop from side to side, squawking at each other. I want to scare them away, but a part of me wonders why I should bother. What's the point?

There's the sound of hooves on the stony ground, and the big ugly birds flap angrily up and away. It's Old Jack, and Masters walks beside him.

"They're gone." Masters sits beside me, his face unreadable even in the low light.

"I thought they got you."

"I'm a ghost, you fucking idiot. I'm already dead."

"They nearly got me!"

"But they didn't. Fuck 'em. You're haunted, boy, you know that. It's how I found you, after all. You let me in and gave me strength. Don't you let them in too, and they'll stay weak."

"I guess." I don't believe a word of it. Next time, the time after. How much more is in me for them to take?

"Finish this business," Masters says. "Get some peace of mind for you and your momma. And for me. They'll have less to hang onto."

"Really?"

Masters stands over me, eyes dark and foreboding. "Get up, you weak prick."

"I don't care any more."

"Yes you fucking do. Look."

I follow his pointing finger and see a jack-rabbit sitting on a mound of prairie not thirty yards away.

"Slow and quiet," Masters says.

The boom of my pistol in the cold air is staggering, and the jack-rabbit's head is gone.

♦

IT'S WELL PAST noon when the silhouettes of a small town appear on the horizon. It gives me renewed strength, and I'm smiling as I ride down the main street that's lined with wooden buildings, brightly painted awnings, and fancy signwriting in the windows. I can see homesteads spreading out beyond the town, people working, wagons rolling. Hills swell up into mountains to the west.

I tie Old Jack to a post outside a saloon, give him a pat on his hot neck. I pull the heavy sleeves of my baggy shirt down to hide my new iron bracelets and walk in through the double swing doors. It's dim and cool inside, quiet and still. Dust motes dance in the early sunlight shafting in between the slats of the shutters. A bald guy with a belly like a full sail is polishing glasses behind the bar, and a pretty young thing is sweeping up. I nod to the barman and watch the girl awhile. She's young and slim, with a cascade of blonde hair and a glint in her eye. She holds my gaze for a second or two before looking back to her broom.

What I would give to find a town someplace, settle down and get some work, woo a pretty girl like that and maybe get married, have some kids of my own. Just normal stuff. But this fire burns in me, and I can't do anything normal until it's out, and that's only going to happen when my daddy is brought to account for what he did to Momma and me. She'd have liked to live in a small town like this, I reckon. Far better than the nuns' sanatorium where she's lying now, mind broken and body withering away to sticks and dust.

"Help you?" the barman calls out.

I smile at him, friendly-like. "I could use a good meal. Or even a bad one," I add with a laugh.

He pushes his chin at the girl sweeping up, and she sets her broom aside and disappears out back. I pull up a stool, sit down and put my ragged black hat on the bar beside me. There's a moment's uncomfortable silence as the barkeep measures me up and down.

The girl returns with a tin plate holding some kind of stew and a hunk of bread. She hands it to me with a soft smile, almost like a secret. The gravy is thick like mud and cold, from last night's cooking, but it smells fantastic. The meat is mostly gristle and the bread's stale, but I swallow it down like it's the food of God, my belly aching at the sudden pressure it hasn't felt for too long. That jack-rabbit kept me alive, but he was near as skinny as me. It feels like the first time I've eaten properly in weeks.

"I'm looking for someone," I tell the barkeep as I mop up with the last of the bread.

He's immediately suspicious. "That right?"

"Give me a whisky. Just the cheap stuff."

He nods, puts a glass on the counter and fills it from a bottle without a label. I'm only drinking to be friendly, trade for the information he might have, but the sour burns nicely all the same. I put a couple of coins on the scratched bar.

Graham Masters stands beside me, unseen by the others. He tilts his head at the barman. Impatient fucking ghost. "I'm looking for a fella goes by several names. Mind if I run 'em by you?"

The barman shrugs.

"All right then. Danny Calhoun?"

He shakes his head.

"Seth Cooper?"

Shake.

"Frank Gates?"

This time there's a slight pause, and his eyes narrow just a bit before he shakes his head.

"Frank Gates?" I ask again, one eyebrow raised.

"I said no, dammit. I ain't ever heard of no Frank Gates."

The pretty young girl has stopped sweeping, watches us with a strange expression. Masters is virtually dancing on the spot. "He's lying!" he says to me, like it ain't obvious, even to the tables and chairs. Truth be told, I'm getting damned tired of this game, but my excitement rises too at this reaction.

I nod and stand up, tip my hat. "Much obliged, sir. Guess I'll move along and keep looking."

The barman seems relieved and smiles at me. "Good luck finding him."

I turn to leave and walk slowly to the door, giving the barman plenty of time to pluck up the courage to ask the question that must be burning his lips to get out.

"Say, stranger."

There it is. I turn back. "Yeah?"

"Why you looking for this fella anyway? You mean him harm?"

I laugh. "Shit, no. We have history. We go way back. I'm just looking up an old friend."

His brow creases, eyes narrowed again. He doesn't know what to make of that. I'm too young to be a pal of someone my daddy's age. Eventually he shrugs once more. "Well, like I said, good luck."

"Thanks."

The sun is beating down outside, making me squint. "Back door or front?" I ask Masters, almost invisible in the brightness.

"Surely the back," he says, vengeance clear in his tone. He's at least as hungry for that now as he was for money in his life, I reckon.

"That's what I thought."

We stroll casually around the saloon, keeping to the shadows near the building walls, and peek around behind. Sure enough, the fat barkeep comes hurrying out, rolling up his apron and dropping it by the door as he waddles behind the other shops and slips away between them. I'm sure we're close. I'm so near the quarry I think I can almost smell the bastard.

"Don't lose him!" Masters barks.

I trot back around the front and turn the corner. It's easy to see the fat barman, hurrying up the street. There's not that many people yet in a frontier town like this, but you can see the potential of the place. It's only going to get bigger, like so many others we've seen. Masters says San Francisco is a city that takes hours to walk across, with huge buildings of rock and brick. I can't imagine a place like that.

The barman shouts and waves and a young boy runs across the street to him. There's some frantic chatter and something changes hands, probably a coin, and the boy takes off north out of town like a rabbit running from a gunshot.

◆

OLD JACK TROTS along happily and I can see the young boy up ahead. There's a property on the hill, just a small farmhouse, and I think that's where he's headed until he jumps bareback onto a horse out front and takes off again. He gallops north and I keep Old Jack in check, tailing him at a distance. There's no point in giving myself away now I'm this close.

The kid rides hard for a good hour, grubby white shirt billowing in the wind of his gallop as his bare feet swing at the horse's flanks. He heads into the hills and down a ravine with a river running along it. Masters is getting more agitated all the time, popping up and shouting at me about losing the kid, but it's hard to keep up and not give myself away when there's fuck-all but the two of us out here.

Sure enough, before we're a half-mile into the narrow valley, I've lost all sight of the boy and his horse. I sit on Old Jack and curse. Masters is furious.

"You are one useless fucking idiot!" he yells. "What now?"

"I don't know," I say in a broken voice. It's going to be dark soon, and the ghosts are coming back. Masters is getting worse at holding them away, and I can't see the fucking point any more.

"Don't you sink into some useless funk, you prissy child," Masters says, his face an inch from mine even though I'm on horseback. "You start searching."

The ravine doesn't branch out, and it's getting deeper. If the kid came through, it's likely I can carry on and hopefully stumble across wherever he was headed. Follow the river and pray I find something before dark.

It's slow going, picking along through the rock and scrub. Often we have to climb a steep bank and keep the river in mind by listening more than watching. We could go right by wherever the kid was headed and not even know it, but I don't tell Masters that. He's irate as hell all the time and only getting madder.

I'm tired, hungry and kinda scared, sagging in the saddle, when something pulls me up. Voices, drifting from somewhere. I hold Jack in a clump of trees and let him drink at the river. Once he's safely tied, I have a drink myself. It's at least as cold and fresh as it looks. Going quiet and careful on foot, it's not long before a crackle of fire and the smell of cooking rumbles my stomach. There are men talking, not far away.

I can see down into the camp, six canvas tents and a big cookfire. Somewhere in here is Frank Gates. AKA Danny Calhoun and Seth Cooper. I settle down to wait for night. Time to finish this.

◆

IT'S NICE TO sit by the river until the dusk turns dark. Graham Masters is impatient to get moving. But it's taken this long, so it can wait a little longer. Caution is the key here, or I'm liable to blow it and waste everything. Masters has ever been eager to get on with it and, if I'm honest, he's often been a fairly unreliable companion. He's caused me trouble more than once.

But it's night, and I have a job to do. My heart's beating fast at the thought. I could finally be here, at that point in my life where I can make my bastard of a father pay and shuck this burden from my shoulders. Tell my Momma he's dead and buried; let her find some peace. Then maybe I'll go back to that last town and talk to the pretty girl in the bar.

I creep down towards the tents. All prospector camps are like this; I've seen a few before. I hide in the shadows and watch as the men sit around the fire, eating and drinking and laughing too loud.

I wonder if it's to stem the disappointment of turning up nothing, or in celebration of the fact they've struck yella and know they're going to be rich. Either way doesn't bother me. I'm going to kill my daddy whether he's rich or poor. Although pulling a few nuggets from the pockets of his corpse wouldn't be such a bad thing.

The kid is curled up asleep under a big coat near the fire. There are four men, so I need to be careful. I don't want to end up in a fight with them all. I've honed some skills these recent years, but even I can't be sure I'd manage four on one.

Masters is clear beside me in the darkness. He squints into the gloom and a smile splits his face. "There he is!" He points to one fella and my chest tightens.

"You sure," I ask.

Masters nods without looking at me. "Oh yeah."

"Really sure?" I ask again, staring hard at him.

He turns his glare to me. "That's Frank Gates."

We watch a while longer. Nothing happens except more eating and drinking and then the men start heading for their tents, to bed early to get up with the dawn.

I keep an eye on Gates, staring hard at the man who seeded me for this world, who ruined my Momma's life. He's a rangy bastard, tall and skinny like me, but his hair is dark black where mine is sandy brown. He's got a nose like an eagle's beak, and that ain't nothing like mine either. Nice to know I take after my Momma more than this sack of shit. He wears good clothes, though they're dirty from prospecting, and his boots are finer than any I've ever owned. Son of a bitch. I start preparing for what I'm going to say to him, and I brace myself for the possibility that I won't have a chance to say anything. Ending him is the only important part of this.

And he starts heading straight for us. I catch my breath, shuffle back against the rocks and scrub where I'm hiding. No time to move anywhere else. He walks right past me in the shadows and I see his mean face, eyes set close together, black stubble making his cheeks dark in the night. He seems in decent shape, but I don't reckon he's close to as strong as I am. He walks between some trees into the gloom, and I can't believe my luck.

Creeping like a cat, I follow. Franks Gates, as he's calling himself, grunts and undoes his braces. He kicks a hole in the sandy ground, drops his britches, and squats, elbows on his knees.

"Don't make a sound," I whisper, as the cold steel of that Sheriff's Colt presses against the skin of his neck.

He stiffens, but doesn't move. A muffled cry of fright escapes his lips, bitten off as soon as it starts.

"Pull up your britches and move forward."

He complies. I can see his hands shaking as he buttons his fly. He stumbles ahead of me, my gun barrel pressed to the middle of his spine.

"What do you want?" he whispers, his voice trembling with fear. "You want money? Gold?"

"Shut the fuck up, Frank Gates," I say quietly, pushing him away from the camp. "That's what you're calling yourself now, right?"

"That . . . that's my name, right enough. Who are you?"

"I'm the son you abandoned, you slimy piece of shit."

"What?"

"The son of the woman you left, pregnant, poverty-stricken and a pariah. She couldn't take it, the ridicule, the rejection. She's a fragile bird, and you broke her mind, Frank Gates! Our lives, too!"

His shaking is visible all over, his knees knocking together, hands flapping by his sides. "I don't know what you mean. I don't have a son. I have a wife and two daughters in San Francisco!"

That just makes me furious. "Is that right?" I almost yell. "Treat them a lot better than you did Momma and me, do you?"

His voice is hitched with tears, sobbing like a little girl. "I don't know what you mean!"

"Turn around and face me, Gates."

He stands there, back to me, shaking and sobbing.

"Turn your face to me, Pa!"

He turns slowly, hands raised. His face is twisted in fear, tears and snot shining in the darkness. I look around for Graham Masters, but he's nowhere to be seen. Surely he wants to see this. My own hand starts to shake, the excitement of the situation is getting to me. Fuck it, I can't put this off.

"Here and now you pay for what you did to us!" The flash and bark of the pistol is massive in the silent darkness, and a rush rips through me.

Franks Gates' chest gouts blood as he staggers over backwards, my shot right through his heart. He's dead before he hits the ground, and Masters comes running.

"Stop!" he cries. "It ain't him!"

I can't believe it. "Not again!"

"I lost you in the trees," Masters says. "I tried to catch up, but I couldn't find you. It ain't him."

My euphoria drains away like rainwater on sun-parched earth. I'm shaking all over. "I killed the wrong man!" I yell at Graham Masters. "Again!"

"I'm sorry, it's so hard to tell. I'm a ghost, I don't see real things as well as you do." He sounds altogether too relaxed for my liking.

"You said you were sure. Just like you did when we found Danny Calhoun, and Seth Cooper!"

Something like a smile glimmers across Masters' face, but it's hard to see in the shadows.

I can hear voices shouting and people crashing through the brush. Those gossamer spectral haunts that dog me every night are lurking, reaching, groaning mouths wide in supplication. Are there three now?

"You have to go!" Masters says.

Confusion fogs my brain. "I killed another innocent man!"

Masters' sudden grin is feral. "Part of you likes it!"

"What?"

He grabs at my shirt, dragging icily at my flesh as his hand passes right through me. "Come on! Don't let them catch you."

Is he laughing? I stumble over rough ground, heading back to where Old Jack is tethered. My mind reels, my heart hammers.

"Keep looking," Graham Masters says. "It's your turn now. You'll find him next time, I'm sure." There's no sincerity in his tone.

I look at the ghost of my mentor in the darkness, and his expression is hard to read. "My turn? Next time?"

He nods as I untie Jack and swing up into the saddle. There's a self-satisfied look about him, like a man who's enjoyed his fill of a good meal. His eyes sparkle, and there are creases at the corners as he grins.

"It's your time, boy," Masters says. "Now you get to keep moving, keep looking for your damn pa, free as you like! Vengeance is a selfish business. And you better stay ahead of those night-time ghouls."

"You sound like you ain't coming," I say, shivers wracking through me.

Masters just stands in the night, smiling at me. I can hear the other prospectors crashing closer.

"I need you to identify him!" I say, and curse how scared my voice sounds.

Masters leans his head back and laughs. "Boy, I have no fucking idea who your daddy is. Never did."

His words echo in my mind and his laughter rings through the valley as I gallop away from the river and into the night.

THE OLD MAGIC

MY YOUNGEST DAUGHTER NEVER WANTED to learn the way. *Her* daughter doesn't even believe in it. What kind of world is it where a child doesn't believe in magic? Though Claire is hardly a child any more, grown and beautiful. I remember her, last Beltane, shaking her head, *Grandma, how are you seventy? You don't look fifty!*

It's the old magic, I'd answered, and she'd laughed and swept away. Susan shook her head, my daughter altogether more sad in the face of her child's innocence. Was it fear of the way that stayed her hand? Fear for her child? Her father's words?

I reach out my hand to touch Gareth's stone, caress the carved letters of his name. He reached a mortal seventy, then seventy-five. Then time took him in its embrace and carried him away, like so many before. The way is only so strong. Gareth had accepted that, enjoyed it. He would smile as I lay beside him, no need for pretence or disguise. *How can you still love me, wrinkled and worn like I am. Look at you!*

I would look into those moss green eyes and tell him the truth. *It's love, my sweet. The most powerful spell of all.*

But it's hard to be part of a world where enchantments are locked in electronic devices and everyone talks to each other all at once. After forty-five years with Gareth, I feel time like an anchor on my heart. There with all the others. Did Gareth's love for Susan come to outweigh his love for me?

The grass under me is soft and fragrant, spongy to the touch. A gentle breeze drifts by, carrying the scent of honeysuckle and hope. I can hear and smell the ocean, out beyond the cemetery. It calms me as I recline against the sunlit trunk of a blue gum. How many have I loved and lost?

◆

"YOU'RE A SPECIAL girl, Erin." My mother stroked my hair, smiling at me with deep affection.

"Am I?" Five years old and full of love.

"Certainly. But I have to teach you, and you have to understand that your power is dangerous."

The way was strong in those days. But it was fear and ignorance that made it dangerous, then, now and always. Those happy years while my mother taught me spells and potions, incantations and enduring days. Our tiny one-room wooden shack, a smoky fire always crackling in the hearth, was my world. Our scrubby herb garden behind it my playground. As I grew I ventured further afield, began to ply my mother's trade. She healed with a master's touch I tried to emulate, but back then I hadn't understood. So many times since I've wondered, *How old was she when the people turned on her?* How many daughters were there before me?

When I was fourteen, my mother smiled as she stood tied to the stake, with the pyre stacked below. Her voice floated through my mind as I scowled, defiant in the crowd. *Away now, Erin, before they realise you're the same as me.*

Our village elder had stood tall, official and superior, his voice ringing as clearly in my memory now as it did through that cold winter air. *In this year of our Lord, seventeen hundred and eighty eight, despite the rulings of the modern world, this woman before you has been declared and proven a witch. We will not bear the Devil's children among us.*

More than sixty years since the last official Trial, supposedly protected by law instead of persecuted by it, yet these scared and superstitious fools acted as though they were the very hand of God. As the flames of their hatred touched the dry kindling beneath my mother, I ran, tears blurring my eyes. She was right, they would surely come for me next. I was old enough to be considered a woman. My mother's lessons were deeply ingrained.

I could only leave. So many times since then I've turned and left so much behind me.

I went south, across the border into England, claimed to be the orphan of a midwife and my path was carved.

◆

I TIP MY face up to the summer breeze, let the aroma of life sooth me. Something that has never become stale, the pure scent of spring, life renewed. Life brand new. Gareth's stone is warm against my back. I let the sun drench my closed eyes for a long time before turning my attention to the treasures before me.

I pour a generous dram of the single malt I've saved for so long. There comes a time when saving things becomes pointless, especially as they're made to be enjoyed. The smoky liquor is bliss on my tongue. I pick up the expensive chocolate and take a bite, revelling in its creamy smoothness. The first time I married, solid chocolate had yet to be invented. I'm sure Barnaby would have been appalled at the idea. A gentle smile tugs at one side of my mouth as I imagine his disdain. *Whisky and chocolate, woman! You spoil them both by combination.* But it's a special indulgence for me.

He would have mocked me, but I know dear Barnaby would have found it endearing too.

◆

TWO YEARS BEFORE the nineteenth century began, nearly fifty years before solid chocolate, I married sweet Barnaby. Such a gentle, honest man. A carpenter of rare skill. He built us a house and a future and I gave him a son and a daughter. Our boy, Damien, grew rich in the industrial revolution, though his machines mystified me. How simple that time seems now. And dear Belle learned the secrets my mother taught me, and she is truly adept. Would she understand if she knew? I wonder where she is now. I miss her so, my first little girl.

In the musty summer of eighteen twenty five Barnaby died. Only fifty two years old. Some sickness even the magic couldn't impede. I grieved, wearing black for two years before I decided it was time to move on. Suspicion would surely rise, for I didn't look my fifty one years. My children understood and we all wept as I slipped away. So many times I've wondered what they did with their lives, what my first daughter might still be doing. Am I really a bad mother? The eternal pain of that separation would suggest I am. I've tried so hard to find Belle, never succeeding. Perhaps she harbours resentment still. But I choose to believe she's out there somewhere, thriving.

◆

I LIFT THE glass and toast dear Belle at the memory. I still feel all my progeny in one way or another but it becomes ever harder to tell whether they're living or dead, especially with the girls. I sip and savour the taste, swallow.

A couple walk slowly by along the gravel pathway in front of me. Old by mortal standards, maybe seventies, they cast me a disparaging look as I sit on my most recent husband's grave. They mutter to each other, probably something about young people today, as I smile at them, whisky in one hand, chocolate in the other. If only they knew what children they are to my eyes. I wonder whose grave they're here to see.

As they pass, I turn my attention back to my small, hard leather case of treasures. I've kept a single thing from each of them, all my men and children. I run a finger over Barnaby's handmade chisel, that he used on so many toys and repairs. Belle's first magicked oak stick, curved against nature by her will, smooth as glass now. A small metal cog Damien used to wear on a chain about his neck, that he gave me the night I slipped away. My eyes prickle with tears, but I've long since done with crying. Haven't I?

My stroking fingers find George's medal, the silver and enamel gift from Her Majesty that he treasured over every other possession. *I don't know what I ever did to earn this,* he insisted every time he looked upon it, and it became a joke between us.

◆

I WENT TO London after Barnaby's death, to lose myself in the madness of the modern world. The factories and noise, the multitudes and poverty. My skills were well-suited and well-used. Nine years after dear Barnaby died, I fell in love again.

George. Strong, handsome George, with his jet black hair and pure white soul. He walked with royalty, a footman to King

William IV, the man who ended child labour and emancipated colonial slaves. Such progressive, wonderful men, King William and my stoic George. We had two sons, Wilfred and Alfred, who grew to be proud, strong men like their father, Royal Guards. No daughters that time.

Two years after George and I were married, King William fell victim to illness. George insisted I help, but even my skills could not keep the poor King's lifeblood pumping for long. I managed to give him one more year before his heart broke.

And then Victoria ascended the throne, just eighteen years of age, and my reputation in the court sealed my future. Though I had been unable to save the King, Victoria insisted on my counsel and assistance. She understood the old way and revelled in it, while George turned a blind eye. She loved our "little secret", delighted in dispensing my skills in the right places, learning from me for her own amusement. Sweet, young Victoria was not without some cunning of her own. And dear George, the man I loved more than life itself, stood by us, protecting and serving.

While I had no daughters with George, our sons gave us granddaughters. They're nothing close to girls of my own womb, but they keep the way alive even today, grateful for my teaching. They instruct their own children and grandchildren, sometimes send me news of their lives, but less and less often. I often wonder how far my legacy extends now. How many of them will know? How many will understand?

Poor Victoria, I still feel her pain, the year she lost her mother and husband within months of each other. If only I had understood disease then as I do now I might have been able to save her Albert. Victoria never blamed me, though her grief coloured the rest of her life. Grief I only truly understood seventeen years later when time took George away.

He loved me more than I thought it was possible for any man to love. He grew old, but never tired. Strong as an ox to the end, he slipped away happy, but for one regret. *It pains me that I leave you alone, dear Erin. But I think you've endured this before.*

The only time he ever spoke directly of my unusual nature was with his dying breath, on the opulent bed in our fine quarters at the Palace, his polished shoes beside the dresser. One hundred years to the day after my mother had smiled from the pyre, my dearest George smiled from his pillows and left. He was eighty-two. Our sons were there and they held me, but nothing could contain my pain. My grief knew no boundaries.

My melancholy was insufferable, to myself and to others around me. Victoria and I could not bear each other's anguish and I had to leave. I travelled back to the north, shook off the trappings of royal life, dropped my disguise of age and survived as a young midwife again. How many lives have I coaxed into this cruel, unforgiving world?

As the century turned once more, I knew my Queen needed me. I felt her calling out across the land, drawing against our shared pain. She wanted to say goodbye. I travelled to the Isle Of Wight and stood by her bed with her son and grandson. She squeezed my hand, still dressed in black even on her own deathbed, itself draped in charcoal raiment. *You're as young and beautiful as the day we met,* she said. *Live well, dear Erin.*

I reached out to prevent her passing, I could have done so easily, but she gently shook her head. *It's time. We can't all be like you. I go to my Albert.* She didn't smile as she left, but she took some of my grief for George with her, I think.

It was the first month of the second year of the twentieth century and I had no one left but two sons, themselves old men with families. Their families had lives of their own, my granddaughters taught and sent out into the world. My first son, Damien, long turned to dust, my first daughter, Belle, somewhere, lost to me, surviving as I survived, I hoped. Time to move on again. I drifted, leaving England and its painful memories for the continental temptations of mainland Europe.

◆

I slip the lavish diamond and sapphire ring from my finger and tuck it into my case of treasures, the only item in there not from a husband or child. The ring Victoria gave me when grief pushed us apart. *Ignore its worth,* she whispered, voice still weak from the pain of loss. *Just remember I have worn this every day I have known you and I want you to wear it now.* A true Crown Jewel in my possession still. I have worn it every day since, my Queen. Every single day. Until now.

I put it beside the fountain pen that belonged to Wilfred, and Alfred's polished pocket watch.

I do miss Victoria as if she were a daughter of my own.

◆

NOT LONG AFTER I left the pain of England behind for the Continent, war swept the world. I travelled the trenches as men tore men to pieces and lunacy ruled. I practiced my art with no concern for secrecy, yet barely stemmed the tide of agony and horror by a fraction. Many soldiers returned home with stories of miracles, while so many more never returned at all. I watched atrocity unfurl among the mud and smoke and blood, and I despaired.

Horrified by all I'd seen, I ran as far as I could imagine, sailing to the new world, putting a heaving ocean between myself and all I'd lost. By the mid-nineteen twenties I found a fresh life in Chicago.

Oh, this was the modern world, where illicit drinks were served in jazz-soaked, smoke-filled speakeasies, and no one cared any more. So good to allow myself to be young again, revelling in my beauty and vitality. Wickedness found me and I welcomed it gladly.

And love found me again, with my guard down. Anthony Magrese, mobster and cad. Ours was a torrid and powerful love affair and I bore twin girls. My skills were used more for bullet wounds and beatings than sickness and disease, and the only children I helped into the world in that time were my own. For the first time in a hundred years I had daughters to teach again, my powerful Marlene and Loretta.

The wild nights and crazy days felt as though they would last forever. Sharp suits and tight dresses, vibrant life and new money, there was nothing my heart desired that Anthony Magrese couldn't supply. We lived in a grand house with all the clothes and jewels and decadence I could imagine. So many cars. I soaked up the envy of his peers and the lust of his crew, every inch the queen Victoria had been, in a new kingdom of wealth and booze and corruption. Our girls at my side, a triptych of female grace and power behind the throne of the man with the attitude.

No one disrespected Anthony Magrese, but no one suspected for a minute he'd have been anything without his potent lady wife and his strangely commanding young girls. They knew power as soon as they knew life, those twins, and they were born for it. Embraced it.

I promised myself I would never lose touch with these two, as I had my first daughter. Sons and husbands grow old and die, but daughters are forever. My granddaughters in England and daughters here would always be part of my life. They still contact me from time to time, my Chicago girls, though more from a sense of obligation than desire, I think. It seems time makes strangers of even the closest bonds. They have daughters and granddaughters too now, my legacy spreading like the arms of an ancient oak. I wonder if they'll understand, any of them? Will they even know?

After fifty-four years married to my wonderful George it seemed as if I hardly knew Anthony at all when, after just sixteen years, a Falcone family bullet took him in the summer of nineteen-thirty-nine. The same year war raged across the world again.

◆

ANOTHER SMILE LIFTS my lips as I caress Anthony's solid silver cigarette case. It bears a significant dent from the first bullet that tried for him, and he always said it was proof smoking couldn't possibly be bad for you. A shame the Falcone bullet went between his eyes instead of for his heart again.

Beside the bullet-shot case are the twin silver hip flasks of Loretta and Marlene. So young but already so decadent. Those girls embraced their twinhood and were as adults from twelve or thirteen years old. I encouraged it, endorsed their quick maturity, for their own protection as much as my own. After Anthony was shot and we knew all our transgressions had caught up with us, I had to disappear. His enemies would ever hunt me down. It was time to move on and I faked my death to give my girls a chance. They each filled a flask and gave them to me wrapped in silk. Rum in Loretta's and gin in Marlene's. For all their similarities, they never could agree on liquor.

They assured me, though they were barely halfway through their teens, that they would be fine and care for each other. I believed them and they proved my faith justified. They were a year older, after all, than I had been when I ran from my mother's pyre. Both flasks are still full, that booze untouched, and they'll stay that way for now. They're both enchanted, each containing far more than a secret drink. My girls' magic is strong and those silver vessels hold valuable power. I wrap them in the flowing red silk again.

♦

I COULDN'T BEAR another war, so I ran far away. Marlene and Loretta left for Canada, young but safe together, to build lives of their own. Dead to all but my closest kin, I took a new identity and another long journey across rolling oceans here, to Australia, unaware the war would follow even this far. But everything seemed fresh again, the outback in the nineteen-forties strangely reminiscent of my youth, so very long before. The climate couldn't have been more different, but the desperate survival just the same. Perfect to shake off the debauchery of the preceding years.

For two decades I travelled through outback communities, building health centres and schools. Teaching care and driving back ignorance. For the first time in a long time I felt as though I had some peace. Barnaby was a warm memory, the painful recollections of George began to soften and the incandescent years with Anthony lost their heat.

The sixties arrived and love was all around. It was a time of such freedom and excitement, new hope and aspiration. I met Gareth among the orange sands of Broken Hill and my heart felt whole enough to give away again.

My life began to wrap around itself when we travelled the state of Victoria and I saw their Government House. It gave me a jolt of painful nostalgia to see a building styled so closely to Osborne House on the Isle of Wight, where I'd said my final farewell to the Queen who gave this far-flung state its name. That was perhaps the first sign of what has come to pass.

Gareth soon tired of outback life, wanted to be near the ocean. Sydney was a shining gem in those days, all optimism and promise. We built a house and a life and Susan was born. Two years later, young Adam. I began to love Gareth as I'd loved George all those years before, something I never thought possible, though I knew George approved. A part of him hung around me always, his blessing like a ghostly embrace.

By the mid nineteen-seventies the world had started speeding up and something in Susan changed. When she turned seven and I two hundred, it became clear she mistrusted me, feared the old magic. She didn't want to learn any more. When I healed her grazes she would cry and hide. And I knew I would never teach her again. She would never be like me.

She married young and Claire was born when Susan was barely out of her teens, so desperate was she to be away from my influence, make a life and family of her own. My newest grandchild, another girl, lost to me before she escaped the womb. Susan always so protective, never leaving the two of us alone.

And Claire doesn't believe anyway.

◆

SADNESS WELLS IN me as I look over the treasures in my small leather case. Gareth's horn-rimmed spectacles are there, so old-fashioned, but he always insisted on them. Every time he needed new glasses I would try to convince him to try something different, more modern, but he would smile and shake his head. *What do you know of modern?* he would mock.

Gareth had understood the magic and I always wonder . . .

I have nothing of Susan's in here.

I turn to face his stone and stroke the carved letters of his name once more, the rough, grey surface warm in the bright sunshine. Did you guide Susan gently away from my legacy, dear Gareth? The secrets you'd coaxed from me, your horror at the depths of my experience, perhaps they made your decision for you. Were you protecting Susan from a life like mine and is that why she turned from me? If she doesn't encourage her gift she will age and die like men. Like you.

I make sure all my treasures are safely secure and close the case, then pinch shut the padlock. Such power contained in here. My sweet granddaughter Claire, who doesn't believe, will get the padlock key in the post tomorrow. Along with a letter explaining what each item is, where it comes from. Her legacy, in spite of her mother. The case will find her, there's no doubt about that. My power is strong, after all these years, and this is set in motion. It will happen. And I've left messages for all the others, in the sinister places where they know to look. Whether they will or not, I cannot guess.

But I can't rebuild again, this world has grown beyond me. All things end eventually and I couldn't be more at peace with that. My legacy is legion. Time to walk away again, from everything this time.

The razor blade reflects sunlight as I turn it over in my hand. Leaning back against Gareth's stone, I smile at the high white clouds.

I'm not nearly as afraid as I'd anticipated. A wave of excitement passes over me with the summer breeze.

I make the cut, let the blood from my arm drip to soak into the welcoming earth, and say the words. My connection to all my pasts severs like a snapped twig, so total. So quick. I no longer feel any of my girls, but I know they'll thrive. As will I, alone and for myself. No more husbands, no more life quickening in my womb, son or daughter. No healing, teaching or saving. I still can't decide if I'm being selfish or brave. Perhaps both. Regardless, I think I've earned my solitude and freedom.

Another few words and the case is sent on its way. I have no idea where I'll go, beyond the sure knowledge that I'll be leaving Australia soon.

It's been so long since I experienced anything truly new.

MEPHISTO

"I NEED A VOLUNTEER!" MEPHISTO scanned the crowd, one hand shielding his eyes as if from a bright sun. His red-lined black cape whipped around as he strode from one side of the stage to the other.

Dozens of hands shot up, clamouring to be chosen. Mephisto squinted, heart hammering. He so hated this bit, but had little choice. *There's always choice*, a voice whispered in the back of his mind and he squashed it away into its dark corner.

His gaze fell upon a young boy, maybe eleven or twelve, smiling in anticipation. His hand wasn't raised and of course, that made him perfect. Mephisto singled him out, one long finger bright in the spotlights. "What about you, lad?"

The boys eyes widened and he looked left and right. One trembling hand rose, pointed to his own skinny chest.

"Yes, you. Come on, I'll make you famous!"

The boy's parents sat either side of him nodding enthusiastically. Cajoling from the crowd drove the boy from his seat, up darkened steps and past voluminous crimson velvet curtains. Brass half-shells along the stagefront cupped incandescent bulbs. Mephisto grinned over the brightness at the audience as they encouraged the boy along.

When the young man reached him, Mephisto laid an arm across bony shoulders. "What's your name, lad?"

"Matthew."

Mephisto turned back to the crowd. "Matthew, ladies and gentlemen!"

Whoops and wild applause disgusted the magician, these easily entertained masses. To hide his grimace he made a theatrical turn, swept Matthew along to a tall black wooden box at centre stage. It had a double door, split top and bottom like a stable, with bright silver tape marking its edges that sparkled in the spotlight that struck it like a bullet. The crowd *oohed*. Mephisto pulled open the two half doors. The box was empty. The crowd *ahhed*.

How he hated them.

Matthew looked terrified, pinned by the beam of light from the gallery. Mephisto couldn't blame him. "Please, step inside."

"What are you going to do?"

"I told you, I'm going to make you famous!"

The boy nervously moved forward and turned around, looked out over a sea of expectant faces partially obscured by the glowing coronas before them. Mephisto closed the bottom door. Only Matthew's head and shoulders showed over it. "You've seen me perform all kinds of magic this evening, ladies and gentlemen," the magician called out. "You've been impressed, yes?"

The crowd whooped and hollered.

Mephisto lowered his voice, forced the crowd to be silent to hear. "But do you believe I can make a young boy disappear?"

The crowd assured him they could. Of course they did, they were in the palm of his hand.

He winked at Matthew, closed the top half of the door. The boy's frightened questions came through the wood but he ignored them.

Mephisto addressed the crowd again. "Clap for me, folks, slow and steady, like this." He set a measured, rhythmic applause going. As audience carried it he raised his hands high. The energy from this roomful of sheep was powerful, but that was ever the case. Never underestimate the malleable vigor of people in large numbers. Their desperate need for entertainment, to muffle, however briefly, mundane lives. He let that energy rush through him, absorbed it, mutated it. He spoke the words.

A low roar, like distant water powering through a canyon, rose in the auditorium. It built up, rising with the frenzied clapping of the audience. They felt it more than heard it, clapped faster and faster, began to cheer and laugh and bay. Mephisto drew that power in and the roar rose to a deafening crescendo. Sparks and flames burst out around the box and quickly vanished. The box stood dark and still, the crowd gasped and faltered, the noise sank away like a tide until silence rang in the theatre.

Mephisto slowly lowered his arms and a grin spread across his face. He turned and threw open the doors. Young Matthew was nowhere to be seen. The crowd erupted in applause and laughter. Mephisto strode to the front of the stage and bowed once, twice, thrice. With a sweep of cape he turned and walked swiftly into the darkened wings. The last thing he saw was the nervous smiles on the faces of Matthew's parents, the empty chair between them.

He packed quickly in his dressing room as the crowd's approval sounded slightly muted through the walls. He stuffed his magician's garb into his hard leather case and put on the shabby suit and scuffed shoes that disguised him with their normality. He pulled off the dark hairpiece and ran one hand over stubbly blond hair. It only took a moment to wipe away thick makeup, revealing pocked and pale skin. In just a couple of minutes he was done, grabbed his case and left by the stage door, into a grimy alley.

A dark shadow, vaguely man-shaped, awaited him. Beside the shadow a smaller presence trembled, emanating terror.

"Thank you, George," the shadow said. "Mephisto, really?"

George shrugged. "As good as any. I'm running out of names. It's fitting, isn't it?"

The shadow laughed, a terrible sound. "Same time next year, George."

The magician scowled, pushed past the darkness, wincing at its icy presence. "Yes, yes."

"What's it been now, two hundred and twelve years?" the shadow called after him.

George turned, his face angry and pained. "Two hundred and thirteen. Don't play games with me."

That deep, ominous chuckle again. "Any time you want it to end, just come to me. I'll be happy to have you."

The shadow winked out with a burst of frost before George could reply. He ground his teeth, hating himself, hating people, hating everything, and scurried from the alley. As he turned down the street away from the theatre he heard a woman's voice inside, high-pitched in anguish, screaming for someone to do something. He hunched into himself and made for the train station.

THE DARKNESS
IN CLARA

MICHELLE SAW CLARA'S FEET FIRST, absurdly suspended a metre above the ground, toes pointing to the carpet, ghostly pale and twisting in a lazy spiral. The rest of the scene burst into her mind in one electric shock a fraction of a second later; Clara's wiry nakedness, limp arms, head tilted chaotically to one side. Her tattoos seemed faded against ashen skin. Her so familiar face grotesque and wrong, tongue swelling from her mouth like an escaping slug. And her bulging eyes, staring glassy and cold as Michelle began to scream. Light from the bedside lamp cast Clara's shadow across the wall like a puppet play, glinted off the metal legs of the upturned chair beneath.

I bought her that belt, Michelle thought, as she stared at the worn black leather biting deep into the blue-tinged flesh of Clara's neck, and she drew breath to scream again.

♦

THE FUNERAL WAS typical, a sombre affair overlain with the gentle patina of judgement that always accompanies suicide. Michelle put on her brave face, smiled at all the platitudes. Knowing she would never be able to make it through a eulogy, she stood stoically beside Paul as he gave the most beautiful speech. When he opened with, "People always ask what it was like growing up with two mums . . . " she almost lost it. He gripped her hand behind the lectern and kept talking, voice strong, daring anyone to contradict his tale of twice the love.

At the wake he stayed by her side, remained calm in the face of false sympathy offered with barely concealed disdain. *So difficult without a father. So tough, such an unconventional upbringing.* "My uncle Gary was a better father than most of my friends' dads," was his go-to line, and he always reminded people that two mums was way better than single parent families and those kids turned out great.

"At her fucking wake, still the snide remarks," Michelle said as they stood on the back lawn after the house had emptied.

Paul put a strong arm around her shoulders. "People are idiots, you know that."

She laughed and quickly devolved into tears, the dam finally breaking through the shell of bravado she'd worn all day. Paul turned her to his chest and they sobbed together for what seemed like hours.

◆

SHE ROSE EARLY, the house so quiet, made strong coffee, scrambled eggs, toast. Paul stirred in bed as she entered his old room. She stood with the tray, smiling sadly, so pleased he'd stayed after the funeral. "Still yours," she said.

He dragged himself to a sitting position, rubbed his eyes. "You really should pull down these posters. Redecorate like a proper guest room."

"But it's your . . . "

"It's not, Mum. It's really not any more." He smiled warmly.

She put the tray on his lap, sat on the bed beside him. "No. Honestly, we just never got around to it."

She stroked his leg through the covers while he forked up eggs, nodded appreciatively. Her little boy, now such a big, strong man. She could still see the child in there, but he was buried deep under layers of experience and life. A tear breached her lashes as she remembered the birth, holding Clara's hand and telling her to breathe and push, *Clara, you're doing so well.* Bringing the baby home, the two of them staring into the bassinet in stunned silence and absolute, total love.

"Why did Mama do it?" Paul asked in a whisper.

Michelle shivered at the memory of those gently spiralling toes, ran a hand over Paul's thick, black hair. "I don't know, love. I really don't." The tears came faster.

Paul sat and stared at his fork resting inert on toast. "She had problems, we know that. Her funks. But was she ever really so depressed?"

"She must have been."

"She never talked to you about it?"

"About suicide?"

Paul shrugged, his eyes haunted with lack of understanding. "About being so down, anything like . . . "

Michelle stroked his hair again, luxuriating in the feel of it as much as soothing him. "We talked about everything. How she struggled with her mum dying young, about the abuse she got when she came out, all that stuff. She had tough times, like everyone. Some of her times were tougher than most. But I never once thought she was suicidal."

"Did she leave a note?"

Michelle drew a ragged breath, tried to stem the tears. She knew this had been coming. "Yes."

"Can I see it?"

"Paul, I would never hide anything from you, but . . . It doesn't make sense."

"Please, Mum?"

Michelle nodded, went to her bedroom, *their* room, to retrieve the scrawled scrap. Paul was eating again when she returned, fork rising and falling robotically, purely because his young body needed the fuel. At twenty-two, his appetite was voracious. She held out the note, sat beside him again. She read over his shoulder as his eyes roved the lines.

> *The darkness never stops and it's eating its way through. How long until I draw it all the way to me and it takes us all? I can feel it coming. The connection is my blood. There's one way I can stop this. You can only run from your past for so long. I'm so sorry. I love you M & P xxx*

Paul looked up, eyes red. "You weren't going to show me this?"

"I was. But I waited until you asked. I knew you would. When you were ready."

He nodded, read it again. "What does she mean?"

Michelle shrugged. "I don't know."

"What past is she running from?"

Michelle took the slip of paper back, folded it reverently. "No idea. I'm going to try to find out."

"How much past does she have?" Paul asked. "Before you, I mean?"

Michelle smiled softly. "Some. We met in uni, when we were twenty. I thought I knew everything about her life up until then, thought we'd talked about it all. She certainly knew all about me."

"But something haunted her. Something she never told you."

Michelle pressed the note gently to her lips, nodded. "Yeah."

◆

DRIVING THROUGH THE old hometown brought a kind of dislocated nostalgia. It was Clara's birth place, after all, not hers. But all country towns shared that out of time personality. A sense they were always playing catch-up and always stuck in the past, yet actually happy to be left alone. She passed a service station with two lollipop-shaped petrol pumps, rusted and dinged, still used every day. A ute pulled up to one as she went by, the driver grizzled and dirty, the ute bed full of hay bales.

The road sloped slightly up towards the intersection that marked the town centre. Big sandstone buildings that used to be the post office and bank stood on two corners. A pub on the third, its balcony a federation skirt around three sides. The fourth corner was a memorial park, a cenotaph to those fallen shining bright white in the midday sun. She turned left, pulled into the pub car park. What the hell was she doing here? Were there really answers to be found?

The Clara-shaped hole in her pulsed with hurt again and she gripped the steering wheel until her knuckles whitened. Answers or not, she had to look. She had two weeks compassionate leave to fill. The seeking more than the finding would be the salve her heart needed. She hoped.

The interior of the pub was like that of every other country town in Australia. Paraphernalia adorned the walls, tin signs advertising

Reschs and *Tooheys*, jokes clipped from magazines and photos of locals baring their arses at the camera. Several lunchtime drinkers sat around, all stopping to pay attention to Michelle as she walked in. She smiled crookedly, half-intimidated, half-impressed that her fifty-two year old body could still garner those kind of looks. She kept in shape, dyed her hair to hide the grey, but none of it was for the benefit of men like these. Not for any men. She remembered Clara's stories, rural bigotry. All the abuse, verbal, emotional, even physical. How many of these bastards, leering at her, were responsible for the hell of Clara's teenage years?

Clara's fuck-you attitude had powered her well through tertiary education. It's what had made Michelle idolise her, fall in love with her. When Clara had fallen too, Michelle had thought it a dream. They shared stories of their so similar small town upbringing, but Clara had had it much worse.

"Drink, love?"

Michelle walked to the bar and the overweight man behind it. His head was shiny bald, nose swollen with liquor, eyes red and mean. "I've booked a room actually."

"Ah, you're Michelle Braid? Welcome to town!"

She berated herself for her own prejudice, the man's eyes were only nervous. "Yes, that's right."

He handed her a key on a battered wooden key ring, a 6 burned into it. "End of the row, furthest from the cars. You've got the place to yourself. Not many people stay here." He grinned apologetically.

"Thanks. I could use a shower. Will you still be serving lunch in half an hour?"

"Kitchen's open til two, then again at five. You've got plenty of time to settle in." He paused, smile nervously hanging on his lips. "You, er . . . on holiday or something?"

Michelle looked around the dingy pub, a couple of local eyes still watching sidelong. "Yeah. Something like that."

♦

"I REMEMBER HER well. She turned me down when we were about fourteen. I was really pleased to learn she was a dyke!"

Michelle bit her tongue, reminded herself to look past the words to the man's genuine smile. "Made you feel it wasn't personal, eh Bob?"

Bob laughed, stared into his beer. "Yeah. Can't believe she's dead. Were you and her . . . ?"

"Yes. Together more than thirty years."

Bob nodded without looking up. "Sounds like true love."

Michelle smiled. "It really was."

They were quiet for a moment before Bob looked into her eyes. "How did she die?"

"Took her own life."

"Ah, fuck that. I'm sorry."

"Me too."

"You know why?"

"Not really. That's why I'm here. Looking for answers, I suppose."

Bob looked around the bar, a dozen or so locals in small groups or drinking alone. "We get a lot of that around here."

"A lot of what?"

Bob mimed a rope tugging his neck crooked, unaware of the pulse of grief it caused in Michelle's gut. "Blokes struggle to keep a farm going, struggle to pay bills. Bloody hard to be a farmer these days. And their wives leave 'em, kids grow up and fuck off to the city rather than stay and work the land. Lot of blokes reach the end of their tether, like."

Michelle watched the distance open in Bob's eyes, wondered how many friends he'd lost that way. "You stayed," she said. "You help your dad on his farm?"

"Nah, we own the country store. Dad's retired now and I run it. Still hard to make a living, but not as hard as farming."

"You never thought of going to the city?"

Bob downed the rest of his beer. "Nah. Not interested. I like it here. Another? I should be getting back, but one more won't hurt."

Michelle held out her beer glass. "Sure." She'd had two already and was enjoying the buzz.

Bob went to the bar and she scanned the pub again. The first two people she had spoken to hadn't remembered Clara, and then she'd seen Bob drinking alone on his lunch break. They were of an age, so she thought it likely he might know. She wondered if he had ever really got over the rejection he joked about. She caught the eye of a woman in the corner, overweight and scowling. Michelle raised an eyebrow and the woman continued to stare, hard and disdainful.

Bob returned, put the beers down. "Here, get this into you."

Michelle laughed, without much humour. "Thanks." She sipped the frosty brew, glanced sidelong to see the fat woman still staring. "Who's that, by the pokie machine?"

Bob looked up, laughed. "Wicked Wendy? Staring at you like she means murder?"

Michelle shivered. "That's the one."

Bob shrugged. "Wendy Matthews, twice divorced, runs the newsagents. Always closes for lunch and comes here, like I do, but she really makes the most of her lunch hour. Everyone knows to go in the afternoon when she's so pissed she usually gives too much change."

"Why's she giving me that look? Doesn't like out-of-towners?"

"Don't think Wendy likes anyone."

They drank in silence for a moment. Wendy pulled a pack of cigarettes from a pocket and went to stand out the front of the pub and smoke. Michelle excused herself, strolled outside.

"Wendy Matthews, is it?"

Wendy stiffened, eyes widening. "Yeah."

Michelle had learned her boldness from Clara and it never failed. Matthews was happy to scowl and act tough until she was called on it. "Seems like you have an issue with me," Michelle said. "Doesn't seem fair. You don't know me."

"Doesn't seem fair that my dad died when I was fifteen," Wendy said, venom dripping off her words.

Michelle frowned. "That's terrible, true. Why take it out on me?"

"I heard you asking about that fucking lesbian."

Michelle swallowed anger, took a breath before speaking. "What does Clara have to do with it?"

"Fucking bitch, this town's well rid of her. I'm glad she's dead."

Trembling began in Michelle's knees, tremored through her stomach. She clenched her fists in an effort not to collapse. Or punch Wendy Matthews in her foul mouth. "You piece of shit," she hissed. "Have some respect for the dead."

"Had no respect for her living, got none now. My dad'd still be alive but for that cunt."

"What the hell do you mean?"

Wendy dropped her cigarette, ground it out with a booted heel. "You know nothing. Fuck off back wherever you came from."

She stormed off up the street, left Michelle paralysed with shock in her wake.

"You okay?"

Michelle jumped, turned to see Bob in the doorway. "Yeah, fine."

"I told you, Wendy doesn't like anyone. She's toxic, that one."

Michelle looked up the street at the retreating back of the woman with so much bile inside. "You're not wrong."

♦

RATHER THAN STAY in the pub all day, Michelle spent the afternoon wandering the small selection of shops in town, sitting on a sun-drenched bench at the cenotaph, lightheaded with beer. She tried to imagine Clara growing up here, bored and desperate for something interesting. Desperate to get away from closed-minded judgements, to a place where she was free to be herself. She imagined it like her own youth, only with a particular Clara-flavoured dose of angry angst added in. Michelle had kept quiet growing up, bookish and patient. Clara's tales told a very different story.

Her phone beeped. She pulled it out, saw the reception flickering between one bar and none, a text message notification across the screen. Paul.

Hey Mum. You okay? How's the country?

She smiled, tapped out a reply.

Backwards. ;) You doing okay, love?

The reply pinged back almost immediately.

I'm cool. Been having terrible nightmares. Really dark, cold dreams.

Michelle winced, desperate to gather him into her arms, smooth away his fears. Of course he was having bad dreams. She shifted for better reception, but there was none to be found. *I can try to call you, love. Signal patchy.*

Nah, don't worry, Mum. I'm okay. Love you.

She nodded softly to herself. Her big, strong, grown-up boy. *Love you too, darling. xx*

As evening drew near, she walked in the pleasant warmth across town to find herself some dinner. Every small town had a lawn bowls club with a bistro or restaurant of some kind and this place was no different. As Australian as the backyard BBQ, the bowling club's cheap bar and average food was inevitable. Bob had told her the way.

There was only the one pub, a handful of shops and one club before the town gave way to farms in every direction. Houses clustered around the town intersection like frightened children at their mother's skirts, and then spread apart the further from town they were. The bowling club sat at the end of one street, the country store the last building before the smooth greens and garish lights of the clubhouse. Michelle stopped and looked into the window of Bob's shop, rolls of wire and racks of tools, animal feed and chemicals for killing things or making them grow. She imagined Bob behind the counter. He would be back in the bar again, following the afternoon trade. Pub for lunch, pub all evening. How many places still had stores that closed for lunch? *I like it here.* Did he really? Or did he just not know anything else? Perhaps he was too scared to venture beyond the tiny town. Or maybe she was being judgemental again and he was a genuinely happy man. Happiness came in many shapes and guises. No one had it easy, but some had it far easier than others.

The day was turning to night as she entered the club and immediately felt like she'd made a mistake. Here were the elderly residents of town, too old to bother with the raucous roughness of the pub, with a handful of all other ages scattered among them. Thirty locals turned as one and stared unashamedly as she entered. The bistro, as advertised out the front, $10 *Steaks every night*, was on the far side from the bar. She saw plastic chairs and white tables through there, a scattering of people among them.

Ranks of televisions took up one wall to her left, the only patrons not looking at her were those with eyes glued to the dog races and traps, betting slips in hand. She took a breath, smiled as she strolled over to the bar. The few beers she had enjoyed with Bob at lunchtime had given her a buzz that had mostly faded, but entering the artificial light and low-level noise of the club reminded her she was still a bit drunk. Her rebellious nature rose and Clara's fuck 'em all attitude urged her on. Grief seemed to be making her careless and she didn't mind.

"Schooner of New, please," she said and the young girl behind the bar nodded, not cracking a smile. The girl was eighteen at most, heavily made up with dark kohl eyes and a tattoo on her forearm of a curling rose. The artwork was beautiful and Michelle told her so when she came back with the beer.

The girl looked at her arm in surprise. "Garth Newhaven in the city. He's a master."

Michelle decided there and then she was getting a tattoo, something for Clara. Clara's had always been gorgeous, and she had been able to wear them with a solid pride Michelle had never been able to muster. Now she would. Every day now she would carry Clara's pride with her. She got the girl to write down the name and address of the tattooist, ignored the kid's crooked smile as she did so.

She sipped her beer and walked through to the bistro. She ordered the ten dollar steak, took her number and turned to pick a table. Wendy Matthews stared at her with icy daggers from the far corner, surrounded by three other similarly built women, with matching hate in their gaze. Michelle steeled herself, held Matthews' eye for a moment, before turning away. She chose a table on the other side of the room. She sat with her back to the wall so she could keep watch on the area, but didn't look towards the group of eating women even though she felt their disdain heavy upon her.

This was a fucking mistake.

She thought of Clara again, living through this, all the time. As a child, a teenager. The thought made her angry all over again and she snapped her eyes to Matthews'. The big woman jumped and Michelle stared hard until Wendy looked away.

That's right, bitch. Do not fuck with me.

She didn't know if it was the beer or the ghost of Clara making her so audacious, but she liked it. Clara would be proud. She ate her steak, drank her beer and the whole time stewed on what Matthews had said outside the pub.

My dad'd still be alive but for that cunt.

What did that mean? How could Clara be responsible for a man's death? Michelle pushed her plate away and stood, braced herself. She walked up to Matthews' table and said, "We don't have to like each other, but I really want to know what you meant about Clara and your dad."

Wide eyes and gasps of shock rippled among Matthews and her friends. One of them started to speak and Michelle pinned her with a hard stare. "Shut the fuck up, I'm talking to her."

She turned back to Wendy, knew she was making enemies by the second and just how dangerous that was in a small town. "Please," she said more softly, pleading. "I'm trying to understand."

"You're a fucking lesbo too, aren't you? You her fucking lover?"

"Yes."

"She ever talk about her life here?" one of the other women asked.

Michelle turned to her, took in the scar across one eyebrow, the missing tooth. "Yeah. Told me how hard she had it, how ostracised she was, how she couldn't wait to leave."

The women laughed. "I don't reckon she told you the whole story," another said. "We couldn't wait to be rid of *her*. She made life fucking hard for lots of people." The woman held up a hand as Michelle drew breath to protest. "And not just because she was gay. Yeah, she copped shit for that, but it was never the real problem. Her fucking *activities* were the problem."

Wendy stood, slapped the table. "Sal, that's enough!"

Sal slumped back in her chair, shook her head. "Is it? Really?"

"It's been quiet since she left and we'll keep it that way." She turned to Michelle. "There are no answers here for you, *bitch*. Come on, all of you."

Wendy pushed her chair in, stared at her friends, daring them to defy her. Slowly, reluctantly, they rose and followed her out.

Michelle stood trembling, staring out into the bar, ignoring the faces looking back at her.

◆

SHE LEFT THE club, lost in thought, stung by the words of the local women. What activities was Sal alluding to? As she walked away from the glow of the club into the gloom of closed shops, something struck her from the shadows. Her teeth clacked together and she cried out, more in surprise than pain.

Wendy Matthews swam into view, her fist a blur as she swung another punch. Michelle tried to dodge, eyes wide in shock. She had never been in a fight in her life. She didn't move quick enough and Wendy's knuckles spun her equilibrium away. She hit the pavement with a jarring impact, mind reeling. *My god, she's beating me up!*

Wendy's scuffed and worn Blundstone boot swung in, right into Michelle's stomach, ripped the air from her lungs. As Michelle gagged and gasped, Wendy leaned forward, face twisted in hate. "Don't think the local cops will care about this. Sleep with the door locked tonight and leave in the morning."

Michelle sucked short, desperate breaths, stunned tears blurring her vision. "Why?" she managed.

Matthews turned away, strode off into the night.

Michelle pushed herself back across the path, arms wrapped around her stomach. Her cheek sang with a bone-deep pain. She sat against a shop front, disbelieving. Movement caught her eye and she flinched, thought Matthews was coming back for more.

"You ain't like her, are you?" Sal, the one who had talked about Clara's "activities".

"Like who?" Michelle asked in a weak voice.

"Fucking Clara."

"I don't know what you mean."

Sal looked down the street, where Matthews had gone, back to Michelle. "Your darling lover was a fucking witch." She stabbed a finger after Wendy. "*Her* dad died protecting this town, thanks to your Clara's black fucking magic."

Michelle tried to process the words, her mind still spinning from the attack. "Black magic?"

Sal sneered. "Go see old Jenkins. At The Pines."

Before Michelle could ask more, Sal walked away.

◆

MICHELLE GOT BACK to the pub and ordered vodka and tonic. Regardless of all the beer, she was suddenly not nearly drunk enough. Perhaps she should take Wendy's advice and leave. Although that's not what Clara would do. A witch? Black magic? How backwards was this hick town?

Bob was at the bar, laughing and drinking with a couple of farmhands. She caught his eye and he wandered over.

"Nice dinner at the bowlo?" he asked.

"Decent steak, yeah."

"Told ya." He frowned, leaned sideways to see her cheek. "What happened to you?"

"Walked into a door. Is it bad?"

"Gonna be a good bruise. A door, eh?"

"Yeah." She swallowed her drink, eyed the bar for another. "Old Jenkins at the Pines," she said. "Mean anything to you?"

"Sure. He's bloody mad, everyone knows that. Complete nutter."

"What's wrong with him?"

Bob shrugged, sipped beer thoughtfully. He ran one hand over his ample beer belly. "Ever since I was a kid he's been a weird one.

But after his brother died he really went doolally. Hey!" He looked up, surprise writ large across his face. "Talk about small town. His brother, what died, was that Wendy Matthews' dad."

Michelle nodded, more disturbed than ever. "Where's the Pines, then?" she asked.

Bob told her how to get to the old farm and she ordered another drink, a double. It was an hour and several vodkas later before she went to her room. She did lock the door, but had no intention of leaving in the morning.

◆

DRUNK AS SHE was, Michelle slept hard. She woke with a headache and a mouth like Gandhi's sandal, but no one had come to harass her during the night. At least, not that she'd noticed. Her dreams had been twisted and dark, full of grief and spite and country people with menace in their eyes. The day was already hot as she showered. Walking out into the glaring sun was an assault on her eyes and mind. A couple of cafés competed for business on the main street and she started towards them in search of coffee and bacon.

Something on her windscreen caught her eye, a scrap of paper under the wiper. It bore a hand scrawled message in blue biro.

Go home, dyke.

Michelle shook her head, screwed it up. *That the best you idiots can do?* But she didn't fancy another beating, resolved to stay alert. The first café she came to was called *Poppy's* and she went inside. The smell of cooking and coffee was both nauseating and enticing. She ordered coffee and a full breakfast, ate it in silence, feeling sorry for herself. It did the trick, her hangover began a slow retreat. She ordered a second coffee, drank it down and headed back to her car.

The drive up to the Pines didn't take long. One of the roads out of town led through wide open paddocks, across a struggling river that trickled through its bed desperately, and up a hill towards a ridge lined with the trees that gave it its name. She saw the farm gate from afar, the sign broken and peeling.

The driveway was rough and pot-holed, leading to a weatherboard house equally run down, paint flaking off like the skin of a dying man. The home looked dark, all the curtains closed. She sat in the car for a while, her head pounding softly with each heartbeat. Eventually she dragged herself out and up to the front door.

It opened before she could knock and an old man peered out at her, squinting against the light. He was stick-thin and bent over, pale skin blotched with liver marks. His eyelids hung heavy from red, rheumy eyes and his lips folded back over gums long since devoid of teeth. "Whatever yer selling, I ain't innerested."

Michelle raised one palm. "Honestly, I'm not here to sell you anything. Just wondered if I could talk to you."

"About what?"

And wasn't that the question. "The old days?" she ventured.

Old Jenkins narrowed his eyes. "The last thing I want to talk about is the old days. Off with ya." He started to push the door closed.

"Please!" Michelle said, surprised at the desperation in her voice. "I really need some answers."

"Answers ain't always good to get."

"I'll do anything. I don't know where else to go."

The old man shook his head. "I don't need nothin'." He began to shut the door again.

Michelle stepped forward, put a hand out to stop it closing. "It's about your brother. And Clara Jones."

There was silence for a long moment before his resigned sigh. "Too hot and bright out here." He left the door open and disappeared into the gloom.

Michelle followed him in, bracing for the possibilities of what might lay inside. She was pleasantly surprised and berated herself again for being judgemental. She had expected a terrible smell, filthy floors, rotten food, maybe a mangy dog. But the house was immaculately kept, clean and fresh. She got a nostalgic rush at the scent of furniture polish and marvelled at the gleam on amazing turn-of-the-century tables and dressers, buffed to a high sheen. Paintings and framed photos adorned the walls, the town when it was just two dirt streets, families and farm animals, portraits and landscapes.

Jenkins led her through to a lounge room with a cracked leather sofa and armchairs. A television muttered quietly to itself in the corner, too low to be heard. Jenkins switched it off, dropped the remote onto a coffee table. "Bloody rubbish," he said. "I leave it on for the company."

"You live alone?" Michelle asked with a pang of sorrow.

"Yep. Never married. 'Spose they all told you I was mad?"

Michelle opened her mouth to assure him that no, no one had said anything of the sort. Then thought better of lying to him. "Yeah, they did. But you don't seem mad to me."

"What does madness look like?" he asked, eyes suddenly hard. She shook her head, searching for an answer, and he turned away. "Drink? I got some lemon squash in the kitchen."

"Sure, thanks."

"Wait there."

He shuffled out and Michelle sank onto the sofa, looked around the room. There were a lot of photos, but nothing more recent than the '70s. Was it possible he had been alone all that time?

Jenkins returned with two glasses, ice cubes clinking, handed her one. "I don't like to talk about Stan."

She swallowed some drink, marvelled at just how good it was. "Stan was your brother?"

He looked at her with suspicious eyes. "What is it you want to know?"

"I'm trying to find some answers, that's all. Clara recently took her own life. I'm looking for . . . I don't know. A reason, I guess."

The old man nodded, sank into his armchair. "Stan died for her, you know. And I did, nearly. They all think I'm mad, but they never saw what I saw. What Stan saw. The thing what got him."

Nerves fluttered through Michelle's chest and she drank again, looking for solace in the normality of lemon squash. "Will you tell me what happened?" she managed eventually. "Someone told me Clara was a witch."

"My hateful niece, I 'spose."

"Actually, no. One of her friends. Wendy didn't want to tell me anything."

Jenkins sipped his drink. "You and Clara together, was you?"

"Over thirty years."

Jenkins stared into a corner, off into the past. "She was a good girl, really. Bit messed up, you know? She had this bolshy attitude, this hard as nails thing going on. I reckon you'd know that after thirty years with her."

Michelle smiled, nodded.

"Told folk she was a lesbian when she probably shouldn't have, much too young. It's like she was daring them to have a problem with it and of course, most people did. Town like this. I don't understand it, you're just born that way, ain't ya? Not like there's anything you can do about it."

"Right."

"Right. Anyway, she made life hard for herself and I 'spose she decided if she'd already been marked out as different, she'd be as different as she could. Started wearing black and all this jewellery like five pointed stars and goat's heads. Listened to all this godawful music."

Clara had told Michelle all about her "goth" phase, before there was anything actually known as goth. Some teens turned to the dark regardless of the times. It never really left her, she always favoured the darkness, still liked heavy music. *Did* like heavy music. She always complained the scene was too late for her, there was never anything heavy enough when she really needed it as a kid. Grief flooded up again and Michelle swallowed it down with more squash. "Being a goth doesn't make her a witch, though."

Jenkins nodded, expression sad. "'Course not. But it didn't help what people thought of her. And she did . . . other stuff, to spite people."

"What about her parents?"

"Her dad was friends with me and Stan. We were mates from way back. But her mum was never right in the head. She died about the time Clara started her, what did you call it? Goth thing?"

"That's right."

"Yeah. Well, her dad was the local vet, always busy. Her mum got sick and some people say she died of sadness, but no one can say why. She wasted away and it wasn't talked about much, but John, Clara's dad, told me it was a horrible cancer. Ate her up in no time."

Michelle nodded. "Clara told me her mum died young from cancer."

"There you go. But it was more than that." Jenkins pursed his lips, thoughtful for a moment. "Cancer might have finished her, but there was more wrong with that poor lass. How's old John?"

"Clara's dad? He died about eight years ago. Cancer ate him up too." She remembered Clara's sadness, the way they got through it together. A flash of memory came back with startling promptness as she recalled the man's last days. Clara crying softly, holding his hand. Her dad telling her to be strong, he'd had a good innings.

And then he'd said, *Let it go, Clarabelle, you hear me? You let that thing go, it can't follow you all the way out here.*

Michelle had asked what he meant by that and Clara had laughed it off, said she had no idea, the ramblings of a dying man. But that had been a lie.

"He left town a long time ago," Jenkins said wistfully.

Michelle felt sorry for the old man. Maybe Clara's dad had been his last friend. "He moved into a flat near us when Paul was born," she said. "Retired early."

Jenkins nodded. "We talked on the phone for a while after he left, but eventually got out of the habit. You know how it is."

"Sure." She didn't, but could imagine.

"Did all the townsfolk here think he was mad too?" she asked, knowing the answer.

"'Course they did."

They sat in silence. There was history here, dark history Clara had never shared. Part of Michelle resented that; she thought they had shared everything. And another part of her ached for her lost love and the story she couldn't tell, not even with her partner of so many years. Did it hurt that much? Or was there more to it? Was Clara trying to protect her family? The confusing note that made no sense now seemed to be saying so much.

"You said she did other stuff," Michelle said. "What stuff?"

"Well, there lies the heart of it. At about seventeen she woke something up." Jenkins raised an eyebrow at Michelle's scornful expression. "You think I'm mad too?"

"No, sorry."

"She killed herself for a reason."

Michelle swallowed, nerves trickling through her again. "Please, tell me."

"Clara started reading all kinds of occult stuff, according to John. He didn't like it, but the more he tried to stop her, the more she hid it and did it anyway. He was smart enough to stop pushing. She used to go off to these quiet places of her own and do strange rituals. Her dad followed her one time and saw her raise up something, from a chasm in the ground."

"Raise up?"

Jenkins stared into his glass. "Some monster. She tried to set it against the townsfolk, told it to get them, fuelled it with all her hate, which was their hate really, reflected right back at them."

"And it . . . " Michelle had trouble believing a word, but the man's face was deadly serious. "It did what she asked?"

"Yep. People started getting sick and dying. Those most mean to her. Her dad couldn't stand it, asked me and my brother to go with him one day, see for ourselves. Prove he wasn't crazy, you know?"

"And you did?"

"Yeah. And John had these charges with him. Explosives, like they use for quarrying. We went to the place and hid, watched Clara cut herself, drip her blood and say these things and this . . . this fucking creature emerged and shot off across the paddocks. Clara sat like she was meditating for an hour or more, until it came back. When it did, it kind of wrapped around her, lifted her and, I don't know, molested her. She was in some kind of ecstasy. Then it went back into the ground.

"John looked at us and me and Stan nodded, yes we'd seen it all. We was scared fit to shit our pants, I won't lie. It was one thing seeing it burst free and rush off, but to see it there, with Clara. It's still burned in my mind, that unholy thing."

Michelle tried to picture the scene, but her mind wouldn't fill in the blanks. A seventeen-year-old Clara, doing these things. The existence of a monster like Jenkins described . . . But he hadn't described it. "What was it like, the creature?" she asked.

Jenkins shuddered, a ripple of timeworn terror through his body. "Hard to explain. Like it was there and not there. Like it was black and purple and green and none of those colours, but all those colours at the same time. It was icy cold and oily, kind of sinewy and huge. And it was evil, it stank of absolute harm." He sank into silence, staring back into the past with wide, terrified eyes.

Michelle found it hard to believe, but was in no doubt this old man meant every word he said. "What happened?"

"John burst out of the trees, Clara was shocked, started shouting and screaming. John was furious, threw her aside and told her to go home right away. She ran off, sobbing, and he handed me and Stan those charges and said we had to seal the place up with that thing inside. The three of us went about five yards into the chasm as it sloped down into the ground. We started putting the charges in, running the fuses back. It was cold in there, unnatural cold. We were nearly ready when we realised Clara was still there, she'd only run a little way. She started screaming and hollering again, telling her dad not to mess with it.

"Stan was still back in the hole, John was yelling with Clara, I was standing by the detonator. Stan was tying the last of the charges. And that thing came back up. Stan's scream, my god, it's something I'll never forget. We heard a kind of hiss, felt a wave of icy air flood out and we spun around just as Stan screamed and was pulled back into the shadows. I started forward, honestly, I don't know what I was going to do. Then, for just a second, Stan reappeared in the light. His skin was tight to his bones, like he'd lost all his weight in an instant. His eyes were yellow, so wide and staring, his mouth was open. Then blood shot up from his mouth like he was puking the stuff and he was yanked back out of sight again."

Michelle put down her glass before her shaking caused her to drop it. "My god . . . "

Jenkins nodded, tears on his eyelids. "And John, he pushed past me and slammed that detonator down. By Christ, the noise of that explosion. It threw us all back, showered us in rock and earth. When our ears stopped ringing and the dust settled, that whole chasm had fallen in as though it was never there. Closed up tight, just a pile of rocks."

They sat in silence for a long time. Tears gently followed the deep creases of the man's face and Michelle realised she was crying with him. Eventually she asked, "What did you tell people?"

"John asked Clara if that was the end of it and she promised it was. The thing could only get in and out that way, she said, but it would eventually escape. Old John, he said no one or no thing would be able to move all that rock and she just shrugged. So we agreed to tell people Clara was up to no good in caves, we went to get her out and the caves collapsed, took Stan down. It was sort of the truth.

"Everyone knew there was more to the story, but most chose not to ask. Clara moved away soon after that, only a few months until she finished high school and went off to uni. As the years passed we tried to talk about it now and then, John and I, but people were happier telling us we were mad. And it all seemed like it was over. I'd hoped to die before I ever needed to think about it again, but I guess I didn't quite make it."

Michelle thought about Clara's last words. "She could feel it coming," she whispered. "That's what her suicide note said."

Jenkins nodded. "Right after we blew up that place, she kept telling her dad it wouldn't stop. She would stop, she said, but *it* wouldn't. He said it was dealt with. I guess as the months passed she started to believe him. She had enough else to deal with anyway, everyone blaming her for Stan's death even if they didn't know the half of it. Then she moved away."

Michelle swallowed the new grief that came with the knowledge. The burden Clara had carried through all those years. The guilt and the shame that must have gone along with it. She was only a child, really, how had she even managed to wake something so terrible? How could anyone? Stuff like that shouldn't be real. And a man's death on her conscience. Not to mention she had used the thing to cause the deaths of others in town, if Jenkins was to be believed. Surely, that was unfeasible. Folklore, coincidence. "Her note said there was one way to stop it. That's why she killed herself, I guess. Do you think she was right? Is it stopped?"

Jenkins shrugged. "I hope so. Who knows? Something like that, I wonder if it can ever be stopped."

"Can you tell me where this place was, the chasm?"

"I can, but I wouldn't recommend you go there."

"Please?"

Jenkins sighed, hauled himself out of the armchair. He found a tatty notepad and pencil by the phone and drew her a rough map. "You can only drive this far, then you have to walk this bit."

Michelle took the note, put it in her shorts pocket. "Thank you."

"Now, I'll have to ask you to leave. I don't feel well, bringing up all this stuff, I'm too bloody old. I'm sorry for your loss, Clara was a good girl really."

She could see he was holding back tears and felt her own grief rising once more. She hugged him, thanked him again. She let herself out, drove her car a couple of hundred yards away from his property, pulled over and collapsed in howls and sobs of grief, fear and disbelief.

◆

MICHELLE PARKED BY a worn wooden fence and looked out across paddocks turned yellow and dry by the summer sun. The day was hotter than ever, the sky huge and cobalt blue. The chasm was about a kilometre following the ridgeline, according to Jenkins' map. With a shrug, she left the air-conditioned comfort of the car, hopped the fence and began to walk. She needed to see. Needed closure.

It was relatively easy going despite the heat, the rising gradient shallow. She wondered how Clara had found the place, how she learned the rituals Jenkins spoke of, how the fuck it all even worked. Was the man mad? Was he covering something else? Clara's suicide and note, if anything, backed up the poor old bastard's story. What reason would he have to make up something like that?

Sloping paddock turned to rock and she followed the map to the site of the explosion. The spot was obvious from Jenkin's description, a scar in the landscape. Except he had described it as full of broken rock their charges had put there, but it was no longer blocked. She looked into a black, yawning gap and the trembling began again. Nervously she moved closer, crouching as she went, to look over the edge. The darkness was absolute after just a few metres where the ground sloped down into blackness. Piles of cracked stone stood either side, made the hole like some grotesque parody of a stony-lipped mouth. The sun beat hard on her back, but goosebumps rose on her flesh from the frosty draught travelling up into the hot day.

Had something escaped from here, after all these years? Was such a thing really possible? Maybe it was Jenkins spinning folklore to scare her. Regardless, even if it were all true, Clara had taken the final course of action, paid the ultimate price to end any threat that may have existed. Hadn't she? She had felt it coming, and it was all over now. But the chill subterranean air still breathed gently from below.

Michelle leapt to her feet with a cry, ran back to her car, gasping and pouring with sweat by the time she got there. She fell into the driver's seat, cranked the AC to maximum and drove back to town with no regard for speed limits or personal safety.

◆

SHE WAS TIRED, scared and in no shape to travel far by the time she got back to the pub and her motel room behind. She stood under a cold shower for an age, crying so hard she had to fight for breath. She needed to go home.

She had come looking for answers and what she learned had left her terrified and with no idea what she could do about any of it. It was dealt with and nothing would bring Clara back. Go home and try to forget it all, move on with life and savour the memory of her brave, tortured Clara. Her love, who had taken the most drastic action. It had ever been Clara's burden, a darkness she had released and carried inside for all those years.

An image of the open ground flashed in Michelle's mind. The cold air coming up from beneath. Had something really spent thirty-five years digging itself out? Only to be thwarted by Clara's suicide before it could come for her? So be it. Among everything else so hard to understand, that's what Michelle chose to believe as she stood under the water and slowly her tears stopped. Tomorrow she would go home.

She dried herself, collapsed onto the bed and fell into a troubled sleep.

◆

SHE SLEPT THROUGH the evening and night, occasionally starting awake from nightmares only to fall back into restless slumber. At around seven in the morning, she finally dragged herself out. She noted a long, deep scratch along one side of her car and walked heavily down the street to the café. A few early risers shared the place while she broke her fast and drank coffee after coffee. She could feel their eyes on her, the weight of their suspicions and accusations, but she refused to meet a single gaze.

After breakfast she returned to the pub, paid for her room and thanked the landlord for his hospitality.

"Not much of a holiday," he said. "You've only been here a couple of days."

"I've had enough," she said, shocked at the weak whisper of her voice. "Time to move on."

"Fair enough. Safe trip."

As she walked around to the car park, a ute slowed as it passed on the main street. "You off?" Friendly Bob from the country store.

She forced a smile for him. "Yeah, hitting the road."

He nodded, his eyes heavy and sad. "Probably for the best, eh?"

"Yep. There's nothing here for me."

He gave her a lazy salute. "In truth, love, there's not really much here for anyone. Travel safe." Before she could reply, he pulled away.

She headed out of town and at the last minute made a direction change. She wanted to say goodbye to Jenkins. She realised she didn't even know his first name. And after upsetting him with her questions, she wanted to apologise, wish him well, maybe see if there was anything she could do for him before she left. Try to make some amends for the things she might have stirred up in the sleepy town.

She pulled along the driveway of The Pines and parked. His front door stood half open. She looked left and right, wondering if he was out and about somewhere on the rambling property as a subtle fear wormed into her gut. She entered the house, paused in the hallway. "Mr Jenkins? You here?"

No answer.

Shaking her head, she walked on wobbly legs towards the lounge. Jenkins sat in his chair, knuckles white on the arms, his skin stretched grey and tight across his thin bones. His face was rigid, wide-mouthed in a silent scream, his eyes bulging from their sockets. He was frozen motionless in terror and quite dead.

Michelle staggered from the house, her breakfast threatening to come back up. It wasn't over, of course it wasn't over. Whatever this thing was, it had unfinished business.

A line from Clara's note flashed through her mind.

The connection is my blood.

The bottom fell out of her stomach and she puked, legs folding beneath her. With a cry of grief and fear combined, she drove herself to her feet and ran for the car screaming, *"Paul!"*

She powered to the highway and turned east, put her phone on hands free and hit speed dial for her son. It rang out, went to his voicemail. "It's Paul, leave a message."

"Darling, it's Mum. Please call me, okay? This is really important. As soon as you get this message!"

Wiping tears from her eyes, she put her foot down.

◆

THE THREE HOUR journey to the city was excruciating, pushing the speed limit as much as she dared without risking a police stop. She dialled Paul again and again, every time getting his voicemail. She left several messages, eventually gave up, just redialled every ten minutes with no result.

He lived in a share house on the other side of the city from the suburban home she shared with Clara. Used to share with Clara. They had tried to convince him to stay with them, save money, reluctant to give up their little boy, but he wouldn't have it. An adult, finding his own way in the world. But he wasn't far away, a thirty minute drive, and he visited once a week for dinner, every week without fail. He was a good boy.

She parked in front of his house, ran up the path, hammered on the front door. A gangly young Chinese man answered, pushing long hair from his eyes. Sammy, or Sonny or something, she couldn't remember. "Hey, hello," he said. "You looking for Paul?"

"Is he home?"

"Nah, got lectures probably. And his girl, of course. You tried calling?"

Michelle clenched her jaw, it wasn't this boy's fault. "Yes, I've been calling for hours. He's not answering."

Sammy/Sonny shrugged. "You wanna wait inside?"

"When did he go out?"

"No idea, I only just got up."

Dread ran icy through Michelle's veins. "You didn't see him leave today?"

The young man started to shake his head, expression doleful, as Michelle pushed past him and pounded up the stairs. She had been to the house before, knew it well. She ran to Paul's door and put a palm against it to push it open. She wailed at the chill of the wood, as if it were frozen solid. The handle was colder as she twisted it and flung the door wide.

Paul lay on his bed, shrunken, reduced, skin ashen, his hair frosty white. His chest rose and fell rapidly as he stared wide-eyed at the thing leaning over him. A thing hard to behold, harder still to comprehend. It was as Jenkins had described, so many dark colours at once, both thickly bulked and sinewy thin, man-shaped, bear-shaped, unshaped. The room was drenched in despair and doom, a palpable hatred drifted through the air like fog. All Clara's pain.

"Get away from him!" Michelle screamed, rushing in. She drove herself between the bed and thing leaning over it, pushed it away with hands instantly numb from an unfathomable cold.

The creature stepped unsteadily back, rose to a towering height, hissing in an echoing, distant voice that came from within it and somewhere else far, far away.

Michelle shook like she was palsied, her stomach turned to water. Her mind ran like treacle, but one over-riding thought drove her on. That was her baby on the bed, Clara's baby. Dear Clara, how could she possibly have raised this evil thing?

Its chill snaked out towards her and she felt the malice it breathed. It was made of pain and isolation. She had to stand against it, protect her son.

"You were born of spite and hate and hurt. I don't carry those things!" The words hurt her to say, made her feel a betrayal to Clara, but there was truth in them, kernels of fierce light against the consuming black. Poor Clara, carrying such darkness alone for so long. She gestured back to Paul, still frozen behind her. "He doesn't hold those things. He knows love and care and kindness. And so do I. And so did Clara, if only she had allowed herself to see. *She* gave you power. Poor Clara gave you form, kept you digging for so long. But I don't! He doesn't! And Clara is gone."

The thing seemed to waver slightly, shrink. Refusing to acknowledge the terror churning in her gut, Michelle walked towards it, one hand raised, finger pointing in sheer defiance. "How easily did you kill before? And how weak are you now? How you struggle to take his life. Because Clara is gone. I don't hate the people who ostracise me, I pity them! I don't fear the people who fear me, I try to make them understand!" The creature reduced further, its deep hiss faded. "I will never give in to the darkness because everywhere I look I find light. I know love, for Paul and for myself. And despite everything, I know only love for Clara. I am *not* afraid of you! You have had enough! You have *done* enough. Begone!"

The thing flickered and wavered, shrank away. It became gossamer, insubstantial, and drew back towards the shadows in the corner of the room. It merged with them and disappeared from sight. But it was still there, somewhere, deep and reduced, but not gone. Michelle stared into the gloom, knowing it would never really be gone, not entirely. She pulled open the heavy curtains, let the afternoon sun slam away every darkened corner. Despair leaked from the room. Mostly. Somewhere, some place adjacent to the plane she inhabited, it still lurked.

She turned to Paul, drawn and blinking against the light. His breath was ragged, his eyes wild. "Oh, my baby, are you okay?"

"Mum. I've had the most horrible dream . . . " He looked at his hands, thin and shaking. "I've lost so much weight."

She gathered him into a hug, almost crushing the breath from him. "It's okay, baby boy. It's okay. It's going to be okay."

♦

MICHELLE AND PAUL stood by Clara's grave, holding hands. Paul's weight was slowly returning, his appetite as voracious as ever. But his hair would always be snow white. Michelle absently rubbed her forearm where fresh ink itched as it healed.

"I still don't really understand," he said, eyes scanning the words on the stone.

Clara Jones, forever protected now against the dark.

"Neither do I," Michelle said. "None of it should be possible. It's hard to believe it was real."

Paul ran a hand back over his ivory hair. "But it was."

"Yes, it was. Poor Clara tried to save us from it. We should have stood against it together, but she couldn't know that. We know now."

"There are terrible things in the world, Mum."

"Yes, darling. There are. There really are."

AFTERWORD

THE QUESTION IS OFTEN ASKED, "Why do you write such horrible stuff?" And it's weird, because I don't think I do. I certainly write dark stuff because, in a nutshell, I think it's more honest. But it's not horrible. It's necessary.

We don't live in a world with happy endings. Everyone dies, everything breaks, all things ends. Entropy is the only certainty. Now that's not to say I'm a nihilist. I love life, I think the world and nature and at least a few people are wonderful and beautiful and awe-inspiring. But there's already a lot of people writing about that. I explore things darker, because things darker hold my interest more. If I come to a fork in the road and one way is a well-lighted street and the other a dark alley, I'll take the alley. I apply the same principles to my fiction. If there's a literary rabbit hole leading underground, I won't turn back when the light fails. I'll follow it all the way down, however dark it gets, and I'll see it through to the end, because I want the honesty of its totality.

Though for me it's many-layered. Not unrelenting blackness, but facets of light and shade. There are moments of horror, there are bad people making nasty choices and good people making bad decisions, but there's a fight for good too, and a hope for the light. There's optimism and realism, though perhaps not in equal measure.

G.K. Chesterton said, "Fairy tales are more than true—not because they tell us dragons exist, but because they tell us dragons can be beaten." This is something I think is absolutely true and incredibly necessary in our stories. But you know what? It's not *entirely* true. Because sometimes the dragons win. Sometimes they're not beaten. And survivors need to live with that truth. That's the purpose of dark fiction. To help *us* live with that truth, to prepare us in some way for the shit that will go down.

Bad things happens to good people for no reason at all *every single day*. We can interrogate that with our fiction, and we can look for our own optimism in someone else's tragedy. *There's* a dichotomy on which to meditate. I write dark fantasy and horror wherein sometimes the dragon prevails, but not always. I write it because there are monsters everywhere, and we must face them, win or lose. Sometimes losing is not the worst thing and sometimes the victories are pyrrhic.

Short stories are perfect for this stuff. They are a unique art form that I've loved ever since Roald Dahl blew my mind when I was a child. I'd adored *Danny The Champion of the World* and *Charlie and The Chocolate Factory*, so when I saw a book on my parents' shelves by Roald Dahl, I naturally snatched it up. I was probably eleven or twelve at the time. That book was *Kiss, Kiss*. In it I read short stories like "The Landlady" and "Royal Jelly", and a dark and twisted and wonderful world opened up before me. (If you haven't read Dahl's adult short fiction, remedy that forthwith.)

Since then I've loved the visceral, powerful nature of the short story, its lens focussed tightly on humanity and life. And, of course, it's the dark stuff that I love best of all, that most honest delving into the rabbit hole and not flinching. Using fantasy and the supernatural allows us to create and explore the deepest rabbit holes of all.

I know many people enjoy a little note from the author after each story, discussing that story's genesis and what it means. I decided against that in favour of this afterword because I want the stories to stand on their own. After all, if you read a story and it resonates in some way and you think it's about this one thing, then I come along at the end and tell you it's about something else, I've destroyed the magic. It might sound pretentious to describe my own work as magic, but *all* stories are magic. I hope mine are at least a little bit enchanted. And these stories aren't just mine any more. They're yours, dear reader, and whatever they mean to you, whatever you take from them, you're absolutely right.

All my stories come from one place or another of personal experience, but they are greatly leavened with imagination and *what if*, and live at different levels of emotion. Some are almost frivolous, though none are pure whimsy, while others were made by tapping directly into a deep well of pain and personal trauma. I've always struggled at a gut level with injustice, unfairness, bigotry and ignorance, lack of agency. I've seen way more terminal illness and premature death than I'd like. All these things and more I've explored in my stories. I've also tried to simply tell a good yarn. To spin a tale that will entertain you, discomfort you, confound you, engage or perturb you. Whatever the result, if there's any emotional resonance in here for you, then I'm happy. I hope you've enjoyed this book, and I genuinely can't thank you enough for reading.

Alan Baxter
New South Wales, 2016

STORY ACKNOWLEDGEMENTS

"Crow Shine" Original to this collection.

"The Beat Of A Pale Wing" *A Killer Among Demons* anthology (ed. Craig Bezant, Dark Prints Press, June 2013)

"Tiny Lives" *Daily Science Fiction* (ed. Michele-Lee Barasso and Jonathan Laden, December 2012)

"Roll The Bones" *Crowded Magazine* issue #2 (August 2013)

"Old Promise, New Blood" *Bloodlines* anthology (ed. Amanda Pillar, Ticonderoga Publications, Oct 2015)

"All the Wealth in the World" *Lakeside Circus, issue* 1 (ed. Carrie Cuinn, January 2014)

"In The Name Of The Father" *The One That Got Away* anthology (ed. Craig Bezant, Dark Prints Press, February 2012)

"Fear Is The Sin" *From Stage Door Shadows* anthology (ed. Jodi Cleghorn, eMergent Publishing, October 2012)

"The Chart of the Vagrant Mariner" *The Magazine of Fantasy & Science Fiction* (ed. Gordon Van Gelder, Jan-Feb 2015.)

"The Darkest Shade Of Grey" *Red Penny Papers* (ed. Katie Taylor, February 2012)

"A Strong Urge To Fly" Original to this collection.

"Reaching For Ruins" *Review of Australian Fiction* (ed. Matthew Lamb, Vol. 16, Issue 3, November 2015)

"Shadows of the Lonely Dead" *Suspended in Dusk* anthology (ed. Simon Dewar, Books of the Dead Press, September 2014)

"Punishment Of The Sun" *Dead Red Heart* anthology (ed. Russell B. Farr, Ticonderoga Publications, April 2011)

"The Fathomed Wreck To See" *Midnight Echo Magazine, issue* 9 (ed. Geoff Brown, May 2013)

"Not The Worst Of Sins" *Beneath Ceaseless Skies* #133 (ed. Scott H. Andrews, October 31st, 2013)

"The Old Magic" Original to this collection.

"Mephisto" *Daily Science Fiction* (ed. Michele-Lee Barasso and Jonathan Laden, June 2014)

"The Darkness in Clara" *SQ Mag, issue* 14 (ed. Sophie Yorkston, May 2014)

AVAILABLE FROM TICONDEROGA PUBLICATIONS

WWW.TICONDEROGAPUBLICATIONS.COM

LIMITED HARDCOVER EDITIONS

978-0-9806288-1-4   The Infernal BY Kim Wilkins
978-1-921857-54-6   Black-Winged Angels BY Angela Slatter

EBOOKS

978-0-9803531-5-0   Ghost Seas BY Steven Utley
978-1-921857-93-5   The Girl With No Hands BY Angela Slatter
978-1-921857-99-7   Dead RED Heart ED Russell B. Farr
978-1-921857-94-2   More Scary Kisses ED Liz Grzyb
978-0-9807813-5-9   Heliotrope BY Justina Robson
978-1-921857-36-2   Dreaming of Djinn ED Liz Grzyb
978-1-921857-40-9   Prickle Moon BY Juliet Marillier
978-1-921857-92-8   The Year of Ancient Ghosts BY Kim Wilkins
978-1-921857-28-7   Bloodstones ED Amanda Pillar
978-1-921857-04-1   Damnation and Dames ED Liz Grzyb & Amanda Pillar
978-1-921857-31-7   Midnight and Moonshine BY Lisa L. Hannett & Angela Slatter
978-1-921857-44-7   The Bride Price BY Cat Sparks
978-1-921857-60-7   Everything is a Graveyard BY Jason Fischer
978-1-921857-64-5   The Assassin of Nara BY R.J. Ashby
978-1-921857-78-2   Death at the Blue Elephant BY Janeen Webb
978-1-921857-82-9   The Emerald Key BY Christine Daigle & Stewart Sternberg
978-1-921857-57-7   Kisses by Clockwork ED Liz Grzyb
978-1-925212-06-8   Angel Dust ED Liz Grzyb
978-1-925212-17-4   The Finest Ass in the Universe BY Anna Tambour
978-1-925212-37-2   Hear Me Roar ED Liz Grzyb
978-1-921857-38-9   Bloodlines ED Amanda Pillar

THE YEAR'S BEST AUSTRALIAN FANTASY & HORROR SERIES
EDITED BY LIZ GRZYB & TALIE HELENE

978-0-9807813-8-0   Year's Best Australian Fantasy & Horror 2010 (hc)
978-0-9807813-9-7   Year's Best Australian Fantasy & Horror 2010 (tpb)
978-0-921057-98-0   Year's Best Australian Fantasy & Horror 2010 (ebook)
978-0-921057-13-3   Year's Best Australian Fantasy & Horror 2011 (hc)
978-0-921057-14-0   Year's Best Australian Fantasy & Horror 2011 (tpb)
978-0-921057-15-7   Year's Best Australian Fantasy & Horror 2010 (ebook)
978-0-921057-48-5   Year's Best Australian Fantasy & Horror 2012 (hc)
978-0-921057-49-2   Year's Best Australian Fantasy & Horror 2012 (tpb)
978-0-921057-50-8   Year's Best Australian Fantasy & Horror 2010 (ebook)
978-0-921057-72-0   Year's Best Australian Fantasy & Horror 2013 (hc)
978-0-921057-73-7   Year's Best Australian Fantasy & Horror 2013 (tpb)
978-0-921057-74-4   Year's Best Australian Fantasy & Horror 2010 (ebook)
978-0-925212-18-1   Year's Best Australian Fantasy & Horror 2014 (hc)
978-0-925212-19-8   Year's Best Australian Fantasy & Horror 2014 (tpb)
978-0-925212-20-4   Year's Best Australian Fantasy & Horror 2010 (ebook)

THANK YOU

The publisher would sincerely like to thank:

Elizabeth Grzyb, Alan Baxter, Joanne Anderton, Laird Barron, Angela Slatter, Kaaron Warren, Nathan Ballingrud, Amanda Pillar, Dirk Flinthart, Stephanie Gunn, Kathleen Jennings, Pete Kempshall, Martin Livings, Anthony Panegyres, Cat Sparks, Lisa L. Hannett, Donna Maree Hanson, Robert Hood, Pete Kempshall, Penelope Love, Nicole Murphy, Karen Brooks, Jeremy G. Byrne, Felicity Dowker, Kim Wilkins, Marianne de Pierres, Jonathan Strahan, Peter McNamara, Ellen Datlow, Grant Stone, Sean Williams, Simon Brown, Garth Nix, David Cake, Simon Oxwell, Grant Watson, Sue Manning, Steven Utley, Lewis Shiner, Bill Congreve, Jack Dann, Janeen Webb, Lucy Sussex, Stephen Dedman, the Mt Lawley Mafia, the Nedlands Yakuza, Angela Challis, Shane Jiraiya Cummings, Kate Williams, Kathryn Linge, Andrew Williams, Al Chan, Alisa and Tehani, Mel & Phil, Hayley Lane, Georgina Walpole, Rushelle Lister, everyone we've missed . . .

. . . and you.

in memory of
Eve Johnson
Sara Douglass
Steven Utley
Brian Clarke